Julia James lives in En[g]... verdant countryside and... She also loves the Medi... and history, with its sunbaked landscapes and olive groves, ancient ruins and azure seas. 'The perfect setting for romance!' she says. 'Rivalled only by the lush tropical heat of the Caribbean—palms swaying by a silver sand beach lapped by turquoise water... What more could lovers want?'

Kim Lawrence lives on a farm in Anglesey with her university lecturer husband, assorted pets who arrived as strays and never left, and sometimes one or both of her boomerang sons. When she's not writing she loves to be outdoors gardening, or walking on one of the beaches for which the island is famous— along with being the place where Prince William and Catherine made their first home!

TYCOON'S RING OF CONVENIENCE

JULIA JAMES

A CINDERELLA FOR THE DESERT KING

KIM LAWRENCE

MILLS & BOON

First Published in Great Britain 2018
by Mills & Boon, an imprint of HarperCollins*Publishers*
1 London Bridge Street, London, SE1 9GF

Tycoon's Ring of Convenience © 2018 by Julia James

A Cinderella for the Desert King © 2018 by Kim Lawrence

ISBN: 978-0-263-93544-8

MIX
Paper from
responsible sources
FSC® C007454

This book is produced from independently certified FSC™ paper
to ensure responsible forest management.
For more information visit www.harpercollins.co.uk/green.

Printed and bound in Spain
by CPI, Barcelona

TYCOON'S RING
OF CONVENIENCE

JULIA JAMES

For JW and CE—with thanks.

CHAPTER ONE

THE WOMAN IN the looking glass was beautiful. Fair hair, drawn back into an elegant chignon from a fine-boned face, luminous grey eyes enhanced with expensive cosmetics, lips outlined with subtle colour. At the lobes of her ears and around her throat pearls shimmered.

For several long moments she continued to stare, unblinking. Then abruptly she got to her feet and turned, the long skirts of her evening gown swishing as she headed to the bedroom door. She could delay no longer. Nikos did not care to be kept waiting.

Into her head, in the bleak reality of her life now, came the words of a saying that was constantly there.

"'Take what you want," says God. "Take it and pay for it."'

She swallowed as she headed downstairs to her waiting husband. Well, she had taken what she'd wanted. And she was paying for it. Oh, how she was paying for it…

Six months previously

'You do realise, Diana, that with probate now completed and your financial situation clearly impossible, you have no option but to sell.'

Diana felt her hands clench in her lap, but did not reply.

The St Clair family lawyer went on. 'It won't reach top price, obviously, because of its poor condition, but you should clear enough to enable you to live pretty decently. I'll contact the agents and set the wheels in motion.'

Gerald Langley smiled in a way that she supposed he thought encouraging.

'I suggest that you take a holiday. I know it's been a very difficult time for you. Your father's accident, his progressive decline after his injuries—and then his death—'

He might have saved his breath. A stony expression had tautened Diana's face. 'I'm not selling.'

Gerald frowned at the obduracy in her voice. 'Diana, you must face facts,' he retorted, his impatience audible. 'You may have sufficient income from shares and other investments to cope with the normal running and main-tenance costs of Greymont, or even to find the capital for the repairs your father thought were necessary, but this latest structural survey you commissioned after he died shows that the repairs urgently needed—that *can-not* be deferred or delayed—are *far* more extensive than anyone realised. You simply do not have the funds for it—not after death duties. Let alone for the decorative work on the interior. Nor are there any art masterpieces you can sell—your grandfather disposed of most of them to pay his own death duties, and your father sold every-thing else to pay *his*.'

He drew a breath,

'So, outside of an extremely unlikely lottery win,' he said, and there was a trace of condescension now, 'your only other option would be to find some extremely rich man with exceptionally deep pockets and marry him.'

He let his bland gaze rest on her for a second, then re-sumed his original thread.

'As I say, I will get in touch with the agents, and—'

His expression changed to one of surprise. His client was getting to her feet.

'Please don't trouble yourself, Gerald.' Diana's voice was as clipped as his. She picked up her handbag and made her way to the office door.

Behind her she heard Gerald standing up. 'Diana—what are you doing? There is a great deal more to discuss.'

She paused, turning with her hand on the door handle. Her gaze on him was unblinking. But behind her expressionless face emotions were scything through her. She would *never* consent to losing her beloved home. Never! It meant everything to her. To sell it would be a betrayal of her centuries-old ancestry and a betrayal of her father, of the sacrifice he'd made for her.

Greymont, she knew with another stabbing emotion, had provided the vital security and stability she'd needed so much as a child, coping with the trauma of her mother's desertion of her father, of herself... Whatever it might take to keep Greymont, she would do it.

Whatever it took.

There was no trace of those vehement emotions as she spoke. 'There is nothing more to discuss, Gerald. And as for what I am going to do—isn't it obvious?'

She paused minutely, then said it.

'I'm going to find an extremely rich man to marry.'

Nikos Tramontes stood on the balcony of his bedroom in his luxurious villa on the Cote d'Azur, flexing his broad shoulders, looking down at Nadya, who was swimming languorously in the pool below.

Once he had enjoyed watching her—for Nadya Serensky was one of the most outstandingly beautiful of the current batch of celebrity supermodels, and Nikos had enjoyed being the man with exclusive access to her. It had sent a clear signal to the world that he had arrived—had acquired the huge wealth that a woman like Nadya required in her favoured men.

But now, two years on, her charms were wearing thin, and no amount of her pointing out what a fantastic couple they made—she with her trademark flaming red hair, him with his six-foot frame to match hers, and the darkly saturnine looks that drew as many female eyes as her spectacular looks drew male eyes—could make them less stale. Worse, she was now hinting—blatantly and persistently—that they should marry.

Even if he had not been growing tired of her, there would be no point marrying Nadya—it would bring him nothing that he did not already have with her.

Now he wanted more than her flame-haired beauty, her celebrity status. He wanted to move on in his life, yet again. Achieve his next goal.

Nadya had been a trophy mistress, celebrating his arrival in the plutocracy of the world—but now what he wanted was a trophy *wife*. A wife who would complete what he had sought all his life.

His expression darkened, as it always did when his thoughts turned to memories. His acquisition of vast wealth and all the trappings that went with it—from this villa on exclusive Cap Pierre to having one of the world's most beautiful and famous faces in his bed, and all the other myriad luxuries of his life—had been only the first step in his transformation from being the unwanted, misbegotten 'embarrassing inconvenience' of his despised parents.

Parents who had conceived him in the selfish carelessness of an adulterous affair, discarding him the moment he was born, farming him out to foster parents—denying he had anything to do with them.

Well, he would prove them wrong. Prove that he could achieve by his own efforts what they had denied him.

Making himself rich—vastly so—had proved him to be the son of his philandering Greek shipping magnate father, with as much spending power as the man who had disowned him. And his marriage, he had determined, would prove himself the son of his aristocratic, adulterous French mother, enabling him to move in the same elite social circles as she, even though he was nothing more than her unwanted bastard.

Abruptly he turned away, heading back inside. Such thoughts, such memories, were always toxic—always bitter.

Down below, Nadya emerged from the water, realised Nikos was no longer watching her and, with an angry pout, seized her wrap and glowered up at the deserted balcony.

Diana sat trying not to look bored as the after-dinner speaker droned on about capital markets and fiscal policies—matters she knew nothing about and cared less. But she was attending this City livery company's formal dinner in one of London's most historic buildings simply because her partner here was an old acquaintance—Toby Masterson. And he was someone she was considering marrying.

For Toby was rich—very rich—having inherited a merchant bank. Which meant he could amply fund Greymont's restoration. He was also someone she would never fall in love with—and that was good. Diana's clear grey eyes shadowed. Good because love was dangerous. It destroyed people's happiness, ruined lives.

It had destroyed her father's happiness when her mother had deserted her doting husband for a billionaire Australian media mogul, never to be seen again. At the age of ten Diana had learnt the danger of loving someone who might not return that love—whether it was the mother who'd abandoned her without a thought, or a man who might break her heart by not loving her, as her mother had broken her father's heart.

She knew, sadly, how protective it had made him over her. She had lost her mother—he would not let her lose the home she loved so much, her beloved Greymont, the one place where she had felt safe after her mother's desertion. Life could change traumatically—the mother she'd loved had abandoned her—but Greymont was a constant, there for ever. Her home for ever.

Guilt tinged her expression now. Her father had sacrificed his own chance of finding happiness in a second marriage in order to ensure that there would never be a son to take precedence over her, to ensure that *she* would inherit Greymont.

Yet if she were to pass Greymont on to her own children she must one day marry—and, whilst she would not risk her heart in love, surely she could find a man with whom she could be on friendly terms, sufficiently compatible to make enduring a lifetime with him not unpleasant, with both of them dedicated to preserving Greymont?

A nip of anxiety caught at her expression. The trouble was, she'd always assumed she would have plenty of time to select such a man. But now, with the dire financial situation she was facing, she needed a rich husband fast. Which meant she could not afford to be fussy.

Her eyes rested on Toby as he listened to the speaker and she felt her heart sink. Toby Masterson was amiable and good-natured—but, oh, he was desperately, *desperately* dull. And, whilst she would never risk marrying a man she might fall in love with, she did at least want a man with whom the business of conceiving a child would not be…repulsive.

She gave a silent shudder at the thought of Toby's overweight body against hers, his pudgy features next to hers, trying not to be cruel, but knowing it would be gruelling for her to endure his clumsy embraces…

Could I endure that for years and years—decades?

The question hovered in her head, twisting and cringing.

She pulled her gaze away, not wanting to think such thoughts. Snapped her eyes out across the lofty banqueting hall, filled with damask-covered tables and a sea of city-folk in dinner jackets and women in evening gowns.

And suddenly, instead of a faceless mass of men in DJs, she saw that one of them had resolved into a single individual, at a table a little way away, sitting on the far side of it. A man whose dark, heavy-lidded gaze was fixed on *her*.

Nikos lounged back in his chair, long fingers curved around his brandy glass, indifferent to the after-dinner speaker who was telling him things about capital markets and fiscal policies that he knew already. Instead, his thoughts were about his personal life.

Who would he choose as his trophy wife? The woman who, now that he had achieved a vast wealth to rival that of his despised father, would be his means to achieve entry into the socially elite world of his aristocratic but heartless mother. Proving to himself, and to the world, and above all to the parents who had never cared about him, that their unwanted offspring had done fine—just fine—without them.

His brow furrowed. Marriage was supposed to be life-long, but did he want that—even with a trophy wife? His affair with Nadya had lasted two years before boredom had set in. Would he want any longer in a marriage? Once he had got what a trophy wife offered him—his place in her world—he could do without her very well.

Certainly there would be no question of love in the relationship, for that was an emotion quite unknown to him. He had never loved Nadya, nor she him—they had merely been useful to each other. The foster couple paid to raise him had not loved him. They had not been un-kind, merely uninterested, and he had no contact with them now. As for his birth parents… His mouth twisted, his eyes hardening. Had they considered their sordid adulterous affair to be about *love*?

He snapped his mind away. Went back to considering the question of his future trophy wife. First, though, he had to sever relations with Nadya, currently in New York at a fashion show. He would tell her tactfully, thanking her for the time they'd had together—which had been good, as he was the first to acknowledge—before she flew back. He would bestow upon her a lavish farewell gift—her favourite emeralds—and wish her well. Doubt-less she was prepared for this moment, and would have his successor selected already.

Just as he was now planning to select the next woman in his life.

He eased his shoulders back in the chair, taking an-other mouthful of his cognac. He was here in London on business, attending this City function specifically for networking, and he let his dark gaze flicker out over the throng of diners, identifying those he wished to approach once the tedious after-dinner speaker was finally done.

He was on the point of lowering his brandy glass,

when he halted. His gaze abruptly zeroed in on one face. A woman sitting a few tables away.

Until now his view of her had been obscured, but as other diners shifted to face the after-dinner speaker she had become visible.

His gaze narrowed assessingly. She was extraordinarily beautiful, in a style utterly removed from the fiery, dramatic features of Nadya. This woman was blonde, the hair drawn back into a French pleat as pale as her alabaster complexion, her face fine-boned, her eyes clear, wide-set, her perfect mouth enhanced with lip-gloss. She looked remote, her beauty frozen.

One phrase slid across his mind.

Ice maiden.

Another followed.

Look, but don't touch.

And immediately, instantly, that was exactly what Nikos wanted to do. To cross over to her, curve his long fingers around that alabaster face and tilt it up to his, to feel the cool satin of her pale skin beneath the searching tips of his fingers, to glide his thumbs sensually across that luscious mouth, to see those pale, expressionless eyes flare with sudden reaction, feel her iced glaze melt beneath his touch.

The intensity of the impulse scythed through him. His grip around his brandy glass tightened. Decision seared within him. A trophy wife might be next on his list of life ambitions, but that did not mean he had to seek her out immediately. He had been with Nadya for two years— no reason not to enjoy a more temporary liaison before seeking his bride.

And he had just seen the ideal woman for that role.

Ideal.

* * *

With an effort, Diana sheared her gaze away, heard the speech finally ending.

'Phew!' Toby exclaimed, throwing Diana a look of apology. 'Sorry to make you endure all that,' he said.

She gave a polite smile, but in her mental vision was the face of the man who had been looking at her across the tables. The image was burning in her head.

Darkly tanned, strong features, sable hair feathering his broad forehead, high cheekbones, a blade of a nose and a mouth with a sculpted contour that somehow disturbed her—but, oh, not nearly so much as the heavy-lidded dark, dark eyes that had rested on her.

Eyes that she still felt watching her, even though she was not looking at him. Did not want to. Didn't dare to.

She felt her heart give a sudden extra beat, as if a shot of pure adrenaline had been injected into her bloodstream. Something that she was supremely unused to—unused to handling. She was accustomed to men looking at her—but not to the way she had reacted to *this* man.

Urgently she made her eyes cling to Toby. Familiar, amiable Toby, with his pudgy face and portly figure. In comparison with the man who'd been looking at her, poor Toby seemed pudgier and portlier than ever. Her eyes slid away, her heart sinking. She was feeling bad about what she was contemplating. Could she *really* be considering marrying him just because he was rich?

Guilt smote her that she should feel that way about him, but there it was. Had seeing that darkly disturbingly good-looking man just now made her realise how impossible it would be for her to marry a man like Toby? But if not Toby then who? Who could save Greymont for her?

Where can I find him? And how soon?

It was proving harder than she'd so desperately hoped, and time was running out...

Speeches finally over, the atmosphere in the banqueting hall lightened, and there was a sense of general movement amongst the tables as diners started to mingle. Nikos was talking to his host, a City acquaintance, and casually bringing the subject around to the woman who had so piqued his interest. The ice maiden...

He nodded in her direction. 'Who's the blonde?' he asked laconically.

'I don't know her myself,' came the reply, 'but the man she's with is Toby Masterson—Masterson Dubrett, merchant bankers. Want an introduction?'

'Why not?' said Nikos.

There had been nothing in his brief perusal to indicate that the blonde's dinner partner was anything more to her—an impression confirmed as he was introduced.

'Toby Masterson—Nikos Tramontes of Tramontes Financials. Fingers in many pies—some of them might interest you and vice versa,' his host said briefly, and left them to it, heading off to talk elsewhere.

For a few minutes Nikos exchanged the kind of anodyne business talk that would interest a London merchant banker, and then he glanced at Toby Masterson's guest.

The ice maiden was not looking at him. Quite deliberately not looking at him. He was glad of it. Women who came on to him bored him. Nadya had played hard to get—she knew her own value as one of the world's most beautiful women, and was courted by many men. But he did not think the ice maiden was playing any such game—her reserve was genuine.

It made him all the more interested in her.

Expectantly he glanced at Toby Masterson, who dutifully performed the required introduction.

'Diana,' he said genially, 'this is Nikos Tramontes.'

She was forced to look at him, though her grey eyes were expressionless. Carefully expressionless.

'How do you do, Mr Tramontes?' she intoned in a cool voice. She spoke with the familiar tones of the English upper class, and only the briefest smile of courtesy indented her mouth.

Nikos gave her an equally brief courtesy smile. 'How do you do, Ms...?' He glanced at Masterson for her surname.

'St Clair,' Masterson supplied.

'Ms St Clair,' he said, his glance going back to the ice maiden.

Her face was still expressionless, but in the depths of her clear grey eyes he was sure he saw a sudden veiling, as if she were guarding herself from his perusal of her. That was good—it showed him that despite her glacial expression she was responsive to him.

Satisfied, he turned his attention back to Toby Masterson, moving their conversation on to the EU, the latest manoeuvres from Brussels, and thence on to the current state of the Greek economy.

'Does it impact *you*?' Toby Masterson was asking.

Nikos shook his head. 'Despite my name, I'm based in Monaco. I've a villa on Cap Pierre.' He glanced at Diana St Clair. 'What of you, Ms St Clair? Do you care for the South of France?'

It was a direct question, and she had to answer it. Had to look at him, engage eye contact.

'I seldom go abroad,' she replied.

Her tone still held that persistent note of not wanting to converse, and he watched her reach for her liqueur glass, raise it to her lips as if to give her something to do—something to enable her not to answer more fully. Yet her hand trembled very, very slightly as she replaced her glass, and satisfaction again bit in Nikos. The permafrost was not as deep as she wanted to convey.

'That's not surprising,' Masterson supplied jovially. 'The St Clairs have a spectacular place in the country to enjoy—Hampshire, isn't it? Greymont?' he checked. 'Eighteenth-century stately pile,' he elaborated.

Do they, indeed? thought Nikos. He looked at her with sudden deeper interest.

'Do you know Hampshire?' Toby Masterson was asking now.

'Not at all,' said Nikos, keeping his eyes on Diana St Clair. 'Greymont? Is that right?'

For the first time he saw an expression in her eyes. A flash that seemed to spear him with the intensity of the emotion behind it. It made him certain that behind the ice was a very, very different woman. A woman capable of passion.

Then it was gone, and the frost was back in her eyes. But it had left a residue. A residue that just for a moment he thought was bleakness.

'Yes,' she murmured.

He made a mental note. He would have a full dossier on her by tomorrow—Ms Diana St Clair of Greymont, Hampshire. What kind of place was it? What kind of family were the St Clairs? And just what further interest might Ms Diana St Clair have for him other than presenting him with so delectable a challenge to his seductive powers to melt an ice maiden?

His eyes flickered over her consideringly. Exquisitely beautiful and waiting to be melted into his arms, his bed... But could there be yet more to his interest in her? Could she be a candidate for something more than a fleeting affair?

Well, his investigations would reveal that.

For now, however, he had whetted his appetite—and he knew with absolute certainty that he had made the impact on her that he had intended, though she was striving not to let it show.

He turned his attention back to Masterson, taking his leave with a casual suggestion of some potential mutual business interest at an indeterminate future date.

As he strolled away his mood was good—very good indeed. With or without any deeper interest in her, the ice maiden was on the way to becoming his. But on what terms he had yet to decide.

He let his thoughts turn to how he might make his next move on her...

CHAPTER TWO

DIANA THREW HERSELF back in the taxi and heaved a sigh of pent-up relief. Safe at last.

Safe from Nikos Tramontes. From his powerfully unsettling impact on her. An impact she was not used to experiencing.

It had disturbed her profoundly. She had done her best to freeze him out, but a man that good-looking would not be accustomed to rebuff—would be used to getting his own way with women.

Well, not with me! Because I have no intention of having anything to do with him.

She shook her head, as if to clear his so disturbing image from her mind's eye. She had far more to worry about. She knew now, resignedly, that she could not face marrying Toby—but what other solution could save her beloved home?

Anxiety pressed at her—and over the next two days in London it worsened. Her bank declined to advance the level of loan required, the auction houses confirmed there was nothing left to sell to raise such a sum. So it was with little enthusiasm that she took a call from Toby.

'But it's Covent Garden. And I *know* you love opera.'

The plaintive note in Toby's voice made Diana feel bad. She owed him a gentle let-down. Reluctantly she acquiesced to his invitation—a corporate jolly for a performance of Verdi's *Don Carlo*.

But when she arrived at the Opera House she wished she had refused.

'You remember Nikos Tramontes, don't you?' Toby greeted her. 'He's our host tonight.'

Diana forced a mechanical smile to her face, concealing her dismay. With her own problems uppermost in her mind, she'd managed to start forgetting him, and the discomforting impact he'd had on her, but now suddenly he was here, as powerfully, disturbingly attractive as before.

Then she was being introduced to the other couple present. Diana recognised the man who had brought Nikos Tramontes over to their table. With him was his wife, who promptly took advantage of the three men starting to talk business to draw Diana aside.

'My, my,' she said conspiratorially, throwing an openly appraising look back at Nikos Tramontes, 'he is most definitely a handsome brute. No wonder he's been able to hold on to Nadya Serensky for so long. That and all his money, of course.'

Diana looked blank, and Louise Melmott promptly enlightened her.

'Nadya Serensky. You know—that stunning red-headed supermodel. They're quite an item.'

It was welcome news to Diana. Perhaps she'd only been imagining that Nikos Tramontes had eyed her up at the livery dinner.

Maybe it's just me, overreacting.

Overreacting because it was so strange to encounter a man who could have such a powerfully disturbing physical impact on her. Yes, that must be it. She tried to think, as she sipped her champagne in the Crush Room, if she had ever reacted so strongly as that to any other man, and came up blank. But then, of course, she *didn't* react to men. Had schooled herself all her life not to.

The men she'd dated over the years had been good-looking, but they had always left her cold. A tepid goodnight kiss had been the most any of them had ever received. Only with one, while at university, had she resolved to see if it were possible to have a full relationship without excessive passion of any kind.

She had found that it was—for herself. But eventually not for her boyfriend. He'd found her lack of enthusiasm off-putting and had left her for another woman. It hadn't bothered her—had only confirmed how right she was to guard her heart. Losing it was so dangerous. A policy of celibacy was much wiser, much safer.

Anxiety bit at her. Except such a policy would hardly find her a husband rich enough to save Greymont. *If* she was truly still contemplating so drastic a solution.

With an inward sigh she pulled her mind away. Tomorrow she would be heading back to Greymont to go through her finances again, get the latest grim estimates for the most essential work. But for now, tonight, she would enjoy her evening at Covent Garden—a night off from her worries.

And she would not worry, either, about the presence of the oh-so-disturbing Nikos Tramontes. If he had a famous supermodel to amuse him then he would not be interested in any other women. Including herself.

As they made their way to their box she felt her anticipation rising. The orchestra was tuning up, elegant well-heeled people were taking their seats, and up in the gods the less well-heeled were packed like sardines.

Diana looked up at them slightly ruefully. The world would see her as an extremely privileged person—and she was; she knew that—but owning Greymont came with heavy responsibilities. Prime of which was stopping it from actually falling down.

But, no, she wouldn't think of her fears for Greymont. She would enjoy the evening.

'Allow me.'

Nikos Tramontes's deep, faintly accented voice beside her made her start. He drew her chair back, allowing her to take her seat, which she did with a rustling of her skirts as he seated himself behind her. Louise Melmott sat beside her at the front of the box.

His eyes rested on the perfect profile of the woman whose presence here tonight he had specifically engineered in order to pursue his interest in her. An interest that the dossier he had ordered to be compiled on her had indicated he must show. Because she might very well indeed prove suitable for far more than a mere fleeting seduction.

Diana St Clair, it seemed, was possessed of more than the exquisite glacial beauty that had so caught his attention the other evening. She was also possessed of exactly the right background and attributes to suit his purposes. Best of all about Ms Diana St Clair was her inheritance—her eighteenth-century country estate—and the fact that it *was* her inheritance, bringing with it all the elite social background that such ownership conferred.

An old county family—not titled, but anciently armigerous—possessing crests and coats of arms and all the heraldic flourishes that went with that status. With landed property and position, centuries of intermarriage with other such families, including the peerage. A complex web of kinship and connection running like a web across the upper classes, binding them together, impenetrable to outsiders.

Except by one means only…

Marriage.

His eyes rested on her, their expression veiled. Would Diana St Clair be his trophy wife?

It was a tempting prospect. As tempting as Diana St Clair herself.

He sat back to enjoy further contemplation of this woman who might achieve what he now most wanted from life.

To Diana's relief, the dramatic sweep of Verdi's music carried her away, despite her burning consciousness that Nikos Tramontes was sitting so close to her, and as she surfaced for the first interval it was to be ushered with his other guests back to the Crush Room for the first course of their champagne supper.

The conversation was led mainly by Louise Melmott, who knew the opera and its doubtful relationship to actual history.

'The real Don Carlos of Spain was probably insane,' the other woman said cheerfully, as they helped themselves to the delicacies on offer. 'And there's no evidence he was in love with his father the King's, wife!'

'I can see why Verdi rewrote history,' Diana observed. 'A tragic, thwarted love affair sounds far more romantically operatic.'

She was doing her best to be a good guest—especially since she knew Toby had no interest in opera, so she needed to emphasise her own enthusiasm.

'Elisabeth de Valois was another man's wife. There is nothing romantic about adultery.'

Nikos Tramontes's voice was harsh, and Diana looked at him in surprise.

'Well, opera is hardly realistic—and surely for a woman like the poor Queen, trapped in a loveless marriage, especially when she'd thought she was going to be married to the King's son, not the King himself—surely one can only feel pity for her plight?'

Dark eyes rested on her. '*Can* one?'

Was there sarcasm in the way he replied? Diana felt herself colouring slightly. She had only intended a fairly light remark.

The conversation moved on, but Diana felt stung. As if she'd voted personally in favour of adultery. She felt Nikos Tramontes's eyes resting on her, their expression masked. There seemed to be a brooding quality about him suddenly, at odds with the urbane, self-assured manner he'd demonstrated so far.

Well, it was nothing to do with her—and nor was Nikos Tramontes. She would not be seeing him again after this evening.

It was to her distinct annoyance, therefore, that when the long opera finally ended and she had bade goodnight to Toby, making sure she told him she was heading back to Hampshire the next day, she discovered that somehow Nikos Tramontes was at her side as she left the Opera House. It was a mild but damp night, and his car was clearly hovering at the kerb.

'Allow me to offer you a lift,' he said. His voice was smooth.

Diana stiffened. 'Thank you, but a taxi will be fine.'

'You won't find one closer than the Strand, and it is about to rain,' he returned blandly.

Then he was guiding her forward, opening the rear passenger door for her. Annoyed, but finding it hard to object without making an issue of it, Diana got in. Reluctantly she gave the name of the hotel she and her father had always used on their rare visits to the capital, and the car moved off.

In the confines of the back seat, separated from the driver by a glass divide, Nikos Tramontes seemed even more uncomfortably close than he had in the opera box. His long legs stretched out into the footwell.

'I'm glad you enjoyed this evening,' he began. He paused minutely. 'Perhaps you'd like to come with me to another performance some time? Unless you've seen all this season's productions already?'

There was nothing more than mild enquiry in his bland voice, but Diana felt herself tense. Dismay filled her. He was making a move on her after all, despite the presence in his life of Nadya Serensky. Her hopes that her disturbing reaction to him were not returned plummeted.

'I'm afraid not,' she said, giving a quick shake of her head.

'You haven't seen them all?' he queried.

She shook her head again, making herself look at him. His face was half shadowed in the dim interior, with the only light coming from the street lights and shop windows as they made their way along the Strand towards Trafalgar Square.

'That isn't what I meant,' she said. She made her voice firm.

His response was to lift an eyebrow. 'Masterson?' he challenged laconically.

She gave a quick shake of her head. 'No, but...'

'Yes?' he prompted, as she trailed off.

Diana took a breath, clasping her hands in her lap. She made her voice composed, but decisive. 'I spend very little time in London, Mr Tramontes, and because of that it would be...pointless to accept any...ah...further invitation from you. For whatever purpose.'

She said no more. It struck her that for him to have sounded so very disapproving of a fictional case of adultery in the plot of Don Carlos was more than a little hypocritical of him, given that he'd just asked her out. Clearly he was not averse to playing away himself, she thought acidly.

She saw him ease his shoulders back into the soft leather of his seat. Saw a sardonic smile tilt at his mouth. Caught a sudden scent of his aftershave, felt the closeness of his presence.

'Do you *know* my purpose?' he murmured, with a quizzical, faintly mocking look in his dark eyes.

She pressed her mouth tightly. 'I don't need to, Mr Tramontes. I'm simply making it clear that since I don't spend much time in London I won't have any opportunities to go to the opera, whomever I might go with.'

'You're returning to Hampshire?'

She nodded. 'Yes. Indefinitely. I don't know when I shall be next in town,' she said, wanting to make crystal-clear her unavailability.

He seemed to accept her answer. 'I quite understand,' he said easily.

She felt a sense of relief go through her. He was backing off—she could tell. For all that, she still felt a level of agitation that was unsettling. It came simply from his physical closeness. She was aware that her heart rate had quickened. It was unnerving...

Then, thankfully, the car was turning off Piccadilly and drawing up outside the hotel where she was staying. The doorman came forward to open her door and she was soon climbing out, trying not to hurry. Making her voice composed once more.

'Goodnight, Mr Tramontes. Thank you so much for a memorable evening at the opera, and thank you for this lift now.'

She disappeared inside the haven of the hotel.

From the car, Nikos watched her go. It was the kind of old-fashioned but upmarket hotel that well-bred provincials patronised when forced to come to town, and doubtless the St Clairs had been patronising it for generations.

His eyes narrowed slightly as his car moved off, heading back to his own hotel—far more fashionable and flashy than Diana St Clair's. Had she turned down his invitation on account of Nadya? He'd heard Louise Melmott say her name. If so, that was all to the good. It showed him that Diana St Clair was...*particular* about the men she associated with.

He had not cared for her apparent tolerance of the adultery in the plot of *Don Carlos*, but it did not seem that she carried that over into real life. It was essential that she did not.

No wife of mine will indulge in adultery—no wife of mine, however upper crust her background, will be anything like my mother! Anything at all—

Wife? Was he truly thinking of Diana St Clair in such a light?

And, if he were, what might persuade her to agree?

What could thaw that chilly reserve of hers?

What will make her receptive to me?

Whatever it was, he would find it—and use it.

He sat back, considering his thoughts, as his car merged into the late-night London traffic.

Greymont was as beautiful as ever—especially in the sunshine, which helped to disguise how the stonework was crumbling and the damp was getting in. The lead roof that needed replacing was invisible behind the parapet, and—

A wave of deep emotion swept through Diana. How could Gerald possibly imagine she might actually sell

Greymont? It meant more to her than anything in the world. Anything or anyone. St Clairs had lived here for three hundred years, made their home here—of *course* she could not sell it. Each generation held it in trust for the next.

Her eyes shadowed. Her father had entrusted it to *her*, had ensured—at the price of putting aside any hopes of his own for a happier, less heart-sore second marriage—that *she* inherited. She had lost her mother—he had ensured she should not lose her home as well.

So for her to give it up now, to let it go to strangers, would be an unforgivable betrayal of his devotion to her, his trust in her. She could not do it. Whatever she had to do—she would do it. She *must*.

As she walked indoors, her footsteps echoing on the marble floor, she looked at the sweeping staircase soaring to the upper floors, at the delicate Adam mouldings in the alcoves and the equally delicate painted ceilings—both in need of attention—and the white marble fireplace, chipped now, in too many places. A few remaining family portraits by undistinguished artists were on the walls ascending the staircase, all as familiar to her as her own body.

Upstairs in her bedroom, she crossed to the window, throwing open the sash to gaze out over the gardens and the park beyond. An air of unkemptness might prevail, but the level lawns, the ornamental stone basin with its now non-functioning fountain, the pathways and the pergolas, marching away to where the ha-ha divided the formal gardens from the park, were all as lovely as they always had been. As dear and precious.

A fierce sense of protectiveness filled her. She breathed deeply of the fresh country air, then slid the window shut, noticing that it was sticking more than ever, its paint flaking—another sign of damp getting in. She could see another patch of damp on her ceiling too, and frowned.

Whilst her father had been so ill not even routine maintenance work had been done on the house, let alone anything more intensive. It would have disturbed him too much with noise and dust, and the structural survey she'd commissioned after he'd died had revealed problems even worse than she had feared or her father had envisaged.

A new roof, dozens of sash windows in need of extensive repair or replacement, rotting floorboards, collapsing chimneys, the ingress of damp, electrical rewiring, re-plumbing, new central heating needed—the list went on and on. And then there was all the decorative work, from repainting ceilings to mending tapestries to conserving curtains and upholstery.

More and yet more to do.

And that was before she considered the work that the outbuildings needed! Bowing walls, slate roofs deteriorating, cobbles to reset... A never-ending round. Even before a start was made on the overgrown gardens.

She felt her shoulders sag. So much to be done—all costing so, *so* much. She gave a sigh, starting to unpack her suitcase. Staff had been reduced to the minimum—the Hudsons, and the cleaners up from the village, plus a gardener and his assistant. It was just as well that her father had preferred a very quiet life, even if that *had* contributed to his wife's discontent. And he had become increasingly reclusive after her desertion.

It had suited Diana, though, and she'd been happy to help him write the St Clair family history, acting as secretary for his correspondence with the network of family connections, sharing his daily walks through the park, being the chatelaine of Greymont in her mother's absence.

Any socialising had been with other families like theirs in the county, such as their neighbours, Sir John Bartlett and his wife, her father's closest friends. She herself had been more active, visiting old school and university friends around the country as they gradually married and started families, meeting up with them in London from time to time. But she was no party animal, preferring dinner parties, or going to the theatre and opera, either with girlfriends or those carefully selected men she allowed to squire her around—those who accepted she was not interested in romance and was completely unresponsive to all men.

Into her head, with sudden flaring memory, stabbed the image of the one man who had disproved that comforting theory.

Angrily, she pushed it away. It was irrelevant, her ridiculous reaction to Nikos Tramontes! She would never be seeing him again—and she had far more urgent matters to worry about.

Taking a breath, anxiety clenching her stomach, she went downstairs and settled at her father's desk in the library. In her absence mail had accumulated, and with a resigned sigh she started to open it. None of it would be good news, she knew that—more unaffordable estimates for the essential repairs to Greymont. She felt her heart squeeze, and fear bite in her throat.

Somehow she *had* to get the money she needed.

But not by marrying Toby Masterson. She could not bring herself to spend the rest of her life with him.

She felt a prickle of shame. It had not been fair even to think of him merely as a solution to her problems.

Wearily, she reached for her writing pad. She'd have

to pen a careful letter—thanking him for taking her out in London, implying that that was all there was to it.

As she made a start, though, it was quite another face that intruded into her inner vision, quite different from Toby's pudgy features. A face that was dramatic in its looks, with dark eyes that set her pulse beating faster—

She pushed it from her. Even if Nikos Tramontes were *not* involved with his supermodel girlfriend, all a man like that would be after would be some kind of dalliance—something to amuse him, entertain him while he was in London.

And what use is that to me?

None. None at all.

Nikos slowly made his way along the avenue of chestnut trees, avoiding the many potholes as Greymont gradually came into view.

With a white stucco eighteenth-century façade, a central block with symmetrical wings thrown out, its aspect was open, but set on a slight elevation, with extensive gardens and grounds seamlessly blending into farmland. The whole was framed by ornamental woodland. A classic stately home of the English upper classes.

Memory jabbed at him, cruel and stabbing. Of another home of another nation's upper class. A chateau deep in the heart of Normandy, built of creamy Caen stone, with turrets at the corners in the French style.

He'd driven up to the front doors. Had been received.

But not welcomed.

'You will have to leave. My husband will be home soon. He must not find you here—'

There had been no warmth in the voice, no embrace from the elegant, couture-clad figure, no opening of her arms to him. Nothing but rejection.

'That is all you have to say to me?'

That had been his question, his demand.

Her lips had tightened. *'You must leave,'* she'd said again, not answering his question.

He had swept a glance around the room, with its immaculate décor, its priceless seventeenth-century landscapes on the walls, the exquisite Louis Quinze furniture. *This* was what she had chosen. *This* was what she had valued. And she had been perfectly willing, to pay the price demanded for it. The price *he* had paid for it.

Bitterness had filled him then—and an even stronger emotion that he would not name, would deny with steely resolve that he had ever felt. It filled him again now, a sudden acid rush in his veins.

With an effort, he let it drain out of him as he drew his powerful car to a momentary halt, the better to survey the scene before him.

Yes—what he was seeing satisfied him. More than satisfied him. Greymont, the ancestral home of the St Clairs, and all that came with it would serve his purpose excellently. But it was not just the physical possession he wanted—that was not what this visit was about. Had he wished. he could easily have purchased such a place for himself, but that would not have given him what he was set upon achieving.

His smile tightened. He knew just how to achieve what he wanted. What would make Diana St Clair receptive to him. Knew exactly what she wanted most—needed most. And he would offer it to her. On a plate.

His gaze still fixed on his goal, he headed towards it.

CHAPTER THREE

'MR *TRAMONTES*?'

Diana stared blankly as Hudson conveyed the information about her totally unexpected visitor. What on earth was Nikos Tramontes doing here at Greymont?

Bemused, and with an uneasy flutter in her stomach, she walked into the library. She found her uninvited guest perusing the walls of leather-bound books, and as he turned at her entrance she felt an unwelcome jolt to her heart-rate.

It had been a week since she'd left London, but seeing his tall, commanding figure again instantly brought back the evening she'd spent at Covent Garden. Unlike on the two previous occasions she'd set eyes on him, this time he was in a suit, and the dark charcoal of the material, the pristine white of his shirt, and the discreet navy blue tie, made him every bit as eye-catching as he had been in evening dress.

It annoyed her that she should feel that sudden kick in her pulse again as she approached. She fought to suppress it, and failed.

'Ms St Clair.' He strode forward, reaching out his hand.

Numbly, she let him take hers and give it a quick, businesslike shake.

'I'm sorry to call unannounced,' he went on, his manner still businesslike, 'but there is a matter I would like to discuss with you that will be of mutual benefit to us both.'

He looked at her, his expression expectant.

Blankly, she went and sat down on the well-worn leather sofa by the fireplace, and watched him move to do likewise. He took her father's armchair, and a slight bristle of resentment went through her. She leant over to ring the ancient bell-pull beside the mantel and, when Hudson duly appeared, asked for coffee to be served.

When they were left alone again, she looked directly at her unexpected visitor. 'I really can't imagine, Mr Tramontes, that there is anything that could be of mutual benefit to us.'

Surely, for heaven's sake, he was not going to try and proposition her again? She devoutly hoped not.

He smiled, crossing one long leg over the other. It was a proprietorial gesture, and it put her hackles up. The entrance of Hudson with the coffee tray was a welcome diversion, and she busied herself pouring them both a cup, only glancing at Nikos Tramontes to ask how he took his coffee.

'Black, no sugar,' he said briskly, and took the cup she proffered.

But he did not drink from it. Instead, he swept his gaze around the high-ceilinged, book-lined room, then brought it back to Diana.

'This is an exceptionally fine house you have, Ms St Clair,' he said. 'I can see why you won't sell.'

She started, whole body tensing. What on *earth*? How dared Nikos Tramontes make such a remark to her. It was *none* of his business.

He saw her expression and gave a smile that had a caustic twist to it. 'It wasn't that hard,' he said gently, not letting her drop her outraged gaze, 'to discover the circumstances of your inheritance. And I have eyes in my head. I may not be that familiar with English country houses, but a pot-holed drive, masonry that is crumbling below the roofline, grounds that could do with several more gardeners…'

He took a mouthful of coffee, setting the cup aside on the table her father had used to lay his daily newspaper on. Looked at her directly again.

'It makes sense of your interest in Toby Masterson,' he told her. 'A man with a merchant bank at his disposal.'

Again, outrage seethed in Diana—even more fiercely. Her voice was icy. 'Mr Tramontes, I really think—'

He held up a hand to silence her. As if, she thought stormily, she was some unruly office junior.

'Hear me out,' he said.

He paused a moment, studying her. She was dressed casually, in dark green well-cut trousers and a paler green sweater, with her hair caught back in a clip, no jewellery, and no make-up he could discern—a world away from the muted elegance of her evening dress. But her pale, breathtaking beauty still had the same immediate powerful impact on him as it had when she'd first caught his eye. Her current unconcealed outrage only accentuated his response.

'I understand your predicament,' he said.

There was sympathy in his voice, and it made her suspicious. Her expression was shuttered, her mouth set. Her own coffee completely ignored.

'And I have a potential solution for you,' he went on.

His eyes never left her face, and there was something in their long-lashed dark regard that made it difficult to meet them. But meet them she did—even if it took an effort to appear as composed as she wanted to be.

He took her silence for assent, and continued.

'What I am about to put to you, Ms St Clair, is a solution that will be a familiar one to you, with your ancestry. I'm sure that not a few of your forebears opted for a similar solution. Though these days, fortunately, the solution can be a lot less...perhaps *irreversible* is the correct term.'

He reached for his coffee again. Took a leisurely mouthful and replaced the cup. Looked at her once more. She had neutralised her expression, but that was to be expected. Once he had put his cards on the table she would either have him shown the door—or she would agree to what he wanted.

'You wish—extremely understandably—to retain your family property. However, it's quite evident that a very substantial sum of money is going to be required—a sum that, as I'm sure you are punishingly aware, given the current level of death duties and the exceptionally high cost of conservation work on listed historic houses, is going to stretch you. Very possibly beyond your limits. Certainly beyond your comfort zone.'

Her expression was stony, giving nothing away. That didn't bother him. It made him think how statuesque her beauty was. How much it appealed to him. The contrast of her chilly ice maiden impassivity with Nadya's hot-blooded outbursts was entirely in Diana St Clair's favour. She was as unlike Nadya as a woman could be—and not, he thought with satisfaction, just in respect of the ice maiden quality, but in so much more—all of which was supremely useful to him.

'As I say, you've clearly already considered—and rejected—Toby Masterson as a solution to your problem, but now I invite you to consider an alternative candidate.'

He paused. A deliberate, telling pause. His eyes held hers like hooks.

'Myself,' he said.

Diana's intake of breath was audible. It scraped through her throat and seemed to dry her lungs to ashes.

'Are you *mad*?' came from her.

'Not in the least,' was his unruffled reply. 'This is what I propose.' His mouth tightened a moment, then he went on. 'I should make it clear immediately, however, that my relationship with Nadya Serensky is at an end. She was a woman I wanted two years ago—now I want something, and some*one*, quite different. *You*, Ms St Clair, suit my requirements perfectly. And I,' he continued, ignoring the mounting look of disbelief on her face, 'suit *your* requirements perfectly, too.'

She opened her mouth to speak, to protest, but no words came. What words could possibly come in response to such a brazen, unbelievable announcement? He was continuing to talk in that same cool manner, as if he were discussing the weather, and she could only listen to what he said. Even while she stared at him blankly.

'What I want now, at this stage of my life,' he was saying—perfectly calmly, perfectly casually, 'is a wife. Nadya was quite unsuitable for that role. You, however...'

His dark eyes rested on her, unreadable and opaque, and yet somehow seeing right into her, she felt with a hollowing of her stomach.

'You are perfect for that part. As I,' he finished, 'am perfect for you.'

She could only stare, frozen with disbelief. And with another emotion that was trying to snake around her stunned mind.

'We would each,' he said, 'provide the other with what we currently want.' He glanced once more around the library, then back to her. 'I want to be part of the world you inhabit—the world of country houses like this, and those who were born to them. Oh, I could quite easily buy such a house, but that would not serve my purpose. I would be an outsider. A *parvenu.*'

His voice was edged, and he felt the familiar wash of bitterness in his veins, but she was simply staring at him, with a stunned expression on her beautiful face.

'That will not do for me,' he said. 'What I want, therefore, is a wife from that world, who will make me a part of it by marrying her, so that I am accepted.' Again, his voice tightened as he continued. 'As for what *you* would gain…' His expression changed. 'I am easily able to afford the work that needs to be done to ensure the fabric of this magnificent edifice is repaired and restored to the condition it should enjoy. So you see…' he gave his faint smile '…how suitable we are for each other?'

She found her voice—belatedly—her words faint as she forced them out.

'I cannot believe you are serious. We have met precisely twice. You're a complete stranger to me. And I to you.'

He gave the slightest shrug of his broad shoulders. 'That can easily be remedied. I am perfectly prepared for our engagement to provide sufficient time to set you at your ease with me.'

He reached to take up his coffee cup again, levelled his unreadable gaze on her.

'I am not suggesting,' he continued, 'a lifetime together. Two years at the most—possibly less. Sufficient for each of us to get what we want from the other. That is, after all, one of the distinct advantages of our times—unlike your forebears, who might have made similar mutually advantageous matches, we are free to dissolve our marriage of our own volition and go our separate ways thereafter.'

He took another draught of his coffee, finishing it and setting down the cup. He looked directly at her.

'Well? What is your answer?'

She swallowed. There was a maelstrom in her head: thoughts and counter-thoughts, conflicting emotions. Swirling about chaotically. This couldn't be real, could it? This almost complete stranger, sitting here suggesting they marry?

Marry so I can save Greymont—

She felt a hollowing inside her. That had been exactly what she herself had contemplated—had told Gerald Langley that she would do. She had seriously contemplated it with Toby, then balked at making a life-long commitment to a man she would never otherwise have considered marrying.

But Nikos Tramontes only wants two years.

Two brief years of her life.

Sharply, she looked at him.

'You say no longer than two years?'

He nodded, concealing an inner sense of triumph. That she had asked the question showed she was giving his offer serious consideration. That she was tempted.

'I think that will suffice, don't you?'

It would for him—he was confident of that. Not just because when they parted he would be secure in the social position that marriage to her would give him, but because he knew from his liaison with Nadya that he was unlikely to be bored with the woman in his life before then. For two years, therefore, having Diana St Clair in his life, his bed, would be perfectly acceptable.

He let his gaze rest on her, absorbing her pristine beauty, the pallor in her cheeks from her reaction to his proposition. She was still looking dazed, but no longer outraged. Again, triumph surged in him. He knew he was most definitely drawing her in.

'Well?' he prompted.

'I need time,' she said weakly. 'I can't just—' She broke off, unable to say more, feeling as if a tornado had just scooped her up and whirled her about.

'Of course,' Nikos conceded smoothly.

He got to his feet. His six-foot-plus height seemed to overpower her.

'Think it over. I'm flying to Zurich tomorrow, but I will be back in the UK at the end of next week. You can give me your answer then. In the meantime, if you have any further questions feel free to text or email me.'

She watched him extract a business card and lay it on her father's desk before turning back to her.

Suddenly, he smiled. 'Don't look so shocked, Diana. It could work perfectly for both of us. A marriage of convenience—people made them all the time in the past. They still do, even if they don't admit it.'

He turned on his heel, leaving her sitting staring after him as he left the room. She heard his swift footsteps, the front door opening and closing again. The sound of a car starting. Her heart was pounding like a hammer inside her. And it wasn't just because of the bombshell he'd dropped in her lap.

When he smiles and calls me by my name...

She felt her pulse give a quiver, and deep inside her she felt danger roil. For reasons she could not understand Nikos Tramontes, of all the men she had ever known, seemed to possess an ability to...to *disturb* her. To make her hyper-aware of his masculinity. Of her own femininity. She didn't know where it was coming from, or why— she only knew it was dangerous.

I don't want to react to him like that—I don't want to!

Her features contorted. Nikos Tramontes had walked into her life out of nowhere and put down in front of her what could be the best hope she had of getting exactly what she wanted—the means to save Greymont. As easily and as painlessly as it was possible to do so outside of a lottery win.

Yes, he was a complete stranger—but, as he'd said, they could get to know each other during their engagement. Yes, his announcement had initially shocked her. But, as he'd also said, such marriages for mutual advantage had been perfectly unexceptional to her ancestors. And theirs would be brief—a year or two at most. Not the life-long commitment that Toby would have required...

And yet for all that she heard a voice wail in her head.

Why can't he look like Toby? Overweight and pug-faced! That would be so, so much better! So much safer.

So much safer than the dangerous quickening of her blood that came whenever she thought of Nikos Tramontes.

Deliberately, she silenced her fear. Dismissing it. There was no need for such anxieties. None! That quickening of her blood was irrelevant—completely irrelevant. It had nothing to do with what Nikos Tramontes was offering her.

The formality of a marriage of convenience, for outward show only—a dispassionate, temporary union to provide him with an assured entrée into her world and her with the means to preserve her inheritance. Nothing else—nothing that had anything to do with that quickening of her pulse.

It was because she owned Greymont and came with the social position and connections he wanted to acquire that he was interested in her. Nothing more than that. Oh, he would want her to grace his arm, be an ornament for him—that was understandable. But that would be in public. In private their relationship would be cordial, but fundamentally, she reassured herself, it would be little more than a business arrangement at heart. He got a society wife—she got Greymont restored. Mutually beneficial.

We would be associates. That's a good word for it.

With a little start she realised she was giving his extraordinary proposition serious consideration.

Her mind reeled again.

Could she really do this? Accept his offer—use it to save Greymont?

It was all she could think about as the days went by. Days spent in visits from the architect, and from the specialist companies that would undertake the careful restoration and conservation work on Greymont that would have to be carried out in accordance to the strict building regulations for historic listed buildings, adding to the complexity—and the cost.

With every passing day she could feel the temptation to accept what Nikos was offering her coiling itself like a serpent around her. Tightening its grip with every coil.

Nikos settled himself into a seat in first class. His mood was good—very good. His decision to select Diana St Clair as the means of achieving his life's second imperative goal might have been made impulsively, but he'd always trusted his instincts. They'd never failed him in business yet, enabling his rise to riches to be as meteoric as it had been steep.

A faint frown furrowed his brow as he accepted a glass of champagne from the attentive stewardess.

But marriage is not a business decision...

He shook the thought from him. His liaison with

Nadya hadn't been a business decision, but it had proved highly beneficial to both of them while it had lasted, with each of them gaining substantially from it. There was no reason why his time with Diana St Clair should not do likewise. As well as gaining the restoration of her home, she would gain an attentive husband and a *very* attentive lover.

What more could she—or he—want?

Certainly not love.

His mouth twisted. Love was of no interest to him. He'd never known it, did not want it. And nor, clearly, did Diana St Clair, or she would have sent him packing when he'd set out his proposal in front of her. But she hadn't—and she would accept it, he knew, his expression changing to one of confident assurance.

What he was offering suited her perfectly. And not just as the means to save her home. On a much more personal level too. Oh, she might not yet realise that her inner ice maiden had finally met a challenge it could not freeze off, but when the time came—and come it would!—she would accept from him all the exquisite sensual pleasure that he would ensure she experienced, all the pleasure that he was so hotly anticipating for himself.

It would be his gift to her—opening the door for her to accept the admiration and desire of men at last. Frozen as she was within, he would ignite within her that flare of sensual awareness he'd seen so briefly, so revealingly in her eyes when he'd first looked upon her.

He would not hurry her—he would give her time to get used to him—but in the end... His smile deepened and he took a mouthful of champagne, easing his shoulders as an image of her pale, exquisite beauty formed in his mind's eye, lingering over the fine-boned features, the silken line of her mouth.

In the end she would thaw.
And melt into his waiting arms.

Diana stared at the vast bouquet of exotic, highly scented lilies that sat on the Boule table in the hall, fragrancing the air. Then she stared down at the cheque she was holding in her slightly shaking hands, and the note accompanying it.

An advance, sent in good faith.

She stared at the numbers on the cheque. A quarter of a million pounds. She felt her lungs tighten. So much money—

With a stifled noise in her throat she marched back into her office. But the scent of the lilies was in her nostrils still. Beguiling. Enticing.

Can I do it? Marry Nikos Tramontes?

The cheque in her hand demanded an answer. Accept or reject it. Accept or reject the man who'd signed it.

The phone on her desk rang, startling her. It was her architect, politely, tactfully enquiring whether she was yet in a position to set a start date for the work that needed to be done. Work that could not start without Nikos to pay for it.

Her hand clenched, her signet ring with the St Clair crest on her little finger catching on the mahogany surface of the desk. Emotion bit into her, forcing a decision. The decision she had to make *now*. Could postpone no longer. If she did not restore Greymont it would decay into ruins or she would have to sell. Either way, it would be lost.

I can't be the St Clair who loses Greymont. I can't betray my father's devotion and sacrifice. I can't!

The offer that Nikos Tramontes had put in front of her was the best she could ever hope to find. It was a gift from heaven.

Nothing else can save Greymont.

She could feel her heart thumping in her chest, her mouth drying, suddenly, at the enormity of what she was doing.

It will be all right—it will be all right...

She heard the words in her head, calming her, and she clung to them urgently.

Slowly—very, very slowly—she breathed out. Then she spoke. 'Yes,' she said to her architect. 'I think we can now make a start.'

CHAPTER FOUR

THE WEDDING VENUE WAS the ballroom of an historic London hotel, with impeccable upper-crust ambience and timelessly stylish art deco décor, and it was packed with people.

Apart from the guests who were Nikos's business acquaintances, Diana had rounded up everyone from her own circles whom Nikos Tramontes was marrying her in order to meet: those people who represented upper-class English society, based on centuries of land ownership and 'old money', who had all gone to school together, intermarried over the years, and would socialise together for ever. It was a closed club, open only to those born into it. Or to those who, like her new husband, had married into it.

She was glad so many had accepted her invitation— it made her feel she was definitely keeping her side of the bargain she'd struck with the man she was marrying. He wanted a society wife—she was making sure he got one, in return for funding the repairs now actively underway at Greymont.

The ongoing work had been her main preoccupation during the three months of their engagement, but she had made time to meet up with Nikos whenever he was in London, including attending a lavish engagement party at his newly purchased town house in Knightsbridge. The fact that his business affairs seemed to require his continuous travel around the globe suited her fine.

All the same, he'd taken pains to allow her to get used to him, to come to terms with being his fiancée, just as he'd promised he would. He'd taken her out and about to dinner, to the theatre and the opera, and to meet some of her friends or his business acquaintances.

He was no longer a stranger by any means. And, although she had been unable to banish that unwanted hyperawareness of his compelling masculinity that made her so constantly self-conscious about him, she had, nevertheless, become far easier in his company. More comfortable being with him. His manners were polished, his conversation intelligent, and there was nothing about him to make her regret her decision to accept marriage to him as a solution for Greymont.

Becoming engaged to Nikos had proved a lot more easy than she had feared. He'd certainly set aside her lingering disquiet that her disturbing awareness of his sexual magnetism might cause a problem. He seemed oblivious to it, and she was grateful. It would be embarrassing, after all, if a man to whom she was making a hard-headed marriage of convenience were to be inconvenienced by a fiancée who trembled at his touch.

Not that he did touch her. Apart from socially conventional contact, such as taking her arm or guiding her forward, which she was studiously trying to inoculate herself against, he never laid a finger on her. Not even a peck on the cheek.

It was ironic, she thought wryly, that her friends all assumed her sudden engagement was a *coup de foudre*…

She'd let Toby Masterson think so, out of kindness for

him, and he'd said sadly, 'I could tell you were smitten, from the off,' before he wished her well.

The only dissenting voice against her engagement had come from Gerald, the St Clair family lawyer.

'Diana, are you sure this is what you want to do?' he'd asked warningly.

'Yes,' she'd said decisively, 'it is.'

As she'd answered that old saying had come into her head. *'Take what you want,' says God. 'Take it and pay for it.'*

She'd shaken it from her. All she was paying was two years of her life. She could afford that price. Two years in which to grace the arm of Nikos Tramontes in their marriage of convenience, a perfectly civil and civilised arrangement. She had no problem with that.

And no problem with standing in the receiving line beside him now, greeting their guests as his wife. She stood there smiling, saying all that was proper for the occasion, and continued to smile throughout the reception.

Only when, finally, she sank back into the plush seat of the vintage car that was to take them to the airport, from where they would fly off on their honeymoon in the Gulf—where Nikos had business affairs to see to— did she feel as if she'd come offstage after a bravura performance.

She could finally relax.

'Relieved it's all over?'

Nikos's deep voice at her side, made her glance at him.

'Yes.' She nodded decisively. 'And I'm glad it all went flawlessly.'

He smiled at her. 'But then, you were flawless yourself.'

'Thank you,' she said, acknowledging his compliment. She was getting used to his smiles now. Making herself get used to them. Just as she would make herself get used to the fact that he was her husband for the time being. Theirs might be a marriage of convenience, but it could be perfectly amiable for all that. Indeed, there was no reason why it shouldn't be. The more time she spent with him, the easier it would get.

Even on a honeymoon that was actually a business trip.

'It's been pretty strenuous,' she went on now, easing her feet out of the low-heeled court shoes that went with her cream silk 'going away' outfit—considerably more comfortable than those that had gone with her thirties-style, ivory satin bias-cut wedding dress, which had been four-inch heeled sandals. 'But, yes, I think I can agree it's all gone extremely well. And, of course—' and now there was real warmth in her voice '—the work at Greymont is making wonderful progress. I can't thank you enough for expediting matters in that respect!'

'Well, that *is* my contribution,' he agreed.

It had been a long day, and she'd been on the go from the moment she'd woken in the bridal suite at the hotel, ready to receive the ministrations of hair stylists and make-up artists, to this moment of relative relaxation now, and maybe that accounted for the tightening of her throat, the rush of emotion in her voice.

'It means so much to me—restoring Greymont. It's my whole world. '

Was there a flicker in his eyes? A sudden shadowing? But he said nothing, only smiled before getting out his phone with a murmured apology about checking emails.

She let him get on with it. He was a businessman. And global business ran twenty-four-seven. It didn't stop for weddings.

Or honeymoons.

Yet when they arrived in the Gulf—Diana having managed to get some sleep during the flight—it was to discover that the incredibly lavish hotel they were staying at was most definitely putting the honeymoon into their arrival with a capital H.

As they were conducted to their suite by a personal butler, Diana could not suppress a gasp. The walls seemed to be made of gold, as did most of the furniture, a vast sweep of glass gave a view out over the vista beyond, and the floor looked to be priceless marble. Huge bouquets of red roses stood on just about every surface, scenting the air richly.

'Oh, my goodness…' she said weakly.

Did she really lean slightly against Nikos, half in weariness, half in amazement at the utterly over-the-top gilded lavishness of their surroundings? She didn't know—knew only that for a moment his strength seemed to be supporting her. And then he was leading her forward, to where their butler was opening a bottle of vintage champagne.

'Is it giving you ideas for improving the décor at Greymont?'

Nikos's low voice was at her ear. She cast him a look, then realised that there was a hint of humour at his mouth and in his eyes. She felt a strange flutter deep inside her. Even though she was getting used to his smiles, he should not smile at her like that. Not so intimately. Not in a marriage like theirs—a marriage in which intimacy was not in the terms and conditions.

'It's perfect for *here*,' she allowed.

She took the glass of champagne proffered to her and Nikos did likewise, dismissing the butler.

He raised his glass. 'Well, Mrs Tramontes, shall we drink a toast to our marriage?'

That smile was still in his eyes, but now she was more composed as she met his gaze.

'Definitely,' she said brightly, lifting her glass to his.

It was odd to hear him call her that. She'd heard it a few times at the wedding reception, but it hadn't seemed real then. Now, coming from Nikos, it did.

Well, yes, on the surface I suppose it is *real, in the legal sense. But it's not* really *real—it's simply...*

Convenient.

That was what it was. Convenient for both of them. Almost a kind of business partnership.

Mutually beneficial, perfectly amicable.

She clinked her glass against his lightly. Smiled back at him. Brightly, civilly, cheerfully. OK, she wasn't yet *totally* used to being in his company, but the next few days would see to that.

She just had to get used to him, that was all.

'To us...'

Nikos's voice was deep, but if she'd thought for a second she'd heard something in it that smacked of some kind of intimacy, well, she was sure she was mistaken. He was, she reminded herself, a formidably attractive man, and he would have an impact on any woman without even intending to.

'To us,' she returned, and took a dutiful mouthful.

Nikos slid open the door to the huge balcony and they stepped out to take in the vista of the hotel's gardens and azure swimming pools, and the glittering waters of the Gulf beyond.

She gave a sigh of pleasure and leant against the glass balcony rail. Nikos moved beside her, not too close, but almost in a companionable fashion, looking down with her, taking in the scene below.

His mood was good—exceptionally good.

The wedding had gone superbly, achieving just what he'd wanted to achieve—his entry by marriage into the world that his bride took for granted as her birthright. A flicker of dark emotion moved in his mind—the bitter memory of being ejected from that Normandy chateau, unwanted and unwelcome, rejected and refused, reminding him that *he'd* had no such auspicious start.

His mouth tightened. Well, he did not need what his own mother had denied him! He had achieved it without her acceptance! Just as he'd made himself as rich as the father who'd repudiated him, denied any claim to paternity.

He shook the dark thoughts from him. They had no place in his life—not any longer. They had no more power to haunt him.

His gaze dropped to the woman at his side and his good mood streamed back. For three months—long, self-controlled months—he'd held himself on a tight leash. For three endless months he'd held himself back, knowing that above all the woman he had chosen for marriage was not a woman to be rushed. He must thaw the ice maiden carefully.

This moment now, as he leaned companionably beside her, was the reward for his patience. And soon he'd be reaping the full extent of that reward.

But not quite yet. Not until she was fully at ease with him, fully comfortable with him. The first few days of their honeymoon should achieve that. It would take more immense self-control on his part, this final stage of the process, but, oh, it would be worth it when she finally accepted his embraces. When she accepted the passion that would, he knew with masculine instinct, flare between them when the time was right.

He hauled his mind back to the present. For now it was still necessary for him to exercise patience. Self-denial.

He turned his head towards her with an easy smile, his voice casually amiable. 'What would you like to do for lunch?' he asked. 'We've flown east, so although you may feel as if it's only early morning, here the sun is high.'

She glanced at him, returning his easy smile, glad that it felt natural to do so. Glad that standing here beside him, side by side, seemed quite effortless. She could see how much more relaxed he was—just as she was. It might not be a honeymoon in the traditional sense, and he might have business affairs to conduct, but there was a holiday atmosphere all the same. She was enjoying the easy feeling it brought. Enjoying just being here.

'I don't mind,' she said. 'Whatever you prefer. And Nikos…' her voice changed slightly '…please don't feel you have to keep me company while we're here. I know you have business appointments and, really, in an ultra-luxurious hotel like this I'll be more than happy to lounge around lazily. And if I feel like anything more energetic I can always take a formal tour and go exploring. You know—souks and whatever. Even the desert, maybe. I'll be perfectly OK on my own, I promise.'

She said it quite deliberately, and was glad she had. She wanted to set the right tone, make it clear that she understood the unstated but implicit conditions of their marriage right from the off.

But he was looking at her strangely. Or so she thought. She gave an inner frown of puzzlement.

'Yes, I do have some business appointments,' he said, 'but I believe I can still find time for my bride on our honeymoon.' His voice was dry.

Her expression flickered, then recovered. 'Well, lunch together now would certainly be nice,' she said lightly. 'Do you think there's anywhere suitable to eat poolside? I must say, that water looks tempting.'

'Let's find out,' he returned. 'We'll take our swim-suits—be sure to apply enough sun cream. Your pale skin will burn instantly in these latitudes.'

They made their way down, bringing the champagne bottle with them, and emerged into the hotel's vast atrium, in the centre of which an enormous crystal fountain cooled the already air-conditioned air and the fragrance of frankincense wafted all around.

She gazed openly at the opulence, and then Nikos was guiding her outdoors. The heat struck her again, and the sun's glare, and automatically she fished out her dark glasses from her tote bag. Nikos did likewise.

As she glanced at him she felt her tummy do a quick flip.

They'd both changed into casual gear—she into a floaty sun dress and he in chinos and an open-necked short-sleeved shirt—but somehow, from the moment he put on his sunglasses, there really was only one word to describe him.

Sexy.

It was such a cheap word—so redolent of dire TV reality shows or girlish banter in the dorm. Not a word for a grown-up woman like her.

But it was the only word for him, and that was the problem. He just...*radiated* it. Whatever 'it' was. He had it in jaw-dropping amounts.

She tore her gaze away, grateful that her eyes were veiled with sunglasses too, berating herself silently for her illicit thoughts as they took their places at a shaded table in the open-air restaurant near the pools.

She gazed around in pleasure as Nikos recharged their champagne glasses. 'This really is gorgeous,' she said. 'Completely over the top, but gorgeous.'

He gave a laugh, taking the menu proffered by a

waiter. He sounded relaxed, at ease. 'Well, be sure to mention that to the Prince when we meet him tomorrow.'

Diana stared. *'Prince?'* she echoed.

'Well, not the ruling Prince, but one of his nephews. He's the main driver behind development here—and I have an interest in various of his ventures—but he has to proceed carefully. Several of his cousins oppose him, and several more want to push for a Dubai-style future. As it happens, we've been invited to his palace tomorrow for—of all things—afternoon tea.'

'Afternoon tea?' Diana echoed again.

'Yes, Sheikh Kamal's sister, Princess Fatima, is a big fan, apparently, and she welcomes any opportunity to partake of it.'

'Good heavens!' Diana exclaimed. 'Well, I dare say to an Arabian princess afternoon tea is as exotic as a desert banquet would be for me.' She frowned slightly. 'You'll have to guide me as to etiquette. I'm not at all *au fait* with royal protocol in the Middle East.'

'We'll get a briefing tomorrow morning from a palace official,' said Nikos. 'But I have every confidence in you, Diana.' He paused, then disposed of his dark glasses. His expression was serious. 'It's thanks to *you*, you know, that we've been invited to the palace. Were I here on my own I would only be receiving a brief audience on a strictly business basis, in his office. Whereas with you to accompany me it has become a social engagement and, as you are probably aware, that takes things to a completely different level in places like this. It will open doors for me.'

She met his gaze. 'I'm happy to be of use, Nikos. It makes me feel I'm…well, pulling my weight, I suppose.' Her tone altered as she inserted a lighter note. 'I'd better ensure I don't do anything to shock the Sheikh or his sister. '

'You'll be perfect,' he assured her. 'It comes naturally to you—knowing the correct way to behave in any social situation.'

She gave a self-deprecating moue. 'I can't claim any personal credit, Nikos. I've had a very privileged existence. It's people like *you*, you know, who didn't have those advantages and yet are where they are today by their own efforts and determination, who deserve credit. All of us are who we are completely by accident of birth—and none of us is responsible for that.'

Was there a sudden veiling of his eyes? A sense of withdrawal behind a mask? If so, it made her conscious of just how little she knew about him. He had never spoken of his own background—only those few dismissive remarks about Greece. Other than that she'd gathered that he'd been brought up in France, spoke the language fluently, and he had made a passing reference to studying economics at one point.

As for his relationship with Nadya Serensky—she knew no more than what he had told her and that she did not have to feel any concern over his discarded trophy mistress. Nadya had married a Hollywood A-lister within weeks of Nikos finishing with her and was now queening it up in LA. Diana could not help but be relieved that she did not need to feel bad about helping herself to Nikos Tramontes.

For her own part, Diana had said very little about herself either. Nikos had asked no questions of her—and nor had she of him. After all, with their marriage being little more than a mutual business deal, there was no need for them to know anything much. All that was required was for them to be civil—friendly. Nothing more than that.

They enjoyed a leisurely lunch, and as it had during their engagement when they'd spent time together, Diana found the conversation flowing easily. Again, there was nothing personal in it—it was mostly about the Gulf, with Nikos briefing her as necessary to supplement what she already knew and then moving on to other parts of the world that her widely travelled husband was acquainted with.

It made for a perfectly pleasant meal, and after coffee they repaired to a poolside cabana. Diana changed in the private tented cubicle to the rear, emerging wearing a sleek turquoise one-piece and a cotton sarong in a deeper blue. The sarong revealed no more of her than her sundress had, and yet for all that she was aware of a sense of self-consciousness.

She sat herself down on a lounger, and was starting to anoint herself with sun cream when Nikos strolled up. He'd clearly changed elsewhere, and now dropped his bag on the lounger beside hers.

Diana tried hard not to stare—and failed dismally.

Oh, dear God...

She'd known in her head that he must have a good physique—his wide shoulders, broad chest, and absolutely no sign of any flab on him anywhere was an indication of that. But there was a difference between knowing it and seeing it in the flesh.

Taut, muscled flesh was moulded like an athlete's, each pec and ab sculpted to perfection. She wished she'd jammed her concealing sunglasses back on her nose. Wished she could make her head drop. Wished she could just stop *staring* at him.

Her only saving mercy was that he didn't appear to notice her fixed gaze. Instead, he dropped down on his lounger and reached across in a leisurely fashion to help himself to one of the large selection of magazines that lay on a side table. Diana could see that it took him no effort at all to use simply his ab muscles to take the reaching weight of his body.

Urgently she pulled her gaze away, made a play of putting down her sun block.

Nikos settled back to read. His mood was even better than it had been before. He could see she'd also taken one of the magazines—not a glossy fashion one, he wouldn't have expected her to, but a popular history title. Satisfaction eased through him—and not just because he was very comfortably settled in a poolside cabana at an ultra-luxury hotel in the Gulf.

Because the woman he'd made his wife less than twenty-four hours ago was trying to pretend she was unaware of him right now.

He smiled inwardly. He'd been right to follow his instincts—to stick to his strategy of thawing the ice maiden Diana slowly before he moved in to melt her. He wanted her to relax in his company, lower her guard, become used to his constant presence.

So he gave no sign that he was perfectly aware of how aware she was of him, stripped to the waist, wearing only dark blue swim shorts, his long legs extended, feet bare. Instead he immersed himself in various articles in the financial magazine he'd helped himself to, while she read as well.

Their studied relaxation was only interrupted by intermittent enquiries from their personal butler as to whether they required anything.

He asked for mineral water, so did she, and then a glass of iced coffee, and both of them picked idly at a heaped plate of freshly cut fruit.

Eventually, with sun lowering and the heat of the day

easing as the afternoon wore on, he tossed his reading aside.

'OK,' he announced, 'time for some exercise.' He threw a smile at her and limbered to his feet. 'Fancy a dip?' he asked.

'I'd better, I think,' Diana agreed. 'Otherwise I'm going to snooze off…it's so restful here. And that will screw up my sleep patterns—jet lag's kicking in.'

He held out his hand and she took it, because to do otherwise would look pointed in a way she did not wish it to. He drew her up as though she weighed only a feather, and then loosed his grip as they walked towards the pool.

The sun, starting to lower behind the hotel to the west, shed a deep golden light over the water, which was shimmering in the heat. The main pool was relatively empty and Nikos strolled to the edge of the deep end, executing a perfect dive into the azure water, sending up a shower of diamond drops.

Diana couldn't help but watch him—watch the way his powerful, muscled body drove through the water, demolishing the length in seconds, only to double under in a tumble turn and head back towards her.

He surfaced, dark hair sleek around his face. 'Come on!' he instructed. 'It's warm as milk.'

To her relief, he didn't wait to watch her slip her sarong from her, and moments later she was in the water, dipping under the surface to get her head and hair wet. It was glorious—refreshing and cooling despite the ambient temperature of the pool.

She began a rhythmic traverse, contenting herself with breaststroke, enjoying the feeling of her long hair streaming behind her in the water, aware of Nikos steadily ploughing up and down only from the splashing of his arms in a strong, rapid freestyle. Having done the number of laps she was content with, she came to a halt at the far end and realised Nikos had also paused.

'Call it a day?' he asked. 'Shall we head back up and think about dinner?'

They got out of the water, put on the towelling gowns their butler had laid out for them, and headed back into the hotel. Diana was very conscious of her dripping hair, now wrapped in a turban. It would take a while to get ready.

It did, but Nikos left her to it, using the bathroom in the ancillary bedroom, obviously set aside for a child or a personal servant, leaving Diana in possession of the bridal bedroom and its palatial en suite bathroom. She was grateful for the unspoken tact with which Nikos had appropriated the other bedroom for himself.

By the time she emerged, over an hour later, she was ready for whatever demonstration of extreme opulence awaited her next. It proved to be an ultra-lavish bridal banquet, served to them in a private alcove off the main restaurant which was cantilevered out over the Persian Gulf.

The dress code, judging by the other diners, was formal, so she was glad she'd come prepared. Her silk gown, with its very fine plissé bodice, was in the palest eau-de-nil, and the soft folds of her long skirts brushed her legs as she walked in on Nikos's arm—an extended kind of body contact she was schooling herself to get used to now that she was his wife. With practice, she would soon lose her self-consciousness about it, she knew.

Her face lit up as they approached their table. 'Oh, how beautiful!' she could not help exclaiming.

Over the top it might be, but the table décor was exquisite. Huge bouquets of flowers flanked it on either side, and the floor was strewn with rose petals. More covered the table, which was also set with exquisite flowers, little candles, and napery constructed into swans—an image echoed on the side table, where stood an ice sculpture of two swans, their necks entwined in a heart shape, a feast of fresh sliced fruit and champagne chilling in a silver ice bucket.

With a low murmur of an appreciative *'Shukran!'* to the bevy of waiting staff now ushering them into their chairs, she was aware that they were drawing the eyes of the other diners as they took their places.

Nikos had opted for the restaurant's speciality—a tasting menu. Tiny portions of exquisite and extraordinary concoctions that went on and on...and on.

'More?' Diana all but gave a mock groan as the waiting staff gathered to bestow upon them yet another tender trifle for their delectation.

'Keep going,' Nikos advised her, 'or the chef will be out here, brandishing his knives in rage at your lack of appreciation for his genius.'

She laughed, and got stuck in to yet another delicious morsel filled with flavours that were impossible to identify but which created a fantasy inside her mouth. She gave a murmur of intense appreciation and closed her eyes.

From across the table Nikos's gaze flickered over her. That little moan she'd given in her throat...that look of pleasure on her face...

He dragged his mind away. First their visit to the palace tomorrow, and then... Ah, *then* the honeymoon proper could begin. And how very much he was looking forward to that.

CHAPTER FIVE

'YOUR HIGHNESS.' DIANA dropped her head to the correct degree as she was formally presented to Sheikh Kamal and then his sister, Princess Fatima, who was at his side, also greeting their guests.

The Sheikh was, she had instantly appreciated, extremely handsome, with dark Arabian looks, a hawk-like nose, and piercing dark eyes from which, she suspected, little was hidden. But his manner to his guests was urbane in the extreme, and that of his sister fulsome.

Having been comprehensively briefed by one of the palace officials that morning in their hotel suite, Diana was confident she was not making any mistakes in protocol, and that her outfit of a long-sleeved, high-collared, ankle-length dress, worn with a loose but hair-concealing headscarf, was acceptable, and she found herself beginning to relax, encouraged by the warmth of their illustrious hosts' welcoming attitude.

'Afternoon tea' turned out to be an exact replica of what might be found in the UK, of the very highest standard, and she was not slow to say so. Her praise drew a giggle from Princess Fatima.

'My brother flew in the pastry chef from London this morning, and he brought all the ingredients with him to bake the scones just as you arrived!' Her dark eyes twinkled. 'Now, tell me,' she said confidentially, 'as an Englishwoman, what *is* the correct order in a cream tea? Jam first or clotted cream first?'

Diana gave a laugh. 'Oh, that's an impossible question, Your Highness. In Devon, I believe it is one way, and in Cornwall the other—but I never remember which! I'm afraid I do jam first.'

'So do *I*!' cried the Princess delightedly. She smiled warmly. 'I do hope, my dear, that we can take tea together when I am next in London?'

'I would be honoured and delighted,' Diana said immediately.

Nikos smiled. 'If it pleases the Princess,' he said, 'afternoon tea at Greymont would be our pleasure.'

Diana's fingers tightened on the handle of the priceless porcelain tea cup she was holding. A small but distinct sense of annoyance flared in her that Nikos had presumed to offer *her* home in his invitation to the sister of the man whose approval he needed to make money out of doing business here. Greymont was *hers*—and *she* would choose who to invite to it.

But he'd clearly said the right thing, and it obviously *did* please the Princess. Her eyes lit up. 'I *adore* English country houses,' she exclaimed in her enthusiastic manner.

'So much so that I bought my sister one only last year,' her brother interposed dryly.

'And so he did—he is the most generous of brothers,' Fatima acknowledged.

A chill replaced the flare of annoyance that Diana had been feeling.

If I hadn't married Nikos then Greymont might have been snapped up as the latest amusement for an Arabian princess.

It was a sobering reminder of just why she was sitting here, in a royal palace in the Persian Gulf, next to the man who was legally her husband, but in name only, making small talk with an Arabian princess about her latest acquisition.

The Princess rattled on in her bubbly manner, asking Diana about how great houses used to be run and how best to furnish them in a style to look authentic. Diana contributed as best she could, making several suggestions which the Princess seemed to value.

As she talked to the Princess, all the while taking delicate bites of the lavish cream tea laid before them, she became aware that the Sheikh and her new husband had moved their own conversation on to matters concerning the economic development of this particular Gulf state.

After a while, with the final sliver of Dundee fruit cake consumed, the final cup of Darjeeling taken, the Princess got to her feet.

'We shall leave the men to their tedious affairs,' she announced smilingly to Diana.

Nikos and the Sheikh immediately got to their feet as well, as did Diana, who was then swept off by the Princess. When they were in the Princess's own apartments Fatima cast aside her veiling, then turned to show Diana that she could do likewise with her headscarf.

'My dear, *what* a handsome husband you have.' She gave a theatrical sigh, her dark eyes gleaming wickedly. 'I'm going to tell my brother that he must lend you his…' She giggled even more wickedly. 'His *love-nest* in the desert. It's actually *quite* respectable—our great-grandfather had it built for his favourite wife, so they could escape together, away from his jealous older wives.'

'Oh, my goodness!' Diana exclaimed weakly, not knowing what to say.

'You must demand of your oh-so-handsome husband that he declares his love for you every morning. And even more importantly...' she cast a knowing look at Diana '...every *night*.'

Diana's expression was a study. It was impossible for her to comment, but fortunately for her the Princess took her silence as embarrassment.

'Oh, you English,' she cried laughingly. 'You are always so frozen—so...what is that word? Ah, yes—repressed. Well, I will not tease you—you are a bride. You are allowed to blush.' She took Diana's arm. 'Now, come and see my wardrobe. I am dying to show it to you.'

She led her off into a chamber which made Diana's eyes widen. It was like, she realised, a museum of costume, for along the walls were a parade of gowns arrayed on mannequins set on pedestals, each and every one a priceless haute couture number, a work of art in its own right. Entranced, Diana let the Princess guide her around, enthusing volubly to the Princess's evident delight.

Then, to her dismay, the Princess exclaimed, '*This* one will be my wedding gift to you.'

She clapped her hands and one of her hovering servants hurried forward to receive instructions in rapid Arabic. Diana immediately demurred—a gown like this would cost thousands upon thousands. She couldn't possibly accept.

The Princess held up a hand, imperious now. 'To refuse it would be to offend,' she instructed regally.

Diana bowed her head. 'You do me too much honour, Highness,' she said formally, knowing she must concede.

'And *you* will do it justice,' the Princess returned warmly, adding for good measure 'The colour is all wrong for me. It makes my skin sallow. But you, with your fairness—ah, that shade of palest yellow is ideal.' She smiled.

'I will have it delivered.' The dark eyes gleamed with a wicked glint. 'Make sure you wear it at the *love-nest*.'

Again, Diana had no idea what to say—could only hope that the Princess would forget to speak to her brother about any such thing as a desert love-nest, which was the last place she wanted to go with Nikos. Meekly she let the Princess lead the way into another exquisitely decorated room, this time with a balcony overlooking a beautiful ornamental pool in a pillared courtyard.

'Tea,' the Princess announced, lowering herself onto a silk-covered divan and indicating that Diana should do likewise, 'but this time from *my* part of the world!'

The mint tea that was served proved very refreshing, and their conversation returned to the subject of historic English country houses. Diana waxed enthusiastic, mentioning the exhaustive restoration work she was having done on Greymont.

'You love your home dearly, do you not?' the Princess observed.

'It's the most important thing in the world to me!' Diana answered unguardedly.

The dark eyes rested on her curiously. 'Not your husband?'

Diana started, not sure what to say.

The Princess was still looking at her curiously. 'But surely you are in love with him more than anything in the world? If, after all, you had to choose between your home or your husband, surely there would be no choice at all?'

Diana swallowed. How could she answer?

Then, to her relief, a servant approached, bowing, then murmuring something to her hostess, who immediately got to her feet.

'We are summoned,' she announced.

A servant was there at once, with their headscarves,

and once appropriately attired Diana followed the Princess from her private apartments back into the palace, to take her farewell of their hosts with Nikos.

As they settled back into the limousine that would return them to their hotel, she turned to him. 'How did it go? I hope the Sheikh was as gracious to you as his sister was to me.'

Nikos eased his shoulders back into the soft leather seat. 'Extremely well—just as I hoped after our having been invited socially,' he said with evident satisfaction. 'I have an agreement in principle from the Sheikh—which is essential—and clearance to talk to the relevant ministers. Exactly what I wanted.'

He looked at Diana and smiled warmly in a way that she must wish he hadn't.

'You did wonderfully. Thank you. I don't just mean all the protocol—I wouldn't insult you by implying you might not have been able to handle it—but the personal touch. The Princess clearly took to you…that was obvious—'

Diana cut across him, feeling flutteringly uncomfortable after that warm smile. 'Nikos, Princess Fatima has given me one of her couture gowns. It's worth a fortune, but she insisted. I know I couldn't refuse, but what on earth should I do now?'

'Make her a present of equal value,' he returned promptly. 'I don't mean financial—that would be crass, and anyway they have so much money it makes *me* look like a pauper, let alone you,' he said carelessly. 'I mean something matching.'

Diana furrowed her brow, and then a thought struck her. 'I know! I'll find an antique gown for her—something she can possess but not wear because it's too historic. Maybe she can display it in her English country house when it's all done up.'

'Great idea,' said Nikos. He rested his eyes on her with warm approval, in that way she wished he wouldn't. 'You impressed the Sheikh, too, I could see that—he quoted from some Persian poet about how a beautiful and intelligent wife is the ultimate jewel a man can possess.' He paused, keeping that look on his face. 'And he was right about you being a jewel, Diana, both in beauty and intelligence. You are, indeed.'

For one long, endless second it seemed to her there was no breath in her body. Then, as if urgently grabbing a towel after emerging naked from the shower, she forced a little laugh to her lips.

'Well, I'm glad I came in useful this afternoon,' she said, and now her face was deliberately bright. 'And thank you for the opportunity to see inside a royal Arabian palace. It was like something out of a fairytale, and with a real-life prince and princess inside it too.'

Determinedly she went on to recollect with admiration some of the architectural details that had impressed her, even more determined *not* to mention anything about the Princess's talk about desert love-nests.

Hopefully Princess Fatima would forget all about it. A desert love nest was the last place that could be relevant to a marriage such as theirs.

A marriage in name only had no need of such a place.

'What do you say we dine up here tonight?'

Nikos's voice was casual as they walked into their huge suite and Diana's reply was immediate.

'Oh, yes, let's. I feel today has been quite a strain, and to be honest I could do with an evening just vegging.'

She rolled her head on her shoulders, rubbing at the nape of her neck.

'Need a massage?' Nikos gave a laugh and crossed towards her. He rested his hand on her neck and kneaded it gently with his fingertips.

It was a casual gesture, lasting only a few moments, but Diana froze. There was something about the weight of his large hand on her nape…something about the soft pressing of his fingers into her skin, the brush of his hand against the loosened tendrils of her hair caught into its habitual chignon…something that made her feel suddenly weak. Breathless.

'Better?' he murmured, and she realised that somehow he seemed to have stepped close to her, so that he stood just behind her. Close—so close.

Despite her frozen muscles, she seemed to be feeling a wash of intense relaxation easing through her—an impulse to roll her head forward and let free the low moan in her throat as she succumbed to the seductive touch of his fingers working at her neck.

Seductive?

With a scrambling of her senses she pulled herself together, made herself shake her head. *Seductive?* Was she mad to think such a thing?

She took a step away, freeing herself, and turned towards him with a bright smile. 'Lovely,' she said lightly. 'Thank you.'

She headed towards her bedroom. She needed a bit of sanctuary right now.

'I'm going to freshen up, then maybe order some fruit juice. The terrace looks very appealing at this time of day.'

Chattering brightly, she didn't look at him, just got inside her bedroom. She felt breathless. Determinedly, she inhaled. This had to stop. All this nonsense with her making such a fuss just because Nikos touched her. He hadn't meant anything by it—not a thing. And especially nothing *seductive*, for heaven's sake.

Yet a few minutes later, as she stood under the shower, warm water plunging like rainfall over her body, sluicing over her shoulders, her breasts, down over her flanks and legs, she felt a kind of restlessness inside her. An awareness of her own flesh and blood that was as rare as it was disturbing. As she smoothed the rich, foaming shower gel over herself, running her hands along her arms, her shoulders, her breasts and abdomen, there was a kind of sensuality about it…

As if it were not her own hands running over her body…

For one vivid, overpowering moment she had a vision of Nikos standing beside her in the steamy enclosure, the water sluicing over both of them as she stood in front of him, his strong arms enveloping her, his hands on her body, soothing, easing, smoothing…caressing her as he washed her then turning her towards him, his arms sliding around her waist, drawing her to him…

She cut off the water. Furious with herself. What on *earth* was she thinking of? Nikos might be the man she'd married two days ago but he wasn't her husband in anything but name. It was totally out of order to think of him in any other way.

Determinedly she stepped out of the shower, towel-dried herself vigorously without the slightest hint of sensuality at all, deliberately not looking at herself in the glass as she did so, and got dressed as quickly as possible.

Friendliness—that was the only atmosphere she wanted between them, and that was what she was set on ensuring.

To her relief, that seemed to be Nikos's idea as well for the evening. So it was in an atmosphere of relaxed congeniality that they dined on their terrace, she wearing a simple cotton print dress with a thin lacy shawl around her shoulders, he in chinos and a polo shirt, feet in leather flip-flops, both of them casual and comfortable.

Unlike the elaborate tasting menu of the previous evening they chose more simple fare—grilled fish for herself, a steak for Nikos, followed by ice cream. Their conversation centred on chatting through the events of the afternoon, then Diana asked about his plans for the next day.

'If you're meeting those government ministers I'll either laze by the pool or go and browse in the souks. Maybe both.' She smiled at Nikos, reaching for a piece of fruit to chase down the last of her wine.

He smiled at her in return, the lamp on the table softening his features. In the dim light, Nikos looked less formidable than he so often did.

'You're a very complaisant wife—do you know that, Diana?' he observed. 'How many other brides would be so undemanding?'

She gave a laugh. 'Good heavens, I'm perfectly capable of entertaining myself for a day, Nikos. So you go off and get your business done. Anyway, it's not like I'm a *real* bride, after all,' she finished lightly.

Was there a strange look in his eyes suddenly, or was it just the flickering candlelight?

His voice was lazily amused when he replied. 'That very swish wedding seemed real enough to me.'

She made a face. 'Oh, you know what I mean!' she exclaimed, taking another piece of fruit.

'Do I?' he replied, in that same lazily amused tone.

'Of *course* you do!' she said in mock exasperation.

She made herself look straight at him. She had to put it behind her—*right* behind her—that stupid, totally inappropriate mooning that had come over her when she'd been showering. There was no place for it—*none*, she told herself sternly.

I have to crush it down if it ever strikes again. Blank it and ignore it until it no longer exists.

He didn't answer, only continued to hold her gaze a moment longer with that same quizzical, amused look in his eye which she was making herself meet in a determinedly unaffected fashion. Then he broke contact, reaching for the bottle of wine and moving to refill her glass.

She covered it with her hand. 'I'd better not. I'm starting to yawn already,' she said.

She didn't want any more discussion about the nature of their marriage. It didn't need to be discussed. Let alone questioned. It was useful to both of them. Nothing more than useful. End of, she told herself firmly.

He accepted her decision. 'Well, it's been quite a day,' he said.

'It certainly has,' she said lightly.

Light—that's the way I have to be. Keeping everything nice and light. Or composed and businesslike. And friendly. Easy-going. Bright and cheerful. Or—

She ran out of adjectives that described the kind of behaviour that she needed to demonstrate for the next two years of marriage with Nikos.

A yawn started in her throat and she was unable to prevent it. She made another face. 'That's it, I'm calling it a day,' she said, and started to get to her feet. 'I'm off to bed.'

He stood up, helping her with her chair. He seemed very tall beside her suddenly.

'Goodnight, then,' he said. There was still that lazy note in his voice. 'Enjoy your bridal bed.'

There was nothing but amusement in his voice, Diana was sure, because obviously there couldn't be anything else. Not in a marriage like theirs.

So she answered in the same vein. 'Indeed I shall,' she agreed. 'I wonder if it's been deluged in rose petals again?'

An eyebrow tilted. 'Shall I come and check for you?'

'Thank you, no. I'm sure I can sweep them away with my own fair hand,' she said, lightly but firmly.

Then she beat a retreat. Any banter, however light-hearted, about bridal beds and rose petals was best shut down swiftly. Any banter at *all* between her and Nikos about anything that could have the slightest sexual connotation should not even be acknowledged. It had no place in their marriage. None at all.

And she had to make sure it stayed that way. Absolutely sure.

The following day passed very pleasantly for Diana. Nikos went off to his business appointments and she went browsing in the tourist souks, lunched at the hotel, then had a lazy afternoon poolside.

Nikos returned early evening, just as she got back up to their suite, his mood excellent.

'Good meetings?' she enquired.

'Highly satisfactory,' he said.

He disappeared down to the pool to cool off, and by the time he came back up Diana was ready. They'd agreed to try out one of the other restaurants at the hotel, less formal than where they'd dined their first night. Tonight she wore a cocktail dress in pale blue had used minimum make-up and wore low-heeled shoes. Nikos looked relaxed and casual in an open-neck shirt, turned-back cuffs and no tie.

He looked devastatingly attractive, but she refused to pay attention to that fact. Instead she chattered on about her adventures in the souks as they tucked into the Italian-style dishes.

'Buy any gold?' he asked, with a lift of his eyebrow.

'A few bits and pieces,' she conceded. 'I know it's not hallmarked, but I couldn't resist. And,' she added, 'I bought a carpet! I saw it and thought it would be perfect for the library at Greymont—the one there is very moth-eaten now. I'm having it shipped home directly.' She made a moue. 'I probably got diddled over the price, because I'm not much good at haggling, but it seemed good value to me all the same. Cheaper than a dealer in London, at any rate.'

'A good morning's work,' he said, and smiled.

His mood was excellent, and not just because he'd had a very productive meeting with one of the Sheikh's key people, but also because Diana was clearly considerably more relaxed with him this evening. His careful strategy was working—get her comfortable with him, let her lower her guard, so she would be ready to accept what was inevitable between them. Ready to accept her own desire for him and his her for her.

The ice maiden melted in passion. Made mine at last...

And now, thanks to the Prince and Princess, he was going to be presented with the absolutely perfect setting in which to do so.

'Oh, desperately strenuous!' she laughed. 'So I rewarded myself with lazing by the pool all afternoon.'

He looked her over. 'You're starting to tan,' he said. 'It suits you.'

There was nothing particularly provocative in the way he was inspecting her, but she had to steel herself all the same.

'How sweet of you to notice,' she said, making her voice lightly humorous. 'I'm still using huge amounts of sun cream all the same!'

He smiled. 'Well, make sure you take plenty with you when we head off into the desert tomorrow.'

She looked at him. 'Desert?' Had he planned an expedition? Dune-bashing perhaps?

But it was not dune-bashing.

'Yes. I've had a communiqué from the palace.' He paused, letting his eyes rest on Diana. 'Apparently it has pleased the Princess to request that her brother the Sheikh lends us the use of his…ah…"desert love-nest", I believe is the term the Princess used, since we are here on our honeymoon…'

Dismay filled Diana's face. 'Nikos, we can't *possibly* accept!'

She'd deliberately not told him what Princess Fatima had said to her—had hoped the Princess would forget all about it, or that her brother would turn down any request she might make. But in vain…

His expression changed. 'Diana, we can't possibly *not*.' His tone was adamant. 'It would cause grave offence to do so. It's a singular honour, and an indication of how the Princess has taken to you.'

'To refuse would be to offend…' Diana echoed in a hollow voice.

'Exactly,' Nikos confirmed in that same steely voice. Then his expression softened, and there was a humorous glint in his eye now. 'Think of it as an adventure. You'll be able to dine out on it in years to come.'

She gave a disheartened sigh. 'I suppose so,' she said reluctantly.

Her mood had plummeted. For a start, she felt a total hypocrite. A complete fraud. Here was Princess Fatima, bestowing upon her what she fondly imagined would be a fantastically romantic interlude, when it was the very last thing that was appropriate for her and Nikos.

But there was more to her dismay than the consciousness of being a hypocritical fraud. The thought of being wafted off to a desert hideaway, all on her own with Nikos...

Sternly, she rallied herself. There was nothing she could do to evade this, and it would, after all, be very good schooling for her to get more and more used to being with Nikos. It would help her to get over this ridiculous overreaction to him she had.

It was an instruction she kept repeating to herself as they set off the next day, heading out into the desert in a luxurious leather-seated, air-conditioned SUV with jacked-up wheels that would clear the desert sand, shielded from the burning heat outside.

It was a heat that deepened as they left the coast and drove along black metalled roads that glistened in the sunshine, first across scrubby flat land and then snaking amongst towering sand dunes that signalled the start of the fabled Empty Quarter.

Diana gazed rapt at the desert scenery which was gradually becoming rockier. The road wound through deep gullies and past oases of palm trees, with few signs of habitation and an occasional glint of murky-looking water. Camels—some being herded along in a chain, some merely wandering on their own, presumably either wild or having been let out to graze as and where they could—wandered along the roadside sometimes, but otherwise there was little visible sign of life.

Though they'd set out early in the morning, in order to catch what amounted to the coolest part of the day, it was nearing lunchtime when they finally arrived. They had been through a village of sorts, and what looked to Diana's eyes like some kind of military base, and now, about half an hour's drive thereafter, a building hove into view that at first she thought merely to be an outcrop of rock.

But she realised as they approached that it was a small, square building, made of the same sand-coloured stone as the earth, two storeys tall against the surrounding desert. Only a perimeter fence indicated that there was something special about the place—and the guards standing to attention as they drove through the metal gates to approach the building itself. High, arched double doors opened wide, and the four-by-four drove through with a flourish to enter what was soon revealed to be an outer courtyard.

Along with Nikos she climbed down. Palace servants were running forward to help. At once the heat struck her, clamping around her like a vice. Immediately she felt perspiration bead on her spine, despite the loose cotton shirt she was wearing. The glare of the sun after the tinted windows of the vehicle made her reach for her dark glasses.

'We need to get inside,' Nikos murmured, putting his arm around her waist and guiding her forward.

She craned her head as she walked towards the ornately carved inner doors that were opening as if controlled by a magic genie, and entered what she realised was the inner courtyard—the palace itself.

The love-nest.

CHAPTER SIX

DIANA GAVE A gasp of pleasure.

'Oh, how absolutely beautiful!' she exclaimed spontaneously.

The courtyard was an exquisite garden—an oasis with trickling fountains in stone basins, little channels that wound about bordered by greenery, the whole edged with vine-covered columns creating shady arbours under which marble benches were set.

They were ushered forward by bowing servants into the interior of the bijou palace, and Diana gazed in pleasure at the delicate fretwork archways and the inlaid marble columns as they went up to the upper floor where the royal apartments were. There might be only one bedroom, huge though it was, but the day room—or whatever it might be called in Arabic—contained plenty of silk-swathed divans, which would, she hoped uneasily, solve the sleeping situation.

Quite how she would cope she didn't know, but somehow she would. She must.

For now, though, what she wanted was a bathroom to freshen up in, and she was relieved to discover it was western in style. Even so, as she took a cooling shower she kept her water usage to the minimum, mindful that they were in the middle of a desert. Then she donned a calf-length, floaty, fine cotton flower-printed dress, draped a chiffon scarf over her hair and bare shoulders.

She found Nikos, also showered and changed, waiting for her by an arched colonnade that looked out on the wide room-length balcony. Lunch had been set out for them, and as they took their places, soft-footed servants unobtrusively waiting on them, Diana resolved that however inappropriate being in an Arabian love-nest might be for her and Nikos, they might as well make the most of this privileged stay.

Lunch passed congenially while they chatted in what had now become quite a comfortable fashion, on subjects roaming from the journey they'd had that morning to more intellectual consideration of the geopolitics of the region and the impact on world affairs and global economics.

Nikos was, as Diana already knew, very well informed, and she found it stimulating to discuss such matters with him. It struck her that he was a far more interesting person to talk to than most of her friends and acquaintances. He had a world view that they lacked, a broadness of opinion and a highly incisive intelligence. No wonder he'd come so far in his life.

I never find his company tedious, she found herself thinking.

So often when she was talking to people socially she was conscious of simply going through the motions—saying what was proper, most of it trivial but socially acceptable, anodyne, appropriate to the occasion. She could do it in her sleep, but it was hardly a mental workout. Exchanging views and arguments with Nikos was quite the opposite, and she found that she really enjoyed trying to keep up with him.

We get on surprisingly well.

The thought was suddenly in her head, lingering a moment, and then, as the leisurely meal ended, Nikos brought the subject round to themselves again.

'So, how do you want to spend the afternoon?' he asked her. His tone was easy, relaxed, his glance at her the same.

'Camel riding?' she suggested, with a hint of humour in her voice.

He nodded. 'We must most definitely do so while we are here—but not in the main heat of the day. However, there's a pool if we want it—though for me...' Nikos flexed his long legs '... I wouldn't mind a good workout after our long drive and this highly delicious lunch—there's a gym here too.'

'Well, why don't you?' Diana smiled amiably, then smothered a yawn. 'I have to say that our early-morning start and that large lunch is making taking a siesta very tempting!'

And that was what she did, dozing peacefully for a good couple of hours or more.

The palace had been built long before air-conditioning, and used the ancient Arabian technique of maximising the up-draught of air through cleverly positioned open archways and slatted wooden windows to create a cooling effect.

When she finally arose, much refreshed, it was to be served with mint tea and tiny pastries, before going to change into her swimming costume and sarong and being shown down to the pool. It was situated in the gardens that stretched beyond the palace, away from the entrance they'd arrived at, bordered by a high stone wall and fronted by palm trees for total privacy.

The heat was beginning to ebb, she fancied, and once she was wet it was much cooler as she swam lazily around, feeling her loose hair streaming sleekly behind her. A sense of well-being eased through her. This really was a magical experience, and however inapplicable it was for her and Nikos to be here in the Sheikh's love-nest it was not an experience she would ever have again.

'So this is where you are.'

Nikos's voice penetrated her consciousness and she looked up from her lazy circling of the pool to see him standing at the water's edge. He looked even taller from this low perspective, and he'd clearly done a vigorous workout indeed. His T-shirt was damp, so were his shorts, and his muscles were pumped.

A moment later she saw even more than his shoulders, biceps and quads. He peeled off the damp shirt and chucked it, then yanked off his trainers. A moment later he was in the pool beside her, under the water, then surfacing in a flurry of diamond droplets, shaking the water from his eyelashes and grinning.

'Wow! That feels good!' he exclaimed feelingly. He looked at Diana. 'Apparently the temperature will start dropping once the sun has set, and for that I shall be grateful.' He quirked an eyebrow in his characteristic manner. 'Do you fancy some star-gazing later on? There's a very fancy telescope up on the roof, I'm told, but even without that the show should be spectacular.'

As he spoke, he found himself thinking about Nadya for a moment. He'd never have made such a suggestion to *her*. She'd have looked at him as if he were mad, and then counter-suggested going to a fashionable nightspot instead, where she could enjoy being seen and admired.

He frowned inwardly. Had he really never noticed how limited Nadya was? She was a professional to the hilt in her work, but when it came to anything else—from astronomy to geopolitics—her eyes would glaze over.

Diana's eyes brightened and sharpened—she listened

and responded, sometimes agreeing, sometimes arguing a counterpoint, putting a different perspective and engaging vigorously, holding her corner, but open to new views as well.

She was open to the prospect of studying the night sky too. She was smiling enthusiastically at his suggestion, as he'd thought she would.

'Oh, yes please!' she said eagerly.

'Great,' Nikos returned, banishing the memories of Nadya's time in his life, utterly irrelevant to him now that he had Diana.

Diana, who was opening the door to the next stage of his life with her impeccable background, her very own stately home, the upper-class world she had been born into and which he would now enjoy as her husband, the world she took for granted, the world he himself had had no right to. Diana would give him that and more.

Diana was the woman he desired for her cool pale beauty, the woman he was so close to making his own in the most intimate way.

Soon...so very soon now.

With a flexing of his muscles he executed a perfect duck-dive and disappeared under the water completely, swimming strongly to the end of the pool and back several times before needing to surface.

Diana watched him admiringly. 'That's amazing breath control,' she told him as he finally broke the water.

He grinned again. 'It's just practice,' he said. 'And good lung capacity.'

Diana's eyes went to the smooth, muscled expanse of his chest, with its perfectly honed pecs and taut solar plexus in the flat between his hard-edged ribs. She looked away hurriedly. Feasting her gaze on his near naked body was no way to behave.

She waded to the steps and clambered out, wrapping a towel around herself. 'I'm heading indoors,' she announced. 'Time to shower. What's the drill for this evening?' Her voice held the light, bright tone she was determined to keep with him.

'Sunset drinks on the terrace,' he informed her. 'No rush.'

It was just as well he'd said that, Diana discovered, for when she returned indoors she was immediately swept away by what seemed to be a whole posse of waiting women who, with a flurry of soft-footed, smiling attention, proceeded to get her ready for the evening.

For a brief moment she resisted—then relented. After all, never again would she be staying in a royal hideaway in the Arabian desert—so why not indulge in what was being so insistently offered to her?

With murmurs of *'Shukran!'* she gave herself up to their ministrations.

Nikos stood on the wide upper-storey terrace, edged by a balustrade in the red sandstone that the whole building was constructed with, smooth and warm to the touch still, though the sun was close to setting. To the east, colour was fading from the sky, and soon stars would be pricking out in the cloudless sky. There would indeed be a spectacular show later on.

Ruminatively he sipped his drink, a cool, mint-flavoured concoction that went well with the ambience. There was champagne on ice awaiting Diana's eventual emergence. His eyes narrowed slightly as he recalled that moment in the pool, when she'd made no secret of being oh-so-aware of his body. Finding it pleasing to her.

Anticipation thrummed softly through him. Finally... *finally* he was losing the ice maiden! It had taken him this long, but the thaw was underway. He felt the tug of a caustic smile at the corner of his mouth as his eyes rested on the desert vista beyond. In this heat, how could she help but thaw?

And here, now, in this the ultimate hideaway, she would melt completely, he knew.

Mentally he sent a message of thanks to the Sheikh and his romantic-souled sister. This place was absolutely ideal. The hotel might have been designed to convey the impression of *Arabian Nights*—but this was the real thing.

His smile lost its caustic edge and widened into one of true appreciation. An appreciation he knew Diana shared too. There was an authenticity to this place that appealed to her—it had a history, a cultural heritage. Generations had passed through it, leaving the echo of their presence, and that made it similar in essence to her own country house home. He felt it was a good omen for their stay.

A sound behind him made him turn. And as he did every thought about the edifice he was in vanished. Every thought in his head vanished except one.

It was Diana—and she looked…

Sensational.

She was walking towards him slowly. Slowly, he realised, because she was in very high heels and her dress was very tight. It must, he realised instantly, be the couture gown gifted to her by the Princess. And, oh, the Princess had chosen well!

The superbly crafted gown contoured Diana's figure like a glove, fitting her almost like a second skin. There was nothing at all immodest in the fit—it simply skimmed over her flawlessly, the smooth, pale yellow material creating a sheen that glistened in the fading light, aglow from the setting sun reflecting off the golden dunes.

He gazed at her, riveted, as she approached, the short train of the dress swishing on the marble floor, the delicate beading rustling at her bodice and hem.

She stopped as she came up to him. 'The Princess had this delivered here!' she announced.

She'd been half dismayed to discover that Princess Fatima had kept to what she'd promised, and half dazzled by wearing so exquisite a gown, far in excess of what her own wardrobe ran to.

Nikos's eyes swept over her. 'You look fantastic,' he breathed.

His whole body had tensed, tautened, and he could not take his eyes from her. The incredible gown—haute couture at its most extravagant best—needed no jewellery. The beading served as that, and all that had been added was a kind of narrow bandeau of the same material, embroidered all over with the delicate beading that had been woven through the elaborate coiffure of her hair. Her make-up was subdued, but absolutely perfect for her, her lips a soft sheen, her skin unpowdered, her eyelashes merely enhanced, and a little kohl around the eyes themselves. It made her look sensual and exotic.

'It's incredible,' he murmured, still sweeping his gaze over her. He found himself reaching for her hands—their nails were pearlescent, with a soft sheen like her lips. Slowly he raised them to his mouth. His eyes met hers. 'You were always beautiful,' he said, 'but tonight—tonight you surpass the stars themselves!'

For a moment their eyes met and mingled. Held. Something seemed to pass between them…something that she could not block—did not wish to. Something that seemed to keep her absolutely motionless while Nikos beheld her beauty.

Then, with a little demur, she slipped her hands away

and gave a tiny shake of her head. 'It's the gown,' she said. 'It's a work of art in its own right.'

'Then it needs a toast of its own!' Nikos laughed.

A servant was hovering, waiting to open the champagne, and Nikos nodded his assent. A moment later he was handing Diana a softly beaded flute and raising his own.

'To your gown—to its exquisite beauty.' He paused. A smile lurked at his mouth, and his eyes were not on the gown. They were on Diana. 'And to you, Diana, my most exquisitely beautiful bride.'

She gazed up at him, her own glass motionless, and met his dark, lustrous eyes, so warm, so speaking...

And suddenly out of nowhere, out of the soft desert night that was slowly sweeping towards them from the east, as the burning sun sank down amongst the golden dunes, she felt a sense of helplessness take her over. She hadn't wanted to come to this place—this jewel-like desert hideaway, this royal love-nest dedicated to sensual love—but she was here. Here and now—with this man who, alone of all the men she had ever encountered, seemed to have the ability to make her shimmer with awareness of his overpowering masculinity.

She simply could not bring herself to remember that he was the man who was saving Greymont for her, to whom she was to be only a society wife, playing the role that he wanted her to play at his side.

How could she think of things like new roofs for Greymont and rewiring, restoring stonework and all the bills that came with that? How could she think of being just a useful means for Nikos Tramontes to move in circles he had not been born into? And how could she think of things like marriages of convenience that were nothing more than business deals?

It was impossible to think of such things! Not standing here, in this priceless precious gown, with a glass of vintage champagne between her fingers as she stood looking out over the darkening desert, miles and miles from anywhere, alone with Nikos.

So she raised her glass to him, took a first sip, savouring the delicate *mousse* of the champagne.

'To you, Nikos,' she said softly. 'Because I would not be here were it not for you.' Her eyes held his still. 'And, as you say, this is an experience of a lifetime…'

Something changed in his eyes—a fleck of gold like flame, deep within. 'It is indeed, my most beautiful bride.'

A frisson went through her and she was powerless to stop it. Powerless to do anything but look back at him and smile. Drink him in. Her eyes swept over him. He was wearing narrow-cut evening trousers, but not a dinner jacket. His dress shirt, made of silk, was tieless, open at the neck, his cuffs turned back and fastened with gold links that caught the last of the setting sun and exposed his strong wrists.

He looked cool, elegant and—she gulped silently—devastatingly attractive. His freshly shaved jawline, the sable hair feathering at his nape and brow, the strong planes of his features and those dark, deep-set, inky-lashed eyes that were meeting her gaze, unreadable and yet with a message in them that she could not deny.

Did not wish to deny…

Emotion fluttered in her again. How far away she was from the reality of her life—how immersed she was, here, in this fairytale place, so remote, so private, so utterly different from anything she had known.

It's just me and Nikos—just the two of us.

The real world seemed very far away.

She felt a quiver in her blood, her pulse, felt sudden

breathlessness. Something was happening to her and she did not know what.

Except that she did…

She took another mouthful of the rare-vintage champagne, feeling the rush of effervescence in the costly liquid create an answering rush in herself. She felt as light as air suddenly, breathless.

She became aware that the silent-footed servants were there again, placing tempting delicacies on golden platters on an inlaid table, bowing and then seeming to disappear as noiselessly as they had appeared.

'How do they do that?' Diana murmured as she leant forward to pick at the delicate slivers of what, she did not know—knew only that they tasted delicious and melted in her mouth like fairy food.

'I suspect a magic lamp may be involved,' Nikos answered dryly, and Diana laughed. Then he smiled again—a smile that was only for her—and met her eyes. He raised his glass again. 'To an extraordinary experience,' he said, his slight nod indicating their surroundings.

She raised her own glass and then turned her attention to the darkening desert. 'I shall certainly remember this all my life,' she agreed. Her gaze swept on upwards. 'Oh, look—stars!'

'There'll be a whole lot more later on,' Nikos said. 'For now, let's just watch the night arrive.'

She moved beside him, careful not to lean on the balustrade lest the work of art she was wearing was marked or creased in any way. Her mood was strange.

She had given herself over to the murmuring attentions of what she could only refer to as handmaidens, letting them do what they willed with her. It had started with them bathing her, in water perfumed with aromatic oils, and gone on from there until she'd walked out on to the terrace feeling almost as if she were in a dream.

Because surely it *must* be a dream—standing here beside Nikos, watching the night darken over the dunes, hearing the strange, alien noises of night creatures waking and walking, feeling the air start to cool, the air pressure change. How far away from the real world they seemed. How far away from everything that was familiar. How far away from everything that was not herself and Nikos.

Her eyes went to him again, seeing his elegantly rakish garb, the absence of a tie, the open-necked shirt, the turned-back cuffs, all creating that raffish look, looking so *sensual*.

She felt a ripple of ultra-awareness go through her like a frisson. As if every nerve-ending were suddenly totally alert—quivering. And as she stood beside him she caught his scent—something musky, sweet-spiced and aromatic, that went perfectly with this desert landscape, matching the oh-so-feminine version of the perfume with which she had been adorned. It caught her senses, increasing the tension that was vibrating silently through her as she stood beside him, so aware of his presence close to her, knowing she only had to lean a little sideways for her arm to press against his. For his arm to wrap around her, pull her to him as they stood gazing out over the darkening desert.

From somewhere deep within her another emotion woke. One she should pay heed to. One that called to her to listen. But she would not listen. She refused to listen. Refused to heed it. She would only go on standing here, nestled into the strong, protective curve of Nikos's arm, gazing out over the desert that surrounded them all about, keeping the world beyond far, far away.

She sipped her champagne, as did he, and they stood in silence until the night had wrapped them completely and the dunes had become looming, massy shapes, darker than the night itself. Overhead, stars had started to blaze like windows into a fiery furnace beyond. Behind them torches were being lit by unseen hands along the length of the terrace, and several braziers, too, to guard against the growing chill of the desert night, and the flickering firelight danced in the shadows all around them.

She turned, and realised that through the archways that pierced the inner border of the terrace more light was spilling—softer light—and the characteristic sweetly aromatic scent of Middle Eastern cuisine.

'Ready to dine?' Nikos asked her with a smile, and she nodded, suddenly hungry.

Lunch seemed a long time ago. Her everyday reality a long time ago.

Because this surely wasn't real, was it? Nikos as her very own desert prince, dark-haired, dark-eyed, and she, gliding beside him like a princess, in a gown fit for royalty, her train swishing on the inlaid marble floor.

Servants were guiding them forward, smiling and bowing, ushering them into yet another room. She gave a soft cry of delight as they entered. It was a dining room, the interior constructed out of wood, fretted and inset with tessellations which glinted in the light of the dozens of candles that were the only illumination, burning in sconces on the walls and pillars all around, and on the table set for them with golden dishes, golden plates— golden everything, it seemed. The air was heavy with the fragrance of frankincense from hidden burners.

'*Jamil jaddaan*—very beautiful!' Diana exclaimed, clapping her hands in delight and indicating the exquisite room.

The servants bowed and smiled, and the steward pulled back huge carved wooden chairs, lined with silk cushions, for her and Nikos. She took her place carefully, and Nikos sat opposite her.

The meal that followed was as exquisite as the room they dined in—dishes of rich, fragrant Middle Eastern food, with delicately spiced charcoal-baked meats as familiar as lamb and as unfamiliar as goat and camel, and who knew what else besides, as tender as velvet, all served with rice enhanced with nuts and dates and raisins, sweet and savoury at the same time.

As a mindful precaution for her priceless gown Diana had called for a shawl to be brought, which she'd swathed around her upper body while she ate.

'I couldn't bear to mark this dress!' She shuddered at the thought. 'I doubt it could ever be cleaned—and even if it could the cost would be terrifying!' She looked at it musingly. 'I wonder when I'm ever going to have an opportunity to wear it again.'

He answered instantly. 'When we entertain at Greymont,' he said. 'Once all the work is complete we can give a grand ball—and you shall wear the Princess's gown for it.'

A vision leapt in her mind instantly. Greymont, thronged with guests, and she and Nikos descending the stairs to the hall, her hand on his arm—man and wife, side by side. As if their marriage was a true one.

For a moment longing fired within her. So fierce she felt faint with it.

What if my marriage to Nikos were real?

The thought wound its way around her senses, enticing, beguiling, sweet and fragrant—just as the fragrance of the frankincense was winding its way around her senses, along with the glowing effervescence of champagne, the deep, rich sensuality of the wine, her physical repletion after the delicately spiced foods, the soft golden light of the candles, reflected a million times in the golden dishes...

The light was setting off the man she had married a few short days ago with a golden sheen, softening the contours of his face, giving him glints like flecks of gold in his dark, long-lashed eyes.

Eyes that were resting on her.

With a message in them that was as old as time.

'Diana.'

He said her name in a low voice, setting down his wine glass slowly, paying it no attention. All his focus was on her, now, as she sat there, held in his gaze.

'Diana...'

He said her name again. His voice was husky now. How beautiful she was! Like a rare, exquisite jewel, shining in this jewel box of a room. For him alone.

He got to his feet, oblivious of the servant who was instantly there, drawing back the heavy, carved cedarwood chair. He held out a hand towards Diana. Slowly, very slowly, she got to her feet. Unnoticed, her swathing shawl fell to the floor. Unnoticed, a servant stooped to pick it up, drape it gracefully around her shoulders.

Wordlessly she took Nikos's hand. It closed over hers, warm and strong. She felt faint suddenly, and filled with a subliminal sense of anticipation. His eyes smiled at her—warm, like his handclasp.

'Shall we look at the stars?' he said softly.

Still wordless, she nodded. There was a breathlessness in her—a headiness that had nothing to do with the consumption of champagne and wine and everything to do with Nikos holding her hand, leading her away.

They went back out on to the wide marble terrace and

down to the far end where, Diana realised, there was a flight of steps that would take them upwards to the roof.

As they gained the flat surface she gave an audible gasp. Only a very dim torch, low down, lit the top of the steps. Beyond there was velvet darkness. A darkness that was pierced only above their heads by a forest of stars, the incandescence of them burning through the floor of heaven.

She lifted her hand. 'It's as if I could reach up and pluck one down, they seem so close!' she said in wonder.

Nikos tucked her hand into the crook of his arm, leading her carefully, mindful of her high heels, into the centre of the wide flat rooftop, which was carpeted like a roofless open-air room. Roofed by stars.

The sky was like a bowl, inset with stars down to the horizon, or so it seemed—a horizon marked only by the rounded edges of the dunes, the jagged outlines of rocks and outcrops. She gazed about her, lips parted, awestruck, tilting back her head.

She dimly was aware that she was leaning against the strong column of Nikos's body to give herself balance. He was gazing upwards too, his gaze sweeping in wide arcs to take it all in. He started to name the constellations that were visible at these latitudes, at this season, raising his arm to guide her.

'It's the most glorious thing I've seen in my life!' She sighed, still breathless with awe.

'Do you want the telescope set up?' he asked her, but she shook her head.

'No, for tonight this is enough—I can't take it all in as it is.' She turned to face him. 'Oh, Nikos, this is the most wonderful sight!'

'It is indeed,' he said. 'And we can see them better still if we lie down...'

He gestured to something that had not at first been visible to Diana, but now, with her darkness-adjusted eyes, she saw that—incongruous as it might appear— there was what seemed to be a king-sized divan in the centre of the rooftop, presumably set there for the very purpose of lying down to see the stars. Already her neck was aching with tilting her head upwards, and her feet in their high heels were scarcely prepared for long standing.

Gratefully she let Nikos guide her, help her to ease down, to take off her shoes—not needed now—and then lie back on the myriad cushions piled on the silk-covered divan.

'Oh, that's better,' she said gratefully, able now to gaze straight up at the night sky.

She felt the divan dip slightly as Nikos's heavy form came down on the other side. With half her mind she felt a flicker go through her—maybe she and Nikos lying virtually side by side like this, all alone under the desert night sky, was not the wisest thing. Then she brushed it aside. This was an experience to be made the very most of. They were here to star-gaze—nothing else.

For a while they simply lay quietly, gazing upwards. Speech seemed not just superfluous, but intrusive. The cushion beneath Diana's head was soft, but because of her elaborate coiffure it was not entirely comfortable. She shifted position slightly, and then heard Nikos speak beside her in the dark.

'What is it?'

'It's my hair,' she said. 'This style is designed to be vertical, not horizontal.' She propped herself up, reaching with her other hand behind her head, patting it to see where the pins were.

'Let me help,' said Nikos.

He levered himself to a sitting position and turned

her shoulders slightly, to give him greater access to the back of her head. For reasons she did not want to explore, Diana let him. It was easier for him to do it than for her.

But there was more about this than ease of access. She dipped her head slightly. And as his fingers worked gently over the intricate plaits and coils, seeking pins and grips, she felt a great sensuous languor creep over her. His touch was delicate, feathering through her hair, and as each pin was removed she felt its loosening go through her. Felt a slow surge of blood start to pulse through her.

'Oh, that feels so good...' She sighed as coil after coil was released, easing the tension on her skull. She felt her locks cascading loose to her shoulders, nothing restraining them at all but the beaded bandeau threaded through them.

'Does it?' said Nikos softly.

Her hair was loose now, all the pins and grips discarded—presumably, she thought absently, on the carpet surrounding the divan. But the thought was vague, inchoate. Irrelevant in comparison with that oh-so-sinuous languor that was stealing over her.

Nikos's fingers were still threading through her hair, softly smoothing her locks, gently kneading her scalp, just above her nape. Instinctively she dipped her head further, giving a little sigh of pleasure. She heard his low laugh again, felt his sensuously working fingertips move to the tops of her ears. Then, with another silvered quickening of her pulse, she felt his thumb idly tease at a lobe. A million quivers of sensation went through her. It felt *so* good...

There was a haze inside her, around her. Above, the stars were blazing in their glory, but she felt her eyelids dip, made a little sound in her throat.

As she did so, she felt Nikos's hand stroke down her

throat, its slender column caressed by his long, sensitive fingers. She felt her face being turned towards him, felt her eyelids fluttering open—to see him looking down at her.

And in his eyes, in the starlight, was what she could not deny.

Did not want to deny.

She said his name. Just his name. Breathed it like a sigh.

Who was there to hear it but him and the empty desert? The desert and the night. The night and the stars. The stars and Nikos.

Nikos—who, alone of all the men in all the world, seemed to possess what no man had ever possessed before.

The power to enthral her. Entice her. Tempt her. Tempt her to do what she was doing now—what she *must* do, it seemed, here, now, on this soft silken divan under the burning desert stars, where nothing else existed but themselves and the night and their desire. His for her, hers for him.

I want him so much… So much…

She did not know why—did not care—only knew that her hand was lifting to feather at his temple, to graze the sable hair and drift down the planed cheek to edge along the roughened outline of his jaw.

Her eyes were still half closed, her body still filled with that incredible heaviness. And as she touched him she made that little sound in her throat again, felt as if in a dream that her breasts were tightening, quickening under the second skin that was her precious, priceless gown. The gown given to her by a princess—a princess who'd asked for this desert love-nest to be theirs. For now. For tonight.

It wasn't what their marriage was about—she knew that—but she couldn't think of it now. Could only think and feel what was happening to her here, beneath the desert night burning with myriad stars.

Yearning filled her, and an instinct so powerful she could not resist it. She had no wish to resist it—not here, not now, not under these burning desert stars, not under the heavy-lidded gaze of the man whose mouth was now lowering slowly, infinitely slowly, to meet hers.

His kiss was like silken velvet—infinitely soft, infinitely sensuous. Infinitely arousing. That little sound came from her again, deep in her throat. She felt her neck arch, her loosened wanton hair sliding like satin, felt the hot pulse at her throat strengthen. She felt her hand slip around the nape of his neck, draw him down to her as she rested slowly backwards, moving down upon the waiting cushions, her hair now spilling out across them.

He came down with her, his kiss starting to deepen. She felt her breasts cresting, straining against the bodice of her gown, and still he kissed her as if he would never release her. Desire was sweeping up inside her. A desire whose power she had never known, had only glimpsed in brief glances, crushed thoughts, whenever she'd looked at the man she had married—who was not hers to glance at like that, not hers to think about, not hers to desire…

Except for this night.

She could have him for this night only! Here, where the rest of the world had ceased to exist, seemed as if it might never exist again, might never have existed at all. For only the stars were burning in their own eternity. An eternity she could share for this one night only…

Nikos—the only man to arouse her, awaken her. The only man to whom she was a woman—a woman who could feel what other women felt.

Never... Never have I felt this desire before! Never!

But now she did—now she knew its power, its force and strength. It was arousing and inspiring her, sweeping her along with its tide so that she could not resist, taking her to a new land—a land she had thought was not for her, had never found before.

But she had found now...with him...with Nikos.

The land of sweet desire.

Desire that was mounting in her now, quickening in her blood, in her heating body, in her shallow, hectic breath. She felt her fingers mould his nape, spear into his hair, felt her body turn towards him like a magnet.

Bliss was seeping up inside her at the drowning sweetness of feeling his lips grazing hers—lips that were slowly, remorselessly, teasing from her a deeper response now, a response that began a restlessness inside her, a sense of going over the edge, giving up all control. Giving it up to the feelings filling her body, her mind, her very being.

Of their own volition, in their own mounting need, her lips parted and she gave that low moan in her throat again—of relief, of pleasure, of wonder and bliss as she tasted to the full all that Nikos was offering, all that he was doing, giving to her, with a touch so skilled, so arousing, that she was blind with it.

He was murmuring her name even as he kissed her, tasted her, his hand slipping down, sliding slowly and sensually over the bodice of the dress to mould the contours of her body. Her spine arched into his caress. She was aching for his hand to close over the straining mound of her breast, and when it did, his palm grazing the straining crests, she felt another surge of unbearable desire. And yet another. And another. Each one stronger, more urgent than the last.

She wanted this with all her being. Madness though it was. She didn't care—could not care—could only go on yielding endlessly, urgently, to the hunger that was growing in her with every passing moment, every yearning press of her body into his.

And then suddenly, abruptly, his hand was lifted from her—and his mouth. With a muffled cry of loss she tried to reach for him again, her eyes blind to all but the overpowering need for him that had brought her to this point. But he resisted her reach and instead, with a gasp of shock, he flipped her over so her face was pressed into the pillows.

She tried to raise herself.

'Lie still.'

There was a growl in his voice—a growl that melted her bones. For she knew at a level so deep she did not understand it that this was a command that was for her, not him. And a moment later she realised why.

His hands were at the back of her dress and his fingers were working assiduously, steadily, at slipping free the myriad tiny hooks that fastened the exquisite gown. It seemed to take for ever, and she felt herself grow restless, filled with a sense of frustration that it was taking so long for him to ease the delicate fabric from her skin, exposing, hook by hook, the long line of her spine. She felt her fingers clutch at the silk of her pillow, felt a heat building in her—a heat she could not cool, did not want to cool.

She wanted only to feel as she did when finally the fabric fell aside, and then his long velvet fingertips were easing beneath, splaying out with the most leisurely arousing touch, so that her fingers clenched more tightly, the restlessness in her mounting, wanting more of him, more of his feathered touch, more of the way his mouth was now lowering to her spine, grazing each sculpted contour as swirls of pleasure began to ripple through her.

As his lips grazed down her spine, teasing those swirls of exquisite sensation from her, she felt his hands spread out, easing the gown completely from her until it was all but falling off. Gently, but with a strength that made it effortless, he lifted her from the gown so that it lay like a discarded thing beside her. Gently he lowered her back upon the silken divan, turning her towards him.

She was naked—completely naked. For an endless moment he gazed down at her. Incapable of more. Incapable of anything except letting his eyes feast on the incredible beauty of her naked body. She was everything he'd known she would be—everything and more. Oh, *so* much more!

Her slender frame, the narrow waist, the perfect contours, the sweet lushness of her breasts, bared now for him alone. The swell of her hips, the deep vee below, her long legs, her loosening thighs…

Then with a sudden movement he sat up, seizing the priceless gown. She did not even remark when he dropped it to the floor—her eyes were only for him. Urgently he hauled his own clothing from him—so much more swiftly than he'd just freed her from the gown that had done its job so well—had made her aware of her own beauty, of how precious it was to her, to him, and was now no longer necessary.

Nothing was needed now. Now they had everything they wanted. They had the silken couch, the night sky, the warmth of the desert, the silence and the darkness, the stars their only witness.

They had each other.

It was all that he wanted now. All he had wanted from the first moment he had set eyes on her. This exquisitely beautiful woman, so different from any he had known, offering him so much…

Offering him now the greatest gift of all—the gift that he had waited so many months to claim.

Herself.

She was his at last. The ice maiden was gone for ever. His self-control, his self-denial was finally needed no longer and she was melting in his arms. Melting and then catching fire at his touch, his kiss, his absolute caress.

With a sense of absolute liberty he lowered himself down beside her. Smoothed her golden hair from her forehead. Gazed down at her with a look that told her everything she needed to know, that sent the blood flushing through her, hot and urgent.

'And now,' said Nikos as he started to lower his mouth, his voice rich with anticipation, satisfaction, 'we can begin our wedding night.'

CHAPTER SEVEN

THE SUN WAS RISING, swelling over the rim of the eastern-most dune, bleaching the sky, quenching the stars one by one by one. Rose-gold lit up the horizon, a long, rich line of colour as the sky above turned to azure blue.

In Nikos's arms, Diana slept—as he slept in hers. Her head and torso rested on his chest, that strong, muscle-sculpted wall that could take her weight as if she were feathers drifting from a passing eagle. And around her waist his arm was clamped, heavy upon her, but it was a weight she'd gloried in, holding her to him even as sleep had swept over them in the long, late reaches of the night.

A wedding night that had burned hot as the distant stars whose light had illuminated their bodies—bodies moving in passion, in desire, in endless, boundless need and satiation. Her voice had cried out time after time, each note higher with an ecstasy that had ripped her mind from her body then melded them back, fusing them with the same heat that had fused her body to his. Fusing them as if they were one body, one flesh. They had clasped each other, their tangled limbs impossible to separate.

The sun crept higher now, spilling into the day. It shafted the world with brilliant radiance. Washing up over their naked bodies, covered only by the silken cloths with which the divan was strewn.

Diana stirred. There was warmth moving along her legs now, and she wondered why, her eyes flickering feebly open, blinking at the day. The sun had gained its final clearance of the dunes and now blazed out over the rooftop, instantly heating them. She felt Nikos stir too, his limbs tensing as he moved upwards out of deep sleep.

The arm around her tightened automatically. But he did not wake.

Breathless, Diana eased herself from him. Her body was stiff, unyielding, but move she must. Carefully, very carefully, she stood up. Every muscle in her body ached. She cast her gaze about. She could not stand here naked, exposed on the rooftop. She dipped down, seizing up her cashmere shawl and hurriedly swathing it around herself as consciousness increasingly came back to her.

With a smothered cry she pressed the tips of her fingers against her mouth.

What have I done? Oh, what have I done?

But she knew what she had done. The evidence was there, spread out beneath her gaze—a gaze that could not help but instantly go to the powerful male glory of Nikos's naked his body. An amazed delight leapt in her. Flaring through every cell in her body. Firing every synapse in her dazed brain.

I never knew... I just never knew how it could be!

But she knew now. Knew that Nikos had taken her to a place she had never understood, never realised existed. She felt dazed with the knowledge. Stunned by it.

But it was not knowledge that she could possess freely. She felt her stomach plummet. Dear God, what she had done she should never have allowed herself to do. How *could* she?

This was not what she had married Nikos for.

It was not what he'd married *her* for.

That was the blunt truth of it. The truth that crushed her as she hurried barefoot back down to the interior rooms, rushing into the bathroom. Maybe water would sluice away the madness of what she'd done.

But when she finally emerged from her shower, wrapped in a huge towel, it was to find Nikos waiting for her. He didn't speak—not a word. He was wearing a cotton dressing gown now, and he simply strode up to her. Wrapped her to him.

His bear hug was all-enveloping. Impossible to draw back from.

But I don't want to! I don't want to pull away from him.

The cry came from deep within, from a place she had not known existed. Not until last night.

It seemed an age before he let her go, but when he did he simply said, his eyes alight, his smile wide, 'Breakfast awaits.'

He scooped up a silken robe that was lying draped across the unused bed. It was in sea-green, vivid and vibrant, and he threw it around her and slipped the towel from her.

'You must keep covered,' he growled, and there was an expression in his eyes that she did not need a dictionary to describe. 'Or we'll never get to breakfast.'

His arm around her shoulder, he led her out. She went with him, as meekly as a lamb. For it was the only thing in the world she wanted to do.

Out on the terrace the silent army of servants had set a lavish breakfast table, shaded by an awning, and they took their places. Beyond the terrace and beyond the outdoor pool glittering in the morning sun, the palm trees guarding it, the desert stretched to infinity. All the world was here, in this one place.

In this one man.

Nikos raised his glass of orange juice to her, his smile wide and warm. His eyes warmer still.

'To us, Diana,' he said.

To us? she echoed silently. There was no 'us'—there was only an empty shell of a marriage, designed to make use of each other, with no future in it. None.

But, as she raised her own glass defiance and a reckless daring surged up in her. Beyond this desert hideaway there could be no 'us' for her and Nikos.

But while we are here there can.

And for that... Oh, for that she would seize it all.

'All strapped in?' Nikos said, checking her seat belt. He nodded at their driver. 'OK, let's go.'

With a roaring gunning of the engine the driver grinned and accelerated the four-by-four almost vertically up the perilous slope of the dune.

Within seconds Diana discovered why it was called 'dune-bashing'. She shrieked and covered her eyes as the skilled driver performed manoeuvres that took them to the top, then slid them down the other side, then careered up again to totter precariously at an impossible angle before plunging down in a huge flurry of sandy and sideways sliding.

Nikos hoped that she was, despite appearances, enjoying herself.

By the time the driver finally screeched to a juddering halt, turning back to Nikos with a triumphant grin on his face, he believed she was.

'Oh, good *grief*!' she cried, half-laughing, half-shaking as she finally let go her death grip on the door strap. 'I was absolutely *terrified*!'

'Me too,' Nikos admitted ruefully.

He turned to the driver, exchanging comments on how

he'd performed those almost impossible and certainly potentially lethal manoeuvres on the steep soft sand.

Diana caught at his arm. 'No, Nikos, you are *not* to try doing it yourself!' she exclaimed feelingly.

He turned towards her. 'Worried for me?' he asked, grinning. His eyes glinted. 'How very wifely of you.'

It was lightly said, but it was like a sudden sword in her side, reminding her of just how little right she had to be 'wifely'. But she could not, *would* not think of that now. Not here in the desert, cocooned in this world so distant from their own.

And then Nikos was announcing his need for lunch—for breakfast had been long ago, before they'd set out to try their hands at the ship of the desert, mounting camels as the patient beasts lay on the sand, clambering up with a serpentine grace and starting to move with their slow, swaying gait.

Diana had found the experience unforgettable as her camel trod silently along the way, feeling only the desert wind playing across her heated cheeks, her head shaded by a wide-brimmed hat, the blown sand off the tops of the dunes catching in the light, the burning azure bowl of the sky arching over them, and the endless ocean of sand stretching boundless and bare all around. She'd felt as if she were in a different world. Ancient and primeval, timeless and eternal.

Far, far away from the real world beyond.

But this world here, now, timeless and primeval, was the world she was giving herself to—and she was giving herself to the man here with her, to this time together. She would not think of the world beyond, would not remember it. Not now.

Elation seared through her—a kind of reckless joy as she seized this moment, this time out of time that had come to her unasked-for, unsought, but which she had taken all the same, bestowed upon her like a gift of all gifts.

The gift of this time with Nikos, the man who, out of all men that existed, had taken her to a place she had not believed could ever be for her.

But it is—it is! It's real for me—passion and desire. It's real and now I have it—here, with Nikos, in this timeless place.

That was all she cared about, all she would let herself care about, feel and believe. This time *now*, with Nikos, alone in the desert.

She could see the camels again now, lying down in the shade of high rocks, resting, as their four-by-four descended to the level dirt track again, taking her and Nikos to where a canopy had been set up over carpets laid on the sand.

There they were offered moistened, cooling cloths to wipe their dusty hands and hot faces, before tucking into an array of spiced and fragranced dishes whose delicious aroma quickened her appetite.

And not just for food.

Her eyes slid to the man she was with and she felt that rush of amazement and wonder that came every time she looked at him, feasted on him. He caught her open gaze and smiled—a warm, intimate smile that brought colour flushing to her cheeks. He said nothing, though, only let his long lashes sweep down as he urged her to try yet another dish.

Around them servants stood, pouring cool drinks from tall silver jugs, removing empty dishes, replacing them with yet more food that seemed to be arriving in a procession from the open-air cooking station some way downwind of where they lounged.

Eventually, sated and replete, Diana felt her eyelids start to drift down.

'I'm falling asleep,' she heard herself say as the heat and drowsiness of midday took their soporific toll.

'Then sleep,' said Nikos.

He made a gesture for the servants to clear the last of the bowls and glasses, which they instantly did, then reached across to Diana, drawing her down on the cushions beside him, letting her head loll on his lap. Idly he stroked her hair, plaited into a confining ponytail, but feathering in soft tendrils around her face. Her beautiful, fine-boned face, flushed now with the sun, her hair bleached even paler.

He felt desire stir in him, but held it at bay. It would wait until they were private again.

A slow smile slid across his features and there was reminiscence in his eyes. Their eventual consummation had been everything he'd wanted. Everything he'd intended. Leisurely he replayed in his head that first night—melting her under the stars, seeing the revelation in her starlit eyes as realisation had swept over her, as she'd felt the full intensity of the sensations he'd drawn from her, using all his skills and experience, knowing just what would most sate the desire burning in her like a flame. A desire *he* had kindled, against her own long-held assumption that men were of no sexual interest to her.

His smile deepened, took on a sensual twist. Well, he had made an end of *that*! From now on she would burn for him—burn for however long it took before his desire for her began to wane and the day came when he woke and knew their time together was done with.

Until that time came she was his...

He felt his own lids grow heavy in the somnolent heat. To lie like this, with Diana supine in his lap, her arm across his limbs, warm and close and intimate, was so very good.

Would he *ever* not want her?

The question hung like an eagle over the desert sand, motionless and unanswered, as his eyelids closed and he, too, succumbed to sleep.

'I hate to say this…' Nikos's voice sounded regretful '…but our idyll here is over.'

Diana looked across at him as they sat taking their breakfast in the beautiful inner courtyard, the trickling fountain cooling the air beside them, verdant greenery all around them in the private, enclosed space.

Nikos set down his phone. 'That was the Minister for Development's office. There's another meeting this afternoon with the minister and several other bigwigs. I'll need to be there.'

Diana blinked. The world beyond the desert had seemed so very far away, and yet here it was intruding, downloaded from the ether, summoning them back to reality. She tried to count the days since they'd arrived here from the coast, and failed. One day had segued into the next—indolent, lazy, luxurious, self-absorbed and self-indulgent. A time of passion and desire—a time of bliss.

A fantasy of *Arabian Nights* made real…

And now it was to be ended.

A kind of numb dismay filled her—a sense of dissociation, loss.

Nikos was already getting to his feet. 'I need my laptop,' he said. 'There are some things I must check. Finish your breakfast, though. There is no immediate rush. They're sending a helicopter to take us back to the city.'

The helicopter, when it arrived, was a huge, noisy, angry wasp, churning up the sand, landing just beyond the perimeter fence. It seemed like an invasion to Diana. As Nikos helped her aboard, ducking under the sweeping rotors, it was as if the twenty-first century was crashing back into her.

The machine took off with a deafening roar, wheeling up into the steel-blue sky, casting its wrinkled shadow over the dunes as it headed back to the coast. It took them back to their hotel, but Nikos was not there long—only long enough to shower, change into his business suit, take up his briefcase and depart again, leaving Diana alone and feeling dislocated and bereft in their suite.

Her head was all in pieces. The abrupt change was jarring. From the emptiness of the desert—the absolute privacy of their time there and all that that had brought—back now into the modern world, busy and crowded, demanding and bustling.

Here, time existed. Other people existed. Other priorities. Other realities.

Realities that now forced themselves upon her.

She did not want to face them—but she must.

Restlessly she paced about, netted by tension. There was a deep disquiet within her. A deep, fearful unease.

Danger was lapping at her feet…

CHAPTER EIGHT

NIKOS THREW HIMSELF into the back of his car, his face set. That meeting had *not* gone well. The damned internal politics of the sheikdom were raising their heads again. Sheikh Kamal's cousin, Prince Farouk, who was against *all* development, was leaning on the minister to block him, Nikos, favoured as he was by Sheikh Kamal. So, although the minister had been urbane, he had also been regretful. And adamant.

There would be problems. Difficulties. Delays. It was unfortunate, but there it was.

He gave a frustrated sigh. Sheikh Kamal, shrewd and far-seeing, would, he knew, outmanoeuvre his cousin in the long term, and until then he would have to exercise patience—though it went against the grain to do so. All his life he'd targeted what he wanted, gone after it and achieved it. Wealth, a trophy mistress, and now a trophy wife.

Immediately his mood improved. After all, there was an upside to this delay in his business affairs here. It would give him more time with Diana…

He felt himself start to relax and his body thrummed with anticipation. She would be waiting for him in their suite, no longer the ice maiden but the warm, ardent, passionate woman of his desires, fully awakened by *him*, as by no other man, to the rich glory of her sensuality.

A sensuality that had swept him away.

Oh, Nadya had been a passionate woman—fiery and tempestuous—and he'd always chosen women for their passion. But with Diana... His expression changed, became wondering. With Diana it had been more than passion, that incandescent union with her beneath the stars.

He tried to understand it, to comprehend it. Was it because he'd had to wait so long to claim her? Was that the reason that those days with her in the desert had been so...so *special*? So different from any other days he'd known? Was it because she'd been that untouchable ice maiden, yielding to him only after so long a wait? An ice maiden only he could thaw, who only melted in *his* arms, no other man's?

A frown drew his brows together as he tried to work it out. Work out why it was that those nights he'd spent with her had been so overwhelming.

Because it wasn't just passion or desire—that was why. There was more than that. Oh, yes, there was a sense of triumph that she'd finally yielded to him and his patience had been so lavishly rewarded. But still there was more than that.

It was the sense of companionship they'd shared. Whether it had been watching the stars, knowing she was as beguiled by their majesty as he was—something that Nadya would have found incomprehensible and irrelevant—or laughing as they'd swayed on those poor camels, bearing the load of riders who were rookies, or leaning back into each other's arms as they lounged on the divans by the poolside, under an awning out in the desert heat.

And talking—always talking. Sometimes about world affairs, sometimes just about anything or nothing. Stimulating and energising, or easy and uncomplicated—they could segue from one to the other effortlessly, seamlessly.

I like her company—I enjoy being with her—whether she is in my arms or just spending time with me.

Was it really that simple? If it was, then there was something else, too. Something basic, fundamental—something he'd never thought about before.

She is happy to be with me. She likes my company... enjoys being with me. As I enjoy being with her—for her company, for just being together...

That seemed an odd thing to think, in many ways, because it wasn't something he'd ever considered before when it came to women. It made him realise that the time he'd spent with Nadya, with all of her predecessors had been entirely superficial. It had been about sex—nothing more than that. Nadya had been specifically chosen to be a trophy mistress—showing the world he could have so lauded and beautiful a woman in his bed, on his arm.

Memory flickered in him. He'd thought of Diana as the next step on from that. Did he still think of her that way? Merely as a trophy wife? Or could the woman he'd made his own beneath the desert stars mean something more to him?

Maybe I'll never get bored with her! Maybe I'll never tire of her?

The thought hovered in his mind. It was something that he'd never felt about any woman before and he did not know the answer—not yet. For now all he wanted was what he had had in the desert—Diana in his arms, clinging to him in ecstasy.

Arriving at the hotel, he strode across the vast atrium, hastening up to the honeymoon suite. To Diana—warm and ardent with all the passion he had awakened in her, all the desire he had released in her.

My bride. My wife!

Emotion washed through him—strange and unfamiliar. It was desire for her, yes—strong and powerful—but more than that too. He didn't know what, but it was there, just as strong, just as powerful. He wondered at it, for he did not recognise it, had no experience of it.

Then the elevator doors were opening, and with eager steps he strode along the plush corridor to reach their suite, swiping the key card and going in.

She was there, by the window of the balcony, a coffee tray set out on the dining table in the embrasure where she sat with her tablet, studying the screen. She looked up with a startled expression as he walked in, carelessly tossing aside his briefcase.

'Oh!' she exclaimed.

For a moment there was a panicked look on her face, but Nikos didn't register it. He walked up to her, loosening his tie as he did so, as if it were constricting him.

'Thank God that's over,' he said feelingly. 'That damned meeting!'

Diana looked at him, alarmed. 'It didn't go well?'

Was there strain in her voice? He hardly knew. Instead he answered directly.

'A set-up by Sheikh Kamal's rival for power,' he expostulated. 'I'm being blocked—and it's because of an internal power struggle in the royal family.'

'Oh, I'm sorry...' Diana's voice was concerned, but distracted.

He shook his head. 'Well, it's not that bad. Things will come about. I put my money on Kamal—he's a smart guy and won't be outmanoeuvred. But I'll have to hold fire for a while.' His expression changed. 'In a way,' he said, and there was a glint in his eye now, 'it has its advantages. Gives me more free time while we're here. We can enjoy ourselves all the more. Starting...' there was a growl in his voice '...right now.'

He drew her upright, made to slide her into his arms, into his waiting embrace. It was good, *so* good to have her here for him. So good to feel her slender body, so pliant, so beautiful, to see her upturned face, her mouth waiting for the kisses which she had come to yearn for in their desert idyll, returning them as ardently as he bestowed them. Diana, his beautiful, exquisite Diana—*his*, all his, completely, all-consumingly.

'I've been aching for you,' he said, his voice a low, husky growl, his eyes alight with sensual desire. 'Aching…'

His mouth lowered to hers, his arms around her tightening. But there was something wrong—something different. She was tensing her body, straining back from him.

'Nikos—'

There was something wrong in her voice, too.

He drew back a moment, loosening his clasp but not relinquishing her. 'What is it?' he said. Concern was in his voice, in the searching frown of his eyes.

She slipped her hands from her sides to rest them against his shoulders—to brace herself against them. Hold herself away.

'Nikos—we…we can't!'

His frown deepened, as did his expression of concern.

'What is it?' he asked again. 'What is wrong?'

She did not answer, then carefully she drew away from him. He let her go and she walked to the far side of the dining table, as if to put it between them.

'We need to talk.'

He stared at her. There was distress in her voice, in her face—her eyes.

His brows drew together in a frown. 'What is it?' he said, and now his voice was different too. Edged.

She took a breath. Cowardice bit within her. And temptation. Sweeping, overpowering temptation! The temptation not to say what she was steeling herself to say. To keep silent. To hold out her arms to Nikos and let him sweep her against him. To carry her through to that preposterous bridal bed smothered in rose petals and take her to the place they had found in each other's arms, each other's ecstasy.

But if she did...

Emotion devoured like the jaws of a wolf. If she succumbed, as she so longed to succumb, then what she had tried to keep at bay out in the desert, what she had denied, refused, would happen.

And I cannot let it happen. I dare not!

All her life she had kept intimacy at bay, kept herself safe from what she had seen destroy her father. The hurt he'd suffered that she dared not risk for herself! So now she must say what she must say. Do what she must do.

Nikos's voice was cutting across her anguished thoughts.

'Diana—speak to me. What is it?'

There was steel in Nikos's voice now. He wanted answers, explanations. Something was going wrong, and he wanted to know what it was. *Why* it was. So that he could fix it. Whatever it was, he could fix it.

Her breath caught—then she forced herself into words. Words she had to say. *Had* to...

'Nikos—what happened in the desert...it shouldn't have happened!'

Disbelief flashed across his face. 'How can you say that?'

His voice was hollow. As if the breath had been punched from his body by a blow that had landed out of nowhere. His mind was reeling, unable to comprehend what she had just thrown at him. It made no sense. *No sense.* How could she possibly be saying what she had just said?

'And how can you *not* see that?' she cried in response. 'It's not what our marriage is about! It never was—it was never anything more than...than convenience! A marriage that would suit us both, provide us both with something that was important to each of us—restoring Greymont for me, an *entrée* into my world for you! And then we'd go our separate ways! You *said* that, Nikos—you said it yourself to me. It was what you proposed!'

She took another ragged breath.

'And that's what I agreed to. *All* I agreed to.'

He was staring at her. Every line in his face frozen. Disbelieving.

'Are you telling me,' he said slowly, 'that you actually believe our marriage should be *celibate*?'

Now it was Diana looking at him as if he were insane. Her eyes flared. 'Of *course*!' she said. 'That's what we signed up to. Right from the start.'

An oath sprang from him. 'I don't believe I'm hearing this!' he said.

His voice was still hollow, but there was an edge to it that made her blench.

He took a heaving breath. Lifted his hands. 'Diana, how can you possibly have thought our marriage should be celibate? When did I *ever* give you cause to think so?'

Consternation filled her features. 'Well, of course I thought you thought that! You gave me every reason to believe so. Nikos, you never laid a finger on me in all the time of our engagement. Nor when we first arrived here!'

He ran his hand agitatedly through his hair. He still could not believe what he was hearing. It was impossible—just impossible—that she should have thought what she *said* she'd thought. Impossible!

'I was giving you *time*, Diana. Time to get to know me,

to get used to me. Of *course* I wasn't going to be crass enough to pounce on you the moment we'd signed the marriage register. I wanted the time to be right for us.'

He made no reference to ice maidens—what help would that have been? She probably hadn't even been aware that she *was* one—that she'd radiated *Look but don't touch* as if it had beamed from her in high frequency.

The very fact that she was talking now, in this insane way, of celibacy—dear God, when they were *married*, when they'd just returned from that burning consummation under the desert stars—was proof of how totally unaware she was of how unaroused, how frozen she had been. It was a state she'd thought was normal.

His mind worked rapidly. Was that why she was being like this now? Was this just panic—a kind of delayed 'morning after the night before' reaction as she surfaced back in the real world, away from the desert idyll that had so beguiled her—beguiled them both? That must be it—it was the only explanation.

His mood steadied and he forced himself to stay calm. Reasonable. He took a breath, lowering his voice, making it sound as it needed to now. Reassuring.

'And we *have* come to know each other, haven't we, Diana?' he went on now, in that reassuring tone. 'We've got used to one another now that we've finally had time to be with each other, now we're married—and we've found each other agreeable, haven't we? We get on well.'

His expression changed without him being aware of it. It was vital that she understood what he was saying now.

'Maybe if we hadn't had that invitation from the Sheikh to stay at his desert palace it might have taken longer for our relationship to deepen. To reach the conclusion that it has. A conclusion, Diana, that has *always* been inevitable.'

He took a step towards her, unconscious of his action, only of his need to close the distance between them. To make everything all right between them again. The way it had been in the desert.

His voice was husky. He had to tell her. He had to make things clear to her, cut through the confusion that must be in her, the panic, even, which was the only way he could account for what she was saying.

'It's always been there, Diana, right from the start. That flame between us. Oh, it was hardly visible at first—I know that—but I know, too, that you were not indifferent to me, however much you might have been unaware of it at a conscious level. And, Diana...' his voice dropped '...believe me, I was the very opposite of indifferent to you from the very moment I first saw you. But it took the desert, Diana, to let that invisible flame that has always run between us flare into the incandescent fire that took us both.'

He strode around the table. Clasped his hands around her shoulders. Gazed down into her face. Her taut and stricken face. He ached to kiss her, to sweep her up into his arms and soothe the panic from her, to melt it away in the fire of his desire—of *her* desire.

'We can't deny what's happened, and nor should we. *Why* should we? We're man and wife—what better way to seal that than by yielding to our passion for each other? The passion you feel as strongly as I do. As powerfully. As irresistibly.'

His voice was low, his mouth descending to hers. He saw her eyelids flutter, saw a look almost of despair in them, but he made himself oblivious to it. Oblivious to everything except the soft exquisite velvet of her lips.

He drew her to him, sliding his hand around her nape, cradling the shape of her head, holding her for his kiss—

a kiss that was long and languorous, sensual and seductive. He felt the relief of having her in his arms again, of making everything all right. It was a kiss to melt away her panic, her fears. To soothe her back into his embrace.

He heard the low moan in her throat that betokened, as he now knew, the onset of her own arousal—an arousal he knew well how to draw from her, to enhance with every skilled and silken touch. His hand slid from her shoulder to close his over her breast, which ripened at his touch, the coral peak straining beneath his gentle, sensuous kneading. He groaned low in his chest, feeling his own arousal surge. Desire soared in him—and victory. Victory over her fears, her anxieties. He was melting the ice that was seeking to freeze her again, to take her from him. To lock her back into a snow-cold body, unfeeling, insensate.

He would never let her be imprisoned in that icy fastness again! In his arms he would melt away the last of her fears. The ice maiden was never to return.

He heard again that low moan in her throat and he deepened his kiss, drawing her hips against him, letting her know how much he desired her and how much *she* desired him.

The low moan came again—and then, as her head suddenly rolled back, it became a cry. Her face was convulsing.

'Nikos! *No!*'

He let her go instantly. How could he hold her when she had denied him?

She was backing away, stumbling against the edge of the mahogany table, warding him off with her hand. Her face was working…she was trying to get control of her emotions. Emotions that were searing through her like sheet metal, glowing white-hot. Emotions she had to quench now—right now.

*He talks of a flame between us as if that makes it better—
it doesn't! It makes it worse—much, much worse! It makes
it terrifyingly dangerous! Just as I've feared all my life!*

So whatever it took, however much strength she had
to find—desperately, urgently—she had to keep him at
bay. *Had* to!

'I don't want this,' she said. Her voice was thin, almost
breaking, but she must not let it break. 'I don't want this,'
she said again. 'What happened in the desert was a...a
mistake. A *mistake*,' she said bleakly.

There was silence—complete silence. She took another razoring breath, then spoke again, her voice hollow. Forcing herself to say what she *had* to say.

'Nikos, if I had thought...realised for one moment that
you intended our marriage to be anything but a marriage
in name only, that you intended it to be consummated, I
would never have agreed to marry you.'

Her jaw was aching, the tension in her body unbearable, but speak she must. She had to make it crystal-
clear to him.

'It wasn't why I married you.'

She forced herself to hold his gaze. There was something wrong with his face, but she could not say what.
Could do nothing but feel the emotions within her twisting and tightening into vicious coils, crushing the breath
from her.

The silence stretched, pushing them apart, repelling
them from each other.

As they must be.

There was incomprehension in his eyes. More than
that. Something dark she did not want to see there that
chilled her to the bone.

Then he was speaking. The thing that was wrong in
his face, in his eyes, was wrong in his voice, too. It had

taken on a vicious edge of sarcasm that cut into her with a whip-like lash.

'I thank you for your enlightening clarification about our marriage,' he said, and coldness iced inside him. 'In light of which it would therefore be best if you returned to the UK immediately. Tonight. I will make the arrangements straight away.'

He turned, and with a smothered cry she made to step after him.

'Nikos! Please—don't be like that. There's no need for me to leave. We can just be as we were before…'

Her voice trailed off. The words mocked her with the impossibility of what she was saying.

We can never be as we were before.

His face had closed. Shutting her out as if an iron gate had slammed down across it.

'There is no purpose in further exchange. Go and pack.'

He was walking away, picking up the house phone on the sideboard, uttering the brief words necessary to set in motion her departure.

'I have work to do,' he said.

His voice was as curt as it had been to the person at the front desk. He walked over to where he'd tossed his briefcase, picked it up. Walked into the spare bedroom.

She heard the door snap shut.

Then there was silence.

Silence all around her.

CHAPTER NINE

BLACK, COLD ANGER filled Nikos. Like dark ink, it filled his veins, his vision. His gaze, just as dark, was fixed on the blackening cloudscape beyond the unscreened porthole of the first-class cabin of the jet, speeding into the night as far and as fast as it could take him.

Australia would do—the other side of the world from Diana.

Diana whom he had made his wife in good faith. Concealing nothing from her, having no hidden agenda.

Unlike his bride. His oh-so-beautiful ice maiden, his look-but-don't-touch bride, who'd never intended, even from the start, to make their marriage work.

Over and over in his head, like a rat in a trap, he heard that last exchange with her. Telling him what she thought of him. What she wanted of him.

What she did not want.

Not him—no, never that.

'It wasn't why I married you.'

Her words—so stark, so brutally revealing—had told him all. All that she wanted.

Only my money, in order to give her what she wants most in all the world.

His eyes hardened like steel, like obsidian—black and merciless. Merciless against him. Against her.

And what she wants most in all the world is not me.

It was her house—her grand, ancestral home—and the lifestyle that went with it. That was all that was important to her. Not him. *Never* him.

Memory, bitter and acid, washed in his veins, burning and searing his flesh. A memory he could not exorcise from his mind. Driving up to that gracious Normandy chateau bathed in sunlight, so full of hope! Hope that now he was no longer a child, and now he had been told who his parents were by the lawyer who had summoned him to his offices on his eighteenth birthday, he had found the mother who had given him away at birth.

He had been hoping he would discover that there was some explanation for why she had disowned him—something that would unite them, finally, that would see her opening her arms to him in joy and welcome.

His mouth twisted, his face contorting. There had been no joy, no welcome. Only cold refusal, cold rejection. He'd been sent packing.

All I was to her was a threat—a threat to her aristocratic lifestyle. To the lifestyle that came with her title, her grand ancestral home. That was all she wanted. All that was important to her.

The revelation had been brutal.

As brutal as the revelation his wife, his bride, had just inflicted upon him.

He tore his mind away as anger bit again, and beneath the anger he felt another emotion. One he would not name. Would not acknowledge. For to acknowledge it would infect his blood with a poison he would never be able to cleanse it from. Never be free of again.

The jet flew on into the night sky.

Out of the brightness of the day into the dark.

* * *

The taxi from the train station made its slow way along the rutted drive that led up to Greymont. The state of the drive was still on her 'to-do' list like a great deal else—including all the interior décor and furnishing work, conserving curtains and restoring ceilings. But the majority of the essential structural work was nearing completion, and work on the electrics and the plumbing were well underway.

Yet the very thought of them burned like fire on Diana's skin.

How could I have got it so wrong? So disastrously, catastrophically wrong!

The question went round and round in her tired, aching head as she walked into her bedroom, collapsed down upon her bed. It had been going round and round ever since she'd walked out of the hotel and into waiting car waiting to take her to the airport, her suitcase having been packed by the maids, her ticket all arranged.

Nikos had stayed immured in his room, the door locked against her. Refusing to have anything more to do with her. Sending her away.

She'd walked out of the hotel like a zombie, feeling nothing. Nothing until she'd taken her seat on the plane and faced up to what the reality of her marriage was.

Completely and utterly different from what Nikos had thought it would be.

That was what she could not bear. That all along Nikos had assumed their oh-so-mutually convenient marriage was going to include oh-so-mutually convenient sex…

He'd assumed that from the start! Intended it from the start!

And she'd blinded herself to it. Wilfully, deliberately,

not wanting to admit that right from that very first moment she'd seen him looking at her it had been with desire.

I told myself he was just assessing me, deciding whether I would fit the bill for his trophy wife, if had the right connections, the right background—the right ancestral home.

Bitter anger at herself writhed within her. How could she have been such a fool not to have realised what Nikos had assumed would be included in their marriage deal? What he'd taken for granted would be included right from the start.

But it was easy to see why. Because she'd wanted to believe that her only role in his life would be to give him an entrée into her upper-class world. Because that had meant she would be able to yield to the desperate temptation that he'd offered her—the means of saving Greymont.

It meant I could take his money and get what I wanted. Easily and painlessly. Safely.

Without any danger to herself.

A smothered cry came from her and she forced her fist into her mouth to keep it from happening again.

Danger? She had wanted to avoid danger—the danger she'd felt from that very first moment of realising that of all the men she had ever encountered it was Nikos Tramontes who possessed the power she had feared all her life.

I walked right into the lion's den. Blindly and wilfully.

And now she was being eaten alive.

The smothered cry came again.

What have I done? Oh, what have I done?

But she knew—had known it the moment she'd surfaced on that rooftop, in the arms of the man she should never have yielded to. She had committed the greatest and most dangerous folly of her life.

Into her head that old saying came: *Take what you want, says God. Take it and pay for it.*

Her eyes stared out bleakly across her familiar childhood room, where she had learned to fear what she must always fear... Well, now she was starting to pay.

Tears welled in her eyes. Anguish rose in her heart.

Nikos was back in London. He'd spent three weeks in Australia, returning to Europe via Shanghai, and then spent another week in Zurich. He had, he thought grimly, been putting off going to London. But he could not put it off for ever.

When he arrived at his house in Knightsbridge his expression darkened. He'd imagined bringing Diana here after their honeymoon, carrying her over the threshold, taking her to bed...

Well, that would not happen now. Would never happen. The black, dark anger that he was now so familiar with, that seemed always to be there now when he thought of her—which was all the time—swilled in his veins. His mouth set in a hard line.

He reached for his phone. Dialled her number. It went to voicemail, and he was glad of it. He did not want to hear her voice.

His message was brief. 'I'm in London. I require you. Be here tomorrow. We have an evening party to go to.'

He disconnected, his expression masked. Diana—his wife, his bride—might have made clear what she thought of him, what she thought of their marriage, but that was of no concern to him right now. She had duties to perform. Duties he was paying her to perform.

However reluctant she might be to do so.

* * *

Diana arrived, as summoned, at the end of the following afternoon. The housekeeper admitted her. Nikos was still at his London offices, but he arrived shortly afterwards. She had installed herself in a bedroom that was very obviously *not* the master bedroom. She'd brought a suitcase with her and was hanging up her clothes—including several evening dresses.

As he walked in she started, and paled.

'Nikos—'

There was constraint in her voice, in her face—in her very stance. Yet the moment her eyes had lit upon him she had felt the disastrous, betraying leap of her blood.

He ignored her, walked up to the wardrobe she was filling with her gowns and leafed through them, extracting one and tossing it on the bed.

'Wear this,' he instructed. 'Be ready to leave in an hour.'

He walked out again.

Behind him, Diana quailed. She had dreaded coming up to town, dreaded seeing him again, but knew she had to. Could not evade it. Could not hide at Greymont any longer.

I have to talk to him—stop him being like this. Try to make it like it was originally between us—civil, friendly...

The words mocked her. Agitation and worse, much worse, churned inside her.

Joining him in the drawing room, changed into the gown he wanted her to wear, steeling herself, she felt them mock her again. He was wearing evening dress, tall and dark and devastating, and as her eyes lit on him a ravening hunger went through her, blood leaping in her veins. She almost ran towards him, to throw herself into his arms, to hold him tight.

Memories exploded in her head of herself in his arms, he in hers...

She thrust them from her.

I cannot let myself desire him.

Desperately she schooled herself to quench that perilous leaping of her blood, the flood of memories in her head. Too dangerous.

He turned his head at her entry, and for just a second she thought she saw the briefest flaring of his eyes as they alighted on her. Then the light was extinguished. He let his gaze rest on her.

'Very suitable,' he said.

His voice was flat, his face closed. She made herself walk towards him, his chill gaze still upon her, feeling the swish of her silken gown around her legs, the low coil of the chignon at her nape, the cool of her pearl necklace around her throat. On the little finger of her left hand her signet ring glinted in the lamp light—the St Clair family crest outlined. A perpetual reminder of why she had become his wife—to keep the house that went with this armorial crest.

She fancied she saw Nikos's shuttered gaze flicker to it, then away.

'Nikos…' She made herself speak, lifting her chin to give her courage—courage she did not feel, feeling only a hollow space inside her. 'Nikos, we have to talk.'

He cast her a crushing look. 'Do we? Have you yet more to tell me, Diana?'

There was a harshness in his voice she had never heard before. An indifference. Absently he busied himself adjusting his cufflinks, not looking at her.

She swallowed again, her throat tight. 'Look, Nikos, our marriage was a mistake. A misunderstanding. I'm sorry—so very sorry—that I got it so wrong in understanding what you…' She swallowed again. 'What you expected of it.'

She couldn't look him in the eyes. It was impossible. He wasn't saying anything, so she went on. Making herself continue. Say the next thing she had to say.

'I've stopped the work on Greymont.'

She said it in a rush, her eyes flying to him, but he gave no indication that he had heard, only went on inspecting his cuff. If she'd thought she saw a nerve work in his taut cheek she must have been mistaken.

She took another breath.

'I've made a tally of all that has been done so far, and anything I'm contracted for. But everything else has been halted. As for what has already been done—the total sum it amounts to…' She faltered, then made herself go on. 'I will do my best to repay you. It will take time—a lot of time, because if I had been able to raise the capital myself I would have done so. And if I realise all my capital, sell my stocks and shares, I'll lose the income from them that I need for maintenance. That's always been the problem—trying to find money both for the restoration and simply keeping Greymont going. The maintenance costs are high—from local taxes to utilities, to just keeping everything ticking over. The place has to be heated in winter or damp gets in, and rot. And I can't throw the Hudsons out on to the street…'

She was rambling, trying to make him understand. He simply went on not looking at her.

'But I will repay you, Nikos. However long it takes me.'

He looked at her then. Finally spoke. 'Yes, you *will* repay me, Diana, of that I am certain.'

She paled. There was something in his voice that felt like a blow. Her lips were dry, but she made herself speak. Tried to reach him.

'Nikos, I'm sorry! I'm sorry this has gone so wrong. I

blame myself—I was naïve, stupid. I really thought you
wanted a marriage in name only—'

'What I *want*, Diana—' his voice cut across hers like
a guillotine '—is for you to honour your agreement with
me. To make your repayment in the only way you can.
The only way I want you to.'

The blood drained from her face and she seemed to
sway. He saw it and wanted to laugh. A savage, baiting
laugh. Emotions were scything through him, slicing and
slicing. She was standing so close. A single step would
take him to her. Crush her to him.

But she was beyond him now. Beyond him for ever.

His expression changed. Became mocking. Savagely
mocking. Mocking himself.

'It's what you signed up for, Diana. To be—what did
you call yourself? Ah, yes. My "society wife". At my
side, graceful and poised, beautiful and elegant—the
envy of other men, a trophy on my arm, with your impeccable background, your absolute self-assurance in
how to conduct yourself, whether in palaces or in stately
homes, or anywhere else I take you. Opening a door for
me into your upper-class world. And that's what you will
do, Diana, my chaste and beautiful bride.'

His face was set, grim now.

'It will be your full-time job. If you've halted restoration work on Greymont, so much the better. It will give
you all the time you require to do your work here, at my
side. Starting…' he glanced at his watch '…right now.'

He crossed to the door and opened it, pointedly waiting for her to walk through. As she did so she strained
away from him, and he saw that she did. Saw that she
was as tense as a board, her features taut. He didn't care.
Would not care. Would do nothing at all but steer her to
the front door.

As he opened it he turned to her. 'I'll brief you in the car about where we are going, who our hosts are and why they are important to me.'

His tone was businesslike, crisp. And as remote as a frozen planet.

She could not look at him. Could only feel a stone forming in her throat, like a canker growing inside her. Melding to her flesh. Choking her.

The house in Regent's Park was lit up like a Christmas tree, but for Diana it was dark and cheerless. She stood, wine glass in hand, her drink untouched and a stiff smile on her face, and forced herself through the ritual of polite chit-chat that the occasion required.

Nikos was standing beside her. Occasionally his arm would brush against hers, and she had to try not to flinch visibly.

He was no longer the person she'd thought she had come to know. He'd become a stranger—a stranger who spoke to her with chilly impersonality, looking at her but not meeting her eyes, withdrawing behind an expressionless mask. She'd had no option but to do likewise and play the part he wanted her to play—Mrs Nikos Tramontes, the oh-so-elegant, oh-so-well-bred, oh-so-well-connected society wife, with her impeccable background and her magnificent stately home—the home her husband's vast wealth had saved for her.

Exactly the marriage she had wanted.

Take what you want...take it and pay for it.

The words mocked her with a cruelty that she had never thought they could possess.

I brought this on myself! I did it to myself! Fool that I am!

A memory as blazing as the desert stars sought entry,

but she held it at bay with all her remaining strength. To remember… No, no, she could not bear it! Could not bear to think of what she should never have permitted herself to have.

It had left her here, now, in this hollow shell of a marriage she should never have made, mocking her with bitter gall. Demanding a price from her that was anguish in every way. And she must go on paying, go on enduring…

Over the weeks that followed—weeks that were spent at Nikos's side, at his direction, on his requirement, she played her part. Performing her social role as Mrs Nikos Tramontes, immaculately dressed whatever the occasion, behaving just as the situation demanded, whether it was luncheon parties at Thames-side mansions, cocktail parties in Mayfair, dinners in top restaurants in London or attending the theatre or opera at Nikos's side. Always she was there, always perfect, always smiling. The perfect wife.

Trapped in a marriage that had become a torment and an agony.

Nikos was angry. He was angry all the time now. With the same dark, cold anger that had possessed him when he'd sent Diana—his beautiful, enticing wife, his beautiful, *untouchable* wife—back to what she loved most of all in her privileged world. Her grand house and the gracious lifestyle that went with it, all that was important to her.

As the weeks passed a kind of pall settled over him. Outwardly he went through the motions of life, but it was only for show. Deadness was filling him. Numbing him. With part of his mind he knew he should let Diana go, that it was achieving nothing but torment keeping her in their impossible marriage, and yet letting her go seemed even worse.

He could not face it.

It wasn't supposed to be like this!

His marriage should have given him everything that he wanted! *Everything.* Diana, his trophy wife, would grant him the place in the world his mother's rejection of him had denied him. Diana, so elegantly beautiful, so perfect a wife, would show him off to the world.

And Diana, his ice maiden, would melt for him and him alone...

And now she had brutally, callously rejected him— refused him.

He felt that perpetual anger bite again. Oh, he had his trophy wife, all right, chained to his side, but it was like dust and ashes in his mouth.

She melted in my arms, burned in my embrace under the desert stars! I thought that it was me that she wanted! How could I not have thought that after what we were to each other those precious days? Those days that seemed to bring us so close together—in body and in even more than that.

Into his head came the memory of what he'd felt that day he'd rushed back to her from that disastrous meeting with the Minister for Development, and the question that had formed in his head of what Diana might be to him...more than he had ever envisaged. What she might yet be to him...

He had not answered the question. But now he knew the answer for the savage mockery that it was.

A silent snarl convulsed in his throat. Fool—arrant fool that he'd been! Fool to think he'd melted her. There was nothing in her to melt—not at the core of her. Nothing at all. At the core of her being was only one thing, the only thing she wanted and the only thing she valued.

And it was not him.

All she wanted was to preserve her precious lifestyle, her grand ancestral home—that was all that was important to her!

It's all she values.

Just as it was all his mother had valued.

Not me.

And his wife—his glitteringly beautiful, icily cold, frozen-to-the-core trophy wife Diana—was the same. The same as the woman who had thrust him from her chateau, ordering him away. Rejecting him.

Just as Diana had.

That was the truth slamming into him day after punishing day. It burned in him like acid in his throat, in his guts. Eating him alive.

He could feel it now, biting invisibly as it always did, by day and by night, as he stood, an untouched glass of champagne in his hand, at this reception at the headquarters of a French investment bank in Paris by whom he was being wooed as a prospective client.

The valuable business he might potentially bring guaranteed that he had the full attention of one of the top directors, but as they talked about business opportunities his mind had scarcely been on the conversation.

He tore his thoughts away. Forced himself to focus on what the director was saying to him.

With a flicker in his eyeline he became aware of someone else coming up to them. A man older than himself by a few years, obviously French, and... Nikos felt his eyes narrow suddenly. He looked vaguely familiar. Did he know him?

The man came up to him, politely but pointedly waiting while the bank's director finished speaking. Then he interjected.

'Monsieur Tramontes, I wonder if I might have a word with you?'

He must be someone notable, for immediately the bank director made a murmuring conclusion and took his leave.

Nikos turned his attention to the man who had addressed him, trying to place him. 'Have we met?' he asked, with an enquiring look and a slight civil smile.

The man did not smile in return. 'No,' he said with a shake of his head.

Nikos frowned. 'Forgive me, you seem familiar…'

The man nodded, acknowledging the comment. He reached inside his jacket pocket, took out a silver card case and extracted a card. He proffered it to Nikos.

'This may account for it,' he said.

Nikos took the card, glanced down at it.

And froze.

All thoughts of Diana, his cold, frozen trophy wife, vanished.

CHAPTER TEN

DIANA WAS IN the rose garden, cutting blooms. Summer sun slanted through the trees that sheltered Greymont from the world beyond, birdsong twittered overhead, and a woodpigeon pecked hopefully nearby. Warmth enveloped her—and peace.

But not in her heart. Not in her soul. Only torment filled her.

How long can I bear this?

Two years, Nikos had told her, holding her to the damning contract she had made—made when she had not known the price she would have to pay, when she had not realised the danger in which she stood, deluding herself, never dreaming she would not be able to bear to pay, but must. Two endless years to endure this hideous, bitter existence. Chained to a husband she had once thought a gift from heaven, who was now keeping her in this hell.

Her only respite was the time she could spend here, at Greymont, when Nikos went abroad and did not want her at his side. Then and only then was she allowed to flee back here, take consolation in the refuge it offered her.

The irony was biting—it was *because* of Greymont that she was trapped in her tormented mockery of a marriage to Nikos. A marriage she could not escape for it was the price she was paying to keep Greymont, to keep it safe.

And safe it was. That was her only comfort. Yes, she had halted all the repairs, but the most critical work had already been completed. The structure of the house was secure, and that was her greatest relief. As for the rest of it—well, she could not even think that far…not yet, not now. Perhaps in the distant future, when she had finally freed herself from Nikos, she would be free…

Free?

The word mocked her, sliding a knife into her flesh.

She could never be free of him.

It was too late.

With a smothered cry she went on cutting, placing the scented blooms—their petals so perfect, so fragrant, so beautiful—into the willow basket at her feet, then, sufficient gathered, she headed indoors. She would arrange them for the drawing room, a task she always found solace in.

But as she left the rose garden and glanced down the long driveway curving far away along the rising ground towards the distant lodge gates she paused, frowning. Two cars were heading along the drive. She could just make them out through the lime trees bordering the avenue. Both cars were long and black, with tinted windows.

Who on earth…? She wasn't expecting anyone.

She made her way indoors, through the garden room door, hastily depositing the blooms in water but not pausing to arrange them. Then she washed her hands and went out into the hallway to open the front door, not troubling to call for Hudson to do so.

She stepped out on to the wide porch. As she did so the two cars drew up in front of the house and immediately the one behind disgorged a handful of dark-suited men, looking extremely businesslike. A moment of fear struck Diana, then astonishment. One of them came up to her, and as he spoke she realised they were all of Middle Eastern appearance.

'Mrs Tramontes?'

She nodded, and then, with another ripple of astonishment, saw that one of the men was opening the passenger door of the first car, and someone was emerging. A woman who was sailing up to her, imperiously dismissing the dark-suited men who backed away dutifully, still scanning the environment as if sharpshooters might be lurking on her roof.

A gasp escaped Diana—she could not help it. 'Your Highness!' she heard herself exclaim, with open astonishment and incredulity in her voice.

'My dear Mrs Tramontes!'

Princess Fatima greeted Diana warmly. Then she turned to another woman, who had now emerged from the huge dark-windowed car, saying something to her in rapid Arabic. The other woman—chaperon, maid, lady-in-waiting? Diana wondered wildly—glided up to the front door, pressed it open, and then stood aside to admit the Princess.

Helplessly Diana followed suit, wondering what the bodyguards—as she now realised these men must be— would do. Her attention was all on the Princess, who was now addressing her again.

'I hope you will not mind my unexpected arrival, my dear Mrs Tramontes,' Princess Fatima was saying, 'but I could not resist paying you an afternoon call!'

Diana gathered her manners. Seeing the Princess again was overwhelming—releasing a storm of memories and emotions. With an effort she made herself say what had to be said, while inside her head everything seemed to be falling into a million pieces.

'I'm honoured and delighted, Your Highness,' she said mechanically, forcing a welcoming smile to her lips. Then she shook her head. 'But, alas, I am quite unprepared— you will find my hospitality very poor.'

The Princess waved an airy hand, dismissing her apology. 'The fault is mine for not giving you notice,' she said.

She was looking around, gazing up at the marble staircase, the walls lined with paintings, the cavernous hall fireplace.

'Your house is as beautiful as you told me it was,' she said, her voice warm. 'I am eager to see it all.'

'Of course, Your Highness,' Diana assented faintly.

'But first, would it be too much to hope that I might partake of afternoon tea with you?'

Immediately calling on all her training to behave impeccably, whatever tumult was inside her, Diana assured her it would not be too much to hope at all, and ushered the Princess into the drawing room. Hudson was hovering in the doorway and Diana instructed that tea must to be served by Mrs Hudson, and, please, she was to bake fresh scones.

Back in the drawing room, Princess Fatima was settling down on a sofa. The other woman was standing by the windows looking out, almost as if on guard.

The Princess turned to Diana. 'How very good it is to be here,' she said warmly. 'Please do be seated,' she invited.

Diana sat down on the sofa opposite, her limbs nerveless, and Princess Fatima launched into an enthusiastic panegyric of the charms of Greymont, then graciously accepted the arrival of Mrs Hudson with the tea tray.

'Ah, scones. Delicious!' she exclaimed enthusiastically, and Diana murmured her thanks to the housekeeper for having baked them in record time.

The Princess ate as enthusiastically as she praised, chattering all the while—to Diana's abject relief, for she felt utterly unequal to conversing. She told Diana about the progress being made on the English country house that her brother the Sheikh had bought for her, and expressed absolute delight in the gift Diana had made to her of a historic costume—a mid-eighteenth-century heavily embroidered silk gown with wide panniers—that she planned to display in her private sitting room.

As she expressed her delight shadows fleeted across the polite expression on Diana's face. Memory as vivid as poison stung through her, of she and Nikos discussing what gift she should make the Princess as they returned from the royal palace.

Pain twisted inside her. It was hard, brutally hard to see the Princess again, to be reminded with bitter acid in her veins of the wedding gift she and Nikos had been given. The gift of the Sheikh's desert love-nest.

More memory seared inside her—unbearable yet indelible.

Had the Princess caught that fleeting shadow? All Diana knew was that as they finished their repast the Princess gave a brief instruction to the veiled woman—servant, lady-in-waiting, chaperone, female bodyguard?—and the woman bowed and left the room.

Only then did the Princess turn to Diana and, in a voice quite different from her gay chatter, asked, 'My dear, what is wrong?'

Diana tensed. 'Wrong, Your Highness?' She tried to make her voice equable, as it had been during their social chit-chat just now.

But Princess Fatima held up an imperious hand, her rings and bracelets flashing in the afternoon sunlight. 'There is a sadness in your face that should not be there. It was not there when we first met. What has put it there?'

Her dark eyes held Diana's grey ones, would not let them go.

'Tell me,' she said. It was half an invitation—half a command. 'I insist.'

And Diana, to her horror and mortification, burst into tears.

Nikos's expression closed like a stone as he stared down at the gilt-edged card in his hand, read the name on it.

'We have nothing to say to each other,' he bit out.

He made to walk away, but his arm was caught.

'But *I* have much to say to *you*!' the other man said.

There was hauteur in his voice, but there was something else as well. Something that made Nikos stop.

The man's eyes—almost as dark as Nikos's, and as long-lashed—bored into his. Refusing to let Nikos go. The next words the man spoke turned him to stone.

'Our mother wishes to see you—'

Instantly Nikos's face contorted. 'I have no mother.' The savagery in his voice was bitter.

Emotion flashed in the other man's eyes. This man who was his half-brother—son of the woman who had given birth to Nikos, a bastard child, unwanted and unacknowledged, thrust away from her unloving arms, given away to foster parents, spurned and discarded.

The other man was implacable. 'That may soon be truer than you know,' he said, his voice grim. He took a breath, addressed Nikos squarely. 'She is about to have an operation that is extremely risky. She may well not survive. For that reason…' Something changed in his voice—something that Nikos recognised but would not acknowledge. 'For that reason I have agreed to seek you out. Bring you to her.'

Nikos's expression twisted. 'Are you *insane*?' he said, his voice low, enraged. 'She threw me out when I tried to see her. Refused to accept me. Refused even to admit that she *was* my mother!'

Pain flashed across the other man's face. His own half-brother. A stranger. Nothing more than that.

'There are things I must tell you,' he said to Nikos. 'Must make clear to you. Mostly they concern my father.' He paused. 'My *late* father.'

Dimly Nikos's mind clicked into action. The card that this man—this unknown half-brother—had given him.

He lifted it to glance at it again. Read what it said in silvered sloping engraved script.

Le Comte du Plassis

He frowned. But if this man was the Count—?

'My father is dead,' his half-brother told him. 'He died three months ago. And that is why…' He paused, looked at Nikos. 'That is why everything has changed. Why there are things I need to tell you. Explain.' He took a breath. 'Where can we talk in private?'

He took another breath—a difficult one, Nikos could tell.

'It is essential that we do so.'

For a long, timeless moment Nikos looked at him. Met the dark eyes that were so familiar in the face that was as familiar as his own. Slowly, grimly, he gave his assent.

Inside his chest his lungs were tight, as if bound in iron bars.

* * *

Diana was still sobbing. She was appalled at herself, but could not stop. The Princess had crossed from her sofa to plump herself down beside her, pick up her hands and press them.

'Oh, my dear friend—what is wrong?' She patted Diana's hands, her dark eyes huge with sympathy and concern.

Helpless to stop herself, Diana let all her anguish pour out in a storm of weeping. Gradually it abated, leaving her drained, and she reached for a box of tissues from a magazine holder by the fireplace, mopped at her face mumbling apologies.

'I'm sorry. *So* sorry!' Dear God, how could she have burst into tears like that in front of the Princess? Was she insane to have done such a thing?

But Princess Fatima did not seem either offended or bemused. Only intensely sympathetic. She leant back, indicating that Diana must do the same. Then poured her a new cup of tea with her own royal hands and offered it to Diana, who took it shakily.

'You must tell me everything,' the Princess instructed. 'What has gone wrong between you and your handsome husband? No, don't tell me it hasn't. For I will not believe you. No new wife weeps for any other reason.'

Yet still Diana could not speak. Could only gulp at her tea, then set it down again with still shaky hands. She stared at her royal guest with a blank, exhausted stare.

The Princess took a delicate sip of her own tea and replaced the cup with graceful ease on the table. Then she spoke, slowly and carefully, looking directly at Diana, holding her smeared gaze.

'Here in the west,' she began, her tone measured, but meaningful, 'I am well aware that it is the custom for marriages to be based on emotion. Love, as you would call it. It is the fashion, and it is the expectation. But for all that it is not always the case, is it?'

Her eyes were holding Diana's fixedly.

'You will forgive me for speaking in a way that you Europeans with your propensity for democracy might find old-fashioned, but for those who are born into responsibilities greater than the acquisition of their own happiness such a custom may not always be appropriate.'

She smiled, exchanging another speaking glance with her hostess.

'Perhaps we are not so unalike, you and I? At some point I must make a marriage for reasons greater than my own personal concerns—and perhaps that is something that you yourself can understand? Something you have also done?'

She patted Diana's hand again, holding her gaze questioningly as she did so.

'I teased you when you visited me,' she reminded Diana, 'about having so handsome a husband that surely he must be the most important aspect of your life—more important than anything else. But perhaps...' She paused, then went on, glancing around her. 'Perhaps that is not so? You gave me reason to suppose that when you answered me...'

Diana's eyes dropped and she stared into her lap. Spoke dully as she replied. With heaviness in her voice.

'I thought I was saving my house...my home. It is dearer to me than anything in the world. I thought—' she gave a little choke '—I thought I would do anything to save it.'

She lifted her eyes, met those of the Princess who, perhaps alone of anyone she knew, would understand.

'Even marry for it.' She took a breath, felt it as tight

as wire around her throat. 'So that's what I did. I married to save my house, my home, my inheritance. To honour what my father had done for me.'

She gave the Princess a sad, painful smile.

'My mother left my father when I was a child, but he chose never to remarry. It was for *my* sake. You will not need me to tell you that in England it is the tradition for sons to inherit family estates, not daughters—unless there is no son. My father knew how much I loved Greymont, how important it had become to me. It gave me the sense of security, of continuity, I so desperately needed after my mother abandoned and rejected me. So he gave up his chance of happiness to ensure mine.'

She sighed.

'When he died, and I found I needed so much money to honour his sacrifice for me, I made the decision to marry money. Forgive me,' she said tightly, 'for such vulgar talk—but without money Greymont would eventually decay into a ruin. You know that, Your Highness, from your own house that you are saving.'

The Princess nodded. 'So you married the handsome man who just happened to have the wealth that you required for this?' She gestured all around her. She paused, then, 'It does not sound so absurd a decision. It was a marriage that made sense, no? Your husband ensured the future of your home and you, my dear Mrs Tramontes, provided the beauty that any husband must treasure!' She paused again, her eyes enquiring. 'So, what is it that has gone so very wrong?'

She searched Diana's face.

Diana, filled with misery, crumpled the sodden tissue in her hands, meshing her fingers restlessly.

'I thought… I thought he married me out of self-interest. Just as I had married him! Because we were *useful* to each other. I—I thought,' she said, her voice faltering, 'that was the only reason and that it would be enough. But then—' She broke off, gave a cry. 'Oh, Your Highness,' she said in anguish, 'your kindness, your brother's generosity, worked magic that was disastrous for me! Disastrous because—'

She felt silent. Incapable of admitting what had happened out under the scorching desert sun in the *Arabian Nights* fantasy she had indulged in so recklessly. So punishingly stupidly...

The Princess took her writhing hands. Stilled them. 'Tell me,' she said. 'Tell me why it was so disastrous for you.'

There was kindness in her voice, and command as well—but not the command of a princess, but that of a woman, knowing the ways of women. The mistakes they made—mistakes that could ruin lives. Devastate them.

And with a faltering voice, stammering words, Diana told her.

There was silence. Only the sound of birdsong through the open window and the sound, very far off, of a lawn being mowed beyond the rose garden.

'Oh, my poor friend.' The Princess's voice was rich with sympathy, with pity. 'My poor, poor friend.'

The small café was all but deserted. Nikos sat with an untouched beer, his half-brother likewise.

'My father,' said Antoine, 'was not an easy man. He was considerably older than our mother. A difficult, demanding man whom she should never have married. That *no* woman should have married,' he said dryly. 'But there it was—too late. She was his wife. His *comtesse*. And required to behave in a manner he considered appropriate. Which demanded, above all, her producing an heir.'

Antoine's voice was dryer still.

'Myself. And so I duly made my appearance.' His eyes grew shadowed. 'Did my mother love me? Yes— but she was not allowed to spend much time with me. I had nurses, nannies, a governess—eventually a tutor, boarding school. Then university, military academy— the usual drill.'

He shrugged with an appearance of nonchalance.

'In the meantime my mother was lonely. Her life sterile. When she met your father…' his eyes went to Nikos's now, unflinching '…despite his philandering reputation she believed she had met the love of her life. His betrayal of her—his repudiation of any loyalty to her after their affair had resulted in the disaster that was your conception—broke her. And then…'

His voice hardened, with a harshness in it that Nikos recognised—recognised only too well.

'And then my father broke what was left of her.'

Antoine reached for his drink now, took a long swallow, then spoke again. The harshness was still in his voice.

'He made her choose. Choose what she would do with the remainder of her life. She was entirely free, he told her, to fly to Greece that same day—to throw herself at the feet of the philandering seducer who had amused himself with her. Or, indeed, she was entirely free to raise her bastard child as a single parent on her own, anywhere in the world she wanted. But if she did then consequences would follow.'

He looked at Nikos, with dark, long-lashed eyes.

'She would never set eyes on me again and I would be disinherited of everything but the title. My father could not take that from me when the time came, but everything else would be sold on the day of his death. My entire inheritance—the chateau, the ancestral lands, all the property and wealth of our name. I would be landless, penniless.'

Nikos saw his half-brother's hands clench, as if choking the life-force from an unseen victim.

'She would not do it. Would not leave me to the tender mercies of my father...' His voice twisted. 'To grow up knowing that nothing but an empty title would be his legacy to me. Knowing that she had abandoned me.'

A shadow went across his eyes.

'She felt her responsibility was to me rather than you. That you would be better off raised in a foster home, never knowing her. Thought it would give you some form of stability at least, however imperfect.'

Nikos watched him take another deep draught of his beer, feeling emotion swirl deep within him, turbid and muddied, as if sediment that had long sunk to murky depths was being stirred by currents sweeping in from unknown seas.

Antoine was speaking again, his glass set down.

'When you came to see her all those years ago, as a young man, she knew that nothing had changed and nothing *could* change. Oh, I was an adult then myself, of course, and even my father could not have kept me apart from her, but still he held the threat of disinheriting me over her head. She knew you were financially protected— that your biological father had settled a large amount of money on you, to be given to you when you came of age.'

'He can rot in hell too!' Nikos heard his own voice snarl. 'I never took a penny of that money. He'd disowned me from birth!'

For a moment Antoine held his half-brother's gaze. 'We have not had good fathers, have we?' he said quietly. 'But...'

He held up a hand, and in the gesture Nikos saw a thousand years of aristocracy visible in the catching of light on the signet ring on his brother's finger.

'But I do not think that of our mother.' He was silent a moment, then spoke again. 'Come to her, Nikos.'

It was the first time he'd used his half-brother's name.

'She has a serious heart condition. This operation is risky, and requires great skill from a top surgeon. She deferred the operation deliberately for years, waiting for her husband to die. Only now, with my inheritance assured, can she take the risk.' He took a breath that was audibly ragged. 'The risk that she might die before seeking to make what peace she can with you.'

Antoine gave a long sigh.

'You blame her—I can understand that. I too would be bitter. But I hope with all my heart that perhaps you can at some point bring yourself if not to forgive her, to understand her. To accept the love she has for you despite all she did.'

Nikos closed his eyes. He could not speak. Could not answer. Could only feel, deep in that part of him he never touched any longer, where the sediment of bitterness, of anger, had lain for so long, that there could now be only one answer.

His eyes flashed open. Met those of his half-brother.

'Where is she?' he said.

Diana stood at the wide front entrance to Greymont, with the lofty double doors spread to their maximum extent. Dusk was gathering in the grounds and she could hear rooks cawing in the canopy, an early owl further off, and she caught the subliminal whooshing of a bat.

The warmth of the evening lapped around her, but she could not feel it. Her eyes were watching the slow progress of the two-car cavalcade driving away, down towards the lodge gates.

Princess Fatima was leaving.

But not without leaving behind a gift that was priceless to Diana.

A gift she had immediately, instantly demurred over.

'Highness, I cannot! It is impossible. I cannot accept.'

An imperious raised hand had been her answer. 'To refuse would be to offend,' the Princess had said. But then her other hand had touched the back of Diana's. 'Please...' she'd said, her voice soft.

So, with a gratitude she had been able to express only falteringly, Diana had taken the Princess's gift. And now, as she watched her uninvited but oh-so-kind guest take her leave, the same profound gratitude filled her.

The black cars disappeared down the long avenue and Diana went back indoors. Went into the estate room—her office—sat down at the desk and withdrew her chequebook. With a shaky hand she wrote out the cheque she had longed with all her being to be able to write for so many long, punishing months.

The cheque that would set her free.

Free of the one man in the world she could never be free of.

However much money she repaid him.

Nikos sat in his seat on the jet, curving through the airspace that divided France from England. He stared out over the broken cloudscape beyond the window, his thoughts full. Emotions fuller.

She had been so frail, that woman in the hospital bed. So slender, so petite, it had hardly seemed possible that she had given birth at all—let alone to the two grown sons now standing at the foot of her bed. The son she had

chosen over her baby, who had now brought that lost child
back to her. And the son who had hated her all his life.

Who could hate her no longer.

Her eyes had filled with tears when they had gone to
him. Silent tears that had run down her thin cheeks so
that her older son had started forward, only to be held
at bay by the veined hand raised to him. Nikos's half-
brother had halted, and she had lifted her other hand with
difficulty, lifted it entreatingly, towards the son she had
abandoned. Rejected.

'I am so sorry.' Her voice had been a husk, a whisper.
'So very, *very* sorry.'

For an endless moment Nikos had stood there. So
many years of hating. Despising. Cursing. Then slowly
he had walked to the side of her bed, reached down,
and for the first time in his life—the first time since his
body had become separate from hers at his birth—he'd
touched her.

He had taken her hand. For a second it had lain lifeless
in his. And then, with a convulsion that had seemed to
go through her whole frail body, she had clasped his fingers, clutching at him with a desperation that had spoken
to him more clearly than words could ever do.

Carefully, he had lowered himself to the chair at her
side, cradled her hand with both of his, pressing it between them. Emotion had moved within him, powerful,
inchoate. Impossible to bear.

'Thank you.'

The voice had been weak and the eyes had flickered—
dark, long-lashed, sunken in a face where lines of illness
had been only too visible—moving between them both.

'Thank you. My sons. My beloved sons.'

She'd broken off, and Nikos had felt a tightening in his
throat that had seemed like a garrotte around his neck.

Antoine had come forward on jerky legs, sitting himself on the other side of the bed, taking her other hand, raising it to his lips to kiss.

'Maman...'

In his brother's voice Nikos had heard an ocean of love. Had felt, for one unbearable instant, an echo of the word inside himself. An echo that had turned into the word itself. An impossible word...an unbearable word. A word he had never spoken in all his life.

But it had come all the same. The very word his brother had spoken.

Maman.

He heard the word again now, sitting back in his seat as the plane banked to head north. He felt again the emotion that had come with that word. Felt again the spike of another emotion that had stabbed at him—at his half-brother, too—as their heads had turned at the entry of a man in theatre scrubs.

'*Monsieur,*' the cardiologist had said, 'I regret, but it is time for you to leave. Madame la Comtesse is required in surgery.'

Fear had struck him—a dark, primitive fear. A blinding, urgent fear.

A fear that had one cry in it.

Too late.

In his head the cry had come—primitive, urgent.

Let it not be too late! Let me not have found my mother only to lose her to death.

And now, as the powerful twin engines of the private jet raced him back across the Channel, he heard that cry again. Felt that fear again.

But this time it was not about his mother.

Let it not be too late. Dear God, let it not be too late.

Not too late to learn the lesson that finding his mother

had taught him. The lesson that meant he must now take a risk—the essential, imperative risk that was driving him on. Taking him back to England.

To Diana.

But as he opened his laptop, forcing his mind to a distraction it desperately needed, his eyes fell upon the latest round of emails in his inbox, and he realised with a hollowing of his guts that it was, indeed, too late.

The first email was from his lawyers.

His wife was filing for divorce.

And the money he had spent on Greymont—the money that she owed him—had been repaid. Every last penny of it.

CHAPTER ELEVEN

DIANA STARED AT Gerald across his desk. 'What do you mean, he says no?'

Memory thrust into her head of how she had sat here in this very chair, in this very office, after her father's death, refusing to sell her beloved home. Telling Gerald she would find a husband with deep pockets.

Well, she had done that all right. She'd done it and she'd paid for it.

But not with money. She was abjectly grateful that Princess Fatima had insisted on lending her the money—however long it took her to pay it back over the years ahead.

No, she had paid for what she'd wanted with a currency that was costing her far more. That would never be paid off. Try as she might by breaking the legal bonds that bound her to her husband. They were the least of the bonds that tied her to him. That would always tie her to him...

Her lawyer shifted position and looked at her directly. 'I'm afraid he says he has no wish to agree to a divorce.'

Diana's expression changed to one of consternation—and a whole lot more.

Gerald shook his head. 'I did warn you, Diana, about this rash marriage. And as for that disgraceful pre-nup he insisted on—'

She cut across him. 'This has nothing to do with the pre-nup. I don't want a penny from him. Just the opposite. That's why I've paid off the sum of every last invoice he settled, direct to his account. He has no *reason* not to agree to a divorce.' Her mouth set in a tight line. 'He has no grounds for refusing me.'

'Except, my dear Diana,' Gerald said in his habitually infuriating manner, 'the law of the land allows him to do so, irrespective of any grounds you might imagine you have. And you don't have any, do you? He hasn't been unfaithful. He hasn't inflicted any cruelty upon you—'

She blenched. Cruelty? What else had it been, these past nightmare months since he'd insisted on having his pound of flesh from her?

Oh, not in a physical sense—her thoughts shrank away from that; it was forbidden territory and must always remain so—but in requiring her at his side, as the perfect society wife. Beautiful, ornamental, decorative, the envy of all who knew him. The immaculately groomed society wife who could move in any circles he chose to take her, always saying just the right thing, in just the right way, wherever they went.

Outwardly it was a wealthy, gilded life—how could that possibly be considered cruel?

How could anyone have seen how she bled silently, invisibly, day after day, drained of all hope of release in the frozen chill of his obvious anger with her?

Anger because she'd refused to have the kind of marriage that he'd expected, had assumed they would have— taking it for granted that it would be consummated and then refusing to see why it was impossible...*impossible*!

She dared not think *why* such a marriage as Nikos had wanted was so impossible! She must not let in those memories that made a lie of all her insistence that she did not want a marriage such as Nikos had wanted.

She couldn't afford to let those memories surface. Memories that haunted her…memories that were a torment, an agony of loss…of their bodies entwined beneath the burning stars, bringing each other to ecstasy.

Gerald's dry voice sounded in her ears, making her listen. 'Well, Diana, if you have no grounds for divorce then you will simply have to wait until you can divorce him without his agreement. That will take five years.'

She stared aghast, disbelieving. *'Five years?'*

'Unless you can persuade him to consent to end your marriage.'

He shifted position again, leafed through some papers in a fashion that told Diana he was looking for a way to say what he had to say next.

He glanced across his desk at her. 'You may be able to change his mind, Diana,' he said. 'Your husband has indicated that he will discuss the matter with you personally.'

'I don't want to see him!' The cry came from her. 'I couldn't bear to see him again.'

'Then you will have to be prepared to wait five years for the dissolution of your marriage,' he replied implacably.

She closed her eyes again, emotion tumbling through her. To see him again—it would be torment, absolute torment! But if it was the only way to plead with him to end this nightmarish façade of a marriage—

She looked across at her lawyer. 'Where and when does Nikos want to meet me?' she asked dully.

The uniformed chauffeur who was waiting for her at Charles de Gaulle Airport gave no indication of where he

was driving her, but she could see it was not into Paris,
but westwards into the lush countryside of Normandy.
There was no point asking. Nikos had demanded this
meeting and she was in no position to refuse—not if she
wanted to be free of the crushing chains of her tortur-
ous marriage.

Apprehension filled her, and a clawing dread—
knowing she must face him, plead with him for her freedom. She could feel her stomach churning, her breathing
heavy, as the car drove onwards.

The journey seemed to last for ever, longer than the
flight had, and it was past noon before they arrived at
their destination, deep in the heart of the countryside.

She frowned as she got out of the car, taking in the tur-
reted Norman château in creamy Caen stone, grand and
gracious, flanked by poplar trees and ornamental gardens, and the little river glinting in the sunshine, winding past.

It was a beautiful house, like something out of a fairytale, but she was in no frame of mind to appreciate it.
Its beauty only mocked the tension in her, her pinching
and snapping nerves. Why was she here? Did Nikos own
it? Was he renting it? Simply staying here? It could be a
hotel for all she knew.

A man was emerging from the chateau, tall and dark-
haired, and for a moment, with a tremor of shock, Diana
thought it was Nikos. Then the rush to her bloodstream
that had come just with thinking she was seeing Nikos
again subsided.

'Welcome to the Chateau du Plassis,' he said. 'I am
Antoine du Plassis. Please come inside.'

Numbly she followed him, having murmured something in French, she knew not what. Inside, the interior
was cool, and there was an antiquity about the place that

was immediately was familiar to her. It was a magnificent country house like Greymont—but in another country.

'Is Nikos here?' Her voice broke the silence as she followed her host.

The tall, dark-haired man, who for that heart-catching moment she had thought was Nikos, glanced back at her.

'Of course,' he said.

He threw open a pair of double doors, standing aside to let her enter first. She saw a beautiful salon, much gilded, and a huge fireplace with the characteristic French chimneypiece. But she took in little of it. Nikos was getting to his feet from his place on a silk-upholstered Louis Quinze sofa, and her eyes went to him with a lurch of her stomach.

He said something in French to her host—something too low, too rapid for Diana to catch—and nor could she catch Antoine's answer.

Her eyes were only for Nikos, and she was wishing with all her heart that her pulse had not leapt on seeing him, that her eyes were not drinking him in like water in a parched desert. He was looking strained, tense, and she found herself wondering at it.

Then, as her eyes went back to her host, Diana's eyes widened disbelievingly.

The Frenchman was slightly less tall than Nikos, less broad in the shoulder, less powerfully made, with features less distinct, less strongly carved, and there was more of a natural Gallic elegance in his manner. His hair was slightly longer than Nikos's, less dark, as were his eyes, but the resemblance was immediate, unmistakable.

Her gaze went from one to the other.

'I don't understand…' Her voice was faint.

It was Nikos who answered. 'Antoine is my half-brother,' he said. 'The Comte du Plassis.'

A faint frown formed between Diana's brows as she tried to make sense of what she did not understand—that Nikos had a half-brother she had not known existed. It was the Count who spoke next, his voice with a similar timbre to Nikos's, but his accent decidedly French, lighter than Nikos's clipped baritone.

'I will leave you to your discussion.'

Antoine gave a little bow of his head and strode from the room. As he closed the double doors behind him the large room suddenly felt very small. A great weariness washed over Diana and she folded herself down in an armchair, overwhelmed by tension, by all the emotions washing through her, swirling up with her being here.

'I don't understand,' she said again.

The three words encompassed more than just the discovery that he had a half-brother. Why had she been summoned here? To what purpose?

She gazed at Nikos. It hurt to see him.

It will always hurt to see him.

That was the truth she could not escape. She could escape their marriage—however long it took her to do so—but it would always hurt to see him. Always hurt to think about him. Always hurt to remember him.

For a moment he was silent, but beneath the mask that was his face a powerful emotion moved. He stood by the fireplace, one hand resting on the mantel, and his gaze targeted Diana.

'I have to talk to you,' he said. He took a ragged breath. 'About things I have never talked about. Because I need you to understand why I have been as I have been towards you these last difficult months. Why I have been so harsh towards you.'

She stared at him, her insides churning. She was here to beg him to end their marriage, beg him to release her from the misery of it all. She did not need to hear anything from him other than agreement to that.

'You don't need to explain, Nikos,' she bit out bleakly. 'It was because I didn't want sex with you. And since you'd assumed right from the off that, contrary to what *I'd* been assuming, sex was going to be on the menu, my refusal didn't go down well.'

There was a brusqueness in her voice, but she didn't care.

Dark fire flashed in his eyes—anger flaring. Her jaw tightened. So he didn't like her spelling it out that bluntly? Well, tough—because it was true, however much it might offend him.

But his hand was slashing through the empty air, repudiating her crude analysis. 'That is *not* why. Or not as you state it like that! Hear me out.' His expression changed suddenly, all the anger gone. Instead, a bleakness that echoed her own filled his face. 'Hear me out, Diana—please.'

His voice was low and his eyes dropped from hers. His shoulders seemed to hunch, and it struck her that she had never seen him like that before. Nikos had always been so sure of himself, so obviously in command of every situation, never at a loss. Self-confident and self-assured. And in the last unbearable months of their marriage he'd steeled into his stony, unrelenting determination to keep her at bay, yet chained inescapably to his side.

Was the change in him now because she had finally broken free of him?

No, far more had shaken him than the repayment of her debt to him, her demand for a divorce. And as she let her gaze rest on him she felt emotion go through her— one that she had never in all her time with him associated with him.

She tried to think when *she* had ever felt such an emotion before, and what it might be. Then, with a shiver, she realised—and remembered.

It was for my father—when my mother left him.

Pity.

Shock jagged through her as she looked across at Nikos, at the visible strain in his face. Was she feeling *sorry* for him? After all his harshness to her?

She couldn't bear to feel pity! Couldn't bear to see such painful emotion in his eyes. Why was it there? There was no need for it—no cause.

He was speaking again and she made herself listen, fighting down the emotion she did not want to feel for him. She was here to end her misery of a marriage, that was all. Nothing he could say or do would alter that.

'It was because, Diana, your reaction after we came back from the desert showed me that I had never realised just what kind of a person you truly are.'

He paused and she felt his gaze pressing on her, like a weight she could not bear.

'A woman like my mother.'

She stared and saw his gaze leave her, sweep around the room.

She frowned—felt confusion in her mind, cutting through her tortured emotions at his accusation. Why was Nikos here, in the home of a half-brother she hadn't known he possessed?

Her confusion deepened as she remembered how Nikos, when he'd proposed their stark marriage of convenience, had told her that he wanted to marry her for her social background, in order to give him an entrée into her upper-class world of landed estates and stately homes.

But he has that already, here with his brother the Comte. So why—?

His sweeping gaze came back to her. Unreadable. Masked. He moved suddenly, restlessly, breaking eye contact with her. Looking instead somewhere else. Into a place she knew nothing about.

His past.

She heard him start to speak. Slowly. As if the words were being dragged from him by pitiless steel-tipped hooks…

'My mother, Comtesse du Plassis. Wife of Antoine's father.' He paused. His eyes were on her now. 'Who was not *my* father.'

He shifted again restlessly, his hand moving on the mantel, lifting away from it now as if he had no right to rest it there.

'The man who fathered *me*,' he said, and Diana could hear a chill in his vioce that made her quail, 'was a Greek shipping magnate—you would know his name if I told you. He was notorious for his affairs with married women. He liked them married, you see.' Something moved in his eyes, something savage, and her chill increased. 'Because it meant that if there were any unfortunate repercussions there would be a handy husband on the scene to sort them out.' He paused again, then, 'As Antoine's father duly did.'

Restlessly he shifted his stance again, his eyes sliding past her.

'I was farmed out when I was born. Handed over to foster parents. They were not unkind to me, merely… uninterested. I was sent to boarding school, and then university here in France. At twenty-one, after I'd graduated, I was summoned to a lawyer in Paris. He told me of my parentage.'

An edge came into his voice, like a blade.

'He told me that my father would settle a substantial

sum on me, providing I signed documents forbidding me from ever seeking him out or claiming his paternity.' The blade in his voice swept like a knife through the air. 'I tore up the cheque and stormed out, wanting nothing from such a man who would disown his own son. Then I drove out here to find my mother—'

He stopped abruptly. Once again his eyes swept the room, but this time Diana could sense in his gaze something that had not been there before. Something that made her feel again what she had felt so unwillingly when he had first started speaking. The shaft of pity.

His face was gaunt, his mouth twisted. 'She sent me away. Saw me to the door. Told me never to come here again—never to contact her again. Then she went back inside. Shutting me out. Not wanting me. Not wanting the child she had cast aside.' He paused. His voice dropped. 'Rejecting me.'

That something moved again in his eyes, more powerfully now, and it hurt Diana to see it. It was that same look her father had had in his eyes when he'd remembered the wife who had not wanted him, who had rejected him.

'I drove away,' Nikos was saying now, piercing her own memories with his, 'vowing never to contact her again, just as she wished, washing my hands of her just as I had my father, as both of them had washed their hands of *me*. I took a new name for myself—my own and no one else's. Cursing both my parents. I was determined to show them I did not need them, that I could get everything they had on my own, without them.'

There was another emotion in his voice now.

'I've proved myself my father's son,' he ground out, his eyes flaring with bitter anger. 'Everything I touch turns to gold—just as it does for him! And, having made as much money as my father, I gained all the expensive baubles that he possesses, the lavish lifestyle that goes with such wealth—and, yes, the celebrity trophy mistress I had in Nadya! But it wasn't enough. I wanted to get for myself what my mother had denied me in her rejection. My place in the world she came from—the world *you* come from, Diana.'

He paused, his eyes resting on her, dark and unreadable.

'By marrying you I would take my place in that world—but I would also obtain something else. Something I wanted the very first moment I saw you.'

He shifted his position restlessly, and then his gaze lanced back to her. And in it now was an expression that was not unreadable at all. It blazed from him openly, nakedly. It made her reel with the force of it.

'I could get *you*, Diana. The woman I've desired from my very first glimpse of you. The woman I thought I had finally made my own—the woman I transformed from frozen ice maiden to warm, passionate bride, melting in my arms, burning in her desire for me!'

His voice changed, expression wiped clean. There was harshness in his voice now—a harshness that had become all too familiar in these last hideous months while she had been chained to his side.

'Only to discover that after all we had together in the desert it meant nothing to you. *Nothing!* That to you all I was good for was supplying the money that would save Greymont for you. That only your precious ancestral home was important to you, your privileged way of life. You did not want me disturbing that with my *inconvenient* desire for you.'

She stared at him. The bitterness in his voice was like gall.

He spoke again. 'Just as my mother valued above all

else her privileged way of life here at this elegant chateau, undisturbed by the *inconvenient* existence of an
unwanted bastard son.'

Diana felt her face pale, wanted to cry out, but she
couldn't. He was speaking again, his words silencing her.

'All these months, Diana, I have blamed you for being
like her. For valuing only what she valued. For rejecting
me.' He paused. Drew breath. 'It made me angry that
you should turn out to be like her. Valuing only the privileged lifestyle you enjoy.' His mouth twisted. 'Nothing
else. No one else.'

She could read bitterness in the stark lines of his face,
savage and harsh, but there was something else beneath
it. Something that seemed to twist her up inside.

He was speaking again, and now there was a tension
in his voice, like wire strung too tight, and his strong
features were incised with that same tension.

'And *that* is what I need to know! Was I right to be so
angry with you? Right to accuse you of being no better
than my mother, who only valued all of this?'

His hand swept around the room, condemning in a
single gesture all that it represented. His gaze was skewering her, nailing her where she sat. She saw his mouth
twist again.

'Are you the same, Diana? Is Greymont all that you
are capable of wanting, valuing? Is Greymont and all that
goes with it all you care about?'

His eyes were dark—as dark as pits. Pits into which
she was falling.

Her voice was shaking as she answered him. Inside
her chest her heart had started to pound, like a hammer
raining blows upon her. 'You...you knew I married you
to protect Greymont, Nikos. You *knew* that—'

A hand slashed through the air. 'But is that all you

are, Diana? A woman cut from the same cloth as my mother? Caring only for wealth and worldly status and possessions?'

She reeled. Suddenly, like a spectre, she saw her father, shaking his head sorrowfully, looking at her with such desolation in his face she could not bear to see it. Nor to hear his words.

'I wasn't rich enough for her...your mother—'

She felt her insides hollowing as the echo of her father's words rang in her ears.

She stared at Nikos, eyes distended. There was a spike in her lungs, draining the air from her, and his bitter accusation was stinging her to the quick, the echo of her father's words like thorns in her soul.

Words burst from her as she surged to her feet. His words had been blows, buffeting her. In agitation and self-defence she cried out at him.

'Nikos, I'm sorry—*so* sorry!—that your mother hurt you so much! Because I know how that feels. I know it for *myself.*'

She took a hectic breath, feeling her heart pounding inside her, urgently wanting to defend herself—justify herself. Protect herself from what he'd thrown at her.

'When I was ten my mother walked out on my father. And on me!' Her expression changed, memory thrusting her back into that long-ago time that was searing in her heart as if it had only just happened. 'Like your mother, Nikos, she didn't want me. She only wanted the huge riches of the Australian media mogul she took off with. A man twice her age and with a hundred times my father's wealth!'

She could hear the agitation in her own voice, knew why it was there. She saw that Nikos had stilled.

Her gaze shifted, tearing away from him, shifting

around the elegant salon in this beautiful chateau. Shadowing. Taking another breath, she made herself go on. It was too late to stop now.

'She cut all contact. I ceased to exist for her. Was not important to her. So I made her not important to me.'

Her eyes came back to Nikos. He was standing stock-still, his eyes veiled suddenly.

Shock was detonating through him. He had summoned her here to find the truth. The truth he had to discover. The truth on which so much rested. So much more than he had ever dreamt.

Well, now he had the truth he'd sought.

I thought she rejected me because she was like my mother—as I thought my mother to be.

But it was himself. All along it was himself. That was who she was like. Like him she had been abandoned, rejected, as he had felt himself to be, by the one woman who should have cherished her.

A chill swept through him.

She was speaking again.

'My father became my world—he was all I had left. And Greymont—'

A low ache was starting up in her, old and familiar, from long, long ago. Without realisation, her arms slid around herself. As if staunching a wound.

With a dry mouth she forced herself on.

'It was the same for my father. We—Greymont, and myself—became his reason for going on after my mother left him. And it was because...' Her voice changed. 'Because he saw how desperately I loved Greymont—how I clung to it, to him—he vowed to make sure I would never lose it.'

She shut her eyes a moment, her jaw clenching. Then her lids flew open and she looked straight at Nikos. He was stock-still, his face unreadable, his eyes unreadable. It didn't matter. She had to say this now. *Had* to.

'And to ensure that I did he gave up all hope of ever finding anyone else to make him happy. Gave up all thoughts of marrying again. For *my* sake. Because…' She gave a sigh—a long, weary sigh. 'Because he would not risk having a son who would take precedence over me— inherit Greymont, dispossess me of the home I loved so desperately.'

There was a heaviness inside her now, like a crushing weight, as she lifted her eyes to his, made herself hold them, as impossible as it was for her to do so.

'His sacrifice of any chance of happiness for himself made it imperative for me to honour what he'd done. He ensured I'd inherit Greymont—so I had to save it, Nikos, I had to! I *had* to make it the most important thing in the world to me. Saving Greymont. Or I would have betrayed his trust in me. His trust that I would keep Greymont, pass it on to my descendants, preserve it for our family.'

She looked about her again, at the elegant salon with its antiques, its oil paintings on the walls, the vista of the grounds beyond, the sense of place and history all about her—so absolutely familiar to her from Greymont.

Her lips pressed together. She had to make him see, understand…

CHAPTER TWELVE

HER GAZE WENT back to him, with a pleading look on her face.

'It's something those not born to places like this can never really comprehend—but ask your brother, Nikos, whether he would ever want to part with his heritage, to be the Comte du Plassis who loses it, who lives to see strangers living here, knowing it's not his any longer, that's he's had it taken from him?' She shook her head again. 'But places like this demand a price. A price that can be hard to pay.'

She did not see the expression on Nikos's face change, the sudden bleakness in his eyes. He knew just what price had been paid for his brother to inherit. And who had paid it.

There was a hollowing inside him. Yes, he had paid the price, had been farmed out to foster parents. But his mother had paid too. Had stayed locked in an unhappy marriage in order to preserve her son's inheritance. Her husband had been pitiless, refusing to release her, punishing her for not wanting him whilst chaining her to him.

As he, Nikos, had kept Diana chained to his side, punishing her for not wanting him.

Again a chill swept through him.

No! I am not like him!

Denial seared in him. And memory—memory that flamed in his vision.

Diana in my arms, with the desert stars above, her face alight with passion and ecstasy. Diana laughing with me, her face alight with a smile of happiness. Diana asleep in my embrace, my arms folding her to me, her head resting on me, her hair spread like a flag across me.

Each and every memory was telling him what he knew with every fibre of his being, every cell in his body.

She wanted me just as I wanted her. That desire that flamed between us was as real to her as it was to me. So how could she deny it—how?

A 'mistake', she'd called their time in the desert. The word mocked him, whipped him with scorpions.

But she was speaking again, her voice heavy.

'And so I married you, Nikos, to keep Greymont safe. That's why I married you—for that and only that.'

His gaze on her was bleak. 'A man whose touch you could not tolerate? Would not endure? Despite all we were to each other in the desert?'

A cry broke from her—high and unearthly. '*Because* of it! Nikos, are you so blind? Can you not *see*?'

Her arms spasmed around the column of her body, as if she must contain the emotion ravening through it. But it was impossible to contain such emotion, to stop it pouring from her, carrying with it words that burst from her now.

'Nikos—when you came to Greymont and put down in front of me your offer of marriage I wanted to snatch it with both hands! But I hesitated—I hesitated because—'

Her eyes sheared away. She was unable to look at him directly, to tell him to his face. But emotion was tumbling through her, churning her up, and she had to speak—she *had* to! Her arms tightened about herself more fiercely.

'I'd seen the way you looked at me at that dinner. Seen the way you looked at me at *Don Carlo*, and in the taxi back to my hotel. I saw in your eyes what I'd seen in men's eyes all my adult life. And I knew I could not...' Her voice choked again. 'I could not have that in our marriage!'

She did not see his expression change. His face whiten. She plunged on, unable to stop herself.

'But I was desperate to accept your offer and so I persuaded myself that it wasn't there. I believed what I wanted to believe—confirmed, as I thought, by the way you were during our engagement.' She gave a high, hollow laugh, quickly cut short. 'And all the while you were just biding your time. Waiting for the honeymoon to arrive.'

She shut her eyes, not able to bear seeing the world any longer. Not able to bear seeing *him*.

'And arrive it did,' she said, her voice hollow.

Into her head, marching like an invading army that she had so long sought to keep at bay, came memories. Images. Each and every one as fatal to her as a gunshot.

Her eyes sprang open, as if to banish those memories that were so indelible within her. But instead of memory there was Nikos, there in front of her. So real. So close.

So infinitely far away.

As he must always be.

Nikos—the man who had caused her more pain than she had ever known existed!

'Oh, God, Nikos!' The words rang from her. 'You think me an ice maiden. But I've had to be—I've *had* to be!'

Slowly, very slowly, she made the crippling clenching of her arms around her body slacken, let her hands fall to her sides, limp. She was weary with a lifetime of exhaustion, of holding at bay emotions she must not let herself feel or they would destroy her.

'Being an ice maiden kept me *safe*. Having a celibate marriage to you kept me *safe*.'

There was silence. Only the low ticking of the ormolu clock on the mantel.

'Safe,' she said again, as if saying it could make it so.

But the word only mocked her pitilessly. *Safe?* It had been the most dangerous thing in the world, marrying Nikos—the one, the only man who had set alight that flare of sexual awareness inside her with a single glance. That single, fateful glance that had brought her here, now, to this final parting with him.

Pain seared inside her—the pain she had feared, so much all her life. A wild, anguished look pierced her eyes as she cried out.

'I *needed* to be an ice maiden! I didn't want to feel anything for any man. I had to protect myself! Protect myself from what I saw my father go through! Because what if what happened to my father, happened to *me*? He broke his heart over my mother! Because she never loved him back—'

She broke off, turning away. She had to go—flee! However long Nikos made her wait for her divorce. The divorce that would free her from the chains he held her by.

But he holds me by chains that I can never break! Never!

The anguish came again, that searing pain. A sob tore at her throat and her arms were spasming again, as if she would fall without that iron grip to hold her upright.

And then suddenly there was another clasp upon her. Hands folding over hers. Nikos's strong, tall body right behind her. Slowly, deliberately, he was turning her around to face him.

His hands fell away from her, and she suddenly felt so very cold. She stood, trembling, unable to lift her head to look at him. He spoke. His voice was low, with a resonance in it that had never been there before.

'Diana…' He spoke carefully, as if finding his step along a high, perilous path, 'Your fears have haunted you, possessed you—you must let them go.'

She lifted her head then. Stared at him with a wide, stricken gaze.

'That isn't possible, Nikos,' she answered, her voice faint. 'You, of all people, should know that.' Her expression contorted. 'Those nights we had in the desert… You could not understand why I so regretted them—why I told you it should never have happened. But now you know why I said that to you. Just as I, Nikos…' her voice was etched with sadness '…know why my rejection of you made you so angry. Because it made you think me no better than your mother—the mother who rejected you so cruelly.'

His expression was strange.

'Except that she did not.' He saw the bewilderment in Diana's eyes. 'Antoine came to me—the half-brother I never even knew I had took me to her,' he said. 'He told me the truth about why she had to do what she did.'

Sadly, he told her the bleak, unhappy tale—and then the miracle of his reconciliation with her.

'It was realising how wrong I had been about her, how I had misjudged her, that made me fear I had misjudged *you*, too!' His expression was shadowed. 'And fear even more that I had not.'

His expression changed, his voice becoming sombre now.

'We've both been chained by our past. Trapped. I was trapped in hating the mother who had rejected me, only to find that she had been trapped by her need to protect my brother. And you, Diana, were trapped by the wounds your mother's desertion inflicted on you—trapped by your gratitude to your father, your guilt over his sacrifice for you, your pity for him—the fear you learnt from him. The fear I want so much to free you from.'

'But that fear is *real*, Nikos!' she cried out. 'It's real. It was real from the first moment I set eyes on you, when I knew, for the first time in my life, that here was a man to make me feel the power of that fear. And it was terrifyingly real after our time together in the desert!'

There was a wild, anguished look in her eyes.

'Oh, God, Nikos, that time we had there together only proved to me how *right* I was to be so afraid. You thought I rejected you afterwards because our time in the desert meant so little to me. But it was the very opposite!'

Her voice dropped.

'So I can't be safe from such fear—it's impossible.' She closed her eyes, felt her hands clench before her eyes flew open again. 'I can only try to insulate myself from it, protect myself.'

Even as she spoke she knew the bitter futility of her words. It was far too late. But she plunged on all the same, for there was no other path for her. None except this path now, lined with broken glass, that she must tread for the rest of her life.

'Just give me my divorce, Nikos,' she said wearily. 'It's what I came here to beg for.'

'So you can be free of me?' He paused. 'Safe from me?'

Her eyelids fluttered shut. It was too much to bear.

'Yes,' she whispered. 'Safe from you.'

She could not see his face. Could not see his eyes, fastened upon her. She could only hear him say her name. The words he spoke.

'Diana—what if you could be safe? Not *from* me, but safe *with* me?'

Emotion was welling inside him. An emotion that he scarcely recognised, for he had never felt it in all his life, had never known until he had seen it in his mother's eyes, as she lay so frail, so pitiful, awaiting the operation that might take her from him for ever.

He felt it again now, fresh-made, rising up in him like a tide that had been welling, invisible, unseen and unstoppable, for so, so long.

Since he had held Diana in his arms beneath the burning desert stars.

'Safe *with* me, Diana,' he said again.

That strange, overpowering emotion welled again. It was an emotion full of danger—a danger that the woman he spoke to now, whose clenched hands he was reaching for, knew so well.

Yet it was a danger he must risk. For all his future lay within it. All *her* future.

All our future.

Urgency impelled him, and yet he seemed to be moving with infinite slowness. Infinite care. So much depended on this.

Everything that I hold precious.

That emotion seared him again, rising like a breaking wave out of that running tide within him, so powerful, so unstoppable.

He felt her hands beneath his touch, her pale fingers digging into the sleeves of her jacket. He gently prised them loose, slid them into his hands, drew them away from her body into his own warm, strong clasp.

'Diana…' He said her name again, softly, quietly. Willing her to lift her sunken head, open the eyes closed against him.

'Safe *with* me. *Safe.*'

He took a breath—a deep, filling breath that reached to his core, to his fast-beating heart, and with his next word he risked all—risked the fear that had crippled her for so long, wanting to set her free from it.

'*Always.*'

Her eyelids were fluttering open…her head was lifting. His hands pressed hers, clasping them, encompassing them. Drawing her towards him, closer and yet closer still.

She came, hesitant, unsure, as if stumbling, as if she could not halt herself, as if she were walking out across a precipice so high she must surely fall, catastrophically, and smash herself on rocks. Her eyes were wide, distended, and in them he saw emotions flare and fuse. *Fear.* And something else. Something she tried to hide. Something that was not fear at all—something that filled him with a rush, an urgency to speak. To say what must now fall from his lips.

The most important, the most vital, the most essential words he would ever say. Words that he had never dreamt in all his life would be his to say. They were filling his whole being, flooding through him, possessing him and transforming him. Fulfilling him.

They could never be unsaid.

They *would* never be unsaid.

'Safe, Diana, in my love for you.'

They were said! The words that had come to him now, burning through all the doubts and fears, all the turbulent emotions that possessed him, burning through like the desert sun burning over the golden dunes.

Love—bright love.

Love that blazed in the heavens.

Blazed in *him*.

Now and for ever.

He folded her to him, releasing her hands, and as his strong arms came around her he felt the sweet softness of her body against his, felt her clutch at him, heard the choking sob in her throat.

He let her weep against him, holding her all the while, smoothing her hair, his cheek against hers, wet with her tears.

'Do you mean it? Oh, Nikos, do you mean it?' Her voice was muffled, her words a cry.

'Yes!'

His answer was instant, his hugging of her fierce. That wondrous emotion was blazing through his whole being now, illuminating the truth. The truth that had started to form out in the desert, under the stars with Diana—so beautiful, so passionate, so precious to him!—whose rejection of him had caused him so much pain.

Pain he had masked in anger. Pain that he no longer had to mask. No longer had to feel. Because now he knew the emotion blazing in him by its true name.

'I love you, Diana. I love you. And with all my heart I hope and pray that you will accept my love. That you do not fear it or flee it! The love,' his heart was in his voice now, heaved up to her, 'I hope that you can share with me, together. '

She pulled away from him, leaning back into the strength of his hands at her spine, her tear-stained face working. At last she was free to say what she had so feared to say—even to herself. What she had kept locked within her, terrified that she had brought about the very fate she had guarded herself against for so long. The tormented and tormenting truth she had admitted to no one—least of all herself—denying it and rejecting it until that fateful day when, with a simple question, it had been prised from her.

One simple question from the Princess—*'What is wrong?'*

And Diana had told her. The truth pouring from her. As she was telling Nikos now, the words choking her.

'I do! Oh, Nikos, I fell in love with you out in the desert. I could not stop myself—could not protect myself. You swept away every defence, every caution. But I knew that I'd condemned myself to heartbreak!' Her eyes were anguished, her voice desolate. 'Because when our marriage ended—as end it must, just as we'd agreed it would—you would move on and then I would become like my father, mourning the loss of a love I should never have let myself feel, but which it was far too late to stop.'

Sudden fear smote her, ravaging her.

'And you *will* move on, Nikos! Whatever you say now, you'll move on. One day you'll be done with me—'

An oath broke from him and all self-control left him. He hauled her back into his arms.

'I will love you *always* Diana.' His voice changed and he cradled her face between his hands. 'I have never known what love is—never experienced it in all my life. Until I found my mother's love for me, learnt the truth about her, about how I had misjudged her. And I feared then that I had misjudged you, too. And I recognised at the very moment you were demanding a divorce what it was I felt for you—what I feared *you* did not feel, *could* not feel, were incapable of feeling.'

She silenced him. With a smothered cry she pressed her mouth to his. Sealing his lips with hers, her love with his. Only drawing back to say, her eyes full, tears still shimmering on her lashes, 'Oh, Nikos, we both bear scars from wounds that nearly parted us, but love has healed them and that is all we need!'

Joy, and a relief so profound it made her weak, was flooding through her. She hugged him close against her, letting her cheek rest on his chest, feeling his strength, his arms fastening around her again. How much she loved him—oh, how much! And she was *safe* to love him—always.

She gave a sigh of absolute contentment. Felt his lips graze her hair, heard him murmuring soft words of love. Then he was drawing a little apart from her, smiling down at her. She met his gaze, reeling from the love-light blazing in his eyes. She felt her heart turn over, joy searing through her more fiercely yet.

And then the expression in his eyes was changing, and she felt her pulse give a sudden quickening, her breath catching, lips parting, breathless with what she saw in his face. She felt her body flush with heat.

'How fortunate,' he was murmuring, 'my most beautiful beloved, that we are already man and wife. For now I do believe a second wedding night must fast be approaching.'

She gave a laugh of tremulous, sensuous delight, and it was a sound he had not heard for so many long, bitter months. Not since they had found their paradise in the deserts of Arabia—a paradise that now would be in their hearts for ever.

'It's only midday!' she exclaimed, her hands looping around his neck, her fingertips splaying in the feathered softness of his hair. Glorying in the touch of her palms at his nape.

Her eyes were alight with glinting desire. Hunger for him was unleashed within her. And all the memories that she had barred were freshly vivid in her mind, heating her bloodstream. How achingly long it had been since she had held him in her arms!

'Then we shall have an afternoon of love,' he proclaimed, his voice a husk of desire, his gaze devouring her.

There was a cough, discreet, but audible, and a voice spoke from across the room.

'Indeed you shall.' The voice was cool and accented, and very obviously amused.

They turned instantly. Antoine, Comte de Plessis, was standing in the open double doorway, his light gaze resting on them, the slightest smile on his mouth.

'But not, I implore you, until *after* lunch!'

His smile widened, and in his gaze Diana could see fond affection as well as humour.

'I am delighted beyond all things,' the Comte continued, his voice more serious now, 'that the reconciliation which I know my brother longed for has successfully been accomplished.' He bestowed a slight nod upon Nikos, and then Diana, and again that amused smile was flickering at his mouth. 'And I am even more delighted that I may now properly welcome you, *ma chère* Madame Tramontes.'

And now he was walking towards them, as Nikos changed his stance so that Diana was at his side, his arm around her waist and hers around his, drawn close against each other. With Gallic elegance he possessed himself of Diana's free hand, raising it to his lips.

'Enchanté, madame,' he murmured as he lowered it again, released it. 'I can see,' he said, and now his smile was warm, 'that it is quite unnecessary for me to say that you have made my brother the happiest of men. I profoundly hope that it is within his capabilities to make you the happiest of wives.'

His smile deepened.

'And with that concluded…' he raised his hands in another very Gallic gesture and turned to walk back to the doors '… I must, I fear, warn you that your presence in the dining room is required *tout de suite*, for the culinary genius of my chef—upon which he has called in measures previously unsurpassed to present us with a celebratory *dejeuner du midi*—is exceeded, *hélas*, only by the volatility of his temperament. In short, I beg you not to arouse his wrath by a tardy appearance.'

He flung open the doors in a dramatic gesture, infused still with humour.

'*Venez,*' he invited. 'Love can wait—luncheon cannot!'

Laughingly, their arms still entwined around each other, as their hearts would be entwined all their lives, Nikos and Diana followed him from the room.

From now on, all their days—and all their nights— would be with each other.

For each other.

EPILOGUE

DIANA SAT AT the dressing table in her bedroom at Greymont, putting the finishing touches to her appearance,
ensuring she looked her best for her beloved Nikos. And
for his brother, and his mother, recovered now from her
operation, who'd both arrived this evening to celebrate
with herself and Nikos their wedding day on the morrow.

Our real wedding, thought Diana, feeling a wash of
love and gratitude go through her. *Which will take place
in the little parish church.*

There would be no guests but Antoine and the Comtesse, who would be their witnesses. Witnesses to the
union that would not be the empty marriage of convenience that had brought herself and Nikos together, but
a marriage of their hearts that would bind them, each to
the other, all their lives.

The marriage she longed to make.

She left her bedroom—*their* bedroom, hers and
Nikos's—and paused for a moment at the top of the stairs,
wondering how she could be so happy. How she could
be so blessed. Her beloved home, her beloved Nikos...

*But it's the other way round! It's my beloved Nikos
and then my beloved home! And it is ours together—and
our children's after us.*

She descended the marble staircase, glancing in approbation around her. Everything at Greymont was now fully restored as it should be. And now, its beauty renewed, she and Nikos could make plans to open Greymont to the public for periods during the summer. How pleased her father would have been at that!

And at her married happiness. She sent a wish towards him, full of love and gratitude, then smiled at Hudson as he waited benignly at the foot of the stairs.

She walked into the drawing room, her silken skirts swishing. Nikos and his brother rose immediately, and Nikos came to take her hand, walking with her to the woman sitting by the fireside. So petite, so frail, but despite the lines of fatigue around her eyes her gaze on Diana and her son was filled with an emotion Diana knew only too well—for it was in her own eyes too, whenever she gazed at Nikos.

Diana stooped to kiss her, welcoming her to Greymont. It was the first time Nikos's mother had been strong enough to make the journey, and Diana knew that both Nikos and Antoine were treating her like precious porcelain. It was a cherishing kind of care that drew the two brothers ever closer together, and Diana rejoiced in it. They had so many years to catch up on.

She rejoiced, too, that shortly after her *belle mère* and her brother-in-law had returned to Normandy Greymont would be host again—to royalty this time.

Princess Fatima had wasted no time, on receiving payment in full of the loan she had made to Diana, paid by Nikos, in discovering what had transpired to bring this about—and she was thrilled at what she had discovered. She wanted to see for herself, she informed Diana, and therefore she would honour them with a visit—'to take afternoon tea!' she had exclaimed gaily.

And in the early spring, when the weather would be

perfect in the Gulf, the Princess was insisting that Nikos and Diana visit again. *Especially* to take a trip to her brother's love-nest.

'It is where you fell in love with your husband,' she had said, looking sternly at Diana. 'To refuse would be to offend,' she'd warned. But there had been a glint of humour in her eyes as she'd spoken. And there had been a glint of answering humour in Nikos's face as he'd bowed his grateful assent.

'Only a madman would refuse to take the woman he loves more than life itself to the place where the stars themselves blessed their union,' he'd said.

The Princess had sighed in romantic satisfaction.

And taken another scone.

* * * * *

A CINDERELLA
FOR THE
DESERT KING

KIM LAWRENCE

For Herb, my much missed writing companion
and friend—best dog ever!

CHAPTER ONE

ABBY FOSTER WAS HOT, her feet ached—part of the photo shoot had involved her walking up a sand hill in shorts and four-inch heels—and something had bitten her on the arm. The thick layer of make-up had disguised it but not stopped it throbbing and itching like hell.

All that was bad enough but what was *really* the icing on the cake was the fact that their transport had broken down. She'd been meant to be in the first four-wheel drive, the one she had travelled out of Aarifa city to their desert location in, but the stylist had pushed past her, bagging a seat next to the photographer's assistant the girl had a crush on.

So, thanks to young love, Abby was now stranded in the middle of who knew where, trying without success to tune out the raised, angry voices outside. So far she had resisted the urge to add her own voice to the melee, but her clenched teeth were beginning to ache with the effort.

Leave well alone remained the best strategy, though, so along with Rob, who had reacted to being stranded in a desert by promptly taking the opportunity to grab a nap and falling asleep, she'd waited inside the broken-down vehicle.

It was a decision she was starting to rethink as the temperature inside the dark car rose and Rob, the person who had made her climb that damned sand dune ten times before he was satisfied he'd got the shot, began to snore.

Loudly!

Rolling her eyes, she pulled a bottle of water from the capacious tote bag she always carried with her. Despite the frequent-traveller miles she had clocked up since she'd embarked on her modelling career, Abby had never mastered the art of travelling light.

She had half-unscrewed the top before caution kicked in and she realised she may need to ration herself. Before he'd fallen asleep Rob had confidently claimed they would be rescued in a matter of minutes, but what if the photographer was being overly optimistic?

What if they were stuck here longer?

The internal debate didn't last long. Her grandparents had raised her to always be cautious—pity they hadn't displayed the same quality when it came to financial advice, considering they'd been swindled out of their life savings by a crooked financial advisor. But caution won out.

Gregory's good-looking face, complete with that boyishly sincere smile, materialised in her head as she tightened the lid with a vicious turn and put the bottle back into her bag. Her jaw clenched, she fought her way through the familiar toxic mixture of guilt and self-contempt she experienced whenever she considered her own part in her grandparents' situation. They put a brave face on it but she knew how unhappy they were.

It didn't matter which way you looked at it, it *was* her fault Nana and Pops had lost their financial security.

If *she* hadn't been fool enough to fall for Gregory's sincere smile and the blue eyes that went with it, and if *she* hadn't imagined herself in love and taken the sweet man of her dreams home to meet her grandparents, then they would still have the comfortable retirement they had worked so hard for to look forward to.

Instead they had nothing.

Her throat thickened with emotion, which she dismissed with a tiny impatient shake of her head. Tears, she reminded herself, weren't going to fix anything; what she needed was a plan.

And she had one. At last.

A militant gleam lit her green eyes as her rounded chin lifted to a determined angle. By her calculations, if she took every single piece of work that came her way—barring those that wanted her to pose minus clothes, and there were quite a few—in another eighteen months she'd be able to buy back the retirement bungalow her grandparents had lost because of her conman boyfriend. She'd brought him into their lives, he'd got them all to trust him and then he had vanished with her grandparents' life savings. In a vicious parting shot he'd emailed her a photo of him with another man, the pose they were in making the salt-in-the-wound footnote 'You're not really my type' slightly redundant.

Gregory's *patience* with her inexperience and his reassurance that he was prepared to wait because he respected her now made perfect sense.

Shutting out the humiliating memories before they took hold, Abby peeled off a wet wipe from a packet in the inner pocket of her bag. Eyes closed, she wiped her face and neck, removing the last of her make-up along with some of the dust and grime.

She was repeating the action while thinking long-ingly of a cool shower and a cold beer when one of the two men outside put his head into the cab. He fiddled with something beside the steering wheel before turn-ing reproachfully to Abby.

'You might have said something, Abby—we've been trying to open the damned engine for hours.' He gave the lever he'd located a sharp tug and yelled to the man outside. 'Got it, Jez!'

By her count it had actually only been ten minutes. 'It felt more like days,' she retorted, more bothered by the swelling bite on her arm than defending herself from this unfair criticism. Teeth gritted, she rolled up the sleeve of her blouse to take the pressure off the area, not that the shirt was actually *hers*—she was still wearing the outfit selected for today's shoot, the shorts and shirt apparently meant to convince viewers that if a girl chose the new shampoo the company was unveiling with this campaign, they too could go from a casino table to trek-king up sand dunes in the desert all while maintaining perfect, glowing hair. They might, but they'd also have blisters if they wore these wretched heels.

The developments through the fly-speckled window didn't look good. The men had both stepped back hast-ily from the scalding steam that billowed out from the engine.

And then they both started shouting again.

She nudged Rob's foot with her own—luckily for him she had swapped the spiky heels for canvas pumps.

'We should go out and see if we can help.'

Or at least stop them killing one another, she thought as she grabbed a scarf from her bag and pulled the strands of sweat-damp hair back from her face, securing the flaming waves at her nape in a ponytail that was neither smooth nor elegant.

As she got to her feet, head down to avoid banging it on the door frame, Rob opened one eye, nodded, then closed it again and began to quietly snore.

Cool was the wrong word, but at least the temperature outside was marginally less oppressive than that inside the car.

'So, what's the verdict, guys?' she asked, adopting a cheerful tone.

Her attitude did not rub off on the two men.

On the occasions she had worked with the lighting technician previously, Jez had always had a joke up his sleeve to lighten tense situations, but his sense of humour had clearly deserted him today. Frowning heavily, he stepped away from the inner workings of the steaming engine, his face glistening with sweat as he dropped the bonnet back into place.

'It won't go and, before anyone asks, I haven't got a clue what's wrong or how to fix it. If anyone else feels the urge...be my guest.' The thickset technician tossed a challenging look in the direction of the younger man but the intern's aggression had drained away and he was standing biting his nails, suddenly looking very young and very scared.

'No need to worry, Jez. I'm sure once they realise they've left us behind they'll come back to look for us,' Abby said, determined to look on the bright side, despite the fact that the sun was quickly setting and darkness was starting to steal across the desert around them.

'We shouldn't have stopped,' the younger man muttered under his breath as he kicked a tyre.

The older man nodded his agreement. 'What's *he*

doing?' He nodded towards the vehicle where the self-acknowledged photographic genius lay sleeping, exhausted, presumably by the effort of taking several dozen shots of an unusually shaped rock with a lizard sitting on it. By the time he had been satisfied with the result, the two lead vehicles in their small convoy had vanished back towards the city they'd come from earlier in the day.

'He's asleep.'

Abby's announcement was greeted with astonished looks and a cry in unison. *'Un-bloody-believable!'*

The two men looked at one another and laughed, their mutual disgust for Rob draining some of the hostility out of the situation. The smiles didn't last long though.

'Anyone got a phone signal?'

Abby shook her head. 'Well, what's the worst that could happen?'

'We die a slow and painful death from thirst?' Rob's voice suddenly cut in as he made a graceful and yawn-filled ascent from the vehicle.

Abby threw him a look. 'Seriously, what *is* the worst that can happen? At least we'll have a story to tell over dinner when we get home.'

'Guys.'

They all turned to look at Jez, who grinned broadly as he stabbed a finger towards plumes of dust in the distance. 'They've come back for us!'

Abby sighed and wiped the moisture from her forehead. 'Thank God!' She frowned at the sound coming from the direction of the fast-approaching vehicles. 'What was that?'

The young man shook his head, looking as puzzled as Abby felt. The two older men exchanged sharp glances, Rob turning to her. 'Maybe you should get back inside, Abby, love.'

'But—' This time the sharp cracking noises were louder and Abby felt her initial relief at being found slip away, replaced by the first flurries of fear as she stared at the approaching dust cloud. 'Was that gunfire?' she whispered.

'We're fine,' Jez said, shading his eyes. 'We're in Aarifa… It's safe as houses. Everyone knows that.' Another volley of gunfire cut across his words. He glanced at Abby. 'Maybe just to be on the safe side you should go inside and keep your head down…?'

The pure-bred Arab horse picked his sure-footed way through a darkness that was profound, a thick, velvety blackness against which the flowing white robe of his rider stood out.

Rider and animal, at full gallop, moved in harmony across the sand, slowing only when they reached the first rocky outcrop. At a distance, the column of rock seemed to rise vertically from the ground, but in reality the spiralling path to the summit, though not one recommended to someone without a head for heights, was a series of shorter ascents punctuated by relatively flat sections.

The highly bred horse was panting by the time they crested the summit and paused, the animal drawing air through flared nostrils, the rider waiting for the usual sense of peace this spot gave him.

Not tonight though.

Tonight, even the three-hundred-and-sixty-degree panorama—incredible any time of day but especially magnificent at night, set against the backdrop of a velvet sky sprinkled with stars—failed to penetrate or lift Zain Al Seif's black mood. The most he could claim was the relaxing of a little of the tension in his muscles as he drank in the view, the illuminated ancient walls of the palace with its towers and spires making it visible for miles around. Tonight, however, there were more lights than usual, lights that spread into the old town, built within the shadow of the citadel walls and extended beyond into a geometric pattern created by the brightly illuminated tree-lined boulevards of the modern city with its tall, glass-fronted buildings.

There were a *lot* more lights tonight because today the city...the whole country, in fact...was celebrating. There had been a wedding. A *royal* wedding.

And the world loved a royal wedding, Zain reflected, his sensually sculpted lips twitching into a cynical curve. On this occasion, the world minus one.

He couldn't escape it even here.

The horse responded to Zain's tight-lipped curse with a snort that was loud in the stillness. His mount, picking up on his own mood, began to paw the ground and dance around in circles that would have sent a less experienced rider catapulting over his head.

'Sorry, boy...' Zain soothed, patting the spooked animal's neck, an action that sent out a puff of the red dust that clung to everything in this desert. He waited for his horse to calm down before dismounting, an action he performed in one supple, well-practised action, his boots making no sound as he landed lightly on the uneven stone surface.

Releasing the reins, he took two steps forward and stood on the edge, not noticing the dizzying drop into blackness as his deep-set electric-blue eyes were drawn to the city's lights. As he stared the faint smile that had curved his lips disappeared, those same lips flattening into a grim line. His dark, angled brows drew together in a parallel line above his hawkish, narrow nose as he embraced a fresh surge of self-contempt.

He deserved to feel like a fool, because he had *been* a fool. A complacent bloody fool.

Yes, he'd had a lucky escape but that was the problem—he'd needed luck. He prided himself on being such a great judge of people but the beautiful bride being toasted by an entire country and assorted foreign dignitaries had totally fooled him with her act. The only positive he could see in the situation was that his heart had not been involved. His pride, however, was another matter and it had taken a serious hit.

Of course, *now* Zain could see the clues, but during the pleasurable six-month affair he had remained oblivious even when he had crossed his own self-imposed very clear line; the progress towards it had been so insidious he hadn't heard the alarm bells when he had started thinking of what they shared as a *relationship*... Who knew where that could have led?

Luckily, he never had to find out, because Kayla had got tired of playing the waiting game and when she received a better offer she took it. Zain, still under the illusion they were playing by *his* rules, had never for a moment suspected that lovely...lovely, *poisonous* Kayla had been playing him.

She had turned up at his apartment in Paris earlier than expected after her trip home to Aarifa to see her family. He'd been pleased enough to rearrange his schedule so they could spend the afternoon in bed. Afterwards, as he lay in bed, his attention was divided between the laptop propped on his knees and Kayla, who had dressed before taking a seat in front of the mirror and beginning to repair her make-up.

'You really don't need that,' he'd said offhandedly.

They had been enjoying a discreet affair for six months and he had never seen her without her make-up. On the admittedly few occasions they had spent the night together she always vanished to the bathroom before he woke, emerging looking flawless, a silent signal there would be no repeat performance that morning as she didn't want her hair mussed or her lipstick smudged.

She had turned to him at his words, lipstick in hand and a hardness in her smile he had not seen before. 'Sweet of you to say but,' she paused and applied a second layer of red to her lips before standing up and strolling back to the bed, 'although I was prepared to pretend to like art and opera and even be interested in supremely boring politics for you, I've never been prepared to settle for the fresh-faced look you seem to like in your women.'

The shrillness in her laugh had made him wince, so unlike her usual placating style designed to stroke his ego.

'No-strings-attached sex…did you *really* believe that was all I wanted? Do you *really* think we met by accident, that I took that awful pittance-paying art-gallery job because I want a career? Oh, well, at least it wasn't a complete loss. I certainly never had to pretend with you when we were in bed…' The concession emerged on a deep sigh. 'You know, I'm really going to miss this.'

Zain, still processing the contents of her confession, had not yet reacted as she sat down on the edge of the bed and trailed a red fingernail down his bare, hair-roughened chest, but his lips curled in distaste now at the memory.

'I thought I owed you…' she paused '…well, nothing actually, but I figured one more time, for old times' sake, wouldn't hurt. My family are formally announcing my engagement to your brother next weekend, so I'm afraid, darling, we won't be able to do this for a while. Don't look so shocked! It is kind of your fault. All I ask is that you try and look a teeny bit heartbroken at the wedding. It would make your brother's day.'

Now, alone in the desert, Zain felt his lips curl into a thin-lipped smile. He might not have inherited his father's physical characteristics but it seemed that he had inherited a genetic predisposition to be blind to women's faults. Then the smile vanished as he scanned the moon-silvered landscape and pushed away the self-contempt.

Acknowledging a weakness meant you could guard against it.

His father had lived the last fifteen years of his life consumed by a combination of self-pity and pathetic hope, not accepting the reality of a situation. It had been the man's downfall.

It would *not* be Zain's.

He stared out into the darkness as the scene in his head continued to replay with relentless accuracy.

'Of course, I'd prefer to marry you, darling, but you never did ask, did you?' Kayla had reproached with a pout, the truth of her anger showing for the first time. 'And I put *so* much effort into being perfect for you. Still, once things have settled we can pick up where we left off in bed, at least, so long as we're discreet. And that's the beauty of it all—Khalid isn't…well, let's just say he's in no position to object, as I have enough dirt on him to…'

Zain abruptly closed down the conversation playing in his head.

People wrote bucket lists of things they wanted to do before they died. At nine, practical Zain had penned a list of things he would *never* do while he lived. Over the years, some had fallen by the wayside—he'd actually grown quite fond of green vegetables, and kissing girls had proved less awful than he'd thought—but others he had rigidly stuck to. The primary one being that he would never allow himself to fall in love or get married—he was determined never to repeat the mistakes his father had made.

Marriage and love had not only broken his proud father as a man but also had threatened the stability of the country he ruled and the people he owed a duty to. Watching the process as a youngster, Zain had been helpless to do anything, the love and respect he once felt for his father turning to anger and shame.

The situation could have had more serious consequences—not that his father would have cared—had the sheikh not been surrounded by a circle of courtiers and advisors loyal to him. Somehow, they had shielded him and managed to maintain the illusion of the strong, wise ruler for the people.

Zain had not been shielded.

He shook his head, aware that he was indulging in a pastime that he would have been the first to condemn in others, and he didn't tolerate those who lived in the past.

A movement in the periphery of his vision interrupted his stream of thought.

Head inclined in a listening attitude, Zain turned his

head and stared hard through the dark towards where the invisible border between Aarifa and their neighbour Nezen lay.

He was on the point of turning away, deciding he'd imagined it, when suddenly it was there again...a flash of light that could be a flashlight, or possibly headlights. The light was accompanied this time by a distant sound that drifted across the moonlit emptiness... It sounded like voices shouting.

This time, lights stayed on. Definitely headlights.

He sighed, feeling little enthusiasm for rescuing what would inevitably turn out to be some damn idiot tourist—they averaged about ten a month—with no respect for the elemental environment. Zain loved the desert but he also had a healthy respect for the dangers it presented.

He sometimes wondered if the deep emotional connection he felt with the land of his birth was made stronger by the fact that, growing up an interloper, he'd had to prove his right to belong.

Things had changed, though sometimes an overheard comment or knowing glance would make him wonder just how much.

Admittedly, no one called him names these days, no gangs egged on by his brother threw stones, excluded him or simply beat him up, but scratch the surface and the prejudices were still there. His existence continued to be an insult to many in the country, especially those members of the leading Aarifan families.

He was more of an annoyance than his mother, who at least was living on another continent. It would have been easier in many ways if he had been a bastard, but his parents had married, not letting a little thing like his father's already having a wife and an heir get in the way of true love.

Love...!

A growing noise of distaste vibrated in his throat as, with a creak of leather, he heaved himself back into the saddle and turned the horse. That word again. In his mind it was hard to be sane and celebrate something that people over the centuries used to justify...well, pretty much anything from bad choices to full-scale war!

Love really was the ultimate in selfishness.

He didn't have to look much farther than his own parents to see its destructive power—there was no doubt of his father's enduring love for his mother, but it was as if their love story had been perfectly designed to increase tabloid turnover.

The sheikh of a wealthy middle-eastern state—married to a wife who had already given him an heir—had fallen for the tempestuous Italian superstar of the opera world, a diva in every sense of the word... Zain's mother.

Despite its progressive reputation, setting aside a wife was not unheard of in Aarifa—in fact, there were circumstances, even in these more enlightened times, when it would be positively encouraged, and even by the discarded bride's family if brought on by the need for a male heir, especially when that heir would one day be the country's ruler.

But Zain's father had already had an heir and the wife whom he dishonoured by setting her aside came from one of the most powerful families in the country. The humiliation of the sheikh's betrayal of the family with impeccable lineage was compounded by the unsuitability of the bride Sheikh Aban al Seif took in her stead, and the fact that the unsuitable bride had won over all her critics with her charm and smiles.

A nation had loved her and then fell dramatically out of love with her when she had walked away from her husband and eight-year-old son to resume her career.

The irony was that her humiliated, proud husband, the leader who had never dodged making tough decisions, the man known for his strength and determination, had not fallen out of love despite her betrayal. He'd have taken her back in a heartbeat and both his sons knew this, which perhaps accounted for the fact that they had never been what anyone could term *close*.

And in many ways, just like their father, Khalid was stuck in the past. His eyes still shone with pure malice when he looked at the half-brother whom he still held responsible for every bad thing that had happened to him and his mother. He still wanted whatever Zain had, be it success, accolades or, now, the woman on his arm. Ultimately it was about depriving not possessing and, once he had whatever it was he coveted from Zain, Khalid usually lost interest.

Would he lose interest in Kayla now he had her?

Zain shrugged to himself in the darkness. It was no longer his concern.

CHAPTER TWO

ZAIN HAD COVERED half the distance to the stranded vehicle when he came across signs that made him slow, stop and, after circling, finally dismount to investigate.

He lost the attitude of disgruntled resignation with which he had embarked on the task as he studied the impressions of tyre tracks that stood out, dark in the moonlight. He picked up one of the shell casings that littered the area, holding it in the palm of his hand for a moment before flinging it away and leaping back into the saddle.

It took him ten minutes before he reached the car that stood with its headlights blazing. He yelled out a couple of times before the three men hiding inside revealed themselves, the drift of the hissed exchange between them suggesting to Zain that his ability to speak English without an accent made him friend not foe in their eyes.

Having halted the garbled explanations they all started to share, he demanded they speak one at a time and he listened, struggling to hold his tongue as he heard them describe what was a list of ineptitude that was in his mind approaching criminal, but there was a limit to his restraint.

'You had a woman with you, out here?' He could not hide his contempt.

'We didn't plan to get stranded, mate,' the older man, who was nursing a black eye, said defensively. 'And we told Abby to hide inside the cab when that mob drove up, but when they started laying into Rob,' he nodded towards the taller man and Zain noticed the wound on his hairline that was still seeping blood, 'she jumped out and laid into the guy with—'

'It was her bag. She hit him with it.'

'And then they hit her back.'

'Was she conscious when they took her?'

It was the oldest man who responded to the terse question. 'I'm not sure but she didn't move when they chucked her in the back.'

The youngest, who looked little more than a boy to Zain's eyes, began to weep. 'What will they do to her… Abby, what will they do to Abby?' he wailed.

The older man laid a hand on his shoulder. 'She'll be all right, son. You know Abby—she's tough, and she can talk her way out of anything. She'll be all right, won't she?' he repeated, throwing a look of appeal at Zain.

Zain saw no need to wrap up the truth. 'They'll keep her alive until they've assessed whether she's worth money.' It had been two years since the last border raids from Nezen. His father's defence minister, Said, would be alarmed when he heard about this new incursion by the criminal gangs who lived in the foothills.

The brutal pronouncement drew a strangled sob from the boy.

What happens if I die here—who will pay off Nana and Pops's debts? You're not going to die, Abby. Think!

She lifted her chin and blinked, flinching as the yelling men riding up and down on camels fired off another volley of bullets into the air.

She'd lost consciousness when they'd thrown her in the truck and when she'd come to she'd had a sack over her head—a situation that had escalated her fear and sense of disorientation to another frantic level. What time was it? Where was she and what was going to happen next?

She still didn't know the answer to either question and she wasn't sure she wanted to know any longer.

She stiffened, her nostrils flaring in distaste as one of the men grabbed her hair in his filthy hand and tugged her towards him to leer in her face. She stared stonily ahead, only breathing again once he had let her go and moved away.

Ignoring the panic she could feel lapping at the edge of her resolve, she lifted her chin. *Think, Abby. Think.*

The effort to make her brain work felt like trying to run in sand, an apt analogy considering that the gritty stuff coated everything.

She clenched her jaw and ignored the pain in her cheek from where one of her captors had casually backhanded her when she'd tried to stop them beating Rob. She had to work out what she was going to do and how much time she had lost while she was blacked out. It seemed like another lifetime that the jeeps loaded with men wielding guns had surrounded their broken-down four-wheel-drive but it couldn't have been that long ago.

It was still dark but the surrounding area was lit up not just by a massive bonfire, which was throwing out enough heat to slick her body in sweat, but also by the headlights of upwards of twenty or so cars and trucks parked haphazardly, enclosing the dusty area on three sides.

She pulled surreptitiously on the rope around her wrists but they held tight. Though her feet were unbounded and she was tempted to run, she doubted she'd get far. It would take only seconds for the half a dozen whooping men who rode back and forth on camels to catch her.

And where would she go?

There were no women.

Abby had never felt more isolated and afraid in her life. She had never known it was *possible* to feel this scared, but, though initially the fear had made her brain freeze, it began to work with feverish speed and clarity as one of the men who had dumped her down came across and said something in a harsh voice.

She shook her head to indicate she didn't understand but he shouted again, and then when she didn't react he bent forward and dragged her to her feet, pushing her forward until they reached an area where a dozen or so of the men were gathered in a half-circle.

When she pulled away from the group the man towing her pushed her hard in the small of her back and produced a long, curved, wicked-looking dagger. Expecting the worst, she fought against tears as he pulled her arms. Then the tears fell—partly in relief and partly in pain—as he sliced through the cord that held her hands behind her back.

She was rubbing her aching wrists when he began to speak, addressing the men gathered around and pointing at her. Someone shouted something and he grabbed her hair, holding it up to the firelight and drawing a gasp from the men with greedy eyes all fixed on her.

She cringed inwardly, her skin crawling at the touch of the eyes moving over her body. Desperately conscious of her bare legs, she wanted to pretend this wasn't really happening to her, but it was. The sense of helplessness boiled over as she stood, hands clenched stiffly at her sides, shaking from a combination of gut-clenching fear and anger.

The man beside her spoke again, and as other yells echoed in answer she realised what was happening—she was being auctioned off to the highest bidder.

Outrage and horror clenched in her as she began to shake her head, trying to yell out and tell them that they couldn't do this. But the words shrivelled in her throat, her vocal cords literally paralysed with fear.

She closed her eyes to shut out the nightmare of the leering faces, opening them in shock when the man beside her tore open her blouse to the sound of applause from the watching men as it gaped, revealing her bra.

Anger pierced the veil of fear and spurred Abby into retaliatory action. She didn't pause to consider the consequences of her actions, she just lifted a clenched fist and swung. The man moved at the last moment but she caught his shoulder with a hard blow that drew a grunt of pain from him.

Someone laughed and the initial look of open-mouthed shock on his face morphed into something much uglier. There was no point running. There was nowhere to run *to*. The determination not to show her fear was suddenly stronger than the fear itself and Abby lifted her chin, clinging to her pride as she drew the tattered shreds of her shirt tightly around her against the imminent threat. The man advanced towards her, snarling angry words she didn't understand, not that a dictionary was needed when his intent was pretty clear.

He lifted a hand to strike her when suddenly he froze. Everyone did, as a horse with a robed rider galloped full pelt into the semicircle, causing chaos as the men threw themselves to one side to avoid the slashing hooves. Just when it seemed as if man and horse were about to gallop straight into the flames of the bonfire, the horse stopped dead.

The rider, having achieved the sort of theatre-hushed entrance that film directors would have traded a row of awards for, calmly looked around, taking his time and not seeming to be bothered by the guns aimed at him.

After a moment, he loosed the reins and let them fall. The animal didn't move an inch as his rider casually vaulted to the ground, projecting a mixture of arrogance and contempt.

Any idea that the hauteur and arrogance he oozed had anything to do with his superior position on the impressive animal vanished since, if anything, his air of command was even more pronounced as he began to move with long-legged purpose towards the spot where Abby stood as transfixed as everyone else by the tall figure in the flowing white robes. His elegance liberally coated his every move, oozing a level of undiluted male sexuality that had nothing to do with the way he was dressed or even the fact that, even without the dusty riding boots he wore, he had to be at least six foot six, with the length of leg and width of shoulders to carry off the height.

The rest of the men present wore Arab dress but there the similarity ended. The dregs of humanity who had been part of this degrading scene were bedraggled specimens. This man was...*magnificent*.

Abby registered this fact while not losing sight of the truth that he was probably just as much of a threat to her...maybe even more so. She ought not to care about such things in her position, but his face had perfectly sculpted features, symmetrical angles and hollows so dramatically beautiful that she experienced an almost visceral thrill of awareness looking at him.

He held the eyes of the man beside her until the man lowered his arm. The stranger gave a curt nod and then his gaze moved on to Abby. His scrutiny lacked the leering quality of the other mens' but it was equally disturbing, though in an entirely different way. Her tummy fluttered erratically in reaction to his blue-eyed stare.

She lifted her chin and planted her hands on her hips, staring right back until a draught made her realise that her ripped blouse was still displaying a lot of skin. Head bent, cheeks hot, she clumsily attempted to pull the sides closer together across her chest as she awkwardly fastened the buttons with shaking fingers. The top button had gone so she used the one below and, as it was either cover her breast or her midriff, she chose her breast.

She thought she might have imagined the flicker of something close to admiration in the horseman's lean face before he turned and spoke to the man who appeared to be the auctioneer.

His voice was low, a throaty, abrasive quality giving the deep, velvet drawl texture.

Whatever he said caused one of the men who had been bidding to step forward, shouting and gesticulating in protest. As the shouting man reached Abby she leaned back, her nostrils flaring in distaste as his foul breath wafted over her face. She winced and closed her eyes as he grabbed her hair, steeling herself against the pain she anticipated. But it never came.

Instead, the man's grip loosened and fell away, the stench receding. Head bent, she half-opened her eyes and saw the man who had grabbed her standing some feet away. He was still close but his focus was not on her, it was on the tall, white-clad figure who stood smiling with his hand curled around the man's upper arm, seemingly oblivious to the wicked-looking blade pointed at him.

Abby held her breath, her heart continuing to fling itself against her ribcage with bone-cracking force, while this fresh top-up to the adrenaline already flowing through her veins made her head spin.

She felt strangely dissociated from the scene she was watching, as though it were the cliff-hanger in a soap opera finale…but this was real. As was the metallic taste of fear in her mouth.

The silent war of attrition lasted a few seconds before the lesser man's eyes widened and he turned his head and slid the blade back into the concealed sheath on his robe.

He had lost face and he was not going to retire gracefully. He began to gesticulate angrily as he shouted, but Abby noticed that the few growls of agreement from the audience of watching men were subdued. Clearly in the 'lay it on the table and measure it' stakes he had lost out big time.

The tall horseman appeared oblivious to the growing tension as he addressed his soft comments to the man who had been in charge of the flesh auction.

Her would-be purchaser bent in to listen and threw up his hands, turning to his audience and inviting them to share his contempt. The response was a low growl.

For his part, the tall stranger seemed utterly oblivious to the threat that lay heavy in the air as he held out a hand and slid a ring off one long, brown finger, dropping it into the palm of the waiting man's extended hand, then sliding a metal-banded watch from his wrist and adding it to the auctioneer's spoils.

The man produced a flashlight from his pocket and turned away, his shoulders hunched as he examined his haul. Without another word he nodded and called out something to another man, who came across holding a rolled-up sheet of paper. He unrolled it and laid it on top of a crate that was acting as a table.

Was it a bill of sale?

The idea filled her with a mixture of revulsion and disbelief. This could not be happening; it was too surreal.

Without even looking at her the horseman took her arm and tugged her with him to the makeshift table. He took the offered pen and wrote what she presumed was his name on it.

He then turned and held the pen out to Abby, who stared at it as if it were a striking snake before she shook her head and tucked her hand behind her back.

'What is it?'

The music being blasted from several of the trucks that had masked the noise of his arrival came to Zain's aid again, covering his murmured response.

'You can read the small print later,' he said, his words betraying an urgency suggesting the odds of them getting out of here diminished the longer they remained.

'If you ever want to see your home and family again sign it right now, you little fool.'

Her eyes fluttered wide as they flew to his face— she had not expected a reply to her question, let alone one in perfect English.

She took a deep breath then let it out slowly. Why was she even hesitating when the alternative was even more grim? Abby gave an imperceptible nod. The words on the paper blurred as she bent towards it and the pen that had been thrust into her hand trembled.

She would have dropped it but for the steadying grip of the long brown fingers that curved over her hand and guided it to the paper.

She looked from the big hand that curved her trembling fingers around the pen to her shaky signature appearing on the paper but felt no connection to it.

She stood there like a statue while the horseman physically took the pen from her fingers, conscious of a low buzz of argument just to her right that became loud and a lot angrier as the horseman rolled up the paper and put it inside a pocket hidden inside his robe.

The girl looked up at him with glazed green eyes— shock, he diagnosed, stifling a stab of sympathy. He pushed it away; empathy was not going to get them out of here. Clear thinking was. There was nothing like the danger of a life and death situation to focus a man, Zain thought with a smile. A bit of luck thrown in would also help.

In the periphery of his vision he was aware of the argument that was escalating, fast becoming a brawl... others were drifting towards it and sides were being taken.

'Come on,' he said through clenched teeth.

As his fingers curved around her elbow he could feel the tremors that were shaking her body. He pushed away a fresh stab of sympathy. His priority right now was getting out of this camp before someone recognised him and realised that he was worth more money than any girl, even one with flaming hair, curves and legs... He cut short his inventory and lifted his gaze from the shapely limbs in question.

'Can you walk?' There wasn't a trace of sympathy in the question.

Ignoring the fact her knees were shaking, the woman lifted her chin and responded to what he could admit had been a cold, vaguely accusing question.

'Of course I can walk.' She was unsteady but she fell into step beside him. It was clear that he was still a danger in her eyes but she clearly saw he represented her way out of this awful place.

'We don't have all day.' Behind his impassive expression he was impressed that she was still walking, and she wasn't having hysterics... This was going to be easier if she was not having hysterics.

'Keep up.'

Clearly unused to looking up at many people, the woman tilted her chin to lob a look of resentment at his patrician profile. 'I'm trying,' she muttered between clenched teeth.

'Then try harder before they realise they could attempt to retake you despite the bride price I paid.' His glance travelled from the top of her flaming head to her feet and all the lush curves in between before trailing to his own hand, which looked oddly bare without the ring he had worn since his eighteenth birthday. 'Or me,' he added softly.

Luckily, he was the spare and not the heir.

Through the dark screen of his lashes he calculated how many people could get between them and the waiting horse. It was encouraging to see that most had moved to join in the fracas they were swiftly moving away from. Zain was content for the men to fight amongst themselves. It was the possibility of their stopping long enough to unite against a common foe— namely himself and the redhead—that bothered him.

None of the thoughts passing through his head showed in his body language, however, as he had learnt a long time ago that appearances *did* matter. It wasn't about a macho reluctance to show weakness; it was common sense. Weakness would always be exploited by enemies, and that went pretty much double when the enemies in question were carrying weapons.

A spasm of impatience flickered across his lean features as the girl slowed and came to a nervous halt when they got within a few feet of the stallion.

'He won't bite…unless you annoy him.'

Abby's experience of equines had until this point in her life been restricted to a donkey ride on the beach. Even at eleven, her long legs had almost touched the floor as she straddled the little donkey, who had plodded along and looked at her with sad eyes. This animal, with his stamping feet, looked about ten feet tall and his rolling eyes were not kind.

'I don't think he likes me.'

The mysterious stranger ignored the comment and

vaulted into the saddle before reaching down and casually hauling her up before him.

Landing breathlessly, Abby clutched at the first thing that came to hand, which was the horseman, seizing on cloth. His body was hard as rock with zero excess flesh.

It wasn't until the horse had stopped dancing like a temperamental ballerina and she had not fallen off that the comment hit her. *'Bride price...?'*

'Can you do something with that hair? I can't see a damned thing...' Holding the reins in one hand, he pushed a skein of her copper hair away from his face and urged the horse into a canter. 'Yes, we just got married.'

She turned her head to stare in wide-eyed alarm as he urged all several hundred pounds of quivering, high-bred horse flesh underneath them into action, and the animal hit full gallop in seconds.

Her shriek was carried away by the warm air that hit her face. Abby tightened her white-knuckled grip and closed her eyes, sending up a silent prayer...or maybe not so silent. She felt rather than heard his heartless laugh as the sting of sand hitting her face made her turn it protectively into his broad shoulder.

'Just hang on.'

She had no intention of letting go or, for that matter, opening her eyes again as her stomach lurched sickly. She couldn't see a thing anyway as they left the lights of the encampment behind. It was pitch-black. How on earth could he see where they were going?

Where *were* they going?

And were they really *married*?

The horse's thundering stride didn't falter. In fact, after a short time, the rhythm of its hoof beats seemed to have a *soothing* effect on her. Although perhaps that was too strong a word to describe the calm, almost hypnotic sensation allowing the rigidity of terror to slip from her body by degrees, allowing her to even lift her face from the man's shoulder.

'Are they following us?'

'Maybe. I only managed to disable half the engines before—' He cut off abruptly as he felt an echo of the swell of rage that had consumed him when he saw the guy raise his hand. 'Did they…hurt you?'

'Not in the way you mean.' She pressed a hand to her mouth to stifle a yawn. It wasn't fear that kept her eyes closed now but the fact that the mere effort of lifting her eyelids was a struggle.

But she had to try—there were questions she needed to ask. Not deep, meaningful stuff, just the basics, like who was he and where were they going?

'This is mad,' she said as another yawn escaped her. She felt weirdly numb and even her bitten arm seemed to have stopped hurting. Eyes closed, hurtling along like this felt strangely like flying, the hand that was looped casually around her ribs keeping her safe.

'No, it's physiology. Shock releases chemicals.'

And never underestimate the power of chemicals, he thought, the memory of the burst of raw rage that had hit him like a tsunami when he had seen the redhead paraded like a piece of meat for the benefit of the pack of rabid scum still fresh in his mind.

For a man who had always taken his ability to approach problems from the vantage point of cool detachment, the knowledge that his struggle to control the initial primal instinct, the rush of visceral hatred, to rush in without considering the consequences when it could have gone either way was disturbing.

'I'm not in shock,' she told him, a hint of challenge in her voice as she prised her eyelids apart and gave her head a tiny shake.

He flashed a look downwards at the woman who sat in front of him. The angle meant her face was hidden from him and he could only see the top of her glossy head and the angle of her jaw. It was a stubborn angle, but it had taken more than stubbornness to stand there and throw a punch. It was stupid, yes, but also just about the gutsiest thing he had ever seen.

'The danger is over and your adrenaline levels are dipping.'

Abby gave a tiny choking laugh, as if she thought the idea she was out of danger was funny.

'You've found something to laugh about in this situation?'

'I can have hysterics if you prefer,' she said with annoyance, a strange look coming over her face. Then, 'I feel sick,' she warned him suddenly.

'Don't be,' he said, knowing it was an unfeeling response but also knowing they couldn't stop now. It wasn't safe.

Luckily for them both her nausea passed, but the bone-deep exhaustion didn't as he felt her fight the losing battle to stay awake. At last she gave in and when her head next slumped against his chest it stayed there, her breathing deepening and her body relaxing into his.

Zain dragged her soft, limp body in closer, giving the powerful animal free rein, and found the quiet place in his head that had eluded him all day. It turned out that all it took was being fired at, giving away a priceless gem that had been in his family for generations, and having a beautiful, albeit filthy and bedraggled, woman snore softly in his arms. Just when he'd thought life was getting predictable.

His narrowed glance moved once more towards the east, where he could see a ribbon of distant lights that indicated they were being pursued, but they had had a head start and if he made a detour to the Qu'raing oasis their paths would not cross.

The danger was over...so why did he feel as if he was about to face another?

CHAPTER THREE

'TIME TO STRETCH your legs.'

Abby murmured sleepily and ignored the voice but couldn't ignore the creak of leather and the abrupt removal of the hard warmth she had been pressed against—as illusions of security went, this one was on an epic scale.

Abby fought her way through the layers of sleep and blinked… The ground was a long way off and the horse she sat astride was stamping and snorting restlessly.

She'd been asleep. How on *earth* had she actually slept?

She arched her back to stretch out the cricks in her spine and felt herself slip, so she grabbed the first thing that came to hand—a piece of horse mane—to regain her balance. Feeling slightly more secure, she risked letting go for a moment to brush away the hair that had fallen across her face, effectively blinding her.

She was half-inclined to pull the silky curtain back in place when her eyes connected with those of the tall man standing, arms folded across his chest, watching her.

Of their own volition, her eyes made the journey up from his dusty boots to the edges of the gold embroidery along the traditional gown he wore. Her throat drying as they reached his face, she lost interest in moving away. He was beautiful in a sharp-intake-of-breath, tummy-clenching way. The carved symmetry of his dark, dramatic features framed by the pale head-covering was riveting.

She quickly shook off her rapt expression, looking away and silently blaming her fascination with the carnal curve of this man's mouth on the situation… Everything that had happened felt more akin to an out-of-body experience than reality.

'I'd prefer not to stop,' she said.

'Is that a fact?'

His tone made her flush. 'I just meant…the thing is… I wasn't alone when they—' She stopped as, without warning, a wave of revulsion tightened like a fist in her stomach, an echo of the fear she had felt when she had been thrown in the truck. It took her a couple of swallows to regain enough composure to finish huskily, 'When they took me.'

He watched her thoughtfully as she fought for control.

'They, the rest of the group I was travelling with, are stranded—we *have* to…' She stopped, frustrated because he didn't seem to grasp the urgency.

'They are three grown men.'

Relief rushed through her; she'd asked her captors what had happened to the men left behind but the only response she'd had she hadn't been able to understand. 'You saw them?' she said eagerly.

He tipped his head in acknowledgement.

'They're not hurt? Did they get the car going?'

'They have shelter; they can survive a night in the desert.'

'You haven't reported their whereabouts to anyone?'

'Following you seemed a priority at the time.'

She bit her lip. 'And obviously I'm very grateful. I'm just worried about my friends.'

'One special friend perhaps?'

The insinuation made her flush. 'They are work colleagues. I'm a model. Now, if you don't mind, I would like to go and check, just to be sure.'

'Be my guest.'

He took a step back and spread an arm in a sweeping gesture towards the miles upon miles of undulating ochre sand. The first fingers of the rising sun had drawn a line of deep red along the horizon and he knew she was seeing a vast, terrifying emptiness, but Zain also knew that it teemed with life and all around them the nocturnal creatures that inhabited the vastness were hiding away from the oncoming day and the heat it brought.

'Which way do you suggest we go?'

She took refuge from frustration in a childish retort. 'So what you're telling me is to shut up and do as I'm told because you know best.'

Head tilted, he considered her comment. 'In the desert, I definitely know best,' he retorted calmly. 'You coming down?'

'Where are we?'

Not civilisation; the pale grey light of dawn revealed that much. There was something that looked like grass under their feet and a few scrubby trees to their left which blocked the view beyond. Behind them lay the seemingly endless miles of bare, bleak desert blushed pink by the dawn. She shivered again.

He had never seen skin so smooth, features so crystal-clear... He brought his list of her attributes to an abrupt halt. Her beauty had made her a victim today, but it was inevitable that there had been many occasions when it had played to her advantage, when men had made fools of themselves over her.

Zain dragged his eyes, which were inclined to linger on the long length of her slim, shapely legs, upwards. The twist of his lips held self-mockery as he observed, 'It's a bit late in the day for caution, don't you think?' His heart might be in cold storage but it seemed his libido was still active and functioning.

Maybe that was the way forward?

Not here, not now and *definitely* not with a woman who probably didn't even realise how vulnerable she was. But empty sex, while not exactly an original way to move on, was a tried and tested method and appealed to him a hell of a lot more than drowning in self-pity or becoming celibate.

Sex was healthy if you kept it free of emotions. And he had learnt to control his years ago…mostly… Unbidden, the moment he had got his first glimpse of the kidnapped woman flashed into his mind.

When he set out to find her he'd had no mental image in his head of the woman he was seeking—she hadn't actually been a person for him. Regardless, nothing he could imagine would have come close to the reality.

He hadn't needed the cacophony of competing music blaring from the trucks to cover his entrance into the ramshackle encampment. All attention had been fixed on her. In a heartbeat the electric air of anticipation in the place had been explained. It had taken Zain a moment to absorb every detail of her lithe, lush body, the impossibly long legs, the sinuous curves, the pale skin and tangled skein of flaming auburn hair. There was nothing plastic or air-brushed about her—just a warm, luscious, desirable woman.

It wasn't difficult to imagine her on a billboard selling anything and maybe causing a few accidents. She was the sort of woman to make a man forget about his troubles. Not that he was that man but, even so, the last few miles with her soft body pressed against his had made for an interesting journey—just him, the sleeping girl and his testosterone. There was a simplicity to it that, after a day of his calculating his every expression and verbal intonation, had been a strange sort of relief.

It took a couple of seconds for Abby's exhausted, stress-racked brain to pick its way through the man's critical comment.

'You think it was *my* fault I got kidnapped? I *asked* for it maybe…? You know, one of the things I despise most is victim-blaming…not that I am—a victim, I mean—but…oh, hell!' She threw up her hands, immediately losing her balance and a couple of wild, flailing moments later falling straight into his open arms.

The impact of hitting a chest that was as hard as steel expelled a soft whoosh of air from her lungs as the arm banding her ribs loosened enough to let her slide slowly all the way to the floor. It was obvious before she made land fall that the rest of him was equally hard—the man was built of solid muscle—and falling had felt less alarming than the head-spinning, stomach-fluttering sensation that made her world spin. The sensation was so strong it was a breathless moment before she managed to get her erratic breathing under control enough to protest.

'Let me g…go!'

He did, with a care that bordered, unexpectedly, on tenderness. 'I'm not the one doing the holding,' he pointed out, angling a quizzical look at her fingers still clutching the sleeves of his robe.

Before she could react to the taunting reminder, the blades of his dark brows drew into an interrogative straight line above his spectacular, dazzling blue eyes. 'What's *that*?'

She lifted a hand to the puffy, swollen area on her arm where his accusatory glance rested. 'A bite, I suppose.'

He laid one hand on her forehead, caught her wrist with the other and extended her arm, bending in closer to inspect the area.

'Do you mind? That hurts!' she protested, turning her head away and tugging on her arm; after what had happened it seemed bizarre that he had fixated on this minor problem.

'So you dress like you're off to play a game of beach volleyball, and for good measure don't use mosquito repellent. Do you know how dangerous this desert is?'

Fighting the urge to pull at the hem of her shorts to cover herself from his contemptuous gaze, she lifted her chin a defiant notch and cut across him.

'It was a photo shoot. I don't choose what I wear, and I did use repellent.' It had been in the sunscreen that she had virtually bathed in. 'If it's all the same to you, I'd prefer to go straight back to my hotel,' she announced.

He looked startled, then, after a short, stunned-seeming silence, gave a laugh. 'I am not a taxi service.'

The amused hauteur in his response made her feel marginally less awful about coming across like some sort of snooty tourist, but she could see he had a point.

Her descent from snooty was rapid and clearly not at all what he'd expected. 'Of course not. Sorry. And I suppose it's a bit late but I'm tremendously… Thank you,' she said, her gratitude as genuine as her hope he really was one of the good guys. She felt the ball of fear in her stomach tightening and refused to acknowledge it.

The groove between his brows deepened. Her rescuer hadn't expected the back-down and it threw him, as did the obvious genuineness of it. 'I don't require your thanks.'

The lingering shock in her system made her response teary. 'Tough, I'm grateful.'

'What were you doing all the way out there alone anyway?' His question had an unexpected throaty quality.

Abby took a breath, feeling tears press against her eyelids, and tried to flatten out her emotional response. Facts, she could do facts.

'We were meant to be much closer to the city, but nobody had factored in the wedding. Did you know? Sorry, it doesn't matter.' All her efforts focused on not sounding weepy, she avoided his eyes. That bright, glittering stare made it hard for her to concentrate. 'But it did complicate things—there was a no-fly zone, diversions and a lot of restrictions.' They had sat in an airport lounge drinking coffee while emails between the firm paying for the jaunt and the director decided their fate. 'I even wondered at first when I was…' Catching herself up short, she gave a self-conscious little nod. She swallowed, her hand pressed to her throat as she relived those awful moments when the men had grabbed her. 'I wondered, actually *hoped* it was a set-up for publicity…' She swallowed again and rubbed her hands over her forearms, remembering the sensations of total, overwhelming helplessness. 'I feel grubby.' She wasn't talking just about the sand clinging to her skin and hair or the assorted smears of dirt on her inadequate clothing.

'Then come.' He tipped his head towards the trees. 'Bathe.'

She blinked at the unexpected response.

'A horse needs water.' He took hold of the horse's reins and approached the scrubby undergrowth.

The incline had not been apparent from where they had stood but it explained why she hadn't been able to see the taller trees or the palms. An oasis meant water and soon they reached it, a bubbling trickle that rose up from the ground and ran in a thin silver ribbon through the trees. Neither horse nor rider paused; instead they carried on, the reason becoming clear a few moments later when the stream fed into a pool of turquoise water framed by palms.

Her exposure to life's ugliness had given her a new appreciation of life's beauty, and emotion deepened her voice as she stared at the shimmering, postcard-perfect image and gasped. 'It's beautiful!'

The stranger watched her battle to subdue the tears, blinking and sniffing but stubbornly determined not to add any new tear tracks to her face as she pressed a hand to her soft, trembling lips. Standing there, bedraggled, her face filthy and scratched, she knew she looked ridiculously fragile. Stubborn pride was the only thing holding her up.

'We need to do something about your arm.'

The first hint of gentleness in his voice released the floodgates and the tears began to overflow, sliding down her cheeks as first one sob escaped her lips then another. They just kept coming…deep, subterranean sobs that shook her entire body.

Without thinking, Zain reacted to her distress. He moved in closer, took her by the arms and stood there, bodies close but not touching, his chin on her head while she wailed like a banshee. One look at her tear-filled eyes and the fear warring with pride there had touched him in a corner of his heart he hadn't known existed.

The sobs and tremors shaking her body subsided and finally she pulled away, looking embarrassed rather than grateful.

'I must look terrible,' she sniffed, not quite meeting his eyes.

'Yes,' he agreed, too distracted by the scene playing in his head to display any tact.

She was under him, her warmth pushing up into him, her body arching as he slid deep inside her.

He'd known her barely a few hours and already it was becoming a recurrent theme that his imagination was intermittently adding erotic details to. More a man for action, Zain had never thought fantasies were any substitute for reality. What he hadn't realised until this moment was just how frustrating they were!

His distracted response made her forget her determination not to look at him. As she did, the startled indignation on her face melted into amusement and she broke the silence with a gurgle of laughter. 'Well, at least I know you're honest now. Which means… I'm safe.' She paused, as if giving it time to sink in. 'I didn't think that…'

She had a very expressive face and he could virtually see the nightmare scenes playing through her head.

'Then don't think,' he recommended, guilt at his lustful thoughts making him sound abrupt. She had just escaped hell and his empathy amounted to fixating on the lush promise of her incredible mouth—and for that matter the lush promise of the rest of her. Hell, but you're a sensitive guy, he told himself sardonically.

'I'm just relieved that I'm safe.' And with relief came a deep exhaustion and she made no protest when he urged her down onto the grass beside the pool.

Leaving her there, Zain walked over to where the stallion was grazing and pulled out a thermos that was tucked into one of the saddlebags. Dropping down into a squat beside her, he unscrewed the top and handed it to her.

She drank greedily, wiping her lips when she'd finished then handing it back.

He couldn't keep calling her 'the redhead' and he'd forgotten what the men had called her. 'Do you have a name?'

'Abby. And you are?'

'Zain.'

'Let me see your arm, Abby.'

He inspected it gently before nodding, then looking around. 'Stay put.'

Abby doubted of she could have moved even if she'd wanted to. Still, she followed him with her eyes—he was easy to watch and the way he moved…the combination of power, grace and perfect co-ordination… her stomach gave a lazy flip before she snatched her glance guiltily away.

There was no harm looking, was there?

Actually, if she *hadn't* been looking she really would need the medical attention as badly as he seemed to think she did. If she met a woman who could pronounce herself indifferent to what this man oozed she would know she was in the presence of a liar!

'This might sting.'

Might...? She bit her lower lip to stop herself crying out when he poured water over the bite. 'Are those leaves?' she asked, watching doubtfully as he laid something over the red, swollen area.

'Neem leaves... Hold it there.'

This time he walked down to the water. He unfastened the gold rope that held his headdress in place before pulling the white cloth of his head-covering free.

Abby felt a little stab of shock; she had just assumed that his hair would be long, in keeping with the whole Bedouin thing...but it was short, very dark, but for a fairer streak near the hairline at the front.

Her fascination increased as she watched him run his hand across the short strands, making them stand on end in sexy tufts before he squatted down, splashed water on his face and head, and pulled a knife from a fold in his gown.

He turned his head and she looked away quickly, guilty that she'd been caught staring like a child with her nose pressed to the window of a sweet shop, except the thoughts that went through her head when she looked at him were not innocent or childlike.

'What is neem?' she asked, watching as he split the white fabric with the knife, tearing it into several strips.

Still in the crouching position, he leaned back on his

heels and pointed upwards. 'A tree—that one there and those over there.'

She shaded her eyes and looked up into the canopy of the tree he indicated.

'People have been using neem medicinally for centuries for any number of conditions; it's said to have antiseptic properties, so here's hoping.'

'That it's not an old wives' tale?'

'A lot of scientific research suggests otherwise. Pharmaceutical firms are taking an interest; Aarifa has developed a project farming the trees. They grow fast, literally anywhere, in any soil, and a deep, extensive root system means they can survive drought.'

She looked more impressed than the old guard—all men—had been when he'd explained the same thing to them. They'd all held positions of power in Aarifa for a generation and were negative about any idea that originated in his office, but Zain believed in it and had pushed on regardless. Ultimately, he'd been proven right.

The project he'd proposed had been a commercial success, bringing investment from foreign companies, creating much needed jobs and inspiring home-grown entrepreneurial talent in the shape of a couple who had developed a cosmetics line using the plant.

Abby, holding her hair back from her face, watched him take a leaf and crush it between his long fingers before pressing it into a piece of wet fabric. He did it with the same precision that characterised everything he did.

'You sound like a teacher.'

His eyes lifted momentarily from his task before he continued. 'I'm not.'

He could tell she was curious but her reluctance to reveal her interest stopped her from bombarding him with questions.

'A bit makeshift—it needs grinding to make a proper poultice—but it's better than nothing.'

'How do you know about this stuff...do you live in the desert?' she probed casually and again he framed a reply that told her nothing.

'Life is simpler in the desert.'

And that had a certain appeal, but time was the issue. His yearly month-long sabbatical, when he returned to his roots and his paternal grandmother's family, who still lived a traditional tribal Bedouin existence, had this year become a begrudging two weeks... How long before it was just a memory?

'You can let go now.'

He took the leaf that adhered to her skin and replaced it with the wet fabric wad covered with the ground leaves of the tree, deftly wrapping another one of the fabric strips around to hold it in place.

He arched a brow. 'Not too tight?'

She shook her head, lowering her gaze from his.

'My shoe is though,' she said, waggling her right foot at him. 'One foot is half a size bigger than the other.' He looked at her as though she were mad—she probably was.

'You need to drink some more water.'

Abby clenched her teeth at his order.

'Thanks.' She got the water bottle as far as her lips before something distracted her. A memory, perhaps.

Zain watched her eyes glaze as she stared, unfocused, into the distance. He was ready to catch the bottle when it slipped from her fingers.

The cynic in him wanted to believe her vulnerability was feigned as she blinked up at him like a baby owl, but he knew it wasn't.

'An imagination can be a curse.' His terse delivery hid the reluctant sympathy he felt.

Abby nodded and looked away, patting the damp spot where water had spilled, soaking a patch of her top before pooling in her cleavage. The action drew Zain's gaze and kick-started his own distracting imagination.

A curse, maybe. Painful, definitely.

He breathed his way through a bolt of mind-numbing molten lust—not so easy when in his head his hands were weighing those tight, high breasts and he was bending his head to taste the berry sweetness of the nipples.

'Your bite is infected...'

CHAPTER FOUR

SHE GLANCED AT his face, wondering what she had said to make him sound annoyed...or *more* annoyed.

'You should get it checked out when you get back to civilisation. You need a course of antibiotics asap.' He rose smoothly from his crouched position and stood over her, holding out a hand.

Abby took it. Standing beside him, she was again very conscious of his physical presence. She was used to looking down on men, or at least to looking most in the eye, and not so long ago had gone through life hunching her shoulders, embarrassed by her height and envying petite women.

'How long will it take to get back?' she asked, rubbing her hand against her thigh. The weird tingling impression remained.

'Half an hour or so, now that he's rested,' Zain estimated. The stallion, as though sensing he was the subject of conversation, wandered over and nudged his master's arm, demanding attention.

So, back to normal life... She frowned, wondering why she didn't feel happier at the prospect. I'm lucky, she reminded herself; her life was something that many would have aspired to and it had fallen into her lap.

More importantly, it was a means to an end, a way to give her grandparents back the life that had been stolen from them.

'Were you serious about…? Are we really…married?'

She had hoped he'd laugh, because it was infinitely preferable to be mocked than married to a total stranger.

'Don't worry, I'll sort it out.'

The acknowledgement that there was something to *sort out* tightened the tension curling in the pit of her stomach. 'So, what, you just wave your magic wand and snap your fingers? Or do you have your own legal team on standby?'

'I'll sort it,' he repeated calmly.

She couldn't hide her scepticism but clung to the hope it would turn out there was nothing to *sort*. 'I assume I should report what's happened to someone.' The thought of explaining to a foreign and not necessarily sympathetic police force what had happened was pretty daunting.

'I'll drop you off at the British Embassy. They'll sort things out for you.'

'Thank you.' She extended a hand to shake his then was struck by the sheer ludicrousness of the formality and leaned in, the leaning coinciding with the exact moment the restless horse chose to butt her bottom quite firmly with his nose, literally pushing her into his master.

Zain's arms opened to stop her falling—strangely the sensation in her head was also exactly like falling as she looked up into his lean, darkly beautiful face. Safe in his embrace, she wriggled her elbows, trying to free herself from the emotions the feelings of his arms around her unleashed. Her arms were squashed between their bodies but the urgency faded as her eyes drifted across the marvellous angles and planes of his face.

'I...' Her voice faded away as she felt a hard shudder run through his body and excitement sparked, kicking up the volume of her heartbeat. She could hear common sense issuing an irritating prissy whisper at the back of her mind and ignored it. Life was short—a fact that had been driven home today—and if you didn't take a chance, what was the point?

She couldn't take her eyes off the nerve she could see beating through the stubble on his lean cheek.

She expelled her breath on a long, gusty sigh. 'I really...'

Zain swallowed; in his head his fingernails were hanging on to the last shreds of his vanishing self-control. He felt like a man walking a tightrope—he wanted to grab on to all that lovely softness and not let go. Her cushiony lips looked so soft and inviting...would they taste as good as they looked?

She slid her hands up from between their bodies, her fingertips shaking as she touched his face, her expression rapt as she trailed them down his stubble-dusted cheeks.

Every cell in his body froze. Digging into reserves of control he didn't know he possessed, he took hold of her wrists and leaned back.

Zain had never had anything but contempt for men who took advantage of women. The boss who misused a position of power, the guy in the bar who honed in on the woman who couldn't walk straight, the best 'friend' who moved in to offer comfort after a tough divorce. They were *weak* men who took advantage, men like his brother, who would and had shown contempt for anything resembling scruples.

The idea of being the man his brother was filled Zain with utter blood-chilling horror.

But God, he was tempted.

'Abby.'

'I really want to say thank you.' She raised herself on tiptoe and closed her eyes, tilting her face up to his in silent invitation.

His head lowered and for a split second their glances connected and the deep, desperate need he felt was reflected in the drowning green of her eyes. Abby gave a tiny sigh as his mouth covered hers and his eyes squeezed closed as he surrendered himself totally to the sensation of the slow, sensuous brush of her lips.

This was insanity but it was a beautiful insanity. It made no sense but it didn't matter…it was not about logic, just need. A need she had never felt before, a need a million miles from the feelings Gregory's awkward kisses had summoned.

The sound of the groan that vibrated in his powerful chest escalated the dizzying excitement swirling through her veins. And when he dragged her in tight, sealing their bodies together and flaunting the hardness of his erection against her belly, Abby felt a primitive thrill sweep through her as she kissed him back.

And then, as quickly as it had begun, it was over. He had physically picked her up and set her a few feet away from him.

She blinked like someone coming up for air and then

the realisation hit home and a moment later scalding humiliation.

'Sorry.'

What for? she thought. *Not fancying me?*

'I know it's not me…it's you.' Papering over her humiliation with pride, she lifted her chin. At least now she had that ability to take control of an awkward situation, unlike in her teens, when her much-anticipated date with one of the cool boys was revealed as a joke… *Like kissing a wet fish!* he'd told his friends at school. 'I never thought otherwise,' she lied.

'You need medical attention, not—'

'A roll in the hay…' she inserted, having learnt from bitter experience that it was always better to mock yourself before your detractors got the chance. 'You are *totally* right,' she agreed, thinking, The only medical attention I need involves a shrink's couch!

What the hell was she doing? She'd never acted like this in her life… The memory of his hands and mouth on her only moments ago made her want to hide from embarrassment, a feeling she remembered from her school days when she had been isolated, become a target for the cool girls and sniggered at by their boyfriends because she was too tall and thin and that swot who put her hand up in class. The situation had culminated in the fake date that had made her retreat even farther into her shell—at least she had got incredible grades.

It was hard to find an equivalent bright side to this situation.

'I'm ready when you are…oh, and I hope you're keeping a tab of how much I owe you for your time and…' She stopped, biting down on her inside lips as her eyes fell from his—what was the going rate for saving someone's life?

Zain shrugged off the insult. If he'd taken offence it would have been easier but his understanding expression made her feel even more of a total idiot!

'How about we call it…?' An expression she couldn't put a name to flickered across his face before he produced one of his inimical shrugs. 'Let's just call it good timing.'

He could call it anything he liked. She still didn't have a clue what he really meant.

'Fine.'

It was hard to project 'distant and aloof' when you were sitting in front of someone on a horse going very fast, so Abby was deeply relieved when the walled city with its iconic towers and minarets came into view.

It was bizarre but after everything that had happened to her it was the humiliation of throwing herself at him like some sort of sex-starved groupie that was eating away at her.

She was mad at herself, mad for setting herself up for the knock-back and for caring about it, and mad at him. Especially mad at him!

It wasn't until the first security checkpoint, some way outside the city limits, came into view that it occurred to her that they might have some difficulty re-entering the city.

Getting out had been complicated enough and then they had had a stack of stamped and signed documents. Now she didn't even have her passport and the man with her looked exactly the sort of dangerous character that would ring alarm bells.

Maybe he was thinking the same because he brought

the horse to a halt before they reached the actual check-point, dismounting and telling her to do the same.

She ignored the hand he extended and, though her solo dismount almost ended in disaster, she hadn't accepted his help, which at that moment was all that mattered, a childish display of defiance but the only defence she had against her humiliation.

'Have you got the right permits? Shall I talk to them?'

'Stay here.'

It wasn't clear if he was talking to her or the horse but he didn't look back, so presumably it never crossed his mind that either of them would disobey his command.

She watched as he walked straight up to the men in uniform and hoped he wasn't going to take the same high-handed attitude with them.

The conversation only lasted a few minutes and the guards' guns had stayed across their shoulders. That had to be a good sign, didn't it?

Her anxiety climbed as the minutes ticked by. Were they grilling him? When he turned and began to walk back towards her she felt a wave of relief that vanished when one of the guards followed him, jogging to catch up with the tall, dominant figure. A telltale flame of desire that Abby wanted badly to deny ignited low down in her belly as she watched him.

It took for ever for them to reach her and the expression on his arrestingly beautiful face gave her no clues as to how the discussion had gone, but no one was waving any guns, which was a step in the right direction.

The guard tipped his head to Abby and said something that didn't sound aggressive—in fact it sounded almost deferential.

'He said he is sorry about your experiences and hopes that it has not given you a bad impression of our country.'

Abby smiled and nodded at the man. 'Did he really say that?'

'Word for word,' Zain responded but the look in his eyes suggested he had missed a few things out in his translation.

'So, what happens now?'

As if in response to her question a jeep drove towards them stopping only a few feet away. A driver wearing a military uniform got out and walked towards them and for a split second she thought his extended hand held a weapon or at least a set of handcuffs, but then she saw that the metal the sun had glinted off was a bunch of keys attached to a key ring.

Zain held out his hand for the keys, delivered some sort of instructions to the driver and then sent him on his way.

Abby hadn't understood a word of the one-sided conversation and felt her confusion grow as she watched the man lead the stallion away.

'You can't let them take your horse,' she protested.

'I thought you did not like horses.'

'That's not the point—you can't trade an animal for a...a...'

'The horse doesn't have air-conditioning. Relax, I am joking.'

'Joking?'

'I have not exchanged my horse.' His lips twitched at some sort of inside joke she wasn't privy to. 'They are merely going to look after him for me.'

'And let you use this in the meantime?' She continued to regard him with extreme scepticism. 'Did you bribe them or something?' she called out as he got into the driving seat.

Zain leant out of the window. 'I simply explained the situation. Now get in.'

Abby did so, not that she was in any way convinced by his story. She knew she was missing something, but what? He started the engine almost before she had closed the door.

'You're not telling me everything. Have you got connections or something?'

'I have an honest face and they have my horse as hostage. It was a simple negotiation.'

It sounded plausible but the conviction she was missing something persisted.

Clearly he knew the city well, as he drove quickly and efficiently, diverting on numerous occasions down side streets when they encountered traffic jams or when some of the parties that still seemed to be going on had blocked entire roads.

The party atmosphere seemed to have infected the policemen on duty as well because they were waved through the numerous security checkpoints without being stopped once. It couldn't have gone smoother if they'd been part of the wedding party.

'This is it.'

He pulled the jeep up outside a building with wrought-iron railings, the only thing differentiating it from the other buildings lining both sides of the affluent-looking but narrow street the small, discreet sign above the door.

She turned in her seat. 'I don't know your name, and you've… People say the words "you've saved my life" all the time.' She done it herself when someone handed her a coffee she needed particularly badly. 'But you *really* have. You're a genuine hero.' For the first time, she saw him look acutely uncomfortable. 'And just when I thought you didn't have a weak spot,' she murmured, half to herself.

'Right place, right time…that's all.'

She shook her head and reached for the door handle, inadvertently knocking her injured arm. She clenched her teeth as fighting the pain was a lot easier than fighting the throb of awareness she felt every time she looked at this man. It was so strange because she didn't normally react this way to men—she never had, certainly not with Gregory, whose appeal had been the fact he seemed safe…turned out, of course, he was anything but!

Zain was opening the passenger door before she had even registered he was getting out. While Abby nursed her throbbing arm against her chest he took her other and helped her out. 'Be careful and get that arm checked out straight away.'

'I will,' she promised, looking at him and feeling the traitorous trickle of heat between her legs. Why did she react to him this way, a way she had never reacted to a man before? 'It's actually feeling better, I think.'

She thought about shaking his hand but remembered how that had turned out the last time and thought better of it, instead tipping her head solemnly in thanks.

He nodded, turned and strode back to the car. She had the craziest impulse to run after him before he vanished from her life, but common sense prevailed before she had made a fool of herself for a second time—he never had been part of her life so there was no reason to change that now.

Abby walked to the embassy door, glad he couldn't see the tears that filled her eyes, unaware that someone else could.

In the basement of the British Embassy a man sitting beside several monitors turned and called out to his colleague, who was dozing in a chair.

'Call Mr Jones; I think he'll want to see this.' He scrolled the image back several frames and froze the streamed recording, zooming in on the face of the man that many privately called the man who should be the next sheikh.

Pity Zain Al Seif was only second in line.

CHAPTER FIVE

Ten months later

EVEN IN AN area where conspicuous wealth and status symbols were the norm, the low-slung silver designer car sitting glinting in the afternoon attracted attention and covetous stares, but not as much attention or as many stares as the man who walked along the tree-lined boulevard towards it. Even had he been dressed in charity-shop rejects, the man would have stopped traffic. He had an almost tangible aura, authority mingled with masculinity in its most raw form.

Zain was oblivious to the swivelled heads and raised designer shades as his attention was focused not on the car, but on its owner.

He was a few feet away when the crowd of giggling young women that had surrounded the man when he got out of his car parted to reveal someone he didn't immediately recognise.

When recognition did strike, his eyes widened behind the darkened lenses of his shades and he made a rapid mental calculation. In the—what?—six weeks since he'd last seen his brother, Khalid, whose dissipated lifestyle, lack of self-control and love of excess had made him pile on the pounds and look older than his thirty-two years, had lost a good twenty pounds.

Perhaps it was the speed of the dramatic weight loss that was responsible for the drawn look on his brother's face, and Zain's jaw tightened as Khalid curved his hand around the bottom of one of the giggling women. The waistline might have improved but clearly his brother's morals had not, as, for better or most probably for worse, his brother was married.

So are you. Zain's lips twisted into an ironic half-smile as he recognised the element of hypocrisy in his disapproval—or, at least, it would have been hypocrisy had his marriage existed anywhere but on a piece of paper signed under a desert sky.

There was an added irony to the situation in that he was the one brother who hadn't actually cheated.

Of course, his fidelity was of the purely accidental variety and nothing to do with respecting his marriage vows or the lingering memory of the redhead he had married—that would have been insane. Instead his celibacy had been the consequence of a non-stop work schedule so intense that he hadn't yet got around to doing something about the marriage certificate still sitting in his safe.

He had considered the simpler option of burning the offending sheet of paper but after a period of reflection he had opted to retain the document rather than destroy it. Less 'doing the right thing' and more the conviction that history was littered with men brought down not by the mistakes they made but the denial of their mistakes—the cover-ups and the lies that turned a minor blip into an earthquake of scandal.

Zain had never doubted there *would* be a scandal.

The only question was the degree of damage caused by a story, so in the interests of damage limitation it had made sense to find out as much as he could about Miss Abigail Foster.

But so far there had been no approach from her agents, no tabloid headlines, no talk of book deals, no rumours circulating at all that he had been made aware of. The only reference to a rescue had been at a British Embassy dinner by one of the anonymous suits, who, letting him know *he* knew, had assured Zain of his *complete discretion.*

The man had also made a suggestion that might explain why there had been no attempt to cash in on the story.

'I'm not sure that Miss Foster, a rather naïve young lady, I think, actually knew who you were.'

The image that floated into his head slowed his stride as he recalled the details of that perfect oval face, which was dominated by extraordinary eyes framed by dark lashes the same sooty black as the sweeping brows.

'Zain, glad you could make it.' Pushing away the distracting image, but not before his body had hardened in reaction, Zain held his brother's eyes as Khalid slid an arm around the waist of the nearest blonde and, leaning in close, said something that made her giggle.

It took effort but Zain didn't deliver the reaction the provocative action had been designed to shake loose and his facial expression stayed locked in neutral, the contempt in his eyes concealed by the mirrored lenses of his designer shades.

After a moment, Khalid let the girl go, his expression petulant as he nodded to one of the minders standing a few feet away, the man quickly reacting and ushering the fawning crowd away.

Khalid did not speak until the sound of their high heels had vanished.

He stood to one side and pulled open one of the doors, inviting his brother with a nod to look inside the interior of the expensive plaything. 'So, what do you think? They have only made five of these beauties...'

'I think that the people affected by the cuts to the health budget might question your priorities.'

Khalid's laughter was not a pleasant sound and neither was the hacking cough that followed it.

As the paroxysm of coughs continued Zain's brow creased in a frown of reluctant concern, though his eyes remained wary as he framed his brusque question. 'Are you all right?'

A white linen handkerchief pressed to his mouth, Khalid straightened up, his eyes above the white filled with glittering black enmity that was in stark contrast to his words as he took away the handkerchief and made his response without answering his brother's question. 'So, you think the health cuts are a bad idea?'

Zain lifted one darkly defined brow. 'And I'm meant to believe that you are actually interested in what I think?'

The handkerchief spoilt the line of his tailored trousers as Khalid shoved it back into his pocket and pulled the passenger door wide. 'We don't have to be enemies, do we?' His sigh was deep and his tone wistful.

An olive-branch moment. Logic and experience should have made Zain walk away, but he didn't. Instead he called himself a fool and stood there thinking optimistically that maybe it was true what they said about blood being thicker than water. Either that or he was certifiable.

Zain dragged a hand across his dark hair, the action weary. 'I'm not your enemy, Khalid.' Something flashed in his brother's eyes but it vanished too quickly for Zain to tell if it was anything more than a trick of the light.

'I've always been jealous of you, you know. Your friends, your—'

'You have friends.'

Khalid gave a hard laugh. 'I buy people...that doesn't make them my friends.'

Zain had never imagined his brother capable of such insight, let alone the courage to admit it aloud.

'Come, let's not argue. Take a drive with me.' Khalid pulled the door wider. 'I haven't put her through her paces yet.'

After a pause, Zain got in.

'All buckled up?' Khalid asked, glancing at his brother. 'You can't be too careful. I thought we'd take the scenic route.'

Zain glanced at the speedometer as they hit the first bend. His brows lifted at the number on the dial, but he didn't feel nervous—his half-brother was bad at many things but driving wasn't one of them.

By the time they hit the third bend on a road famous for its hairpin turns and the crashes they had caused, a layer of tension had descended onto his shoulders.

'Do you want me to slow down, little brother?' Khalid mocked as he overtook a lorry on a bend, pulling in just in time to avoid a car coming in the opposite direction.

'Are you high?' Zain asked.

'High on life...high on...actually I probably am,

though the drugs don't really work the same now. You see, little brother, I'm dying. I have lung cancer and it's already spread. I'm terminal.'

'Medical—'

'Advances are made every day. I know. But I also know they won't work for me.' The low purr of the car became a growl as he floored it once more around the next bend.

'It's not too late for us to—'

'Bury the hatchet? How heroically noble and so very *Zain*…' he spat. 'But it's too late for that. Don't look sad, brother, we all die. But knowing the when and the how…that changes things, gives you back the power. Yes,' he said, watching with a smile as Zain's hand moved to the door handle. 'It's locked, but going at this speed you'd die even if you could open it.

'You know, the worst thing about learning I was going to die was knowing that *you'd* be there after me, taking my place on the throne…in my wife's bed…but now it's fine because I've realised that death is actually a gift. Because I can take you with me.'

Zain lunged to take the wheel but his brother kept the car on its trajectory, a trajectory that would send it sailing off the cliff and into space. Zain transferred his attentions to the door, slamming and kicking to gain his freedom.

'Relax and enjoy it, little brother. I intend to.' Khalid's laugh turned into a cry of rage as the door finally gave and Zain threw himself through it.

Wide, cool corridors radiated out from the octagonal central atrium, where light from the glass dome sparked rainbow reflections off the water cascading from the fountain into a mosaic-lined pool.

It felt more like a five-star hotel than any hospital Abby had ever experienced, certainly nothing like the ones she remembered from her childhood. She'd been six when she had first arrived at one in the back of an ambulance. She remembered the rush of cold December air that brushed over her before the trolley she had lain on was pushed through a wide set of double doors and whisked along what had seemed a never-ending corridor. The lights shining down from the ceiling had made her head ache.

There was a gap in her recollections between that point and later when she'd found herself sitting in a hard-backed chair, her feet not touching the floor as she swung them. She had been counting in her head the trail of bright red splodges on the tiled floor that stopped at the curtain that hid from view the people who were making the loud noises, the people who were trying to save her parents.

They'd tried for a long time. Abby had climbed out of the chair and wandered off long before they'd admitted defeat. Her gran told the story of how she'd been found later, thumb in mouth, asleep on the floor of a sluice room.

'Sorry to keep you waiting.'

Abby dropped the hand she'd raised to shade her eyes from the rainbow colours dancing on the water and turned, the motion displacing the silk scarf that her British escort had handed her before they stepped out of the car... *Not essential but a nice gesture,* he'd said.

She knew the green filaments in the scarf emphasised the deep emerald of her eyes and she adjusted it again over the burnished waves of her hair, which seemed determined not to be covered.

'Will we be able to fly back tonight, Mr Jones?

'We all want this situation to be resolved as swiftly as possible,' came the frustratingly vague response.

His voice, like everything else about the man, was nondescript and unmemorable. Abby had only encountered him once before and if it had not been for the extraordinary circumstances under which they'd met, she doubted she ever would have remembered him. And circumstances didn't get much more extraordinary than the ones that had preceded her arrival at the British Embassy in the Aarifan capital city ten months ago.

She'd told her story to at least half a dozen people before Mr Jones appeared, and over another cup of tea she had related her tale yet again. He had listened, then pressed her on a few specific points. Had she actually read the document she'd signed? Had the man who'd come to her rescue given his name?

His gentle persistence had sent alarm bells ringing in her head.

'I'm not actually married though, right? It wasn't real…?'

He'd been very soothing on that point and told her *absolutely not*. He'd then advised her to forget what had happened and to go home and get on with her life.

So Abby had. Well, she had got on with her life. Forgetting was another thing. Her memories had taken on a surreal dream-like quality, the man who rescued her the stuff fantasies were made of.

Fantasies had no place in Abby's life though; she was too busy for that nonsense. Though the tall fantasy figure did insert himself into her dreams, and even then she frequently didn't recall the details of the dreams he'd invaded but she'd know he'd been there by the heavy, nameless ache in the pit of her stomach that lingered when she awoke...*too soon*, it always felt.

Mr Jones had been the last person she had expected to see waiting outside her flat door when she arrived home yesterday afternoon after a particularly depressing appointment with the agents selling her grandparents' old home.

The timing couldn't have been worse. She had just about put together enough money for the deposit and she had a mortgage in place... She'd assumed all she'd have to do was sign on the dotted line. The man had not laughed outright in her face, but he had come close.

'I'm afraid, Miss Foster, that the housing market has been buoyant since your grandparents sold. The present vendors are asking—' He scrolled down the page on his tablet and read out a number so crazy that initially Abby thought he was joking. Sadly, he wasn't.

Mr Jones also hadn't been joking when, flanked by two men in Arab robes, he explained that it turned out she *was* married after all and her 'husband' was the younger son of the Sheikh Aban Al Seif, the ruler of Aarifa.

And all before she'd even got through the door!

Abby was still assimilating this news when, seated on her sofa that was badly in need of reupholstering, Mr Jones worked his way up to his next big reveal, fortifying himself first with a Rich Tea biscuit.

'There is no need to be upset, Miss Foster; the mistake was little more than an unfortunate clerical error.'

'So, can I sign something?' she asked.

'Ah, well, there is the rub. Normally I would be able to say yes but, well, the accident means that the doctors are unlikely to agree to Zain Al Seif travelling for some weeks, and the legal process means that your signatures both need to be witnessed by...'

One word in the bland, meandering explanation had leapt out at Abby as an image flashed into her head so real that, for a moment, Zain seemed to be standing there, physically imposing, the same way he'd looked when she had first seen him striding into the encampment—a beautiful man exuding an arrogance and command that was mesmerising. 'What do you mean, "accident"?'

'Yes, both Zain and his elder brother, Khalid, were involved in a crash in... I believe they call it a *super car.*'

The buzz in Abby's head had got louder as the blood drained from her face...not just her face—even her oxygen-deprived fingertips tingled.

'I do not know the extent of the younger Prince's injuries but sadly his brother died, which means that the man you...*married*,' he gave a light laugh, 'is now the heir.'

'So how is...?' she'd paused, unable to reconcile the idea that her rescuer was also a royal prince, let alone put a name to the man who for so long had been anonymous '...he?' she'd finished weakly.

'The hospital is unwilling to reveal details to anyone but relatives.'

'Miss Foster?'

Abby started, her skittering glance moving from the Englishman to the two daunting figures in flowing Arab dress pretty much identical to those worn by the four who had shadowed her ever since she'd left her London apartment yesterday.

'I just want to confirm…you told no one, no one at all, about the…marriage document?'

'No one.' There had obviously been a lot of interest when she had had to recount the story but she'd played the kidnap down, preferring to turn the incident into a joke gone wrong rather than admit to the visceral, gut-churning nightmare it had been.

Her lashes flickered downwards as she ran her tongue across her lips to moisten them. She purposely kept her expression impassive even though inside her heart was thudding, the memory of visceral fear metallic on her tongue.

She pushed hard at the memory as she exerted control just as she'd practised. The memory belonged in another world a million miles from her own, where a disaster was a facial blemish—imagined or otherwise—that would spoil a fashion shoot.

'Excellent.' He turned his head as another robed figure approached. 'Will you excuse me?'

Abby watched as the men spoke for a few moments before Mr Jones returned. She had the immediate sense that under the emollient smile he was not happy.

'It seems that you may go in.' He gestured to the new arrival, who tipped his head in Abby's direction. 'Abdul will show you the way.'

'Aren't you coming in with me?' Abby asked, struggling to conceal her panic at the prospect of facing her 'husband' alone.

Beneath the little moustache the man affected, his lips thinned. 'It seems not.'

CHAPTER SIX

ABBY TOOK A deep breath, lifted her chin and walked through the door held by someone who looked more Security than medical, and who bowed low as she passed.

The soft, respectful murmur as she walked down the hallway seemed to be addressed to her. It would have been disconcerting had she had any thoughts to spare for anything but the question of what waited for her inside the room she was about to enter.

She slipped inside and as she closed the door behind her she hitched in a deep breath, straightened her shoulders and turned, wishing in that moment that she had asked more about Zain's condition. She had no idea what she was about to be confronted with—tubes, machines…was he even conscious?

Her sense of disorientation deepened as she found herself looking at what appeared to be an office, an office where a meeting seemed to be in progress at a long, rectangular table between several men wearing traditional Arab dress, and several more wearing business suits.

One of the men stood in front of what appeared to be a PowerPoint presentation, but moved towards Abby, who was already backing away mumbling apologies when he noticed her.

'Sorry. I think must be in the wrong...'

The man bowed and, after a momentary pause, the other men seated around the table got to their feet and followed his example.

This situation was just getting weirder, she thought, fighting the urge to curtsey or something.

'Not at all. This way, Amira...please...' His attitude deferential, he gestured for her to precede him towards a half-open door.

After a pause, she responded to the softly spoken invitation, even though as she approached the door the conviction that this was a case of mistaken identity grew stronger.

Then say something, idiot!

She half turned, ready to explain that this was a mistake, but her guide was backing out of the room with his head bent in a bow and it was hard to explain anything to someone you couldn't make eye contact with.

Her nerves were so stretched by this point that the soft sound of the door closing with a definitive click was enough to make her jump. Ignoring the chill of trepidation skittering down her spine, she turned.

This second room was not as large as the one she had entered, but still, was not small. It had the look of an upmarket hotel bedroom complete with a TV covering half of one wall and leather sofas around a glass coffee table covered with artistically stacked books.

The only thing that suggested she should not ring for Room Service was the hospital bed. It was empty, though the rumpled condition of the sheets and the drops of blood standing out against the white linen suggested it had been recently occupied by someone who had been attached to the bag of fluid that hung empty on a stand beside it.

She released a sigh, tried not to look at the blood and walked warily across the room towards the bed. Without thinking she put her hand on the sheets…they still retained the body heat of their recent occupant.

Abby clutched her head—all she wanted to do was get this over with and go home and she couldn't even find the man! 'Where the hell is he?' she murmured to herself.

'Behind you.'

At the sound of the soft, deep voice Abby jumped a foot off the floor as if a starting pistol had been unexpectedly fired in the room. She spun around, the action causing the silk veil on her head to slide off the slippery satin of her fiery curls.

She blinked and fought against the urge to retreat as the owner of the voice took a single step through a doorway that was half-concealed behind a screen and, without taking his eyes from her face, casually captured the fluttering fabric in his hand.

While his reflexes were clearly in excellent shape, Zain's bruised and battered body was not. Though he clenched his teeth against the pain zigzagging through his body as he straightened up, a muffled groan escaped his compressed lips.

The shock that had frozen her to the spot disappeared and was instantly replaced by concern. Abby laid a hand on his arm, her eyes widening as she registered the tense, rock-hard muscle through the fine fabric of his white shirt—more blood was spattered down one arm. Her stomach tightened before she looked away.

'Are you all right?'

Ah, well, someone always had to ask the stupid question. Might as well be her.

One hand pressed to his ribs, Zain lifted his eyelids and produced a look that managed to be both ironic and lazy through eyes that were every bit as blue as she remembered. They were shaded by lashes which looked almost ridiculously long and dark against the pallor that had robbed his vibrant, toned skin of its usual golden colour.

The memory of the first time she'd seen him floated into her head and, for a moment, the antiseptic room vanished and Abby was back in the desert encampment, the scent of woodsmoke and sour sweat almost as strong as the metallic taste of fear in her mouth.

At first she hadn't understood why the raucous cries and yells had faded, but then she'd seen the magnificence of the figure who rode into their midst, entirely ignoring the hostile stares and rifles aimed at him.

'Do I *look* all right?'

He looked incredible!

In that first startled moment when she had turned all she'd got was a blurred impression of the man she remembered—perfect face, perfect body and an aura of high-voltage *maleness* that had delivered a gut-punch blow to her unprepared nervous system.

'Should you be—?'

Standing there looking gorgeous?

Rising above the unhelpful prompting of her subconscious, she took a breath and tried again, focusing on the fact that, though her first impression was correct—he *was* still off-the-scale gorgeous—he also looked as though sheer willpower was the only thing keeping him on his feet.

'I decided that it might be hard to garner respect when any false move is likely to reveal my rear; however, getting dressed was not quite as simple as I thought.'

It was not his growled admission that brought a rush of colour to her cheeks but the mental image that flashed into her head. She was not in the habit of imagining men's bottoms...

'You could have asked someone for help...' Abby imagined that his position of power would make it likely that the staff would knock the door down to offer him assistance. 'Shall I...?' She paused and felt a flush bloom on her cheeks as she struggled to banish the half-formed image in her head of herself performing the required assistance...only in her mind she was taking the clothes off rather than helping him put them on.

'Shall I get someone to help you?'

'Someone who is not you?'

Her alarmed eyes flew to his face... *Relax, Abby; he can't read your mind.* 'One of those men in the—'

'No!' He barked out the injunction and then paused and took a deep, obviously painful breath before continuing in a more moderate tone. 'They are not nurses.'

'Who are they...? Sorry, I didn't mean to be nosy—'

'They are the men who run Aarifa.'

The comment shocked her into an uncensored response. 'Isn't that your father?'

'My father lost interest in the job a long time ago.'

Her curiosity was interlaced with empathy as an image of a frail and elderly ruler flashed into her head. 'So he relied heavily on your brother.'

The suggestion drew an odd laugh that terminated in another wince.

'I think I should call a nurse or—' Her concern morphed into something far less elevated when he lifted a hand, causing his unbuttoned shirt to gape open a few extra inches, revealing a hard, taut, muscle-ridged torso. The tendrils of shameful heat unfurling in the pit of her belly cooled into empathy as he winced and she realised his injuries were not restricted to his face.

Abby dragged her eyes upwards towards his face. Under the long-sleeved ankle-length silk dress she wore her heart continued to thud hard as she tilted her head back to meet his heavily lidded eyes. That in itself was a novelty—her own height meant it was rare that she ever had to look up at anyone.

'I think this is a mistake...' She stopped and shook her head. 'No, it *is* a mistake; I really don't know why I'm here...we could do this by email when you're feeling better, or...'

He placed a hand on the side of her cheek. The touch of his long fingers was light but the electrical tingle it sent through her nervous system was anything but.

'I prefer the personal touch.'

Abby fought the hypnotic tug of his electric-blue eyes and focused on the damage to his face, the bruising along the crest of one razor-sharp cheekbone that extended over the chiselled planes of his dramatically handsome face. Bruising that the dark shadow of stubble dusting his lean cheeks and angular jaw could not disguise.

'I don't.' She got nowhere near the level of cool she was aiming for but to her relief his hand fell away, though that may have been simply because he looked as though he needed all of his control just to stay standing up.

'Even if you manage to get dressed, you'll probably pass out…is that really worth it?'

An expression of hauteur spread across his lean features as he responded with chilly dismissal. 'I'm fine.'

'Well, you can be snooty if you like but I was only trying to help.'

The hauteur faded from his face, to be replaced by a smile that she found much more disturbing. 'As forthright as ever… I had forgotten.' His eyes slid from her face down her body, his gaze possessing a caressing quality that made her stomach muscles quiver. 'You scrub up rather well…'

She looked quickly away from the heat in his eyes, but not soon enough to stop the lick of flame that slid through her body.

'And it is very hard to tell that your feet are mismatched.'

Her wide eyes flew back to his face. 'You remember that?'

Something moved at the backs of his eyes. 'I remember everything.'

'You have a photographic memory?' she said, searching her own memory for any incriminating things she might have said.

He gave a low chuckle then stopped, lifting a supportive hand to his ribs. 'You take things very literally. I just meant that you are memorable.'

She lifted her chin. 'I'm assuming that's not a compliment.'

'It is a statement of fact. For a beautiful woman,' he observed, 'you seem to find taking a compliment graciously a struggle.'

The heat in his eyes was hard to escape, but then

escaping when you didn't really want to was never going to be simple. It took her to the count of ten to regain control of her chaotic, jagged respirations. This was far too close and personal for her taste...injured or not, this man had a raw sexual aura that she found massively disturbing, but she had fought the hypnotic tug of his eyes before so she knew it was achievable if she tried.

Her confidence wilted when she lifted her eyes and found his gaze now trained on her mouth. While the heat low down continued to unfurl its very disturbing tendrils she fought to maintain a passive expression... or, at least, a *relatively* passive expression.

Zain quite literally couldn't stop staring at her mouth. He put down his lack of self-control to his weakened condition but in his head he saw that lush pinkness parting under the pressure he applied before he sank into...

The sabre-sharp stab of pain helped him distance himself from the sexual fantasies swirling in his head. Having her here was not about indulging his fantasies—it was far more prosaic.

His views on marriage had not changed but his position had. He was no longer the spare, he was the heir, and the forced desert marriage to this enticing redhead was all that stood between him and Kayla, who was waiting in the wings like a praying mantis in Prada.

He understood that continuity and the smooth transition of power was important, and he was fully prepared to accept the burden of duty that came with the role that he had been thrust into, a position the several people who he had awoken from the crash to find standing around his hospital bed had been eager to inform him of.

But, they added when several of the machines he was attached to had begun to beep loudly, he was not to concern himself with securing a bride. A wedding to his late brother's widow, a union that would ensure stability and the line of succession, could be performed as soon as he could leave his hospital bed.

He had felt the darkness coming to claim him and there had been no time for subtlety as he'd croaked out, 'I'm already married, Jones at the British Embassy will confirm.'

He had slept through the subsequent diplomatic storm his revelation had created, and by the time he'd been conscious again the marriage had been confirmed as genuine.

Abby had adopted a businesslike expression, though it was clear maintaining it was becoming difficult. 'So, is there something you want me to sign?'

'You're in a hurry.'

'The thing is, I think I'd prefer to get out of here before you kill yourself with all this unnecessary effort,' she husked out as her glance moved from his blood-stained shirt sleeve to the beads of moisture he could feel along his upper lip…and the deep lines of strain he knew were bracketing his mouth.

Her concern spilled over into exasperation. 'For heaven's sake, I know you're big and tough, but you're in pain. It doesn't make you a lesser man to admit it!' She rolled her eyes.

Her outburst startled him into silence but that quickly gave way to a low, throaty laugh. 'Fine, I'm not too proud to ask for help.' He nodded towards the bed. 'Will you lend me a shoulder?'

Abby's eyes were wide as she moved seamlessly from lofty female superiority to something approaching panic.

He lifted an arm. 'I'm swallowing my pride, and asking for your help.'

CHAPTER SEVEN

ABBY FOUND HERSELF staring at his abs, the muscles perfect enough to make her stomach flutter helplessly in reaction. She caught her lower lip between her teeth, disturbed more than slightly by her body's helpless reaction to his physicality.

It was mystifying and definitely bad timing! Lord, what was it about this man that made him the one member of the opposite sex capable of awakening her dormant sex drive? Recognising this was a question for later when she was safely back home and far away from temptation, so she huffed out a resigned but determined sigh and lifted her chin, responding to the internal challenge of not acting like a sex addict with as much dignity as she could manage.

'Fine. So what do you want me to do?'

He *almost* looked as if he was going to tell her something very different, but at the last second he seemed to regain some control and dragged his eyes off her mouth. 'I just need to sit down for a minute.'

'All right, lean on me,' she said, trying to sound brisk and not breathless at the thought of contact with his hard, lean maleness.

'No, it's fine.'

She shot him a glance from under the sweep of her thick, straight lashes, discovering as she did that he was looking tense. 'You really don't have the hang of this accepting help thing, do you?' she sighed out. 'It was *your* idea,' she reminded him. 'And don't worry, I'm stronger than I look.'

An image of her landing a right hook on her captor's jaw flashed into her mind.

'I remember, *cara*,' he said, the look he gave her hinting that he was seeing the same replay in his own head.

The unexpected approving warmth in his voice brought a flush to her cheeks. 'I don't normally need rescuing,' she husked out, not sure why it felt important to establish this upfront, but it did.

The tentative half-smile that had begun to twitch the corners of her mouth upwards wilted then vanished completely as their glances connected. Abby had the weirdest sensation of time slowing as the air seemed to buzz with an invisible static. She had no idea how long the moment lasted, but when she did manage to wrench free she took refuge in resentment.

'Why didn't you tell me who you were?' Had it been some sort of joke to him? she wondered, remembering their smooth negotiation of the security checkpoints, which of course made perfect sense now.

'I was trying hard to forget myself.'

Abby had not begun to decipher this cryptic response when he moved in closer and laid a hand across her shoulders. She fought against the impulse to tense, the effort making her body quiver as she struggled to focus on the mundane, the ordinary, the smell of antiseptic to distract herself from the massive hormone rush that sent wave after wave of heat through her body.

Whether he was injured or not, the animal magnetism that poured off him had a mind-blanking force.

Get a grip, Abby told herself sternly as she followed her own advice, literally, and slid her arm very carefully around his narrow waist, feeling ludicrously self-conscious.

'Is that ok?' she asked, tilting her chin up to look into his face. The veil of his lashes lifted and she was instantly skewered once more by the mesmeric tug of his electric-blue stare. When she managed, after a short delay, to react to his head jerk of acknowledgement, she was too flustered to notice that he looked as disconcerted as she felt.

She cleared her throat. 'Good, then lean on me and take your time…say when you need to stop.'

She hadn't wanted him to stop…

The memory surfaced and she felt a stab of shame. Oh, hell, now was *not* the time to relive a moment that was indelibly printed onto her mind for all the wrong reasons!

Her jaw quivered and her teeth clenched as she closed the door on the memory of the mortifying moment when she had come on to him with all the subtlety of a sledgehammer and then—as if that wasn't enough to make her cringe—been firmly rebuffed.

It was an embarrassing memory but that, she reminded herself, was all it was. It wasn't exactly rocket science—she'd been vulnerable and he hadn't taken advantage…humiliating at the time and, yes, she had hated him for it then, but now she was glad he'd been a gentleman.

Common sense told Abby that it had been the circumstances as much as the man that had fanned into life instincts she didn't even know she possessed. Chances were she might never experience a moment like that again. She didn't know whether to be relieved or depressed by the thought.

At several points during the transfer his breathing sounded laboured but they didn't stop, their progress slow but steady.

'Thanks. I'll be fine now.' Zain straightened up and took the last steps under his own steam, then lowering himself down onto the edge of the bed. 'It's easing.'

She tossed him a sceptical look but shrugged; clearly, showing weakness was not his thing, another reason on the list she'd compiled that he really wasn't her type. The macho stuff really tried her patience; she liked men who didn't mind showing their vulnerable side. There was just one vital ingredient missing, however. The thought of kissing them, let alone anything more intimate, left her feeling...well, nothing really.

The silence stretched until Abby decided that getting straight to the point was probably the best policy—she knew what she wanted to say, as she'd been rehearsing it on the journey here, not sure when she'd have the opportunity to deliver her speech and wanting to be ready when it came.

'I wasn't sure if you'd be well enough for me to—'

He spread his hands in a mock-submissive gesture. 'I'm weak but willing.'

She cursed the flush that she felt run up under her skin but tried not to react to it. Being flippant was probably his way of coping; the man had almost lost his life and had seen his brother die, so having a fake wife revealed was the least of his problems but one she had no doubt he could do without.

She took a deep breath and decided that even though he was injured there was no point skirting delicately around the elephant in the room, and she could at least reassure him on some points. 'I just want you to know that I've no intention of…there is *no* question of me making any claims, if we really *are* married.' She paused, shaking her head slowly in an attitude of disbelief—she still couldn't quite believe they actually were. 'I'm assuming that under the circumstances an annulment will be straightforward. I can see what you're thinking.'

Well, that, Zain thought, made one of them!

'But you don't need to worry, I'll fully co-operate. I'll sign whatever you need me to sign,' she added earnestly. 'Including a confidentiality clause.' She pressed a finger to the small furrow between her brows as if mentally ticking things off a list. 'I don't think I've missed anything out.'

'Is your lawyer here with you?' Her expression was confirmation that she wasn't here to negotiate. She didn't, incredibly, seem to be aware that she had the advantage; she wasn't thinking about what she could get…she just wanted out.

'Do I *need* a lawyer?'

Everyone has an angle.

Zain had probably learnt this fact of life before he had had the ability to communicate it and now he had met someone who, it seemed, hadn't.

'And what sort of settlement did you have in mind for delivering these guarantees?' As he appealed to her avarice part of him *wanted* to see her fail the test, and silence the soft whisper of his freshly awoken optimism,

but to his frustration Abigail Foster didn't even seem
to recognise his gentle prompt; instead she reacted as
though he'd just offered her an insult.

'Settlement...?' Her puzzled frown faded as the
angry heat climbed into her cheeks. '*Money*, you mean?
I don't want anything from you!'

'Because such things are above you? You expect me
to believe money means nothing to you?' he cut back.
Nobody was that wholesome and sweet.

Her chin lifted but she didn't react to his challenge.

'I admire your principles' he said, a scornful curl
turning his smile mocking. 'But are you really in the
enviable position to refuse money?'

'You make it sound as though everything...every-
one...is a commodity or has a price.'

'Oh, in my experience they do, *cara*, they do.'

'Then I pity you. I never want to be that cynical.'

'Don't get me wrong, I'm impressed, especially when
you consider that you are supporting your grandparents.'

She went rigid, her delicate jaw quivering as her suspicious gaze narrowed on his face. 'Who told you that?
What do you know about my grandparents?'

He produced an enigmatic smile that he saw made
her teeth clench and intensified the uneasy look on her
face.

'There should be no secrets between husband and
wife.'

'I don't have any secrets.'

'True,' he drawled. 'The stories of your love life are
pretty well-documented. And I'm assuming there has
to be a built-in life expectancy to your kind of work.'

She'd gone on the huffy offensive to the suggestion

she deserved to profit from the situation but the idea of losing her looks drew a laugh from her.

And he thought he knew women! This one seemed determined to challenge all his preconceptions.

'Before everything goes south, you mean,' she said cheerfully. 'Oh, I don't intend to stay in the job long enough for that to happen, just long enough to...' She broke off, giving a self-conscious shrug as her eyes slid from his. 'It's not my life's dream, I sort of fell into modelling. I was spotted at a shopping mall. I actually thought it was a set-up when the photographer approached me. I looked around for hidden cameras and told him the name on the card he gave me meant nothing to me.'

'I would have thought it was an obvious avenue for someone with your looks,' Zain observed, expelling a frustrated hiss from between clenched teeth as he gave up trying to fasten the button on his shirt. Apparently it took losing your healthy body to make a man appreciate having everything work. At least his debilitation was temporary, he thought, sending up a silent prayer of thanks for that.

'You mean the height,' she held a hand flat on top of her head, 'and *the* face?' She gave a gurgle of laughter.

The attractive sound brought his attention zeroing in on that face, and this time he felt not only his libido stir, which it had done the moment he laid eyes on the supple curves of her luscious body, but also his curiosity. He was forced to accept the seemingly impossible—that there was nothing feigned about her lack of vanity and yet she worked in an industry where looks were everything.

His eyes drifted down the long lines of her superb body. 'You don't seem to take your looks very seriously.'

* * *

'If I'd taken my looks seriously I'd be…' She paused and brought her lashes down in a protective sweep before adding lightly, 'I was five-ten at twelve years old. My nickname was freak or giraffe. As for my face,' her fingers moved lightly across the delicately angled features, 'someone said I looked like their cat and it kind of followed me, not that I expect you to understand,' she said without heat—people couldn't help the way they looked, and he probably didn't even realise that he made other men feel insecure, especially other men with wives, she mused, not struggling at all to imagine the effect he had on her own sex.

She was just grateful that she possessed the ability to consider her own reaction to his sexual aura with objectivity… *Yeah, you carry on telling yourself that, Abby.*

'Why wouldn't I understand?'

She resisted the temptation to dodge the question while she endured the heat as a flush travelled up her neck, but delivered her reply with as much composure as she could manage.

'Because I'm doubting you were ever an ugly duckling, Prince…is that what I call you…?'

'You call me Zain.'

Abby suppressed the childish impulse to tell him she didn't want to call him anything, she wanted to go back home.

'You think of yourself that way? As an ugly duckling?'

Abby was thrown enough by the question to miss a beat. Yes, she supposed deep down, no matter how other people saw her, she was still the ugly duckling. It was ironic really that what had set her apart at school had been the reason for her success. The length of her neck or her legs was no longer mocked but admired… 'Have I wandered into a therapy session?' How, she wondered, had this conversation got so personal so quickly?

'Aha!' He pounced on her response. 'It's classic avoidance technique, answering a question with a question.'

A much better technique in her experience was to pretend she didn't understand the joke, especially when *she* was the joke. It was the only way to prevent the outside world realising they were getting to her…to that end she'd cultivated a mask, the same mask that was much in demand at photo shoots, only now they called it enigmatic.

And Zain's reference to her love life being well-documented… She had her agent to thank for that, leaking stories about her 'romances' on social media, because, as she put it, *'Abby, darling. you're as dull as ditchwater, and beggars can't be choosers. You're not one of the elite… Relax. It's win-win and you'll get the odd free dinner out of it.'*

The romances were usually with male celebrities who needed the publicity because their career had dipped or younger, media-hungry newbies out to make their mark. It was all part of her image.

'Sorry to disappoint you but I'm not a needy basket case. I always had a warm home to go back to at the end of a bad day.'

'So what did your parents think of your career move?'

'My grandparents,' she corrected, her brow pleating as she recalled his earlier comment. 'My parents died when I was very young and Nana and Pops supported my decision because they understood that I didn't want to leave uni with a massive debt. I wanted to be financially independent.' And after Gregory's betrayal her modelling career had been the lifeline that had helped keep her virtually penniless grandparents afloat.

'It was a hard time for them, though, when I first started out. They were swindled out of their life savings and pensions.' She swallowed as she felt her throat thicken with tears. 'An investment in a project,' she continued in a flat voice that she hoped revealed none of the devastation and frustration and guilt she still felt, 'that never existed and a financial advisor who vanished off the face of the earth.'

His expression was thoughtful as he listened to her. 'You're really very good, aren't you, at pretending it doesn't hurt?'

Her eyes fluttered wide in shock before she coaxed a laugh from her aching throat. 'Are you always this sure of your infallibility or is it the medication? Speaking of which…' Her concern became genuine as she scanned his face; the bruises seemed to have deepened in colour since she'd been in the room, which, now that she thought of it, had to have been a long time ago. 'I should be going…'

'Where?'

It was a good question.

'You missed out one thing in your story. It was your boyfriend who scammed them and stole their life savings.'

Her face flamed with shocked guilt before the colour fled, leaving her lily-pale. 'Have you got a file on me in a drawer somewhere?'

'In a safe.'

He said it so casually that her jaw dropped.

* * *

Zain took advantage of her dumbstruck silence. 'I have a proposition to put to you. How would you like to be in a position to buy back your grandparents' bungalow and restore their savings?'

He really did know everything! 'I fully intend to...' She shook her head. 'You have a *file* on me...?' Her eyes flashed with outrage.

He registered that outrage suited her but didn't allow his appreciation to divert him. 'I don't mean in a year or two years, I mean now, today.'

'Is that meant to be some sort of joke?' Expression stony, she pointed to her face. 'Not sure if you'd noticed, but I'm not laughing.'

'Eighteen months of your life.'

'Eighteen months doing what?' she tossed back.

'Being my wife.'

The moment of dumbstruck silence was followed by her shaky laughter as she said in a flat voice, 'I think you have a fever.'

'Not every woman in the world would consider being my wife such a horrifying prospect.'

'Can't imagine what the attraction is unless...oh, let me think...maybe the life of luxury, the private jet, the holidays...not that I'm judging.'

'Yes, I can tell.' He smiled as the sarcasm earned him another flash from her magnificent emerald eyes. 'Look, just hear me out, and then make an...objective decision based on the facts and not on your emotional reaction. As for marriage, we are both on the same page—I don't want to be married any more than you do.'

Her delicate brows arched. 'Not ever?'

As his eyes swivelled her way it was clear that she regretted having betrayed her curiosity.

'Not ever,' he said flatly. 'However, my situation requires that, as my father's heir, I am married. In this situation, custom would normally dictate that after my brother's death my bride would be his widow.'

It took her a few seconds to process this information. 'That's positively...' The idea of asking a grieving woman to be passed on like a worn-out pair of shoes evoked a response strong enough to lend a sheen of emotion to her eyes. 'Oh, my God...poor woman.'

'Exactly.'

'But you won't, will you...do that to her?'

'I will do everything within my power to prevent this from happening, but it's not just about me; the solution is in your hands.'

'Mine...?'

'Well, if I am already married, Kayla will escape this terrible fate.'

'That's not fair,' she protested at his not at all well-disguised display of moral blackmail.

'Life is not fair; however, I am offering a practical solution, not asking you to bear my children.'

She flushed and pushed away from him.

'I never thought you were,' she assured him with a disdain that didn't fully hide her embarrassment.

'You're not the first person to be taken in,' he began, responding to a need to offer her some comfort that was alien to his nature. 'You really shouldn't beat yourself up about what happened to your grandparents.'

She read the pity in his comment and reacted with anger. 'Like you'd know anything about it!'

'Fine, carry on berating yourself.' He gave an off-hand shrug, unwilling to admit even to himself that the conflict shining in her beautiful eyes stirred something inside him. 'Or, alternatively, you could swallow your pride and accept this offer.' Zain watched as she stiffened and bit down on her full lower lip, her teeth digging into the soft, pink plumpness. Her lashes brushed her smooth cheek as she glanced down but he could see the resentment sparkling through the dark filigree.

'Offer or ultimatum?' she charged, thinking *temptation* might be a more accurate description.

'It benefits us both.'

'It would change my life.' It would also change her grandparents' lives—could she ever look at them knowing that she could have given them back the retirement they had planned and saved for and hadn't?

Could she look at herself?

He didn't bother denying her assertion. 'Yes, your life will change.'

Abby could feel her resistance fading but she clung on, not prepared to concede just yet. 'Isn't a scandal the thing you want to avoid?' If their desert marriage was revealed there was going to be one and she was going to be at the centre of it. Saying yes would mean saying goodbye to any semblance of a private life for the next year and a half…could she cope with that? 'Or are you suggesting people aren't going to notice my sudden appearance?'

His eyes moved from her vivid face to her auburn hair. 'These situations can be managed,' he assured her smoothly. 'There are people whose job it is to put a positive spin on anything.'

An image of her future life of endless ceremony and presence flashed before her eyes, and it was followed immediately by an equally vivid picture of her grand-parents pottering around the garden of their bungalow with a front door that didn't have six bolts on it.

'I wish—' she began.

He cut across her, his tone sardonic. 'I'm sure that his wife wishes my brother were not dead.'

Abby felt a stab of guilty contrition—she'd been so self-absorbed that she hadn't even considered how he must be feeling—and her mouth twisted in a grimace of self-condemnation.

'I am truly sorry.' Belated but better than not at all, she gave her condolences, not that he seemed to recognise them as such.

'Sorry?' he echoed, his dark eyes drawn into an interrogative line above his nose.

'About your brother,' she explained awkwardly.

'Oh…' he grunted as he eased one long leg onto the bed and then the other, murmuring a soft word of thanks when she pushed a couple of pillows under his head, her tummy quivering in sympathy at the sight of the bruises on the golden expanse of his stomach.

His eyes were closed and for a moment she thought he'd fallen asleep, and she was thinking about creeping away when he opened them again; the electric-blue had a febrile quality.

'We weren't close,' he revealed.

'But he was your brother.' She'd always wanted a sibling and had envied the big, noisy family who lived next to her grandparents.

'Half-brother,' he corrected, closing his eyes again. 'So do we have a deal?'

She glanced up from her contemplation of her clenched fists. 'I need to think.'

'Fine.' He closed his eyes.

The tension had barely begun to leave her bunched shoulders when he spoke again.

'Let me know what you decide in two minutes.'

His eyes opened, the glazed glow in the blue depths doing nothing to ease her stress levels.

'I didn't come here to…to…stay married, I came here to disentangle our—'

'Past, present, future?'

'We don't have a *future*.' They both heard the questioning upward inflection in the last word.

'Eighteen months. That's all I ask.'

Abby, the conflict clearly written on her face, shook her head in a slow negative motion. 'No… I can't.' An image of her grandparents floated into her head with their brave smiles, noisy neighbours and no garden. Pops had so loved his garden.

Her shoulders dropped in defeat as she took the step that sent her over the cliff edge she had been balancing on.

'Yes, all right, I'll do it.' The moment she spoke she knew it was the right, the *only* response she could have given, but it didn't stop her feeling sick, literally.

Hand pressed to her mouth, she turned away, in her haste stumbling over the trailing wires that must at some point have been attached to Zain.

That was when the bells started ringing!

CHAPTER EIGHT

'SORRY... SORRY... How do I turn it off...?' Abby picked up the loops of wire she'd sent flying and looked at the space-age machine lit up by red flashing lights.

Before Zain could respond to her frantic question the first white-coated figure burst through the door, several more followed in quick succession and the sheer volume of people pushed a bewildered Abby against a wall, where she stood watching as Zain responded to the medical attention with increasing irritation.

He raised his voice to be heard above the din of the alarms and the medical babble. 'I'm not dead—the fact I'm breathing is the first clue. Will someone please turn that damned thing off?'

The sudden cessation of noise created a freeze-frame moment. Zain broke the silence to order the rapid departure of all the white coats and before she knew it Abby and Zain were alone once again.

'Sorry about that.' She lifted her chin in challenge. 'I'm very clumsy.' Surely he could see now that she was not princess material.

'I noticed. Do you fall off the catwalk often?'

'I'm a professional.'

'Then direct the same professionalism to our contract

and there will be no problem.' He gestured towards the chair she had just vacated.

She didn't accept the invitation but stood there, her hands clasped across her stomach and her brow pleated with a furrow of consternation. 'You know this is crazy—people are never going to believe...' Her hand moved in a descriptive arc from him to herself. 'Nobody will believe that *we* are married.'

'Why not? It's true.'

A tiny flicker of a smile moved shadow-like across her face. 'There were times when I convinced myself I dreamt it.' Her chest lifted in a tiny little sigh of resignation. 'So how would it work? What are you going to tell people?'

'How *will* it work?' he emphasised, before adding with some of the hauteur she remembered from their previous encounter, 'My father is the only person I am required to *explain* myself to, and I will explain to him that you are my soulmate.' His expressive lips curved into a cynical half-smile that left his eyes cold as he continued to reveal their fictional back story. 'We fell in love, and there was a falling-out; I shall be vague on this but we are both, you see, passionate people and so these things happen...then the news of my accident had you rushing to my side because you realised that your life was nothing without me.'

'You should write fiction...or fairy stories,' she husked back.

'Any good writer knows you target your story to your audience.' His voice carried no discernible inflection but the cynicism in his azure stare was painfully pronounced as he explained, 'My father is a firm believer in fairy tales. Are you?'

Unprepared for the abrupt and vaguely accusing addition, she looked confused. 'Am I what?'

'A believer in fairy tales, *cara*?' he drawled.

She clenched her teeth. 'What if I am? It's not a crime,' she shot back. 'And will you stop calling me that—has someone told you Italian makes you sound sexy or something? For the record, it doesn't!' she lied.

After a startled silence his low, husky laughter rang out. 'I wasn't aware I was using it; I've recently spent some time with my mother...the language kind of rubs off.' The long weekend in Venice had turned into a fortnight when the diva had been forced to cancel a booking at the Met due to a throat infection which she had been convinced was about to end her career. Her harassed, much younger live-in lover had been unable to cope with the dramatic declarations that her career was over and so had begged Zain to extend his stay.

Zain had taken pity on the guy because he'd lasted longer than most, and his mother was nobody's idea of low-maintenance.

'Your mother is Italian?' Her brow speared into a speculative furrow. 'Spend some time...?' Her eyes flickered wide. 'Does that mean—?'

'She left when I was eight.'

'She left you?' Abby struggled not to sound shocked at the idea.

'She considered it the unselfish thing to do.' There was no inflection in his voice but the twist of his lips was ironic as he explained his parent's motivation. 'She could no longer deprive the operatic world and her public of her talent.'

Had she *really* said that to a little boy...? Abby couldn't bring herself to ask...she wasn't sure what shocked her most about the story—the seeming total lack of maternal feeling or the impression of total self-absorption.

'So, you see, Italian is quite literally my mother tongue. Most people here in Aarifa speak French and Arabic and a good percentage speak English as well these days, though there are some schools that are giving Mandarin preference. So, to business. If you give Hakim the details of your grandparents' account I will have the funds deposited by the end of the day.'

'From a hospital bed?'

'It is called delegation…*cara*.'

The addition was deliberate but her stomach gave a little kick anyway. 'You've got this planned but aren't you missing the details? You haven't asked how much my grandparents need.'

'Then tell me.'

She took a breath and said the sum she was short of for the house purchase and her grandparents' pension pot very quickly, but it still sounded an awful lot. She looked at him warily through her lashes.

'Per week, it sounds reasonable.'

She looked him as though he were mad. 'Week!' she yelped. 'Are you insane?'

He shook his head. 'I really hope you have an agent for your modelling work, otherwise you'd be paying them.'

Abby watched as he reached for the phone that lay on the locker beside the bed and punched in a number while she stood there wondering what the hell she had signed herself up for as he spoke quickly to someone at the other end.

'Well, that is organised,' he said, sliding seamlessly

into English as he finished the call. 'Hakim has just arrived at the hospital. He was bringing me some personal items,' he added by way of explanation. 'He will escort you back, and have Layla, my housekeeper, settle you in.'

'Take me back where?'

He looked surprised by the question. 'To the palace.'

'Right now…?' Panic gave her question a shrill edge. 'What if I see someone, what do I say, and Mr Jones is waiting…he…?'

'I will attend to Mr Jones, and I imagine you will see several people. None of them will ask you any difficult questions; they are there to make you comfortable. If you need anything just ask Hakim.'

'You're not giving me time to think,' she protested weakly. 'And who is Hakim?'

As if on cue there was a knock on the door before it opened to reveal a man who was so broad you didn't immediately notice he was not above average height.

'This is Hakim, my right hand.'

Excluded as Zain slid into what appeared to be a mixture of Arabic and French—presumably he was issuing instructions because the other man nodded several times—it wasn't until after Zain had finished speaking that Hakim turned and bowed his head once again, this time to her.

'I hope you will enjoy your stay with us, Your Royal Highness.'

'Thank you…' Her glance skittered towards Zain lying in the bed— his position did not stop him manipulating everyone like some sort of chess master but her little blip of resentment faded as she saw the lines of fatigue around his eyes.

'You should get some sleep,' she scolded, missing the thick-set man's startled expression when she added sternly, 'And don't do anything really stupid like getting out of bed!'

Zain did close his eyes after the door closed…and lay there wondering if he'd done something very stupid. Did she have the faintest clue of what she had agreed to?

Though present, the doubts tinged with guilt flickering through his head did not last. Doubts were a luxury, a weakness he could not afford. Opposing a forced marriage to Kayla and making enemies along the way would expend time and energy he also could not afford. His father may have lost sight of the fact that in their position of privilege a personal life must always be secondary to duty, but Zain had not.

He knew it was essential that, as heir apparent, he must establish his authority without delay if he was to stand any chance of bringing about the reform the country needed.

And it did need it.

Always held up as a shining example of liberal thinking and progress over the past few years, Aarifa, without a strong figurehead, was increasingly becoming a country run on a system of patronage and tribal alliances between the ruling families. Corruption was already rampant and worst of all it was becoming an accepted business practice. Zain had watched from the sidelines, painfully aware of the decline but impotent as the younger son to do anything to prevent what was happening. He had watched while the country's oil wealth was siphoned off into tax-haven accounts, while the growing inequality caused discontent and unrest.

For those who would resist his reforms Zain knew the scandal of his mother would resurface and they would try to smear him by association. There was nothing he could do about that but he could stop them weaponising his single state. A temporary marriage of convenience was the obvious solution even if that did mean throwing Abby Foster into the palace life of intrigue and deception…how would she cope?

He ground his teeth as he brushed away the question but not before his thoughts had been infiltrated by guilt once more. She would not lose out by this situation, he reminded himself, and in eighteen months when he had established his authority she would be free to take up her life once more without the burden of debt hanging over her head. She would have the freedom to choose, something that Zain knew he had lost in the moment of his brother's death.

He dug his head a little deeper into the pillow and reached behind his head with a grunt of effort to switch off the oxygen and the irritating hiss. Settling back, he closed his eyes.

Behind his flickering eyelids his thoughts continued to swirl until he closed them down, refusing to allow emotions to rule his actions the way his father always had. He fell asleep not thinking of reform but of a woman with green eyes smiling at him while she wrapped her fiery hair and her slim arms around his body.

CHAPTER NINE

YOU THOUGHT THIS was a good idea why, *exactly?* Abby asked herself as the door finally closed behind Layla. She resisted the temptation to open it to see if the two large men were still stationed there… Were they to keep people out or to keep her in…?

It didn't really matter though; the idea of anyone making it this far into a building that had a dizzying number of corridors and discreet but visible security was laughable. Though really, even if intruders got in they would never find their way out…there were probably skeletons of would-be thieves and assassins gathering dust in unknown marble-floored corners of the building even now.

She was too tired to smile at the fantasy image as the weariness, both mental and physical, went cell-deep. Even a cursory view of one of the bathrooms—the suite had two—did not tempt her to do more than brush her teeth and splash water on her face.

She stepped out of her borrowed dress, leaving it where it dropped. She could imagine her grandmother's horror at such slovenly behaviour but was too tired to do anything more than pull her nightshirt over her head before flinging herself face down on the bed where someone had conveniently pulled back the silk sheets.

She had never seen a bed this big, let alone slept in one. Despite its size it actually looked small in her vast room, which was part of a suite of similarly palatial rooms, but then it was a *palace*.

Perhaps she could ask to be moved to something a little cosier tomorrow, if this place even did cosy…? She was still debating the question when sleep claimed her. She dreamt of the enormous bed she lay in but in her dreams she wasn't alone…

As she emerged from a deep sleep the next morning the dreams that had dominated her night slipped away, leaving just an impression, an odd ache deep inside her and a tight feeling in her chest. As these too slipped away she experienced a moment's total disorientation that tipped over into panic as she stared at the intricately coloured antique-glass panels in the delicately wrought brass chandelier that hung over the bed.

'Where am…?'

Then she remembered, the previous day's events trickling through her head like an old-fashioned slide show. With a groan she sat bolt upright, giving a startled gasp when she saw the young woman standing a few feet away holding a tray.

The girl's smile slipped a little, but who could blame her being scared, Abby reflected, as her morning look tended towards super-scary even on good days? It didn't matter how successfully she tamed her hair during the day, at night it went its own wild way, and, as she had no memory of removing any make-up last night, she probably had panda-eyes as well.

'Good morning…you startled me.' Just as well

her tenure in the palace was temporary because she wouldn't like to think of this as part of her morning routine...of course, Zain's *real* wife might enjoy a very different sort of morning routine. She might wake beside, maybe even entangled with... Abby's eyes half closed and her head extended to one side as she imagined lips moving up the curve of her neck, tracing a sensual path to her mouth. The kiss would be deep and slow, hungry... Her eyes shot open as she sucked in a guilty gasp through flared nostrils.

What are you doing, Abby?

A burn of shame joined the other burn already lit low in her belly and she responded to the young woman's question of, 'Coffee?'

'Lovely, thank you.'

The girl sketched a little curtsey, put the tray on a table a few feet away and turned back.

'The curtains...?' she asked, nodding to the row of four floor-length windows along the opposite wall, all covered by heavily embroidered curtains.

Abby nodded and lifted a self-conscious hand to her hair as she pulled back the sheet and swung her legs over the edge of the bed. The cartoon cat grinning on her chest tugged her lips into a twisted smile—her nightwear looked almost as incongruous in these surroundings as she felt!

That feeling didn't diminish when the young woman approached with a floor-length dressing gown in oyster silk. They probably stocked such luxury items in a selection of sizes on the off-chance that an overnight guest might need one.

Or maybe one of Zain's *personal* overnight guests had left it behind? The fabric might have been impregnated with this faceless woman's perfume… The idea took hold and seemed so strong that Abby found herself taking a step backwards, the young attendant's face making her realise that her own expression must be reflective of the deep repugnance she was experiencing.

She dug deep and forced a smile, standing still as the younger woman slid the gown over her arms. Thankfully it smelt of nothing but *newness*. Frowning faintly, Abby stepped away, fastening the belt around her slim waist and wondering why she had overreacted so much to the hardly surprising idea that Zain slept with women; it would have been naive…actually insane to assume he didn't have an active sex life.

What would have been surprising would be the discovery that he lived the life of a monk. She smiled at the thought, ignoring the inexplicable nauseous knot that still lingered in her belly.

His sex life was not of any interest to her, she told herself, but what *was* of interest to her was the question of whether he intended to continue enjoying his bachelor lifestyle for the next eighteen months…yes, her interest in that was totally legitimate, she decided with some relief.

If she was expected to play her part this was exactly the sort of information she needed. If she was expected to look the other way and pretend she didn't know about his affairs it would be good to know ahead of time what the royal etiquette for that would be.

Oh, yeah, Abby, that should be a really good Q&A session. What would be a good opening line…? I'm not interested in who you sleep with, but…

She spared a moment of sympathy for his real wife when he took one, though she supposed there was any number of women in the world willing to make quite a lot of compromises to occupy the position she had temporarily found herself in.

The knowledge would have been easier to live with if she had been able to pretend that it was his position, his status and conspicuous wealth that attracted these faceless women who in her head were stepping over each other to offer themselves to him, but Abby knew that, even stripped of all the trappings of his position, Zain had more earthy sex appeal in his little finger than any man on the planet.

She sucked in a breath, dispelling the disturbing image forming in her head. 'Too much stripping, Abby.'

The expression of the petite woman who had been holding out the gown was wary as she shook her head to signal she didn't understand what Abby had said.

'Don't worry, I'm mad but not dangerous.'

The girl, continuing to look wary, held out a pair of slippers, delicate little velvet things embroidered with open toes and a tiny wedge heel.

Abby didn't realise her intention until the girl was about to drop down to her knees, and at this point she snatched the slippers and slid her feet into them herself. 'Perfect fit...' Abby arched a delicate brow of enquiry in the younger woman's direction.

'Mina,' the young woman supplied shyly as she dragged her curious gaze from Abby's flamed hair, which seemed to fascinate her.

'Thanks, Mina, but I can take it from here,' Abby said politely but firmly.

It took a few attempts but Abby finally managed to convey her message, namely that she didn't need help to dress, drink or anything else. It had taken five minutes and Abby was on her second cup of reviving strong coffee by the time she walked the younger woman to the door, where she received a startled look in response to her casual parting shot of *see you later*.

'*Morning, guys!*' she called to the men standing outside before ducking back in.

She leaned against the wall, thought *steep learning curve* and began to laugh…hysteria, she told herself as the tears ran down her cheeks. Ah, well, as her nan would have said, better to laugh than cry. She might have entered into a very dubious deal with a sinfully good-looking devil who, pointless to pretend otherwise, she was not immune to, but it was a means to an end and she'd make it clear when she saw him that she was probably going to mess up…royally! She dragged a hand though her tousled hair and wondered when she was likely to see him and what she was meant to do in the meantime.

Zain had seemed convinced that he'd be discharged from hospital today but that seemed unrealistic to Abby.

Floating in a bath into which she had tipped half a gallon of truly glorious-smelling oil from one of the crystal flagons on the marble-topped washstand, she began to feel slightly more relaxed.

She didn't manage to empty her mind but at least she had things more in perspective—a few uncomfortable months of her life was a price worth paying to know that her grandparents would be able to live in comfort for the rest of theirs.

She had just emerged from the decadent sunken tub and was towelling herself dry when she heard the sound of voices. She took a deep breath, wrapped a towel turban-style around her hair and tightened the sash on the silk robe. Clearly she had not convinced the woman that she could cope alone.

She took a deep breath, realising she'd just have to be blunt. 'Thank you, Mina, but I'm—'

The level of calm she'd achieved in the bath went flying out of the window. Mina was there, along with two other women, one of whom was folding items of clothing that were definitely not Abby's into a tall chest of drawers, removing layers of tissue paper as she did so. The other was helping Mina fill a wardrobe with hanger-hung items which all had labels still attached.

This was all disturbing but it was a gnat bite to a mountain lion when compared with the disturbing presence of the man who was standing there supervising them!

CHAPTER TEN

SHOCK HELD HER immobile but was it shock that made her body hum or that made the silk suddenly feel heavy against her sensitised nerve-endings?

In no mood to think about alternative explanations to shock, she caught her lower lip between her teeth, lifted her chin and waited for him to acknowledge her presence, and in the seconds it took she made a comprehensive survey of his tall, dynamic figure, casual in beautifully cut dark trousers and a pale open-necked shirt that didn't make him any less of a dauntingly elegant figure or lessen the impact of his sheer male physicality.

There was nothing that even vaguely suggested his invalid status. The bruises she knew were on his body were concealed and with his left profile presented to her the damage to his face was hidden.

He turned his head then and Abby pulled in a tense breath as their eyes clashed electric-blue on emerald. After a moment that seemed to stretch on for ever he tipped his head in curt acknowledgement.

Breathing again, she watched as he turned back to the women, said something that had them dropping curtsies and murmuring a respectful chorus of *'Amir!'* before they hurried from the room, eyes down.

* * *

Zain waited until the door had closed and then he waited some more before he turned back; it took the extra moments to get his rampaging libido back under some sort of control. Being celibate for too long went some way to explaining the strength of his reaction...some, but not all.

It was crazy and he'd never known anything like it. It had been the slither of silk that had initially alerted him to her presence and sent the rush of aroused heat through his body, the rush becoming a flood when he'd turned and got his first look at her, sinuous curves swathed in silk that clung to her breasts and the long, lovely line of her shapely thighs. It was obvious she didn't have a stitch on underneath.

He lifted his gaze quickly, but not quickly enough to stop the painful pulse of heat from skewering him where he stood. She had the body of a goddess, athletic and toned.

The effort of dragging his eyes upwards caused the muscles along his jaw to quiver. He forced his hands to unclench; the sensation of not being in complete control of himself was a new one—one he didn't like. Thankfully he recognised it for what it was—simple sexual desire.

'Should you be out of hospital?' Abby sounded shrill.

'I have been given a clean bill of health.'

'Who did you bully and intimidate into signing that?' She couldn't resist the retort but as he held her gaze he sensed she immediately regretted it. A long, uncomfortable moment passed before he spoke.

'Is that some subtle allusion...are you trying to suggest that I *bullied* you, Abigail?'

'Nobody calls me Abigail.' She shook her head and sighed. 'All right, this is my decision. I've agreed to do this but—'

'Ah, the *but*…?'

'I don't think I can carry it off.'

'I don't see the problem.'

Her mouth twisted at his unsympathetic response. It was plain that she found it extremely frustrating that he didn't seem to take her concerns seriously.

'That is the problem—you don't. The girl earlier— she tried to put my *shoes* on!' Her voice rose to an incredulous quiver that made his lips twitch.

His glance dropped to her painted toes peeking out through the velvet before returning to her face. 'And that is a problem because?'

'See?' she said, lifting her hands in a point-proven gesture. 'Having people put your shoes on for you is normal for you; for me it's…well, ridiculous, and it makes me feel uncomfortable.'

'It is not compulsory; I have been known to tie my own shoelaces on occasion.'

'You're laughing at me!' she accused hotly.

He huffed out a grunt that could be construed as apology or maybe an admission. 'I appreciate this all might seem strange to you at first.'

'Big of you,' she said, refusing to be mollified.

'I have every confidence that you will fulfil your side of the deal, unless I read you wrong?'

He watched her eyes narrow at the suggestion she was not a woman of her word, and tough to boot, which was the response he had intended.

'I said I'd do this and I will.' The words carried more conviction with an image of her grandparents in her head. 'Obviously I will need to speak to my agent.' He wasn't going to be happy she had work commitments lined up. 'I don't know what I'm going to say to him.' Whatever she said it would be difficult to defend herself against his inevitable accusation of lack of professionalism.

'I'll sort it—give me the name.'

Her lips tightened. 'I don't want *you* to *sort* it.' She cinched the belt on her robe another defiant notch. 'Look, this,' her fluttering gesture took in their surroundings, 'isn't public so I don't have to pretend to be weak and ineffectual. I am more than capable of sorting my own affairs. Obviously in public I will do my best to act as though I think every word you utter is a pearl of wisdom, but in private—'

'In private,' he drawled, 'you will assert your independence just for the hell of it. Sounds like a fun eighteen months. For the record, I was simply trying to smooth things for you, not take over your life.'

'I think you've already done that, considering you *saved* my life,' she admitted. Abby caught her full lower lip between her teeth and pushed out a husky, 'I know… I know it's my choice and I will try not to keep hitting you on the head with it,' she promised. 'My grandparents taught me to take responsibility for my own actions…' Her face fell, a look of dismay widening her eyes. 'Oh, God, Nana and Pops!' How was she going to explain this to them?

'Whatever you want to tell your grandparents, I will go along with it.'

Taken aback by his concession and his quick reading of the situation, shee took a moment to respond. 'I don't know what I'm going to tell them…maybe I don't have to tell them yet—it's two weeks before they get back from their cruise. And delaying the inevitable seems very attractive just now.'

His brows hit his dark hairline, taking her glance with them, and her eyes stayed glued to the blond streak that he knew stood out against the glossy black.

He caught the direction of her stare and lifted a hand to his head. 'My mother come from Northern Italy. There are a lot of blondes there, though she is a redhead these days.' His brow furrowed. '*Cruise...?* I thought that your grandparents were strapped for cash?'

'They are but they won a competition in a magazine that my nan didn't even remember entering...an all-expenses-paid trip in the Caribbean,' she said, looking anywhere but at him...the woodwork over the door was really quite marvellous.

'There was no competition, was there?'

She dragged her eyes away from the doorway. 'What makes you say that? Of course...oh, all right, then, there wasn't, but Pops got really ill starting last winter; he had bronchitis and it really wore him down, so the summer was a total washout.' She looked at him, her chin tilted to a defiant angle. 'Then I saw this cruise advertised—it was massively reduced, they were virtually giving it away to fill empty cabins, and I knew they wouldn't let me pay so I invented the competition,' she admitted, fixing him with a so-hang-me glare.

'So you *can* lie.' Very badly, as it happened. 'There's no need to look so guilty. It was a kind thing to do.'

Her dark eyelashes fluttered against her cheek as she experienced a glow of pleasure that was totally dispro-portionate to the unexpected praise.

'Have you eaten?'

She nodded and looked across to the table where she'd sat earlier, but the dishes had already vanished, along with last night's fresh flowers, which had been replaced by an equally fabulous arrangement of beautiful blooms. The place seemed to be populated by an army of people whose job it was to wait on her hand and foot without her ever seeing them.

'Good, then get dressed and we can be off.'

She blinked and stood her ground even though having one layer of silk between her skin and his eyes made her feel quite ridiculously exposed, and clothes—a wool jumper or something equally covering—seemed a very good idea!

'Off where?'

'I thought I'd give you the guided tour.'

'That's really not necessary,' she said, wondering why he would offer to show her around himself when anyone else in his position would delegate.

He raised a brow and folded his long length into one of the easy chairs set beside the double French doors that opened out onto a balcony. 'What are you planning to do? Stay in here?'

'Why not? A family of six could live here comfortably and I could do with catching up on some reading.' She gave a sigh and added, 'Look, I think that, under the circumstances, it would be better that I keep a low profile.'

'That would defeat the object of this exercise.'

She pursed her lips and tilted her head to one side, angling a feathery brow. 'And that was again...?'

'Showing that the future ruler of Aarifa has a beautiful wife which makes him a strong and dependable pair of hands. The press office have issued a statement this morning.'

'Already!' She fought her way through the panic churning in her stomach. 'So what is expected of me—do I speak or just wear clothes and smile?' The latter ought to be fine…it was just about all she'd done with her life so far, she thought, stifling a slug of resentment. When he came to choose a bride for real, would he want a mannequin then too or a real woman?

'I think wearing clothes is a good idea,' he said with an amused, sensual grin. 'I hope there are some you care for in what I've ordered, but feel free to order anything else you need or want.'

'Where did they all come from?'

'I couldn't tell you exactly, I just gave your measurements to—'

'My measurements? How did you know my measurements?'

A slow smile split his lean face as his glance slid slowly over her slim, sinuous curves. 'I have a good eye for such things, *cara.*'

'And no doubt a lot of practice sizing up women,' she flung back, focusing on the annoyance of him making her blush, rather than the fire zigzagging along the nerve endings under the surface of her skin.

'Oh, and for the shoes I got two sizes of each to accommodate your feet.' He looked down at the items under discussion. 'Shall I come back in, say, an hour and a half?'

'How long do you think it takes me to get ready?'

It wasn't until he had grinned, said, 'Right, half an hour, then,' and left the room that she realised her indignation at his assumption that it took her so long to make herself presentable meant she had missed an opportunity to buy herself more time to recover from the way he was making her feel. Though she could have said three hours and probably should have said at least an hour, she had let him get to her and so he'd given her a tight timeline, knowing that she would be determined not to be a second late.

Walking across to the massive wardrobes, she focused on the positives—at least he wasn't going to sit there and wait—but she quickly met her second challenge…there appeared to be no handle in the smooth wooden surface. It wasn't until she inadvertently pressed her palm to a panel that the doors slid silently open, revealing a massive space.

The new items hanging in their protective covers covered a fraction of what was available, and she dropped to her knees to check the shoeboxes neatly stacked…still not sure if he'd been joking.

He hadn't been.

There were ten pairs of shoes, all in two sizes.

The clothes were all in one size—*her* size—and there was a bigger selection than many shops she knew carried. She didn't buy many clothes for herself normally, though she had an eye for a bargain and she knew what suited her. Ultimately, what she felt comfortable in was quite often plain old jeans and a T-shirt.

Neither was available, so after a short sift through Abby pulled out a pair of palazzo trousers with deep pockets in a subtle silvery blue and a square-shouldered fifties-style shirt in a slightly darker shade brightened by drifts of butterflies.

She used her bra and pants from her overnight bag, though a quick glance in one of the drawers in the an-

tique chest revealed a vast selection of silky under-
clothes in mouth-watering shades and gorgeous fabrics.

She pulled out her one make-up bag from the hold-
all and, after pushing her hair back from her face with
an Alice band she applied that too. It didn't take long—
just her usual moisturisers and sunscreen, a smudge of
blusher across her cheekbones and a smudge of brown
eyeshadow on her eyelids. She tended not to wear mas-
cara as her eyelashes were naturally brown and long,
though they never curled without a lot of encourage-
ment. Finishing off with a defiant slash of bold red lipstick, she let her hair fall loose. Standing in front of the
mirror, she subjected her wild curls to a wrinkle-nosed
scrutiny. The time constraint ruled out straightening
it so, after holding it on top of her head for a moment
while she tried to figure out how to tame it, she released
it with a hiss of dissatisfaction and delayed the decision
by going back into the bedroom to dress. Sliding on a
pair of low-heeled red mules, she went over to one of
the full-length mirrors to judge the results, but before
she reached it there was a tap on the door. The visitor
didn't wait for a response, he just walked in.

The sardonic half-smile curling his mouth at the corners flattened out when he saw her and he walked across
the room towards her. Abby was flustered by his sudden
appearance but she still managed to notice the clenched
tension below his relaxed exterior.

'I'm *nearly* ready.'

'Take your time…' His glance drifted upwards from
her feet to the top of her glossy head, returning to rest
on her lips. 'You look ready to me.' She looked incredible…like a classy, sassy female lead in one of the clas-

sic old black and white Hollywood movies his mother had introduced him to as a kid…elegant but sexy and in full, glorious colour.

She stuck out her chin. 'Are you trying to be funny?' She lifted a hand to her tumbling curls. 'I haven't done anything with my hair.'

'It looks fine to me,' Zain replied in a voice that gave no hint that he was imagining those curls falling down her naked back and over her breasts. It would cover them now it was inches longer than it had been ten months ago… He sucked in a sense-cooling breath through flared nostrils and pushed away the raunchy image. 'What do you still need to do?'

He arranged his long, lean length in a chair, aware her resentment was growing and choosing to push her by adopting a bored demeanour.

'I need to make myself presentable…' She lifted the weight of her hair off her neck and let it fall back in a gesture that suggested it explained everything. For Zain, it explained nothing. 'Presentable for all those people who are probably lined up outside to look at me. Perhaps I should wear a veil…or would that offend people?' Looking suddenly and completely overwhelmed by what she'd signed up for, she grabbed the padded back of a nearby chair, taking a deep breath before adding despairingly, 'You see, I don't have a clue.'

His clicking fingers cut through her diatribe of complaint. He refused to believe that a woman who looked the way she did had any confidence issues. 'Do not play the victim, it doesn't suit you.'

This bracing and unsympathetic advice brought her chin up, a move he was growing used to very quickly.

'And it is also extremely unconvincing. I have seen

you stand up to men wielding knives,' he reminded her. 'And as for presentable...presentable...' he parroted. 'What the hell is that?'

'It's something my nan always said before she left the house... *Do I look presentable?*' The mention of her grandmother brought a wistfulness to her face and she blinked to clear the tears he could see her fighting. Before he could say anything to try and help, a hopeful smile spread across her face.

'Perhaps your sister-in-law,' she began eagerly. 'Do you think if we told her the story she'd help me? I mean, it was her job, so surely she'd be able to give me some pointers.'

'No.' His emphatic response was designed to flatten her enthusiasm, and it worked.

'But—' she began to protest.

'You will not approach Kayla.' He moved towards her as he spoke, his voice not raised, but each ice-edged syllable had a dangerously explosive quality that was echoed in his body language; he looked big and dangerous.

Breath held, her hands tightened on the back of the chair, he wasn't sure if it was pride or paralysis that made her hold eye contact. It was definitely not good sense—that would have had her running for the nearest exit. Instead she tilted her head back, mirroring the tension he knew drew the skin tight across the angles and planes of his face.

He paused a few feet from where she stood and added in the same soft, deadly tone, 'And you will not tell her our story.' He could only imagine what Kayla would do with that sort of information. 'Is that understood?'

'Well, I don't see what the harm would be,' she began mutinously.

'Stay away from Kayla, Abigail,' he intoned grimly. Seeing her opening up to Kayla, all earnest eyes and the best of intentions, would be like watching a kitten ask advice from a tiger. The image in his head was enough to make him break out in a cold sweat.

Refusing to categorise the feeling in his gut as protective, Zain zoned in on the practical measures he would need to put in place to protect Abby from Kayla, who would consider Abby, or anyone else that came between her and what she wanted, the enemy.

'Why?'

The question floored him but before he could think of a suitable response a look of comprehension appeared on Abby's face.

'Oh, God, I'm sorry, I wasn't thinking…you're right.'

Zain made a non-committal sound in his throat, glad she had reached the conclusion but not sure how she had got there.

'I wasn't thinking.'

Slightly thrown by her abrupt capitulation Zain watched her lips twisted in a self-recriminatory grimace.

'She must be devastated.'

'She is, I'm sure.' Though he imagined that fury was a more accurate description of Kayla's likely reaction to having her position at the pinnacle of society being taken from her.

'I won't bother her, I promise. It must be a terrible thing to lose your husband so young… I can't even begin to imagine.' She lifted her hand to her hair. 'Could you wait a minute while I tie it back?'

His eyes moved down the golden red waves. 'Your hair is spectacular just as it is.' It was no less than a statement of fact. 'And no one will be offended no matter how you appear—most women in Aarifa stopped wearing the veil a generation ago…a few of the older or more conservative do when they go out in public but it is their choice. So just relax.'

It took Abby a few moments to recover, not just from her reaction to having him call any part of her spectacular, but also to the flash of sense-incinerating fire she had seen in his eyes that had sent her heart rate crashing through the ceiling.

'Relax…?' She managed a laugh at the idea. 'I'm living in a velvet-lined box.'

'I can have you moved to another room.'

She gave a sigh of frustration. 'Not the room! I mean the *situation*. The lying and the money and—'

'Yes, I get it, but compared to escaping from desert pirates it should be child's play.'

'Pirates. I suppose they were, and the desert is a bit like the sea too,' she reflected, a little shudder tracing a path up her spine as she recalled the vast emptiness. 'I didn't escape. I hung on, that's all,' she reminded him, a glimmer of a smile tilting one corner of her lips as she recalled that journey through the blackness of the desert.

The memory reminded her too that she owed him, big time. He hadn't played that card, he even seemed inclined to play down the fact he had saved her from a fate that Abby considered worse than death. Given how much she owed him, he wasn't, when she really thought about it, asking so very much in return. So it didn't sit

well with her conscience; being uneasy was not much
to ask of her in the grand scheme of things.

'I signed on for this so don't worry, I won't wimp out.'

'I like your hair that way…it is you.'

Before she had the opportunity to decide if that had
been a compliment or an insult he was opening the door
for her to pass through. As she did he stopped her, patting his trouser pockets. 'I've forgotten my phone…hold
on…' He paused. 'What are you scared of?'

'I'm not scared…just…people are going to be curious, to ask questions.'

'I feel confident that they won't, but if they do simply refer them to me.'

Her little chin lifted in challenge once more. 'I don't
need a man to speak for me! Do you even know how
sexist that sounds?'

'You were the one playing helpless,' he pointed out.

The term grated on Abby.

She glared at him through narrowed eyes. 'I wasn't
playing.'

'So you are helpless, then?'

Her exasperated glare morphed into confusion when
instead of moving past her through the door he back-
tracked, heading towards the row of cupboards that
lined the opposite wall.

'What are you do…?'

She stopped, her mouth ajar, as he opened one of the
doors and stepped through.

'What the…?' She followed him, pushing the door
wider and seeing that there was no closet behind it,
there was another room. As she walked through to it,
it became obvious that the room was a bedroom on the
same palatial scale as her own but much more sparsely

furnished than the one allocated to her and very definitely masculine.

She stood there, frozen in the concealed doorway, as Zain went to a desk on one wall and shifted some papers to find what he was looking for. It took her a few seconds for the significance to sink in. When it did she experienced a flare of alarmed fury!

'Got it!'

Her jaw tightened—*was that all he had to say?* 'This,' she said in a frozen voice, 'is a bedroom?'

'Hard to get anything past you.'

Her lips compressed. '*Your* bedroom?' she added, her voice heavy with accusation.

'Right again.'

Her chest swelled. 'Was anyone going to tell me that there was a secret door in my room?'

The conversational tone didn't fool him for a minute—he knew she was mad as hell and yet he appeared to enjoy watching her like this.

'Oh, it isn't a secret, *cara*, everyone knows it's there. My great-great-grandfather had it put in when he moved his favourite mistress into the palace. And as we are married it is almost obligatory to share the same bedroom suite, if not the same bed...' He paused, his gaze sliding down the long, supple curves of her body. 'Unless, of course, you do wish to *share*...? Relax,' he recommended before she could react. 'There's a lock on the connecting door. We can use it if you're worried about your virtue.'

His mockery stung colour into her smooth cheeks, or maybe it was the thrill of illicit excitement low in her stomach.

'I am perfectly capable of defending my virtue, thank

you.' The question that was becoming more relevant, considering that even his voice had the ability to make her quiver, was, did she actually *want* to defend it?

She lowered her gaze as the internal admission brought a rosy flush to her cheeks.

'So I don't need a lock.' A bit of self-control might help though, she thought despairingly.

'I do not doubt it, but the lock is on *my* side.' The lock might be on one side but the attraction, the same attraction that had flared into life in the desert, was mutual, and stronger than anything he had ever experienced in his life.

If the circumstances had been different he would have enjoyed exploring it, and her. His chiselled jaw tightened as he reminded himself that they were to be together for eighteen months, and, while sharing sex might make the first couple of months easier and *definitely* more enjoyable, it still left the months that came after.

In his experience, when lust burnt itself out the very things that had attracted you in the first place became irritants, and then there was the boredom... Under normal circumstances the solution was walking away, but in this situation that was not an option.

Even this sobering thought did not stop his eyes making an unscheduled journey up the long, supple curves of her spectacular body once more, or the heat that pooled in his groin. Jaw clenched, he made himself walk past her before he did or said something he would definitely regret.

The lightning-quick return sliced through Abby's veneer of bravado.

'In your dreams,' she said contemptuously.

He swung back without warning, the speed and fluidity of his action taking her unawares. He was standing so close, towering over her, and he could feel the heat of her body. She reacted instinctively to the force of his sheer male physicality, placing her palms flat and pushing hard against his chest.

Her strength was nothing compared to his resolve and as her eyes became locked with his he slid a hand to the small of her back and pressed her against his chest, trapping her hands between them and doing nothing to hide his arousal.

She struggled for breath, the air emerging from her parted lips in a series of stressed little gasps. Zain was breathing hard too, his breath warm on her face as he bent his head until there were only centimetres of air between their lips.

The breathless stillness could have lasted a second or an hour before it was broken by Zain.

'You want to know about my dreams, *cara*…?' he said thickly. Alarm bells louder than those she had set off the previous day were screeching in his head but he tuned them out. This was just sex.

Abby moaned, her eyelids closing as he moved his lips across her own so lightly it was agony as every nerve in his body tensed and started screaming.

It was the little shudder, the warm lips that softened beneath his that cut through the last threads of Zain's control. He slid his fingers into her silky hair, wrapping them through the fiery strands and letting instinct take over as he kissed her like a starving man.

Abby responded to the searing contact, parting her lips under his probing pressure and welcoming the intimacy, craving it as she fell into the hard, hungry kiss.

They were both breathing like marathon runners when his mouth finally lifted. Warm breath mingling with hers, Zain stood there, his fingers tangled in her hair, the side of his nose resting against her own.

The muscles along his jaw quivered as he gently kissed the corner of her mouth. 'You want to explore my dreams a little longer? Or maybe your dreams…?'

'I don't have those sort of dreams,' she said.

CHAPTER ELEVEN

IGNORING HIS LOOK of disbelief, Abby barged past him and out of the door, mortified, ashamed by her response, but much, much more disturbed by the illicit excitement that remained low in her belly.

'So you've decided to take the lead?'

She flashed him a look of dislike. Her insides were trembling. He looked totally cool and she resented and envied his ability to turn his passion on and off like a tap as if it meant nothing to him.

It meant nothing to *me*, she added firmly to herself, and repeated it just to emphasise the fact—*nothing*. 'Are they going to follow us all the time?' she asked crankily.

He looked blank; he was actually struggling to focus. 'They who…?'

'The two large men with granite faces and…at a guess, automatic weapons over their shoulders, who are ten paces behind us. Is that ringing any bells?'

'Oh…you tune them out after a while.' It was that or go mad. 'Security.'

'I didn't think they were the entertainment…do they follow you everywhere?'

You could get used to anything, she supposed, even

the low, disturbing electric thrum in the air when Zain was around…so long as she didn't touch him, she would cope.

'They try to.'

'It's very intrusive…'

'It's the art of living in a velvet-lined box.'

The reminder dragged a reluctant smile from Abby. 'A figure of speech. It's actually a very beautiful box.' They were walking under arches of marble embellished with intricate carvings. Beneath their feet was a mosaic made of bright blues and golds, the colours so intense it looked as though it had been freshly laid, but it had to be ancient.

'If you slow down you might actually get to see some of it.'

With a slight tip of her head she acknowledged his comment.

'Are you in much pain?' she asked.

'I'm on strong painkillers.'

She tilted her head to look up at his strong profile. 'But are you actually taking them?'

'I put my comfort ahead of my macho reputation.'

'Do you have a macho…?' She caught her breath and rushed across to the archway that had given her a glimpse of the vista that had stopped her in her tracks. 'Oh, my goodness!' She put her hands on the wrought-iron rail that came up to hip height and leaned out.

With a sharp admonition of, 'Careful!' he tugged her back from the railings embedded in the base of the opening that appeared to be cut into a single rose-coloured stone so massive it looked like a rock face.

It took several moments for Zain's heart to slide back down from his throat, where it had climbed, and into his

chest—the image of her leaning out too far and simply
falling out into space was hard to shake.

His chest continued to heave like someone who'd
just had to sprint ten kilometres, his breath hissing out
in fast, measured gasps, his bruised ribs screaming in
protest. As he turned his head to study her profile she
appeared utterly oblivious to the fact she had ever been
in any danger, and utterly oblivious to him, her enrap-
tured gaze fixed on the panoramic vista.

He'd wanted to surprise her, to see her reaction, but
the plan had definitely backfired. He was the one who'd
been surprised…and probably taken twelve months off
his life in the process.

The original city had been built up around the palace on three sides, and this side faced the desert, the
endless sand dunes rising organically from the rock of
the building's foundations.

Nothing broke the undulating miles and miles of red
desert until it reached the mountains, blue in the distance against the even more vivid, eye-aching blue of
a sky that seemed to go on for ever.

Abby was so completely enthralled by the dazzling vista
that it took her a few moments to register that Zain was
standing behind her, his hand on her shoulders. As compelling as the view was, her appreciation was drowned
beneath the awareness of his warm proximity.

She felt the shudder start in her toes and begin to
rise… She stepped forward to break contact but instead
his grip tightened and he swore softly as he turned her
around to face him.

'For God's sake, woman, are you trying to kill yourself?' Without taking his angry eyes from her face he jerked his head in the direction of the drop.

She frowned in bewilderment at his stressed exclamation.

'The drop is two hundred feet.' He spaced the words, enunciating them slowly through his lips.

Her expression cleared. 'Oh, I'm fine with heights.'

His chiselled jaw clenched. 'Well, I am not fine with scraping up pieces of your stupid—' He bit back any further remarks and shook his dark head, his big hands sliding downwards from her shoulders to her upper arms. He seemed at the point of jerking her towards him when instead he stepped backwards, releasing the breath that had clearly been trapped in his chest in a deep sigh.

Relieved there was a barrier of air between them, she might have been able to clear the whirling fog of emotions in her head if he hadn't continued to stare at her with daunting disapproval, mingled with something else she couldn't quite name.

The something else made her heart rate escalate, throwing the stressed organ against her ribcage as her eyes went to his mouth, remembering his kiss as she swallowed to relieve the contraction in her dry throat.

She didn't have a clue how long they stayed there, a frozen tableau, before he finally broke the silence, though not with a kiss this time.

'You scared me witless...this place—'

'It's beautiful.'

You're beautiful, she thought, unable to stop staring at his face.

He nodded. 'Yes, but it is also dangerous.'

So were the currents she could feel shimmering like silken ribbons in the air between them.

'My ancestors used to bring their enemies here and push them to their deaths...'

She gave a shudder at the image his words created in her head.

'When I was a boy I used to be fascinated by the gruesome stories in the way that small boys are always fascinated by gruesome anything. On my twelfth birthday, my brother said he had a present for me... he brought me here...' His head turned towards the ledge. 'By that time I was as tall as Khalid, but two of his friends were waiting. They held me over the edge and threatened to drop me...they wanted me to say my mother was a slut... I wouldn't, so they held me there until I passed out from fear.'

She hadn't felt dizzy standing at the edge but the furious reaction she felt in response to his matter-of-fact recounting of the story of bullying rose up in her now, so strong that her head spun. 'Oh, that's so terrible... wicked...no wonder you are scared of this place!' she exclaimed.

'I'm not scared of this place.'

'It's fine if you are,' she soothed, taking his hand as she began to back away from the stone opening.

It took him a moment to realise the astonishing truth: she was looking after him... With a twisted half-smile he allowed her to drag him away until she stood with her back to the wall and he was facing her a few feet away from the opening.

'Is that better?'

'I'm really not afraid of heights—my father cured me. Somehow, he heard about what had happened. I

never questioned how, I just accepted his omnipotence.'
There was a wistful edge to his soft laugh. 'Anyway,
he brought me here and told me to look over the edge.'

She looked up at him, eyes wide with shock and indignation.

'That was brutal!'

She couldn't believe it when he shook his head in
denial of her condemnation. He actually smiled, and
the poignant quality of the motion made her ache with
sadness.

'I refused point-blank and so he brought a stone out
from his pocket. It was large, smooth and black.' He
extended his hand, rubbing his thumb across his palm
as though he was seeing it, feeling it there.

'A stone?'

'He gave it to me and told me that it was very valuable, he explained that it had magical qualities, that the
person who carried it would never fall. He said it had
been given to him by a famous climber who had con-
quered Everest.'

Abby's shoulders relaxed as she smiled. 'You believed him.' She was taken by the story and the image
in her head of Zain as a little boy.

'I was still afraid of the drop, but yes, I believed him
and actually more than that I didn't want to disappoint
him. So every day we met here and each day I looked
over the edge with a little less fear than the previous
day. After a week of coming here, only to have my father not show up, I got bored and curious so I took the
stone from my pocket and climbed up onto the ledge.
Did I mention I was a rather curious child? I wondered
what would happen if I dropped it…so I did.

'When I turned around my father was standing there. I told him the stone hadn't worked. It had fallen.'

'And what did he say?'

'He just shrugged and said, "Yes, but you didn't." And walked away.'

Abby smiled at the story. 'It sounds as though you had a great relationship.'

'When I was a child, certainly.'

'But not now?' Even before his expression froze over she was regretting her probing. 'I'm sorry, it's none of my business.'

'Why not? It is no secret.' He turned away to stare out of the window, his face in profile remote, his voice devoid of expression as he continued. 'My father was a good man, and at one time a good ruler. He was strong, everyone respected him and the people worshipped him. When I heard the stories of the early days of his rule I wanted to be just like him.'

His bitter, reflective laugh made her wince. 'What happened?'

'There was an enormous scandal when he married my mother—she had a past and he had a wife, Khalid's mother. But he didn't care; his *love* for my mother was an obsession, a *disease*. He put his personal happiness ahead of his duty.'

'Maybe,' she began tentatively. 'He felt he needed the woman he loved beside him to do his job as ruler?'

He whipped around, his mouth twisted into a sneer as he responded to her softly issued suggestion. 'She left him!'

'And you,' she said, her heart aching with compassion for the boy he had been and sad for the man he had become, a man who seemed to have sealed himself off emotionally.

'I survived but my father did not—he went to pieces, he cared about nothing…his duty, this land…and he would take her back tomorrow if she would come.'

'Poor man…' A little shudder ran like a chill down Abby's spine; it must be terrible to love someone you couldn't have…to taste a little of paradise and be thrown out.

'Poor man?' Zain's nostrils flared in outrage at the suggestion. 'He is a leader, a ruler, he has responsibilities—the people, the land relied on him and he left them. Oh, he is still here physically, but he might as well not be.'

'You're angry with him?' Her heart ached for the little boy discovering his hero had feet of clay. His determination to stay single and his contempt for marriage certainly made sense in light of the family history he had revealed.

'I'm ashamed of him.' The words were wrenched from somewhere deep inside him and he seemed almost as shocked to have said them as she was to hear them. Zain turned abruptly away, obviously regretting that he had confided so much in her…and disturbed that he had.

'Are you coming? We have a lot of ground to cover,' he said in a clipped tone as he strode away.

She nodded quickly and ran to catch him up.

He was right, there was a lot of ground and all of it was the stuff of superlatives. Zain spoke of geometric patterns and symmetry but to her the corridors and courtyards, the ballrooms and paved quadrangles had no logical sequence. It was a beautiful, glittering maze, but

Zain was a good guide—he didn't try and overwhelm her with too much detail but instead told her little snippets, gossipy stories that made his ancestors seem very real people and not just the daunting historical figures in portraits that lined the gallery above the ballroom with its mirrored, domed ceiling of blue glass.

But, as fascinating as the stories he told were, Abby could not stop thinking about the present-day story, the sad, tragic tale of his parents.

'Now, this,' he said as they walked along a wide corridor with a vaulted ceiling, 'is the oldest part of the Palace complex. You won't come this way unless you're going to the stables.'

Abby had fallen a little behind and stopped. 'Do you think they will ever get back together?'

Zain inhaled, his nostrils flaring as he turned around to face her.

She stood her ground while his gaze swept across her face. 'Your parents?' she pushed out nervously.

'You like a happy ending?' he sneered.

She gave a little shrug, wishing she had kept her mouth shut. 'Doesn't everyone? Don't you think you would be happier if you could forgive your father? He couldn't help falling in love.'

His jaw clenched before he responded. 'While I am grateful for your unsolicited wifely concern for my welfare,' he told her with blighting insincerity, 'it is not required. You are my wife on paper only, so please don't get carried away by the job description.'

She breathed through the utterly irrational hurt that quivered through her body. 'I'll do my level best,' she promised before miming a zipping motion across her lips.

He said something not in any language she understood before some of his rigidity fell away and something approaching a smile twisted his lips. 'You, silent? That I'll believe when I see it. But for the record you are wrong, you *can* help… Falling implies a helplessness that does not exist; there is always a choice.'

She searched his lean face for any sign of doubt and found none at all; he radiated male arrogance. Her insides shuddered, the mouth-drying sensation dramatic and disturbing as she continued to stare at him.

Always a choice, she mused; well, she had one now: carry on looking and feeling like this or look away; argue or bite her tongue.

She chose the latter in both cases, probably the way to go for the next eighteen months.

'So this leads to the stables,' she said.

'Yes,' he said, experiencing a sense of anticlimax as he let her walk before him under a large stone arch guarded by massive, double-metal-banded doors and into the fresh air.

Abby took a deep breath and took it all in, turning her head towards the sound of thundering hooves as a string of horses with riders on their backs galloped out through the open gates. They left behind a hum of activity she hadn't yet experienced in Aarifa.

She had encountered a few people during the tour but all had bowed to Zain and scooted out of their way, so their functions in this vast complex had not been immediately obvious to Abby.

Here was different, with everyone occupied on a specific task, be it grooming one of the horses, mucking out stables, leading horses across the cobbled yard or walking them into what seemed to be a horse bath.

'Hydrotherapy,' Zain explained when he saw her

staring. He took her arm and steered her towards the nearest row of stables; there were three similar rows that lined three sides of the quadrangle, while the fourth seemed to house offices.

'I know that horses are not your thing, but I thought you might like to say hello to an old friend.' He took her across to a stable door, pausing to speak to one of the stable hands with a lack of formality that surprised Abby.

The young man moved ahead of them, tipping his head towards Abby as he passed. As they reached the stable he had gone inside he emerged leading a horse.

'Malik al-Layl,' Zain said, taking the ends of the reins from the stable hand and leading the stallion towards Abby. 'I think he remembers you,' Zain said as the horse snickered and put his head down towards Abby, who, after a self-conscious moment of indecision, extended her hand towards the animal.

'We were not formally introduced, Malik...' She glanced towards Zain for guidance.

'Malik al-Layl—it means King of the Night.'

'We were not formally introduced, Malik al-Layl, but I don't blame you for that.' She shot a look loaded with meaning at Zain. 'There was a lot of anonymity going on.' She jumped as the horse brushed her hand with velvety lips, her smile spreading. 'I think he *might* remember me,' she said, unable to hide her pleasure at the thought.

'Once seen, never forgotten.'

Their eyes met and the *something* that she had sensed earlier—the crackly charge she had been conscious of several times—surfaced once again. She lowered her gaze quickly but it still hung there in the air as she pretended to look for something in the pocket of her trousers and watched covertly as Zain ran his hand down the stallion's flank, the dangerous male aura he exuded sending little thrills through her nervous system.

'Lost something?'

Like someone caught in the act…well, in some ways, she had been lucky her sin remained in thought and not in action, and Abby pulled her empty hand out of her pocket.

'I was just looking for a tissue…' she improvised. 'I'm fine.' The hasty addition was just in case he decided to send for someone to fetch her a gold-lined box of the things.

'I was wondering if you'd like to have some riding lessons while you're here?'

'You make it sound as though I'm on holiday.'

'It doesn't have to be a punishment—there is nothing that says you can't enjoy yourself.' His eyes connected with hers, the teasing look making her feel warm and *other things*. 'You might even get to like me…'

Her half-smile flattened as she realised that was the problem, the one she didn't want to acknowledge—that it might be far too easy to like him. 'That's pushing it,' she husked out, refusing to analyse why the idea scared her so much. 'But I would like to learn to ride.'

'Fine, I'll…' He broke off, his eyes moving past her in response to the sound of the clatter of hooves.

Abby turned her head, curious to see who had galloped through the gates just as the rider of the first horse dismounted. As the woman landed with almost balletic grace, the two men who had ridden in behind her shadowed the move but with far less elegance.

Before the riders had hit the ground, grooms were rushing up to take the reins of the horses.

The woman pulled off her riding cap and shook back a dark bell of smooth, shiny hair. She barely glanced at the man who took it from her hands then led away her mount, though she did call something out to the two men who were clearly her security detail. They bowed in response.

She then swung around and, shoulders back, head high, helmet in hand, with a swing of her slim hips she walked towards where Abby and Zain stood.

Abby looked towards Zain and found he was not looking at the tiny brunette but at her. He seemed to read the unspoken question in her eyes and nodded almost imperceptibly.

Abby put his tension down to a fear she was about to say or do something that would blow their cover. His concern, she admitted, was pretty well-founded.

'Zain, darling!'

For a moment Zain did nothing but then he took a deep breath, lifted his hand and walked out to greet the woman.

They met somewhere in the middle, close enough for Abby to see what the other woman looked like but not hear what they were saying apart from the odd word that floated out…which sounded French.

Abby wasn't prepared for the flood of peculiar emotions seeing them together released, rising to the surface like oil on water. She examined the woman rather than the feelings.

At a distance, there had been the suggestion of glossy perfection. Closer to, this was intensified; the other woman didn't have a hair out of place, literally. The dark hair that swung to her shoulders in a bell-like curve was smooth and glossy and there wasn't a single crease in the tight-fitting riding breeches that were moulded to her bottom and thighs or a mark on her whiter-than-white shirt. The knee-high riding boots she wore had a glossy sheen and clung to her calves, the darker, fitted jacket on top was nipped in where it buttoned at the waist and the scarf arranged artfully around her neck added the final chic touch.

In profile, her features looked small and neat, and next to Zain she was tiny and delicate-looking. She was just the sort of woman that brought out protective instincts in men.

The sort of woman who always made Abby feel big and clumsy. For a split second she was back at school, towering over the other girls, hearing the popular girls laugh and snigger at her in the hallways. Annoyed with herself, she forced the images away—she had moved on a long time ago, she reminded herself.

The sound of female laughter drifting across to her brought Abby's attention firmly back to the present and she found herself clenching her teeth, her curiosity turning to something else, something that made her want to look away, but she couldn't. She continued to watch as the woman reached out a hand and laid it on Zain's chest… Was the intimacy of the gesture a figment of her imagination?

She watched as Zain turned and gestured in her own direction—clearly he was talking about her, but *what was he saying*…? The woman turned too and, lifting a gloved hand, she waved. It took Abby a split second to respond with a jerky movement of her hand.

Then the couple began to walk towards her.

By the time they reached her Abby had a very credit-able smile painted on her face.

'Kayla, this is my wife, Abby; Abby, this is Kayla, my...brother's widow.' Zain smoothly made the formal introductions.

Abby tipped her head, still in shock at hearing Zain call her *his wife*. 'I'm very sorry...for your loss.'

The woman's red lips stretched into a gracious smile, her mouth the perfect rosebud shape. Her diamond ear-rings flashed in the sunlight. 'Thank you. It has been a difficult time...my mother insisted I go out this morn-ing; she knew that it would help. Zain understands. He feels the same way.'

It was hard to tell from Zain's expression if he felt anything at all. His expression was tight and stony.

Kayla clasped a hand to her chest. Not anticipating the dramatic gesture, Abby stepped back.

'The desert...for us...' Kayla's glance took in Zain. 'It is hard to explain to an outsider...it is an almost spiri-tual connection that cleanses the soul.'

Struggling to know what to say to this, Abby just nodded and heard herself say stupidly, 'That's nice.'

'I'm sorry I wasn't here last night to greet you.' Abby noted how the gracious smile did not quite reach her dark eyes.

'No...not at all,' Abby stammered.

'Everyone wants to meet you—perhaps we could have tea one day? Go shopping... I'm sure we will be great friends.' She leaned in and, stretching upwards, kissed the air either side of Abby's face. Abby's nostrils flared as she was engulfed in a cloud of exotic-smelling cloying perfume.

Without waiting for a response, Kayla turned and lifted her face to Zain.

Abby turned away, tangling her fingers in the animal's mane but aware in the periphery of her vision that the pause before Zain bent forward was one second away from being awkward. She didn't look as he air-brushed her cheek with his lips but turned in time to see the other woman catch hold of his hand, sandwich it between both of hers, the red nails bright against his skin, before pressing it to her chest and only then slowly releasing it.

There were tears in the corners of her dark eyes as she turned to Abby. 'Forgive me; it's just that I nearly lost both *my* men.'

Abby told herself she had imagined the emphasis and nodded, feeling a little guilty that her own sympathy felt so forced.

'Later, Zain...?' The tears dried as the beautiful brunette arched a brow in Zain's direction and nodded to Abby before walking regally away, the two men falling into step behind.

'So that is Kayla.'

'It is,' Zain agreed.

His response gave her no clue as to the cause of the atmosphere she'd sensed between the two of them. 'She's very beautiful.'

She's poison, Zain wanted to say. Instead he gave the stallion one last pat and nodded to the man who appeared to take him away. 'This evening Kayla has asked us to join her for dinner.'

Abby nodded but with little enthusiasm. 'It must be very hard for her.'

'I said you were still too tired.'

He was giving her an out but he fervently hoped she wouldn't take it.

'Will you be all right?'

'Why wouldn't I be all right?' Abby asked in confusion. 'It's not as though we're going to be living in each other's pockets, is it? I'm sure you're going to be busy getting used to your new role...'

He tipped his head in acknowledgement. 'I do intend to be more...hands-on than my brother. It will be a steep learning curve. Concerning your days, things will run smoother once you have a team of staff around you. I have selected some candidates but I wasn't sure of you'd like to interview them personally or have Layla or one of my team do it?'

'Staff...team...me...?' She shook her head in an attitude of bewilderment.

'Obviously you will have your own staff.'

'But surely that wouldn't be necessary—I'm not really—'

He cut across her faltering protest. 'The world is meant to think you are *really*, and what do you intend to do for the next eighteen months—hide in your room? You'll be bored stiff in two minutes,' he predicted.

'So you want me to fill my time with riding lessons, and what, unveiling statues, general good works...?' The barely disguised uncertainty in her voice told him she didn't have a clue what the royal duties of the wife of a prince were.

'It might keep you out of trouble.' And hopefully out of Kayla's way. The only reason he had accepted this evening's invite was to make it quite clear to Kayla that she was to keep away from Abby and to dash any expectation she had that the two of them would ever get back together.

The memory of her propositioning him in a not very subtle manner he assumed had been meant to arouse him, with his wife standing just feet away, was still fresh in his mind. The effect on him had been the opposite to what she'd intended, as Zain had stood there wondering, as he did now, how he could ever have been taken in by her, how he could have missed the naked ambition that motivated her. His response to her inappropriate overture had been constrained by the public place; this evening it would not be.

CHAPTER TWELVE

It seemed to Abby that Zain took a more direct route back to the suite; he appeared lost in his own thoughts and to such a degree that she was struggling to keep up with the pace he set. So after a couple of attempts to break the silence she gave up.

At the door to her room he paused, seeming to notice for the first time that he was a little out of breath, and glanced at the metal-banded watch on his wrist.

'Sorry, I'm late. I have an appointment with my father.' He added, evidently feeling guilty he was leaving her alone, 'Layla will be available if you want anything.'

She nodded absently, still absorbing the fact that she was living in a world where you made an appointment to see your father.

About to turn away, he swung back. 'He lives quite a secluded life and my brother's death has hit him hard, so don't take it personally if he doesn't want to see you.' He sketched a forced smile that left his eyes sombre and shadowed. 'I never do.'

She watched him stride away, tall and powerful, wondering if he'd told himself the same thing when he was a little boy who'd needed his father.

Abby spent some time responding to texts from her

grandparents and a much longer one from her agent, who wanted to know where she was. She ate her supper in the small private sitting room, preferring it to the dining room—which had all the intimacy of a banqueting hall—before sinking gratefully into the scented water of a warm bath. She closed her eyes and floated but the calm she sought eluded her, her brain continuing to fire off in all directions, thoughts and questions swirling in her head.

How had Zain's meeting with his father gone—was the sheikh angry that his son had been secretly married? Was Zain telling Kayla all about it over dinner? Was she making him feel better? Abby couldn't figure out if she had imagined or over-egged the intimacy she sensed between Zain and the widow…in Abby's head she had become the *black* widow, thought that might have just been her jealousy talking.

'Jealousy!' she yelped out loud, sinking under the scented water before coming up gasping and spluttering a second later.

'Do not go there, Abby,' she told her fogged reflection in one of the many mirrors. So yes, she *was* attracted to Zain—all right, *attracted* didn't really cover it… Zain had woken up a dormant sensual side of her that she hadn't even known existed—but she couldn't lose sight of the fact that she was here to do a job, a job that meant they spent a lot of time together in close proximity. But she would be vigilant not to confuse that closeness with real intimacy and in eighteen months she was out of here.

Easing herself out of the warm water, she scrubbed the mist off the mirror and pushed the wet hair back from her face. 'Do you want sex if it's just cheap and meaningless?'

It kind of depends on who's offering it...

Her eyes widened before she closed them with a groan. Sometimes honesty was definitely *not* the best policy. Standing up, she reached for one of the neatly folded bath sheets, muttering, 'Just as well he's not offering,' and keeping her eyes on the floor as she padded back through to the bedroom, afraid the mirrors might evoke some more unwanted insights. She just had to keep reminding herself that she was here to provide a smooth transition of power and nothing else.

The two men who had shadowed him at a respectful distance stopped when Zain halted and waited. It was the fourth such pause he had made since he left his father's apartments, still in a state of shock. As he walked past the two uniformed guards who flanked the entrance to his own private section of the palace he nodded to the men behind him, who peeled away as he shut the door.

He leaned against it. Zain was not a man easily shocked but he was… He closed his eyes as the relevant section of his conversation with his father continued to play on a loop in his head.

'Several members of the council have come to me to express their…concern over this marriage, and your choice of bride.'

Zain, who had expected this, had only half listened while his father recited the names, and none had surprised him. But then his father had said something that *did* surprise him.

'I told them that you have my total support.'

Zain had not doubted his ability to gain his father's support by appealing to his sentimental nature, but to receive it totally unprompted had surprised him.

'I am glad you have found someone,' his father had continued. 'Leading this country can be a lonely job and it's not one I would inflict on my worst enemy, let alone my son, without a great deal of thought.'

'It will not be my job for a long time, Father.'

'It will; I intend to step down and let you take control, Zain. It is something I would have done sooner but your brother...well, let us not speak ill of the dead.'

Repetition did not lessen the shock value, Zain realised as he began to pace the room.

He had never needed a shoulder to lean on or someone to confide his fears to—there was no one in his life to let him down, to leave. But both his father and Abby had spoken about the loneliness of the role.

To Zain, being alone was a positive, but it was not a point of view he imagined he stood any chance of converting Abby to—she rather unexpectedly turned out to have a romanticised view of life which even a profession not known for sentiment had not knocked out of her—and she was stubborn.

One corner of his mouth half lifted as, in his mind, the lines of her face quivered and solidified, becoming so real that for a moment it was as if he could reach out and touch her, but when he blinked and his vision cleared there was just the door she lay behind.

He walked across to it, hand outstretched, only to let it still on the heavy handle for a long time before he dropped it back to his side and walked away, reminding himself that alone was an *advantage* not a disability.

Unlike the previous night, Abby *didn't* fall asleep the moment her head hit the pillow—she tossed and turned as her thoughts went around in dizzying circles, bits of conversation from the last couple of days drifting through as her mind disconnected thoughts and images.

Occasionally her eyes would go to the hidden door to Zain's rooms as she wondered about past times when it had been used for illicit liaisons, about the mistresses and wives of powerful men who had lain in this bed before her, though she was not a mistress…and a wife in name only.

A wife who frequently felt as if she were the only twenty-two-year-old virgin on the planet. It wasn't deliberate; in her teens she had been the butt of male jokes—too tall, too thin, too gawky…too weird—so she had focused on her books and read about true romance. Not the fumbling sort her contemporaries boasted of enjoying, but grand passions, soulmates.

The irony was that now, even though she was essentially the same person, she had plenty of men lusting after her, to the point that she'd had to adopt an aloof reputation to put them off. The last thing she actually wanted to be was untouchable so Abby had decided she was setting the bar too high, which was the reason she'd taken a chance on Greg, working on the theory that, while he didn't set her on fire, she recognised the strong possibility that nobody would, and he was so nice—irony didn't get much darker really.

Maybe it was an evolutionary process and she was a slow starter; she had found unrequited lust now—and frankly she wouldn't have recommended it to anyone— so maybe one day she might discover what love felt like too…she just hoped it was better than this!

This reflection drove her from her bed. Barefoot, she walked across to the windows. She hadn't closed the curtains—there was no one to see in, considering her room and the entire private section belonging to Zain was situated in one of the highest of the three towers the palace boasted.

She could see the paved herb garden far below, the fragrance drifting up on the warm night air, the sound from the series of fountains a distant trickle. It was soothing and as she lifted her face towards the warm breeze it caught the folds of the nightdress that she had taken from the selection neatly folded in one of the drawers; soft chiffon silk in a pale shade of blue, it reached midcalf and gathered under her breasts. One of the ribbon straps slipped as she pushed her hair back from her face.

She froze, one hand pressed to her head, fingers deep in the lush red curls, the other hand on the intricate wrought-iron rail of the Juliet balcony, as a disturbing sound broke the dark silence.

The sound was almost feral…an animal, perhaps, but what sort of animal would be roaming the palace grounds at night? Then the terrible lost sound came again. It was not, she realised, coming from the grounds, but from the room next door and from the throat of a person.

She didn't think, she just raced to the secret door and rushed through. Like her, Zain had not closed the curtains. The moonlight was streaming into the room, giving the illusion that carved wooden bed in the centre of it was spotlit.

The feral-sounding wail that emerged from the figure in it sent a chill through her blood. Heart pounding, she raced across the room and, climbing onto the bed, crammed forward to kneel beside the hunched figure on his knees, the tangled sheet over his body covering him only to waist level, leaving his head, his heaving shoulders and back exposed to the moonlight. The skin gleamed like oiled gold as every individual muscle tensed, tautly defined like an anatomical diagram displaying the perfection of the human form.

The only sound now, to her relief, was Zain's laboured dragging in and sighing out of deep, drowning breaths and the heavy thud-thud of her heartbeat as the blood pounded in her ears.

'Zain...?'

His head lifted fractionally at the sound of her voice. 'Go back to bed, Abigail,' he shook out in a muffled, raw voice that pained her ears like nails on a chalk board.

It was good advice and she knew it.

She reached out, hesitating a moment before she touched his shoulder and felt his muscles tense in rejection. Under the slick of sweat his skin felt cold to the touch.

'Get the hell out!' he growled.

Logic said she should do just that, but in the same way as her physical response to him was something elemental, the response to his obvious suffering was equally instinctive and strong. It went beyond empathy and easily drowned out the voices of self-preservation in her head.

She tucked her legs underneath her and sat there. 'Well, you can be as rude as you like, call the guards to cart me off to the dungeon if you want, but I'm not moving until you tell me what the hell was going on—that was no dream, that was...' She thought of the nerve-shredding sound and shuddered. 'You might as well talk to me. I'm vastly cheaper than a therapist and my confidentiality is guaranteed.'

After a moment he sighed and flipped over onto

his back, eyes closed. In the moonlight the angles and planes on his face took on the aspect of a beautifully carved statue.

The seconds dragged and his silence continued to contrast with the emotions she could feel rolling off him.

She could see the waistband of a pair of boxers just below the crest of his hip bone, his belly flat and ridged, showing each individual muscle with every inhalation. The multi-coloured bruises down one side of his ribcage and upper torso shone through the light triangular dusting of body hair on his chest. His body had a power and beauty that dragged an emotional response from some previously unknown portion of her heart.

'Go away, Abigail Foster. I am not...*safe*.' His smoky blue gaze slid from her face and down her body, betraying the sinful thoughts in his mind.

He closed his eyes as if fighting against a surge of primal possessiveness.

'I'm not prying... I just want...' she began, framing her words carefully before stopping and straightening her shoulders. 'I just want to help and it's no use trying to scare me. I'm not afraid of you.'

His eyes opened and she nodded, smiling serenely down at him as she realised that she was telling the truth. She never had been afraid of him—even that first time when she had not known if he was one of the good guys, she had felt safe with him.

'Is it the accident? Is your memory coming back?'

He huffed out a dry laugh. 'It never went away, *cara*.'

'I know you said you didn't get on with your brother.' Her lips tightened as she recalled the dead man's idea of a birthday present. 'But you *were* brothers...and I know that people feel guilty when they survive and—'

He lifted a hand and touched a finger to her lips.

Abby inhaled and forgot what she'd been about to say as a deep tingle surged through her body from the point of contact.

He took the finger away and she breathed out, watching as he curved his arm on the pillow above his head; the stretch involved a contraction of muscle that inflamed the tingling she was already feeling inside.

'I am not suffering survivor guilt...surviving is my way of...' He broke off, as if at a loss to explain his relationship to someone like her. 'I wish the world were the way you think it is, *cara*—you think that blood is thicker than water, but the brutal reality is that brothers do not always love one another. Some brothers hate... my brother hated me.'

Assailed by a sense of helplessness, she felt the lump of emotion in her throat swelling. She hated to see him hurting like this and beating himself up...guilty for something that no one could have prevented.

'You can't blame yourself, it was an accident, you argued...that is what families do—'

'I really don't feel guilty,' he cut back with savage, biting emphasis that made her wonder if she was missing something.

'Well, then, that's good.'

'Good!' he spat before closing his eyes and clapping a hand heavily to his head. A moment later his hand fell away and he raised himself on one elbow, his free hand going to her chin, drawing her face around to look at him. 'The truth is it was no accident. It was planned.'

'How is that possible?'

'It's possible because...' He paused, a battle waging across his face as he struggled to force the words out.

'You have that wholesome, shiny, dewy-eyed belief that goodness will overcome, don't you?'

'I'm not that naive, Zain, but yes, I do think that if you give people a chance they will mostly do the right thing…yes, I do.'

'The *right thing*!' he echoed. 'Do you think it was the *right* thing that my brother invited me there that day with the intention of ending both our lives?' He must have heard her sharp intake of breath, seen her pale, shocked face, but he ignored both. 'Khalid had found out that his life was ending—he had terminal cancer, the autopsy after the accident confirmed it—and he decided to put his—what do they say?—yes, his "affairs" in order.

'He took great delight in telling me he was going to take me with him—his last revenge. Khalid's last *I love you, brother* moment.' His bitter laugh cut her like a shower of glass shards.

'It wasn't an accident.' Her horrified whisper sounded loud in the silent room. 'It was attempted murder.'

'And he very nearly succeeded. I would be dead if that door had not given at the last moment and every time I close my eyes I see my brother's face and know how much he hated me.'

'I'm so, so sorry. Have you told anyone?'

Something flashed in his eyes as he looked at her and shook his head.

Shock vibrated through him; he had never intended to share the knowledge with anyone, let alone a woman he barely knew. There was nothing between him and this woman except a sexual attraction, he told himself, refusing to examine the suspicious knot of emotion that lay like a lead weight behind his breast bone. She had awoken in him something stronger than anything he had ever experienced and for the first time he realised how some men mistook this sort of primal connection for love.

'My father must never know— it would… Khalid put him through hell over the years. I don't want him to know the truth behind his death…what my brother tried to do. It would kill him.'

She pressed a hand to her heart as though making a vow as she held his eyes and shook her head. 'I won't tell him… I won't tell anyone.'

Their eyes were locked, the silent, deep connection stretching as he reached up his long fingers, digging into the deep, silky mesh of waves at the back of her head.

Her heart thudding audibly, Abby rose up on her knees and placed her palms flat on either side of his head as he dragged her face slowly down to his.

The first brush of his lips sent a jolt of shock fizzing through her body. She tensed and then, with a sigh, relaxed into the pressure of his slow, seductive exploration. Her body arched over him as his hands slid down her shoulders, moving slowly over the thin silk of her nightdress. By the time they reached the curve of her taut bottom she was quivering with need.

'I have wanted you from the moment I saw you,' he said thickly, easing her onto her back and rising over her.

The raw desire in his voice excited her more than Abby would have believed possible. She ran her hands down his back—it was all hard muscle and silky skin—but stopped suddenly, remembering his injures.

In the act of sliding down her body he stopped and lifted his head. 'What's wrong?'

'I want you, Zain, I want to touch you…taste you…'

She shocked herself with the bold admission before adding a half-whispered, 'I don't want to hurt you.'

His laugh held relief and warmth. 'Let me show how much you're hurting me, angel.'

He took her hand and fed it down his body, sliding it under the waistband of his shorts, watching her face as he curled her fingers around the smooth, hard shaft of his erection.

She gasped, her heart pumping as her smoky stare connected with his. The carnal image that flashed into her head of him inside her so hot and hard made her fingers tighten, and she felt rather than heard the feral moan that vibrated deep within the vault of his chest as he took her hand away and held it on the pillow beside her face. With his free hand he stroked down her cheek and, holding her eyes, slid one and then the other thin strap of her nightdress off her shoulders.

He leaned in close, his breath warm on her cheek. 'Your skin is like silk,' he rasped, pressing an open-mouthed kiss to the blue-veined hollow at the base of her throat. 'I want to see you.'

The erotic statement took her breath away and tightened the hard knot of desire low in her belly but also released a flicker of fear that spoilt the moment.

'What's wrong?'

'You do realise that my photos are airbrushed, right?' She looked at him through her lashes, her body language defensive as she pushed out, 'I'm not perfect... and I've never really felt this way before...'

He caught her two clenched fists and brought them up to his lips. 'You are beautiful.'

Her lashes lifted from her cheek.

'And I want... I *need* you.'

The raw, driven quality of his admission started to melt away her doubts and the hungry kiss that followed it completed the job.

She lay there breathing hard as he levered himself far enough away to pull her nightdress down to her waist. His eyes made her think of blue molten fire, and they left a burning trail on her skin as he hungrily absorbed her quivering breasts, cupping one in his hand. When he ran his tongue across the engorged peak, she stopped thinking at all.

It ought to have felt strange to be touched but it just felt gloriously right.

The sight of his dark head against her breast was the most erotic thing she had ever seen. When he lifted his head his cheekbones were scored with dull colour. 'I want to feel you around me, Abigail, holding me tight.'

She struggled to force her response past the aching occlusion in her throat as his words sparked a flame into life inside her. She had wanted him, wanted to give him comfort, wanted to feel it in return—to feel warm and safe—but this was not comfort, it was something hotter and more dangerous, something wild. Her skin felt heated and she was shaking with need as he caressed her breast once more, and then, as she moaned against his mouth, he took hold of the fabric bunched at her waist and pulled.

There was a jagged tearing sound and then a moment later cool air was on her hot skin.

She opened her eyes as he levered himself away and pulled herself into a sitting position, but the protest in her face faded away when she saw he had only left her to kick away his shorts.

As he turned back to her, her greedy glance slid over the strong, perfect contours of his body. The power and the beauty of his fully aroused male body made her head spin with desire that thudded like a hammer in her head and pooled hotly between her legs.

A hand on her breastbone, he pushed her back down and brought his hands to either side of her face as he covered her body with his.

The first skin-to-skin contact of their naked bodies was electric. He parted her lips and sank his tongue deep into her mouth, the repeated penetration a rehearsal for what was to come. Abby sank her finger into his hair and kissed him back with a wild, combative ferocity that matched his.

His hands were everywhere, touching her, caressing her until her pleasure-saturated nerves were screaming for some sort of relief.

When his hand slid between her legs, his finger spreading the sensitive folds and sliding into the warm slickness of her femininity, she screamed his name.

'Zain!'

Her fingers clawed his back as he parted her legs and mounted her, his powerful body, slick with sweat, rearing over her before he slid into her in one powerful thrust.

A slow sigh hissed through her parted lips as, head thrown back, she absorbed the sensation of him inside her, making her aware of herself in a way that she had never experienced before.

Her eyelids flickered as she heard the astonished growl of his exclamation, the words muffled as his head dropped into her shoulder, then lifting fractionally. This time she could make out what he was saying and hear the concern in his deep voice.

'Are you all right?'

All right? She was absolutely incredible! 'Better than all right,' she husked. 'Don't stop, please…?'

'I couldn't even if I wanted to!' The tension in the raw admission was mirrored in the taut, strained lines of his face as he began to move again, drawing a sigh of relief from Abby. The sigh of pleasure became something more as by slow, careful increments he sank deeper before pulling out, repeating the movement, touching places that fed directly to the pleasure centres in her brain.

Her back arching, she grabbed his hips, pulling him deeper into her. There were no barriers of any sort between them, there was no check on the things she said to him, the words she used to urge him on as she wrapped her legs tight around him and let him take her into uncharted territory with each stroke.

She reached the explosive climax a second after she felt his hot release inside her; every muscle in her body spasmed then relaxed, the process repeating until she lay spent and breathing hard, pressed down into the mattress by his weight.

She was still floating some place out of her body when he moved to lie beside her on his back.

A primal surge of possessiveness tightened in Zain's chest, the powerful, fundamental response interwoven with tenderness as he struggled with the realisation that he had been Abby's first, her *only* lover. Something he hadn't thought possible.

'I lost control… I'm sorry.'

The words were heavy with self-recrimination and Abby's head turned sharply towards him on the pillow, their glances locked.

'Take that back,' she hissed furiously. 'Don't you *dare* say you're sorry.'

'I assumed…there is a lot of stuff out there about—' It was no excuse and he felt ashamed for voicing it.

'My multiple lovers? None of it is true—it was only ever my agency trying to get publicity. I've never even met some of the men I'm meant to have been sleeping with—one of them is even gay, though I don't think he actually knows it yet.'

'And you don't mind?'

'It's mostly harmless, and Nana and Pops don't do the internet or read tabloids so there's no harm done.'

'If I'd known you had never been with a man before I would have not been so—'

'You were perfect,' she cut in, blushing ferociously.

'I would be flattered except you've not really had any other experiences for comparison, have you? Another thing…' He hesitated.

'I'm fine. What did I do wrong?'

'Not you, me… I… I didn't use protection; are you…?' She shook her head. 'No.'

'Right, that could be a complication.'

She swallowed. 'It was just one time.'

He reached for her and pulled her down to him, a realisation dawning on him—the possibilities this new development created. 'It doesn't have to be one time… eighteen months is a long time to go without…'

Abby could have pointed out that she had gone twenty-two years *without* with no ill effects, but she didn't. Shading her eyes with her lashes, she asked, 'So does that mean you won't be…?' She broke off, arching her back as he ran a hand over the curve of her bottom.

Zain completed the question for her. 'Sleeping around?'

An image of Zain in bed with faceless and beautiful women floated into her head along with a stab of pain that felt as if a hand had reached into her chest and squeezed hard.

Abby looked away and nodded, hoping nothing in her expression gave away the fact that his reply mattered more than a little to her.

'I have too much respect for you to do that.'

She didn't doubt his words but there was a certain uneasiness in his tone.

'I don't want your respect, I want… I want…' Shaking her head, Abby struggled to sit up but was prevented by the weight and tensile strength of the arm that lay across her shoulders.

A long finger on the angle of her jaw brought her face around to his, her lashes lowered before he could read the answer to his question in her eyes. 'Abby, *what* do you want?'

'I want…' It was as if someone had turned up an invisible volume control and the whisper that had been active in the back of her mind became a loud, deafening and infinitely shocking shout.

Love!

She wanted love!

A strong sense of self-preservation made her rush immediately into rationalisation mode—of course she wanted love; didn't everyone? Only a fool would fall in love with a man who didn't believe in love…a man who had to all intents and purposes walled off his own feelings. But could she really walk away from what Zain was offering after she'd experienced a passion more intense than she had ever thought possible? Love was wonderful but there was also something to be said for a physical connection that defied explanation.

So maybe this was nothing more than strong sexual attraction—*very* strong...primal even—amplified by their first dramatic meeting and the fact she had just made love to the man who had haunted her dreams ever since he rode to her rescue. From a safe distance she could call it temporary insanity, but there was no reason to call it anything else now, not when she could embrace the opportunity Zain was giving her and enjoy the situation as it was.

Her muddled thoughts were interrupted as he kissed her, his lips warm and persuasive, moving over her body. Suddenly none of the questions seemed to matter so much. She would take what was on offer!

'I want this too...' he said against her mouth. 'Besides, I'm not about to give grist to the rumour mill by taking anyone other than my wife to bed, especially considering the new developments.'

'What new developments?'

'My father told me tonight that he intends to abdicate in my favour. I persuaded him to wait before he announces anything, but eyes are going to be watching me very closely once this leaks.'

Which, of course, it would.

'That means you're going to—' The rest was lost in the warmth of his mouth.

'Be very frustrated,' he rasped against her lips, 'if you don't focus on the next lesson.'

His voice in the semi-darkness made her shiver. 'There's a next lesson?'

It turned out there were two more that night.

CHAPTER THIRTEEN

ZAIN HAD LEFT before she woke. She had a vague memory of him kissing her goodbye, but that must have been hours ago, as the bed beside her was now cold.

It wasn't the first time Abby had woken alone since she came to Aarifa and she never liked it, but during the last four weeks she had come to realise that Zain worked harder than anyone she knew.

Having a greater grasp of Aarifan politics after four weeks of immersion therapy on the subject, Abby understood why he worked as hard as he did. He had no choice.

At first Zain had seemed surprised by her questions and Abby suspected he had initially doubted her interest was genuine, as his early responses had been pretty monosyllabic, but as he'd come to realise that her interest was real he had opened up and become more expansive. Now it had reached the point where he volunteered information—be it a breakthrough or an obstacle—without actually waiting for her to ask.

A couple of times recently he'd even asked her opinion. It gave her a little glow to know that he valued it, or, at least, it seemed he did to her.

But they never discussed the widowed princess, Kayla. Over the last few weeks malicious rumours had started to spread, which as far as Abby could make out were intended to harm her reputation. Luckily, the wife of a courtier she had become friendly with had warned Abby that it was Kayla spreading these, and Abby had been able to minimise the damage. There were also rumours that Zain and Kayla had once had a relationship before Kayla's marriage, which had made Abby burn with jealousy. When she had asked the woman why Kayla hated her so much, she'd needed pushing but had finally expanded on her initial diplomatic, *It's not my place to say.*

'Kayla wants what you have, Amira. I went to school with her, and she will do anything to get what she wants. Tell the Prince,' she'd said.

But Abby knew Zain would only tell her to stay away from Kayla. And, besides, she wanted to show him she was strong enough to confront this on her own. It certainly wasn't her place to be jealous of whatever might have happened in the past. Nevertheless, it gave her comfort to know that every night it was *their* bedroom Zain came to.

Sliding out of bed, she headed for the bathroom, humming softly under her breath, but she stopped humming when she became aware of the familiar monthly ache low down in her belly. Since that first night they had slept together they had been careful to use protection, but a tiny part of her had been nagging at her, aware there was some chance she might be pregnant. But now, the evidence to the contrary was clear and suddenly overwhelming.

Without warning, the tears just kept coming, gushing out from some unidentified region deep inside her, before finally they dried to an occasional burble of misery.

Sniffing, Abby walked across to the marble washbasin and turned the cold tap on full, telling her red-eyed image sternly to, 'Get a grip!'

She splashed her face with water and switched off the tap but stayed where she was, leaning on the basin, looking at herself, a questioning frown furrowing her smooth brow.

Her reaction had been inexplicable, and not just the reaction but also the strength of it.

This was a good outcome, the *desired* outcome, she reminded herself. She knew that, and yes, she *was* relieved, or at least part of her was. But there was another part that felt oddly…what…? *Bereft*. The recognition deepened her frown and increased her growing sense of unease.

She hadn't wanted to be pregnant—it would have complicated an already complicated situation and she'd been too scared to even imagine the consequences of an accidental baby, considering their arrangement. Not that the idea of pregnancy scared her; she wanted a child one day but she wanted that baby to be the product of a loving relationship. She wanted to give the man she would eventually love in a 'forever after' sort of way the ultimate gift of his child.

Another sob began working its way past her trembling lips but it never escaped. Instead her eyes flew wide and she literally stopped breathing, the blood seeping from her face and leaving it paper-pale!

The truth hit Abby with the force of a tsunami blast and continued to reverberate through her body: some secret part of her *had* wanted a child because she loved Zain!

Because she *did* love him. As the denial fell away

the pain rushed in to fill the vacuum it left. Loving a man who would never return those feelings was always going to hurt, which was why she supposed she had been in denial, filling her thoughts with enough irrelevant chatter to drown out the words that were now shouting inside her head.

Zain was the last man she would have expected to fall in love with. No matter what he said, Zain was wrong—there was no choice involved; love defied all logic.

Patience was not one of Zain's strengths and Aarifan politics seemed a slow-moving machine. The past few weeks had been at times incredibly frustrating—there had been moments when he had struggled to retain control in the face of the obstacles being put in his way by the powerful politicians who opposed his reforms in any and all ways they could.

But today had been a good day and it was still early, he saw, glancing down at his wrist. The early breakfast meeting had been an unexpected breakthrough. He had brought a previously obstinate opponent around to his way of thinking and he was buzzing with a sense of purpose.

It took days like this to keep him going through all the days when it felt as if he was being blocked at every turn, days when progress seemed impossible and the tightrope of diplomacy slippery as ice. Days when, if it wasn't for the fact he vented in private with Abby, he might have been tempted to forget the advent of civilisation and throw the whole avaricious bunch in a deep dungeon. Abby had proved a very effective sounding board, listening to him rage and talking him down.

She was going to be thrilled when she heard about

this advance...he couldn't wait to— His footsteps slowed, a thunderstruck expression crossing his face...

He couldn't wait!

It was literally true.

He wanted so badly to share the victory with Abby, just as he had shared the defeats and setbacks, and it was something he could not imagine feeling a few short weeks ago.

How far had he strayed from his original game plan...what had it even been? He had rewritten the rules to fit the circumstances and his needs so often it was hard to remember. It was easy to justify his first diversion from the plan because it had been totally unrealistic to expect to fight the intense sexual attraction between them. He couldn't get enough of her and actually he couldn't even see why it had ever seemed so important to take such a masochistic stance, why he had seen danger where in fact there was pleasure.

Sex he could rationalise; what made him more uneasy was the recognition of the emotional, almost symbiotic, connection they seemed to have developed...if this was how he felt now, what was it going to be like when the eighteen months was up?

He made himself walk slowly to the door. It wasn't as if he needed her here; she liked to be involved...she was lonely, and it would have been cruel, he told himself, to leave her to her own devices.

Surely the only thing that had changed was that in eighteen months' time they would part as friends...if ex-lovers *could* be friends. Or maybe they would even be parents...that circumstance still an unknown, the memory of their first time and his thoughtlessness always there in the background.

He walked into Abby's room, almost tripping over the suitcase by the door.

For a split second shock closed his brain down—it closed everything down—then, as the paralysis weakened, something close to panic tightened like an icy fist in his belly. Before he identified it as such it shifted into full-blown, mind-numbing fury. She was running away. She was leaving him.

Didn't everyone?

He was literally shaking as he strode across the room and through the door between the wardrobes that lay open.

Passport in hand, Abby was standing looking adrift, the long, lightweight trench coat she wore open to reveal a plain white silk shirt she had teamed with dark, narrow pedal-pushers.

'What the hell is going on?' Had she intended to slip away while he was absent?

Abby blinked; she was working hard at disguising her misery, at the truth she was sure was written all over her face, and it left little or nothing to register his awesome fury.

'Sorry, it was a last-minute decision.' She managed a smile…held it for a few seconds before it faded, too bright and too brittle. Hell, she really needed some time to sort herself out—if she stayed now she'd do something irreversibly stupid like blurt out the truth. 'I would have rung but I didn't want to disturb your meeting… how did it go?'

'To hell with my meeting!' he growled.

'Sorry,' she said automatically, assuming from his attitude that it had gone badly. A knot of protective

anger tightened in her chest; he worked so damned hard
and for what seemed to her very little thanks. Sometimes she wished she could bang together the heads of
those men making his life tough. 'It's just I've been
putting off going to see Nana and Pops but I need to;
I only told them half the story and they deserve more,
plus the solicitor says the vendors are finally ready to
exchange contracts, and I'd like to give them the keys
in person.'

'You're coming back…' The wildness died from his
eyes as they swept her face, and his body began to unclench as the explosive tension lowered. For the first
time he noticed her pallor, the red rims around her beautiful eyes…the protective swell in his chest so intense
it was a struggle to breathe past.

'Well, not tonight…unless you need me to?'

'I'm fine,' he said with a shrug that made it clear he
didn't need anyone.

'The plane is on standby; I hope you don't mind,'
she said, not quite meeting his eyes.

He frowned and she worried he could see through
her lies.

'Of course not. You'll ring me when you land…?'

She nodded. 'Of course.'

'Come here…'

She went to him and sighed as he drew her body
against his, smoothing her hair back. With one hand he
cupped her chin and drew her mouth up to his… The
tenderness meshing with the passion brought an emotional lump to her throat.

Afraid she was going burst into tears, she pulled
away, sure that if she lost control she might start blurt-
ing out things she shouldn't. She allowed herself to say

'I love you' silently in her head but kept her mouth closed.

Zain didn't want her love and he certainly wouldn't have wanted their baby. But she had, she really had. Until this morning, she hadn't known just how much that hope had flickered inside her.

Hand on the door handle, she turned back. 'Oh, and I'm not pregnant, by the way, so you can relax.' She managed what she hoped was an unaffected laugh before she almost threw herself through the door because this time no amount of determination could stop the tears.

A few days later as Abby returned to Aarifa the sadness was not gone but it was contained. Although she had told herself otherwise, she knew that she had allowed herself to hope.

It had been a selfish thing, wanting a child that was a bit of Zain because she couldn't have him or his love. She recognised that now. A baby should have two parents who loved one another…it didn't always happen, of course, but in a perfect world it would, and didn't everyone want their child to be born in a perfect world?

She had to focus on what she had, not what she didn't have. Her chin lifted as the co-pilot came out to ask her if she'd had a good flight and then continued to make small talk while she only half listened. She would make some lovely memories over the next few months, memories to treasure when she returned to her old life, not that it would ever be the same, she realised, because *she* wasn't the same.

It was weird stepping off the plane and walking into

the wall of heat that not long ago had felt so alien but
now felt like home.

Bubbles of excitement exploded like star bursts in
her stomach as she shifted in her seat, leaning forward
to stare out of the window as first the city gates came
into view and then the palace.

She had told Zain that she would be back late-after-
noon but she planned to surprise him with an early arrival, telling the palace staff to keep quiet. Although,
she realised now, it might not be much of a surprise if
he was tied up in meetings all morning.

Quietly entering the sitting room, which was empty,
she moved through to the bedroom they shared. It was
empty, the bedclothes rumpled, which was surprising,
considering how keen the housekeeping was under Layla's watchful eye.

Ah, well, at least Abby would have time to repair the
ravages wrought by the flight. Dropping her handbag,
she walked across to the bed, automatically twitching
the quilt to pull it into place. As she did so, something
glittered as it fell. Abby bent to pick up the small, shining object and as she lifted it her heart stopped.

She had seen the very distinctive diamond earring
before, she realised. Kayla had been wearing it that
first day in the stables. A whimper escaped her white,
clenched lips.

The hand she pressed to her mouth to contain further
cries shook; she shook everywhere as she stared at the
tiny object that had shattered any and all illusions she
had built up about how Zain might really feel.

She couldn't be angry that their marriage was a
sham—it was *meant* to be a sham—but she could be
angry and hurt and mad as hell that he was a cheat!

She backed away from the bed, unable to bear the things she saw when she stared at it—her bed, their bed...it felt like a violation that he had taken *her* to their bed...maybe not even for the first time.

'Oh, excuse me... I am so sorry.'

Wiping her eyes with the back of her hand, Abby spun around to see a young woman in the uniform worn by the household staff standing there.

The girl dropped a curtsey. 'So sorry to disturb you but I...' She saw the diamond sparkling in Abby's hand and exclaimed. 'Oh, you have found it! I am so grateful.'

Smiling, she went to grab the earring out of Abby's hand but Abby's fingers closed over it. There was something strangely familiar about the girl.

'It is a very pretty thing,' Abby said, realising where she had seen her before—at Kayla's side on those rare events when their paths crossed.

'It's not real but it was a gift. I am most grateful—it must have come out when I made the bed.' The girl held up a hand with a look that was probably meant to feign innocence but was hampered by the hint of a smirk.

Maybe it was the smirk, the connection to Kayla, or maybe just the fact she was able to think past that first blast of hurt, jealous outrage, but suddenly Abby joined the dots and saw what this was about...

So... Kayla wanted Zain, the crown or maybe even both. It had been obvious from the rumours that Kayla didn't like her, but Abby had told herself that it didn't matter, she was not here long enough for it to matter, and she had no intention of running to Zain any time she had a problem. She had wanted to prove to him she could cope.

She had been wrong not to tell him. This was a problem that needed addressing immediately.

'No, I don't think that's what happened at all.' What was Kayla's problem? she wondered, watching the look of revealing shocked apprehension wash over the girl's face. 'Where is Kayla, your mistress? I think I'd like to return this trinket.' She dangled the earring. 'In person,' she added grimly.

The girl looked scared now and as Abby walked towards her she shadowed the steps, backing towards the door. 'I… I don't know, really—the stables maybe, Amira?' She fled.

When Abby reached the stables a stable hand she recognised spotted her and approached shyly.

'You want to see the King of Night?' he asked in halting English.

To Abby, her King of the Night would always be Zain. 'Yes, please, if it's not too much bother?'

The idea of anything being a bother seemed to shock him.

Abby fingered the earring in her pocket. 'Have you seen the Princess Kayla?'

'She was here, Amira, but she left.'

Abby was not sorry to hear this; her appetite for a confrontation had waned considerably as she had walked the corridors. Wasn't there a certain amount of hypocrisy in her reaction? The woman might be trying to break up Abby's marriage but that marriage was a sham. 'Your English is excellent.'

He flushed with pleasure at the compliment. 'I worked in England long time ago at a very important race stable; it was my wish to be a jockey.' He pressed a hand to his stomach and rolled his eyes. 'But I got too fat… I like my food too much.'

'Well, the stables here are beautiful, spotless, and the weather is a great deal better than in England.'

'It is a very grey place,' the man agreed. 'But I enjoyed the fish and chips. Here he is.' He gestured towards the next stable along the row, one with the top door open.

The stallion whinnied as she approached.

'Hello, boy,' she whispered as she pressed her face into his mane.

'He likes you.'

Well, at least someone does, Abby thought, swallowing a sob of self-pity just as the person she least wanted to see in the world at this point appeared.

Not dressed for riding today, Kayla was instead wearing a pencil skirt that ended mid-calf, her legs elongated by the spiky heels she wore. Her silk top had bell sleeves and a square neck above which she wore some massively impressive pearls.

She lifted her chin; this woman was a bitch, but Abby's childhood experiences meant she had had a great deal of practice dealing with mean spirits and she knew that you should never let them see that they had got to you, as fear and pain were the food they fed on.

'Kayla.' She tipped her head in cool acknowledgement and had the satisfaction of seeing an expression of annoyance in the other woman's dark, malicious eyes as the thundering sound of horses being put through their paces on the gallops in the distance got louder and then faded away.

'How was your trip to England…*home*? You must miss it.'

'I miss my family and friends.' But not as much as she missed the sound of Zain's voice, the touch of his hand…his lips.

'Then I am surprised your visit there was so short.'

Abby closed her eyes and shook her head. She had no appetite for the cat-and-mouse fencing. She heaved out a long, sibilant sigh, opened her eyes, lifted her chin once more and prepared to take the metaphorical gloves off.

'Actually, I was looking for you. I think I have something of yours.' She held out her hand, the diamond stud between her fingers catching the light.

The woman's smile was almost as insincere as the sympathy and regret in her response. 'Oh, dear, I wouldn't have had you find out this way for the world.'

Abby's brows lifted as she dropped the earring onto the woman's palm. 'Find out what? That you are totally desperate and wouldn't know a moral scruple if it bit you?'

Kayla's triumphant smile faltered as her lips compressed in a petulant pout, but she recovered quickly and threw out a fresh taunt. 'You probably don't know, but I had a relationship with Zain before you were married.'

'I was here about five minutes before I learnt that on the palace grapevine.'

'But what you didn't know is that it carried on…and is *still* carrying on,' Kayla added before dramatically producing the twin to the earring.

Abby felt a fresh stab of shame for those split seconds when she had allowed her own insecurities and jealousy to make her jump.

'If you expect me to believe that you slept with my husband last night, forget it… Zain has too much…'

her lips quivered and her eyes misted '…too much respect for me to act that way.' She clung tight to this; she might not have his love but by his actions Zain had proved time and time again that it wasn't just words—he did respect her.

The other woman's eyes flashed with pure malice in response to the simple pride ringing out in Abby's confident statement. 'You mean you amuse him right now. It won't last, you know; the novelty value will wear off.' Abby's dignified silence seemed to enrage the woman even more as she snarled out contemptuously, 'You love him, I suppose?'

'Yes.' Even in this situation it felt liberating to be able to say it out loud.

'And you think he loves you…? I suppose it is his great *love* for you that will carry him through the latest polling disaster…' She saw the flicker of shock in Abby's eyes and nodded. 'Oh, yes, not good news at all, but then, no great surprise either,' she drawled. 'His advisors were expecting it; they warned him that seeing you, an *outsider*, with him will always remind people of his mother.' She stepped in closer. 'You're the kiss of death for Zain, and if you really loved him you'd leave!' she hissed, before turning and sweeping majestically away.

Abby stood perfectly still, her thoughts whirling. Kayla was trying to manipulate her but that didn't mean what the woman was saying didn't have an element of truth—more than an element, she realised; it *was* the truth.

Presumably at the outset Zain had calculated that any damage to his reputation that the sham marriage to her might cause could be rectified after they split up down the line, but what if he was wrong…? What if the longer she stayed the more damage she did to his reputation…what if it became irreparable? What if the people he loved rejected him?

She knew that would kill him.

'Amira?'

The young stable boy was standing there looking concerned.

Abby shook her head and turned, pride keeping her head up as she walked away, her firm tread contrasting with the awful icy chills running through her body.

Her chaotic thoughts chased around in her head. She didn't know where she was going or what she was going to do yet she knew she needed space…time…distance… but a moment later the stable hand caught her up.

'Excuse me, Amira, but the driver found this in the car.'

She looked blankly at the tiny charm that had fallen from the bracelet that had been her mother's. 'Oh, thank him…' A sudden thought occurred to her: if she was going to do this it was best to do it quickly, better for Zain. 'Is the Prince here in the palace?' she asked quickly.

'Yes, I think so, Amira…'

Abby reached into the pocket of her trench coat, her fingers curling around the passport she had not removed.

'Do you have paper…a pen?'

Zain stood there for a full ten minutes after he had read the note.

He didn't trust himself to move.

She was gone; the note, the ink blurred, was some drivel about leaving for him…she had left!

He had never chased after a woman in his life and he wasn't about to now.

Last night he'd lain awake longing and aching for something he could not name that she gave him, missing her softness, her scent, her warmth.

But life was a hell of a lot simpler without her. Without her there was no temptation to allow her to do to him what his mother had done to his father. His mother had drained his father, making him grow weak, making him love her so much that she blocked out his responsibilities...to his people and to the son who needed him.

He couldn't silence the counter-argument in his head.

Had Abby made him weak...? Could he have done what he had done these past weeks without her support? She didn't take from him, didn't drain him. She gave instead.

And now she had gone.

The thoughts tumbled in circles around his head until he took a deep breath and blinked like a man waking up and realising he had one more shot. He hit the ground running.

Considering she was not exactly inconspicuous, it took him a long time to find anyone who had actually seen her. It took him fifteen minutes to track her as far as the stables and another five to discover that she had been seen deep in conversation with Kayla, after which it seemed she had been driven away.

A phone call to the private jet confirmed his suspicions. He made it clear that under no circumstances was the plane to take off, and went around to the garages.

His fastest car got him as far as the palace gates, where he found his way totally blocked by a hundred or so banner-waving protestors taking advantage of the

fact that such gatherings were no longer prohibited—
one of his reforms that had definitely backfired!

Frustrated but not defeated, he flung the high-
powered car into reverse and drove back to the stable
yard.

He saddled the stallion himself with stable hands
watching and wondering who knew what? Zain didn't
actually care—the burning frustration that drove his
every action was choking him.

'Shall I stop, Amira?'

Dragged from the depths of her despairing reflections, Abby looked up. It didn't matter how many times
she told herself her life was not over, it felt as if it was
and so she could only try to take comfort from the fact
she was doing the right thing. Maybe this knowledge
would make her feel better in the future but right now
it didn't.

'Pardon?'

The driver nodded to the rear-view mirror and Abby
turned to see what he was looking at. The blood drained
from her face and her heart began to thud as fast and
hard as the hooves of the stallion that was galloping
full pelt towards them.

'No!' she said in a wobbly voice of panic. 'Don't
stop!'

'Amira!'

'Don't stop for anything!' she ordered imperiously as
Zain and the stallion began to overtake the car.

'Yes, Amira.'

He did, of course, but he didn't really have a choice
when there was a rearing stallion in the road ahead, the
hooves inches away from the car bonnet.

'Sorry, Amira.'

Abby barely heard as she watched as Zain, looking just as rampantly male and awe-inspiring as the first time she had seen him, dismounted and walked over to the car.

He wrenched open the door. 'Get out, *cara*.'

She thought about ignoring the order but decided getting out of her own volition would be more dignified than being dragged out, and Zain looked more than capable of that.

While she stood there he leaned into the cab and spoke to the driver, who turned the car around and drove away before her horrified eyes.

Leaving her, Zain, the stallion and a lot of sand.

'Just like old times,' he said, walking towards her with long, purposeful strides.

She shook her head. He was standing almost toe to toe with her and looking at her in a way that made Abby's head spin as she looked up into his dark, lean, beautiful face, her heart lurching wildly in hope.

'What is this about, Zain…?'

'This.' He took her by the shoulders and dragged her into him, covering her mouth with his. The kiss went on and on.

When it stopped she stood there feeling quite crazily bereft.

'That doesn't change anything, except fine… Oh, God, I have no self-control when it comes to you! I'm just—'

'In love?'

She froze and thought, *Am I that obvious?* 'I wasn't trying to fall in love…'

He brushed a strand of hair from her cheek, the ac-

tion so tender that it brought tears to her eyes. 'I know...
I was actively fighting it...' A grin split his lean face...
Suddenly he looked younger. 'I was a fool. It feels great
to surrender to you.'

Golden joy burst inside her but she shook her head.
'You can't stay married to me.'

He looked at her with frustration. 'Are you going to
tell me why?'

'The polls.'

'What polls?'

She gritted her teeth; he really wasn't making this
easy for her. 'You don't have to pretend,' she said, wishing that doing the noble thing felt less absolutely awful.
'I know that the numbers were bad.' Her carefully composed voice acquired a little wobble that required her
to stop and swallow several times before she continued, looking up into his face through a glaze of tears.
'I know that the longer I stay the worse they will get...
the people will reject you because I remind them of your
mother. So, I'm going now before things get worse, and
don't try and stop me,' she warned, knowing that if he
did she wouldn't have the strength to do the right thing.

He didn't look at all impressed by her sacrifice. 'Who
the hell has been filling your head with this nonsense?'

'Kayla. And it's not nonsense, it's the truth.'

His expression darkened. 'Kayla...is poison.' He dismissed the other woman with a contemptuous click of
his long, expressive fingers. 'The woman wants power
and position. She had an affair with me to get it and,
when I didn't play the game like she wanted, she married my brother. I should have kept her away from you.
I thought I had; I'm sorry, *cara*.'

She knew she shouldn't but she leaned in as he

stroked her cheek, the tenderness in his face bringing tears to her eyes. 'The poll…'

He sighed. 'There was a poll, not instigated by me,' he added. 'And the numbers were not good but that was when the news was first broken. Another, this time with my approval, was put out in the field yesterday and the results came back this morning.'

Abby closed her eyes. 'I'm so sorry, Zain.'

'My popularity ratings have soared, all thanks, it seems, to my redheaded wife.'

Her eyes flew wide. 'Kayla lied!'

He arched a sardonic brow and drawled, 'Now, there's a shocker.' All hint of sardonic humour vanished as he framed her face between his hands. 'You're the dream I never even admitted I had, Abby. The dream I was afraid of. I've been a coward, and my only excuse is that I've been guarding my heart so long that I forgot I had one, and I was too cowardly to admit what I felt…felt from that first moment I saw you…so brave, so beautiful, so…'

She raised herself on tiptoes, grabbed his head and kissed him. The kiss led inevitably to another then another…and by the time they surfaced the horse had wandered a few yards away.

'Does this mean…?' Was it possible to explode from sheer happiness? She felt as though she was walking on air as light as the bubbles of happiness popping in her bloodstream.

'Yes?' he prompted.

'You want me to stay longer than eighteen months?'

'I want you beside me every day…' His voice dropped a shivery, sexy octave as he whispered, 'Every night,' against the sensitive skin of her earlobe. He stopped nuzzling her neck and lifted his head to stare down into her face with an expression that stopped her heart as he caught her hand and pressed it to his chest. 'I want you beside me always. I love you and I could not do this… any of it, without you.'

What could she say to that? With stars in her eyes Abby linked her arms around his neck. 'You saved my life; I think I owe you mine.'

'I don't want your gratitude, Abby. I want your heart, your love.'

She looked at him with shining eyes and whispered, 'You have both.'

Zain's eyes blazed with love as he took her hands and pressed them to his lips. 'I will keep them safe, I promise.'

Abby lifted her face to his kiss with a blissful sigh. 'I'm going to have to learn some languages.'

'The language of love is the only one that counts,' he said, leading her by the hand to the horse. Heaving himself with no seeming effort into the saddle, he held out a hand, which she took. A moment later she was sitting in front of him.

'Are we going home?'

'I like the way you say that, but no, I thought we might detour. There is a certain oasis I know.'

The wind caught her hair and whipped her laugh away as he kicked the King of the Night into a gallop across the red sand. It felt as though they were the only two people on earth and she liked it.

* * * * *

COMING SOON!

We really hope you enjoyed reading this book. If you're looking for more romance, be sure to head to the shops when new books are available on

Thursday
9th August

To see which titles are coming soon, please visit
millsandboon.co.uk

MILLS & BOON

Coming next month

THE HEIR THE PRINCE SECURES
Jennie Lucas

He eyed the baby in the stroller, who looked back at him with dark eyes exactly like his own. He said simply, 'I need you and Esme with me.'

'In London?'

Leaning forward, he whispered, 'Everywhere.'

She felt the warmth of his breath against her skin, and her heartbeat quickened. For so long, Tess would have done anything to hear Stefano speak those words.

But she'd suffered too much shock and grief today. He couldn't tempt her to forget so easily how badly he'd treated her. She pulled away.

'Why would I come with you?'

Stefano's eyes widened. She saw she'd surprised him.

Giving her a crooked grin, he said, 'I can think of a few reasons.'

'If you want to spend time with Esme, I will be happy to arrange that. But if you think I'll give up my family and friends and home—' she lifted her chin '—and come with you to Europe as some kind of paid nanny—'

'No. Not my nanny.' Stefano's thumb lightly traced her tender lower lip. 'I have something else in mind.'

Unwilling desire shot down her body, making her nipples taut as tension coiled low in her belly. Her pride was screaming for her to push him away but it was difficult to hear her pride over the rising pleas of her body.

'I—I won't be your mistress, either,' she stammered, shivering, searching his gaze.

'No.' With a smile that made his dark eyes gleam, Stefano shook his head. 'Not my mistress.'

'Then…then what?' Tess stammered, feeling foolish for even suggesting a handsome billionaire prince like Stefano would want a regular girl like her as his mistress. Her cheeks were hot. 'You don't want me as your nanny, not as your mistress, so—what? You just want me to come to London as someone who watches your baby for free?' Her voice shook. 'Some kind of…p-poor relation?'

'No.' Taking her in his arms, Stefano said quietly, 'Tess. Look at me.'

Although she didn't want to obey, she could not resist. She opened her eyes, and the intensity of his glittering eyes scared her.

'I don't want you to be my mistress, Tess. I don't want you to be my nanny.' His dark eyes burned through her. 'I want you to be my wife.'

Continue reading
THE HEIR THE PRINCE SECURES
Jennie Lucas

Available next month
www.millsandboon.co.uk

LET'S TALK
Romance

For exclusive extracts, competitions
and special offers, find us online:

 facebook.com/millsandboon

 @millsandboonuk

 @millsandboon

Or get in touch on 0844 844 1351*

For all the latest titles coming soon, visit
millsandboon.co.uk/nextmonth